W9-BGR-647

Watchers
in the Night

Jenna Black

tor paranormal romance
A TOM DOHERTY ASSOCIATES BOOK
NEW YORK

This is a work of fiction. All the characters and events portrayed in this book are either products of the author's imagination or are used fictitiously.

WATCHERS IN THE NIGHT

A Tor Book
Published by Tom Doherty Associates, LLC
175 Fifth Avenue
New York, NY 10010

www.tor.com

Tor® is a registered trademark of Tom Doherty Associates, LLC.

ISBN-13: 978-0-765-35451-8
ISBN-10: 0-765-35451-9

First Edition: November 2006

Printed in the United States of America

0 9 8 7 6 5 4 3 2 1

For Kris and Dean,
who turned on the lightbulb over my head.

ACKNOWLEDGMENTS

It would take a whole new book to thank all the people who've helped me over this long and bumpy road. However, I don't think that book would make great reading, so here's a highly abridged version. First of all, I'd like to thank my editor, Anna Genoese, and my agent, Miriam Kriss, for believing in me. Then, there are the Heart of Carolina Romance writers—especially my critique partners, Amy, Gayle, and Jennifer E.—who kept me relatively sane along the way. *Merci beaucoup* to Isabelle, who taught me how to swear in Québécois. Any errors are just, uh, "artistic license" on my part. Lastly, I'd like to thank my husband, Dan—AKA Harper Scott—for all his love and support. I couldn't have done it without you.

1

CAROLYN MATHERS FELT RIDICULOUS carrying a gun on a date, but that didn't stop her from donning her shoulder holster and slipping in the Glock. Pathetic, she supposed. Certainly not romantic. But Paul was a cop—he'd understand in some kind of basic way. If she let him get close enough to find out she was carrying, that is.

Grimacing at the thought, she stepped out into the frosty night. The weatherman had said it was ten degrees out. But Carolyn's palms were sweating.

"It's just a date," she muttered under her breath, exasperated with herself. Her words formed a misty white cloud before the bitter wind dispersed it. Sticking her hands into her coat pockets, she braced herself against the cold and descended her front steps, hurrying toward the open parking lot a block and a half away.

She'd chosen ten o'clock on a Wednesday night for this date because when she'd tried to meet Paul at a civilized hour, her work had interfered and she'd had to stand him up. Now, however, she felt tired and unenergetic, and if it weren't for the scrap of pride she had left—the one that told her she was being a coward—she would have begged off again. It appeared that even after three years, she wasn't fully ready to date again.

As soon as her feet hit the sidewalk, the hairs on the back of her neck prickled in a way that was becoming infuriatingly familiar. She stopped and took a slow look around her, searching for the prying eyes her body insisted were upon her no matter what her rational mind told her. Row houses lined both sides of the street, but no faces peeked out from any of the lighted windows. An occasional car passed by—the streets of Philadelphia were never truly deserted—but there wasn't a single pedestrian in sight.

Shaking her head at herself, she started toward the parking lot once more. One of the big street lights in the lot flickered, then went out, leaving her car buried in an intimidating pool of shadow where the light had once been. The creepy-crawly feeling of being watched heightened, and she hunched her shoulders against it.

This was why she'd brought the gun, this constant uneasiness she'd been feeling for several months now every time she went out at night. Most likely, she was just being paranoid. But she'd been a cop for eight years and a PI for three, and in both lines of work she'd naturally made some enemies. It wasn't a bad idea to be on her guard.

If some nut case were following you, he would have made his move by now, she told herself. No matter how nutty they were, they didn't stalk you for months at a time without making some kind of move, if only to let you know you were in danger.

Forcing herself to relax, she strode briskly toward her car. She glared briefly at the burned-out light. It buzzed to life for a second, then died again. She paid this place one-fifty a month to park her car—the least they could do was keep the lights on! There wasn't even anyone at the booth tonight, and with the cold weather keeping most sensible people in their houses, the lot felt deserted. And ominous.

She was just a few steps from her car when she heard

the unmistakable sound of a footstep behind her. She whirled around so fast she almost made herself dizzy.

In the dismal pool of shadow, not ten feet away from her, stood a white male, maybe eighteen or twenty. The street lamp made another feeble attempt to come back to life, and Carolyn got a good look at him. Blond hair spiked with some kind of greasy gel, blue eyes with the color and warmth of a glacier, thin, heavily chapped lips twisted into a menacing sneer. Despite the cold, he wore only a denim jacket for warmth, but from his dilated pupils she gathered he'd found a chemical solution to the cold. His hand moved, and she saw the gleam of a wicked-looking switch blade.

"Well, hello there pretty lady," he said. His gravelly voice should have belonged to someone who'd smoked three packs a day for sixty years or so.

Damn it! When she'd first stepped out of her house, she'd taken a city-girl's care to check out her surroundings, scoping out the area before potentially stepping into danger. But she'd just walked blithely into the darkness of the parking lot with barely a second thought. Trying to prove to herself how tough she was, how unaffected by the constant uncomfortable feeling of being watched. She knew better.

The hoodlum licked his chapped lips. "Whatcha got under that nice coat?"

A Glock with your name on it, she thought. She consciously widened her eyes and made her lower lip tremble, trying to project helpless victim. All she had to do was get her hand under her jacket, and the hoodlum was in for a big surprise.

Her feigned fear must have been convincing, because the kid's eyes gleamed with malicious enjoyment, and his jeans bulged noticeably. Carolyn glanced around the parking lot, but there wasn't another soul in sight.

"Scream, and I swear I'll cut your tongue out," the kid warned, coming closer, brandishing his knife.

"P-please don't hurt me," she stammered. Her eyes focused on the knife and her heart rate shot through the roof as adrenaline pumped through her system. The kid was probably hopped up on something, not to mention armed, so her chances of taking him at hand-to-hand combat weren't good. She had to get to her gun before he made his move.

His smile was sly and cold and ugly as sin. "Oh, I won't hurt you none, lady. Long as you behave yourself. Now why don't you slip out of that nice coat for me?"

She sniffled loudly, not having to feign the sound because the cold was making her nose run. She fumbled with the first button on her coat, making it look like her hands were shaking. Sometimes it helped that she was so petite and looked like such a girly-girl. It had pissed her off when her fellow officers underestimated her, but it wasn't a bad thing at all when the suspects did.

Her world shrank until there was nothing in it but herself, her attacker, and this little pool of shadow in which she stood. She continued slowly unbuttoning her coat, mentally rehearsing the hurried reach into her blazer, the quick draw. The hoodlum would be caught entirely by surprise, and she tried to imagine what he'd do. A sensible guy would probably run for his life, but Carolyn doubted this punk would be sensible considering how high he was.

The kid's breath was coming shorter and shorter as he grew more excited. Oh, he was just loving this show of fear, loving the power he thought he wielded! Carolyn looked forward to turning the tables on him.

The last button slid free, and she shrugged her shoulders out of the coat. She meant to let it fall to the ground behind her, but as it slid down her arms she once again felt that prickle on the back of her neck. Her hands were free of the coat, but it didn't hit the ground. Her attacker's jaw dropped open, and Carolyn caught a glimpse of misty white breath brushing past her cheek.

Reflexes took over, and despite the threat of the knife,

Carolyn whirled and backpedaled at the evidence of a threat from behind. Her hand plunged under her blazer, seizing the butt of the Glock. And then froze.

Standing there, maybe a foot away from where she had been, was a ghost from her past. How he could possibly have come that close to her without her noticing— or without the knife-wielding punk noticing—was beyond her.

The man had her coat in his hands, and he casually laid it over the hood of a car while the punk quickly determined that he was a much greater threat than Carolyn.

"Stay away from me, man," the punk snarled, poking the air with his knife for emphasis. But he'd lost a lot of his cockiness.

Carolyn blinked rapidly, but the ghost didn't disappear. He looked markedly different from how he'd looked three years ago, when she'd seen him last, but there could be no doubt that it was him. Gray James. The only man she'd ever loved. The man who'd stranded her at the altar and disappeared from her life.

He wasn't dead. For three years, she'd told herself and anyone else who would listen that something terrible must have happened to him. For three years, she'd dreaded getting the news that his body had finally been found. Now, here he was standing in front of her, very much alive, and she could hardly believe her eyes.

Gray had lost a lot of weight, she noticed. He'd never been fat, really, but he'd always been just a touch on the heavy side, no matter how carefully he'd watched his diet. His hair, once always cropped close and neat to his head, formed a shaggy black mane around his pale face, which was devoid of the glasses and mustache he'd once worn. He even *dressed* differently. Instead of his dress-for-success outfits, he was now wearing a black leather jacket over faded jeans and well-loved sneakers.

Damn, he looked good.

Then he smiled, and a chill traveled down Carolyn's spine.

"I'd advise you to leave the lady alone," Gray said, and if Carolyn had thought the hoodlum's eyes looked cold, Gray's were arctic. His smile was more like the baring of his teeth, and the air fairly vibrated with menace.

Menace? From Gray? The man was so even-tempered he rarely raised his voice, and so gentle he wouldn't even kill a spider in his apartment but would trap it in a glass and take it outside instead.

But that sense of menace wasn't just Carolyn's imagination—the hoodlum's face had noticeably paled. She tried to shake off her shock and draw her Glock out of its holster. Gray's eyes flicked briefly in her direction and once again she froze, unable to complete the movement. It was like one of those dreams where you were being chased by a monster but you couldn't get yourself to move. She knew it was just the shock of seeing Gray, but that knowledge did nothing to loosen her limbs.

"Don't mess with me!" the hoodlum warned, but his voice held too much fear to be even vaguely threatening.

Gray smiled that terrifying smile again, the one that would have chilled Carolyn to the marrow if it had been directed at her. The hoodlum's knife hand shook.

"I'll do more than mess with you, little boy," Gray said in a low growl, taking a step forward.

The hoodlum broke and ran. Gray took off in pursuit, and Carolyn once more urged herself to draw the Glock. She had to stop this kid, before he terrorized some other woman. Her hand moved sluggishly, the gun catching in the folds of her jacket, and by the time it was out the kid had turned the corner.

Gray pulled up short, then slowly turned to face her once more. He wasn't smiling anymore, but that mysterious aura of danger still clung to him as he came closer. His once plump and rounded face, made even softer and more harmless-looking by his round glasses, was now sharp and angular. Sculpted, even. And yet no matter how different he looked—and no matter that she'd been sure he was dead—she couldn't deny that it was really Gray.

Averting his eyes, he walked past her and picked up her coat from the hood of the car where he'd laid it. She shivered and hugged herself, suddenly conscious of the cold once again.

"Here," Gray said, handing the coat to her.

She shoved her arms into it and clutched it close around her as the chill deepened.

"Come on," Gray said. "I'll walk you back to your house."

She wanted to say something to him, *anything,* but her tongue stuck to the roof of her mouth and her throat closed up on her. Instead she followed mutely as he walked to her front door, not looking at her. His face was almost completely devoid of expression, although occasionally she caught the gleam of some unknown emotion in his eyes.

Her hands shook for real as she unlocked her front door, and she wondered if she were about to wake up from this dream. But no, it was too coldly real to be a dream. Gray brushed past her without waiting for an invitation, making his way into the living room as if he had every right to make himself at home. She paused in the hall to hang her coat, then followed, thoughts and emotions fighting and scrambling over each other within her.

Relief that he was alive quickly faded. If he wasn't dead, that meant he'd left her of his own free will. The conviction that he'd met with foul play had protected her heart, but now that protection was gone. Pain threatened to overwhelm her if she let down her guard enough to let it in.

He'd squatted in front of the dark walnut cabinet that held her liquor stash. He poured a healthy dose of

Scotch into a tumbler, then rose and held it out to her. Nothing for himself, she noticed.

She took the glass from his hand and downed the Scotch in a single burning swallow, grimacing and wrinkling her nose. As a cop, it had practically been a job requirement that she drink, but she'd never particularly liked the taste of hard liquor. Still, she appreciated the warmth right about now.

She cleared her still-burning throat. "So, long time no see," she said, attempting to sound casual and failing spectacularly. She tried to meet his eyes, but he looked away as he unzipped his jacket and threw it over a chair.

Underneath, he was wearing a short-sleeved sky blue T-shirt that clung appealingly to his chest. In the past, he'd always worn his clothes on the loose side to camouflage his extra weight. Carolyn couldn't help noticing that he most definitely did not need to camouflage anything anymore.

Damn it, why was she noticing stupid things like that? Who cared how good he looked, when she'd just found out she'd been mourning three years for a man who was alive and well and hadn't even bothered to say goodbye when he'd left her?

"Are you all right?" he asked.

"I'm fine." Except for the fury that was rising within her, that is. "I thought you were dead."

The corner of his mouth twitched, but he didn't quite smile. "You mean you *wished* I was dead."

He was *amused* by her anger? By her pain? "You bastard!" she spat, and it was all she could do not to cross the distance between them and land a solid right to his chin. She smacked her glass down on the coffee table. Otherwise, she might have thrown it at him.

He sighed heavily and shook his head. "I should go." He managed to take two steps toward the door before she seized his arm in a grip meant to hurt. Up close, she could smell the faint hint of his cologne, and it made her heart clench in her chest. Cool Water. She'd given him a bottle on their first Christmas together, and thereafter he'd always worn it to please her. The scent evoked memories of chilly winter mornings spent cuddled in his arms. She summoned her anger once more before the pain could overwhelm her.

"Oh no you don't! You don't get to just waltz back into my life for ten minutes, play the hero, and then waltz back out again." Her heart was pounding harder now than it had been in the parking lot. "I want to know where you've been for three years."

He pried her fingers loose from his arm. He'd put on his expressionless mask once more, and even his voice when he spoke gave away nothing about how he felt. "I should have just let you handle that hoodlum on your own. I'm sure you could have taken him. I'm . . . sorry. Now please, I have to go."

She grabbed him again. "You're not going anywhere. Not until you've answered a whole lot of questions." Fury still coursed through her veins, but pain was slowly and steadily working its way in as well. "Two days," she started, but the pain caught up with her and squeezed her throat. Her eyes burned, but no way in hell was she going to let herself cry in front of him. "Two days before our wedding, you disappear with nothing but a three-line Dear Jane letter. Three years I've been trying to figure out what happened to you."

In the beginning, she'd tried to let the police handle it, like a responsible citizen. But because of that damning Dear Jane letter, no one except her had really thought there was any foul play involved. The fact that he'd last been seen leaving his bachelor party with a stripper on his arm hadn't helped her arguments any. She'd launched her own investigation, and it had turned into an obsession. When her superiors had given her an ultimatum—quit the investigation or quit the force—she'd walked away, full of regrets, but unable to let go.

She cleared her throat, hoping her voice didn't come out froggy. "Now you just show up here to 'save' me when you know damn well I can take care of myself, and you're just going to *walk away*? I deserve an explanation, don't you think?"

The expression on his face softened just slightly. "You do," he said quietly. "But I can't give it to you. I'm sorry."

The weasely answer inspired another surge of anger. Anger was good, much more manageable and energizing than pain. Carolyn seized that anger and held onto it for dear life. "Sorry? You put me through three years of hell and all you can say is you're sorry? Well that just ain't gonna cut it, mister."

Something sparked in his eyes, but his voice remained calm and level. "I know you're angry with me, and I understand why, but I have nothing to give you, Carolyn. I never wanted to hurt you, but life doesn't always give us what we want." A hint of bitterness tinged his voice, intensifying her anger. What did he have to be bitter about? *He* was the one who had done the leaving!

"If you didn't want to marry me, you could have just said so." Damn, did she detect a trace of a sob in those words? *Anger, Carolyn. Hold onto the anger.* "Instead, you had to disappear mysteriously without a word to anyone. You had to make me worry myself sick over you, convince myself you were dead. And now you just casually stroll into my house and say 'Sorry, Carolyn, I'm not going to explain anything to you?'" She'd latched on to the anger with gusto, and her voice had risen to a shrill level. Perhaps shouting at him wasn't the most effective way to pry information out of him— it had never worked before—but it was better than bursting into hysterical tears.

"You're right," Gray said. "You deserved better then, and you deserve better now, but it doesn't matter. I have my reasons for what I've done, and they aren't reasons I can share with you." Again that hint of bitterness in his eyes. "Gray James died three years ago. It's time you let him go." He turned his back and started heading toward the door.

"You are *not* walking out on me again!" Carolyn shouted, but he didn't slow down. She drew the Glock and pointed it right between his shoulder blades. "Hold it right there!" *Okay,* a rational voice whispered in her head, *now you're taking a step off the deep end.*

Gray glanced over his shoulder briefly but seemed completely unintimidated by the firepower ranged against him. He put his hand on the doorknob.

The bastard really was going to walk out without a word of explanation! Carolyn couldn't believe it, and wasn't about to let him get away with it. She swung her aim down and to the right and squeezed off a shot.

The report was deafening in the enclosed space, and Gray's shoulders hunched protectively at the sound. The bullet dug into the wall beside the door, and a shower of plaster dust sprinkled the carpet. The scent of cordite burned her nostrils, and Carolyn wondered how many of her neighbors were now dialing 911.

Once again, Gray paused to look over his shoulder. She met his gaze and found she couldn't look away. There might have been a hint of reproach in his eyes, but there certainly was no hint of fear. He shook his head briefly, then opened the door. A gust of chill air filled the room. Carolyn willed herself to move, to fire off another shot, to do *something* to make him stay, make him explain himself. But everything was taking on a dream-like quality, and she couldn't seem to make herself move.

The door pulled shut behind Gray and finally Carolyn was able to shake off the strange paralysis. Shoving the Glock back in its holster, she sprinted for the door and threw it open, careening down the short flight of stairs and looking frantically right and left.

But Gray James had disappeared. Again.

2

GRAY HAD GONE THREE blocks before he realized he'd left his jacket draped over one of Carolyn's chairs. He stopped in his tracks for a moment, then continued on his way. He should never have shown himself to her in the first place—why compound his mistake by going back for his stupid jacket? It wasn't like he would die of the cold!

Carolyn was an ex-cop, and a gun-toting one at that. She could have handled one teenaged hoodlum without Gray's help. But every scrap of rational, logical thought had fled his brain when he'd glimpsed the knife, and the hoodlum was damned lucky to have lived through the encounter.

Idiot, he cursed himself. Three years he'd managed to stay out of Carolyn's life, and one knee-jerk reaction screwed it all up.

Gray shook himself out of his funk, turning his mind away from thoughts of the past as he'd learned to do with mediocre success over the last three years. As soon as he did so, he became aware that he was being followed. He gritted his teeth on a surge of anger as he came to a stop and turned to face his damned shadow.

Jules smirked at him, and Gray braced himself for

whatever abuse the older vampire was going to heap upon him.

"Awfully cold night to be trotting around with no coat on, don't you think?" Jules asked.

Gray was edgy enough to seriously consider taking a swing at the prick. He managed to restrain himself. Jules had become a vampire something like a hundred years ago, and with only three years under his belt, Gray was no match for him in strength. A fact he had learned the hard way on more than one occasion.

Jules always dressed like he was on his way to a *GQ* fashion shoot. His coat probably cost a couple grand, his pants looked like they'd been pressed five minutes ago, and his shoes were so shiny they hurt the eyes. In short, he was the kind of man other men would describe as a sissy, and women would drool over. Definitely not the kind of guy Gray wanted to lose a fight to.

"Don't you have something better to do than follow me around all the time?" he asked. He'd thought Jules had given up on being his own personal demon over a year ago. How long had he been watching?

"Sometimes you're so naive it's laughable." Jules's mocking tone once again tempted Gray to take a swing. But that's what Jules wanted—he'd never lower himself to taking the first swing, but he'd love to demonstrate his superior strength and quickness by beating Gray to a pulp in "self-defense."

"And you're such an asshole it's amazing no one's pounded a stake through your heart yet." Perhaps not the most powerful of comebacks, but Gray's oratory skills always seemed to desert him when his nemesis was around.

"Did you think the Guardians were just going to let a free agent wander the night unobserved? In *our* city? *T'es pas une lumiere, mon ami.*" He grinned and looked proud of himself.

Gray curled his lip in a snarl. "What's the matter,

Jules? Afraid of what I might do if you insulted me in English?"

Jules laughed. "Yes, I'm terrified," he said with an exaggerated shiver. He reached into his cashmere coat and pulled out a small paperback book. "I brought you a gift, in case you'd like to look up the words." He held the book out to Gray.

It was a French-English dictionary, but even if he'd been inclined to research the insults, Gray doubted he'd have much luck. Somehow, he didn't think many of the phrases Jules used would be found in polite dictionaries.

Sticking his hands in his jeans pockets, Gray ignored the little book. "Gee, Jules. I didn't think you liked to admit you were *French*."

"Québécois," Jules corrected automatically, stuffing the book back into a pocket inside his coat. "And for that to be as insulting as you wished it to be, you would have to be from Québec yourself. Coming from a foreigner . . ." He shrugged.

"A *foreigner*? Jules, this is Philadelphia, not Montreal." He turned to continue down the street. Naturally, Jules fell into step beside him.

"You seem to have developed an unhealthy obsession for this mortal woman."

"Go fuck yourself."

"She would be your ex-fiancée, no?"

Gray shot him an ineffectual glare.

"This stalking of yours . . . Not a good sign, my friend. It's predatory behavior, you know."

Gray jerked to a stop, his stomach turning over at Jules's sick implication. "You think I would hurt Carolyn?" he cried. Damn it, why did Jules *always* succeed in riling him?

For once, Jules didn't gloat at his success, his expression grave. "Any predatory behavior in a free agent, especially one with your history . . ."

"I would never hurt her!" Gray felt the truth of those words down to his bones. Yes, he had changed dramatically since that night three years ago—the night the real Gray James had died. But never could he change so much that he would hurt the woman who had been—and still was—the love of his life. "It's been three years! If I haven't killed anyone in three years, why would you think I'd start now?" The Guardians had regarded him with unadulterated suspicion since the moment he'd met them, but Gray had thought they'd eventually back off.

"Because you've tasted death," Jules said, leaning into Gray's space. Gray made the mistake of meeting his eyes, and the older vampire's glamour trapped his gaze. "There's no going back, not for you. The beast inside you is awake, and it's hungry, and one day it'll take over and you'll do whatever it takes to feed that hunger. And when it wins the battle, I'll be there to put you down like a dog." A feral, vicious smile spread over his thin lips. He'd lowered his fangs, tonguing them in threat as Gray remained rooted to the sidewalk, eyes locked with his, unblinking.

Moments later, Gray shook his head to clear a sudden fog of confusion. Jules had slipped away. Gray let out a shaky breath. He hated it when Jules did that little disappearing act. He should have known better than to meet the prick's eyes and let his glamour get a foothold.

Gray ground his teeth as he stuck his hands into his jeans pockets and continued on down the street. *Jules is full of shit,* he tried to tell himself. The two of them had taken an instant and comprehensive dislike to each other, so it was no surprise that he'd try to sow seeds of doubt in Gray's brain. But Gray could never be a Killer, would never allow himself to become a true vampire.

You've tasted death, Jules's voice taunted in his brain. But that was three years ago! Three years of liv-

ing in the shadows, neither human, nor fully vampire,
nor even Guardian. If he was going to turn killer, he
would have done so by now, surely.

Unbidden, an image came to his mind of the young
punk fleeing the parking lot earlier this evening. Gray
had let him get away, but there was no denying the
nearly overwhelming desire he'd felt to give chase. If
Carolyn hadn't been there, would Gray have given in
to his instincts? Chased the kid down? Might he have
killed him?

Gray shook his head violently. Jules was screwing
with his mind. He wasn't now, nor ever would be, a
Killer. That was final.

* * *

IT WENT AGAINST JULES'S instincts to let Gray return to his home unwatched, but surely the fledgling
was shaken up enough that he wasn't a danger at the
moment. Besides, even if Jules wasn't watching him,
Gray had to assume he was. No doubt it was safe to
leave him on his own for the remainder of the night.

Disturbed by Gray's unhealthy behavior—it had
nothing to do with his personal dislike of the man,
Jules told himself—he decided to call on the Founder
and give him a full report.

Elijah Cromwell, who had founded the Guardians of
the Night well before Jules was born, lived in a palatial
mansion that overlooked the Delaware River. The
building was an anomaly amidst the row houses and
historic landmarks that surrounded it, a stately Victo-
rian mansion that looked like it was trapped in a time
warp. An expansive, gated garden surrounded the house
like a moat, and a powerful glamour emanated from
the place, a glamour more powerful than Jules had felt
anywhere else in his life. A glamour that caused mortals to pass by it without even a second glance, no mat-

ter how incongruous it looked. Even Jules felt the echo of that glamour, urging him to look away, walk on by.

But the glamour wasn't the only thing that made Jules reluctant to approach the front gate. The wrought-iron fence that circled the mansion made the hairs on the back of his neck prickle, and it took an effort of will to reach out and gingerly press the intercom button no matter how many times he'd come here over his long life. The button sat in an oasis of stone, but it would be easy for the unwary to accidentally touch the surrounding iron and gain a nasty burn.

Jules waited patiently until Eli's voice squawked at him from the intercom. "Who's there?"

"It's Jules," he said, and, after a brief delay, the gates swung open. Jules overcame his natural distaste for stepping into a space enclosed by iron and hurried to the front door. The door was unlocked, as always, for the iron gates would prevent any intrusion by unwelcome vampires, and the glamour kept away the mortals. As soon as he stepped into the house, he heard the faint murmur of voices and realized he'd have to wait his turn for the Founder's attention. He followed the sound until he entered what had probably been a ballroom when the house was first built. Eli had turned it into a meeting hall.

The room was long and rectangular. In the near wall was a massive fireplace in which a crackling wood fire burned merrily. The far wall was a bank of floor-to-ceiling windows, hidden from sight by green velvet brocade drapes. Jules had always wondered why Eli lived in a house with so many windows. But then, mysteries swirled around Eli and if Jules started examining all of them, his head would start hurting.

Jules stopped short in the doorway as he surveyed the scene. The Founder sat in a huge wingback chair in front of the fire. He reminded Jules of a king, sitting on his throne looking wise, and grave, and noble. On

the sofa facing Eli were two Guardians, Deirdre and
Fletcher. Standing noticeably distant from them with
his back to the door was someone Jules disliked almost
as much as he disliked Gray.

"Well, come on in, Jules," Eli beckoned on catching sight of him, and Jules had no choice but to enter
the room.

Drake turned to face the doorway, giving Jules a
jaunty smile. "Yes, do come in. I promise I won't bite
you."

Eli and the two Guardians chuckled, but Jules was
far from amused. Although intellectually he approved
of the Guardians' deal with the devil, he really hated to
work with Drake—a *true* vampire, a Killer.

Jules greeted his fellow Guardians by name, giving
Drake only a nod of acknowledgment, then took an
empty seat by the fire. He wanted to speak to Eli in private, but he would have to wait his turn.

Drake leaned casually against the mantel and turned
his attention to Deirdre and Fletcher. "So, where are
the suspect's usual hunting grounds?" he asked.

"Most of his kills have been on Broad Street, around
City Hall," Deirdre answered. A lovely, doe-eyed
brunette, she was just the kind of woman Jules would
have loved to flirt with when he was a mortal. But Eli
frowned on romantic entanglements—or even unro-
mantic, purely physical entanglements—among the
Guardians, so Jules had kept his distance.

"*His* kills?" Drake said with a raised eyebrow. If
Drake had ever had any qualms about his vampire
state, he had long ago squelched them. To Jules, he always looked resolutely comfortable in his own skin,
and he dressed to heighten his aura of sensuality and
menace—black leather was his favorite, and when he
walked down the street anything with ovaries gave him
a second glance. "You know it's a male?"

Deirdre nodded. "His kills have all been women.
Pretty. Young."

"And soaked in semen," Jules added. He wasn't part of the task force assigned to the case, but he made sure to keep up with their findings. Eli should have asked him to help out before resorting to Drake. Jules bit his tongue, determined to keep his opinion to himself.

But Eli read that opinion easily without Jules having to say a word. "His kills are accelerating," the Founder said. "Should we let more innocent women die while we use only our traditional methods to locate him?"

Jules squirmed under Eli's disapproval. Of course he had no desire to sacrifice more lives, and he knew Eli wouldn't call Drake in unless he thought it absolutely necessary. Drake being a killer, his strength—both physical and psychic—was far greater than that of the Guardians. Who better to catch a brutal, cold-blooded murderer than another brutal, cold-blooded murderer? "Just because it's practical doesn't mean I have to like it." An uncomfortable silence settled upon the room as he sank deeper into the chair. Deirdre gave him a sympathetic smile, while the men looked vaguely disapproving.

It was Drake who broke the silence. "When was his last known kill?"

The tension in the air eased and the Guardians turned their attention away from Jules.

"Wednesday," Fletcher answered. Blond-haired and blue-eyed, Fletcher exuded an all-American boy charm at odds with the cunning that lay beneath his surface. That cunning had allowed him to destroy rogue vampires who far out-powered him. Although Eli frowned on the Guardians keeping tallies of their kills, everyone knew Fletcher was their best hunter. If the Broad Street killer had eluded Fletcher, he must be an old and powerful vampire with a good dose of cunning to top it off.

"Sometime just after midnight, I'd guess," Fletcher continued. "The police think they have a serial killer on their hands. They're calling him the Broad Street Banger."

Drake shrugged. "Well, technically I suppose he *is* a serial killer. Is he trying to cover his tracks?"

"Yes," Deirdre said. "He slashes their throats to hide the bite marks."

"The police think the lack of blood on the scene means the women were killed somewhere else," Fletcher said.

Drake nodded. "Sounds fairly straightforward."

Jules managed to suppress a snort. If it were a straightforward case, Eli would never have enlisted Drake's help! Just the fact that Fletcher hadn't caught the guy should have clued Drake in that this case was anything but straightforward.

"Tread carefully," Eli warned. "If he's managed to evade Deirdre and Fletcher, it probably means he knows he's being hunted. It's far easier to take down the unwary."

Jules allowed himself a slight smirk. Obviously, he and Eli were on the same wavelength. He cast a surreptitious glance at Drake to see how he'd taken the warning that was just short of a rebuke.

Drake looked distinctly unimpressed. "Meaning no disrespect for your people, Eli, but he hasn't really been hunted yet. Merely chased."

Fletcher's pretty-boy face flushed red and he opened his mouth for a retort. Eli silenced him with a glance.

"I expect you all to work together on this," Eli said. "Drake, I'd appreciate it if you would refrain from antagonizing 'my people,' as you call them."

Drake bowed slightly from the waist, and Jules wondered whether that had been a gesture of respect or mockery. Grumbling, Deirdre and Fletcher took their leave, Drake following behind at a discreet distance. Jules stared after him for a long moment after he'd left, feeling tarnished by association.

"You're uncommonly cranky tonight," Eli commented as he moved to the fireplace to put on another log. The fire blazed and crackled, casting a red glow on the dimly lit room.

"Cranky? What am I, a baby?"

Eli chuckled. "Compared to some. But let me see if I can guess the source of your discontent." He tapped a finger against his lips and made a great show of thinking hard.

"Glad to be a source of such entertainment. Do you want to hear what I have to say or not?"

Eli returned to his seat, lowering himself gingerly as if his joints troubled him. But of course, vampires didn't *have* joint trouble. Sometimes, Jules suspected Eli used his physical age as a prop, a way to emphasize that he was older and wiser than the rest of them. Outwardly, he looked to be about sixty, but no one knew how old he really was. Hell, no one was really sure *what* he was. That he was some form of vampire was clear—his psychic footprint gave that away. But so many things about him didn't add up.

His power was undeniable—no vampire Jules had ever met could manage the massive glamour that surrounded this house. But he clearly wasn't a Killer. He made too much of a public figure of himself amongst the Guardians. If he were a Killer, his people would know. Besides, he had founded the Guardians to destroy the Killers—hardly the act of a soulless murderer.

"So," Eli said when he had comfortably settled himself, "what has Gray James done to get under your skin tonight?"

"Remember I told you he was stalking his ex-fiancée?"

Eli nodded.

"He showed himself tonight. Some mugger was trying to attack the woman, and Gray came out of hiding. If you'd seen the way he went after that mugger . . ."

"That he's protective of the woman he once loved is hardly evidence that he's gone rogue."

Jules acknowledged that with a shrug. "I know, but he's on the edge, Eli. I can *feel* it. I can see it in his eyes. Isn't it better for us to put down a Killer *before* he kills?" An idea struck him with a chill. "Or what if he's *already* killed? The Broad Street killer started hunting not so long after you called a halt to the surveillance on Gray James."

"You think Gray is the Broad Street Banger?" To Jules's annoyance, Eli sounded amused by the idea.

"Why not? He's killed before. You know that for some it only takes one taste for the addiction to take hold."

Eli sighed. "I know you're not going to like this, Jules, but I seriously doubt he's the Broad Street killer. I agree that he's in danger of giving in to the addiction, but if he does, I suspect he'll take Drake's route."

Jules couldn't help his grimace of disgust. "Oh yeah, if he only kills 'bad' people, then it's all right."

"That's not my point. My point is he wouldn't be attacking innocent women." Eli leaned forward in his chair. "If he goes rogue, he will be destroyed. One Drake is quite enough. But you are not to act against him on the suspicion that he *might* kill. Understand?"

Jules held up his hands in a gesture of acquiescence. "I hear you loud and clear, Eli." And in truth, no matter how much he disliked and distrusted Gray, Jules couldn't see himself killing the bastard on nothing more than a hunch. "Do you agree with me that we need to put a watch on him again?"

Eli thought about it a moment, then sighed. "I suppose it's best if we do. Your instincts about him might be a tad questionable, but I'll agree his behavior lately has been cause for concern. Do you think you can watch over him without being overly antagonistic?"

Jules grinned. "Probably not, but hey, he's used to me by now."

Eli didn't look terribly amused. "Now that Drake is working the Broad Street case, I suppose I can spare

Deirdre for a little surveillance here and there. Gray seems to like her."

"Any man with a drop of testosterone in his system likes Dee." Jules rubbed his hands together in anticipation. "We can play good-Guardian, bad-Guardian with him."

Eli looked even less amused. "This is hardly a cause for humor, Jules! We're supposed to be dedicated to saving men like him from the blood addiction. Not rooting for them to succumb to it."

Jules hung his head, properly abashed. It wasn't that he wanted Gray to fall victim to the addiction. It's just that his gut told him Gray would fall, that he walked the razor's edge with uncertain balance. "Sorry, Eli. I'll behave myself, I promise."

"I'm sure you will," Eli agreed with an enigmatic smile.

Jules knew better than to ask him what that smile meant.

3

IF HANNAH WAS ANNOYED to be called from her home at eleven o'clock on a weeknight, she hid it well. When Carolyn opened the door, her best friend and business partner flashed her a merry smile. Carolyn returned the smile and let Hannah in.

She hadn't told Hannah what she wanted to talk about—just that she needed a friend tonight. And Hannah had dropped everything to come over with no questions asked. Now, she demonstrated the uncanny powers of observation that made her such a wonderful detective. Her gaze fixed on the chipped plaster beside the door and her eyes widened.

"Jesus, Carolyn! What happened here?" She fingered the small hole, peering closely at it and no doubt seeing the squashed bullet that nestled inside. Hannah cut a look toward Carolyn. "Are you all right?"

A loaded question, and one Carolyn couldn't answer with a simple yes or no. "Come on in. This is going to take some explaining."

Despite what must have been rampant curiosity, Hannah held her questions as they retired to the living room. Carolyn made them each a drink without asking, then sat and faced her best and oldest friend. Hannah, bless her, didn't prod or nudge, waiting for Carolyn to take the first step.

"I saw a ghost tonight."

Hannah's face registered no surprise. "Oh?"

Carolyn swallowed hard. "I saw Gray."

Hannah sucked in a quick breath, her hazel eyes going wide. "No way! Oh, please, tell me you called me over to help you dispose of the body!" She sat forward on the couch, her face all eager anticipation.

Carolyn laughed at her friend's loyalty. Hannah would have been her maid of honor if Gray hadn't pulled his disappearing act. When Carolyn had finally forced herself to consider that Gray might have left voluntarily—though she had never quite been able to force herself to believe it—Hannah had been there to help plot revenge fantasies. And to be a shoulder to cry on, though Carolyn had stoutly refused to use her in that capacity. Raised by a single father who despised tears as a sign of weakness, Carolyn had learned never to let anyone see her cry.

"Come on, Carolyn. Stop laughing and tell me what happened! I'm dying here."

Carolyn swallowed the last of her giggles. "Some punk tried to mug me in the parking lot," she started. She was quite sure the kid had more than mugging in mind, but there was no reason to go into that much detail. "Gray came out of nowhere and chased the kid away. Then we came back here."

"And he told you how he was kidnapped by white slavers who carried him off to deepest darkest Africa to work in a diamond mine. It wasn't until this year that he was able to escape his captors and make his way back to America to find you again. How romantic!"

Carolyn shook her head ruefully. Sometimes, Hannah raised sarcasm to an art form. "Not quite."

"Well, what *did* he have to say for himself?"

"Nothing."

Hannah's mouth dropped open. "Nothing? What do you mean, nothing?"

"Just that. He said he couldn't explain what had happened to him and I should just forget about him. Then he left."

"My God! What an asshole!" Hannah's forehead crinkled. "So what's with the bullet hole in the wall?"

Carolyn managed a sheepish smile. "I tried to get him to stay and talk, but he called my bluff. Apparently, he didn't believe I would shoot him, even after my little demonstration."

"Well, he's got balls, I'll give him that. Of course, if I could get him alone in a dark room, with a rusty, dull knife, I'd be happy to remedy that."

Carolyn snickered. In truth, Hannah had never really liked Gray. She'd always said he was too conservative and stuffy for a free spirit like Carolyn. There might have been an element of truth to the accusation. For one thing, he had absolutely hated her job. They'd had more than one bitter fight in the days leading up to their wedding. Somehow, Gray had assumed she'd quit the force once she married him. Where he'd gotten that impression, she didn't know, but a gun-wielding, risk-taking homicide detective wife didn't fit in with his cozy image of domestic bliss. No doubt he would have been thrilled if she'd been a nurse or a school teacher, or—but no, it was unfair of her to think of it as sexism on his part. All he'd really wanted was for her to be safe.

She rubbed her eyes, suddenly tired. In the end, she *had* quit the force for him, just not in the way he'd meant.

"There's more," she said. Hannah quirked an eyebrow, and Carolyn pointed to the black leather jacket that still lay draped over the chair where Gray had left it.

Hannah's mouth dropped open again. "He left his coat?"

Carolyn nodded.

"It's like minus fifty degrees out!"

"More like ten."

"Don't forget wind chill."

Carolyn smiled. "We both agree it's way too cold to leave your coat behind."

"So you think it's a subliminal message? If you leave something at someone's house, it's supposed to mean you want to go back."

Carolyn figured Gray might *want* to come back, but she knew he wouldn't. He'd made that very clear. "I think it's a clue to where to find him."

Hannah clucked her tongue. "Why, Carolyn Mathers, have you been snooping?"

Carolyn reached into her blazer pocket and pulled out the handful of receipts she'd found in Gray's jacket. "We have here five receipts from a Zip Mart on Thirty-Second and Walnut." She held the receipts out.

Hannah took them and examined them, her brow puckering more and more deeply as she flipped through them. She looked up again when she'd seen the last of them. "He appears to have become a creature of habit."

"And very monotonous diet," Carolyn agreed. According to those receipts, Gray had visited that Zip Mart every Monday night at around six o'clock and bought a quart of milk. Nothing else, just milk.

"Weird," Hannah said.

"Hmm." Carolyn retrieved the receipts and put them back in her pocket. "What do you want to bet that next Monday at around six o'clock he'll be at that Zip Mart?"

Hannah sighed and seemed to consider her words carefully before speaking. "Honey, you need to think long and hard before you do anything . . . rash. You talked to him tonight and he wouldn't tell you anything. Chances are if you confront him again, you'll get the same answer. Why torture yourself?"

Carolyn fought a flush of undeserved anger toward her friend. Hannah was just trying to help. "The man made the last three years a living hell for me. I deserve an explanation. At least it would give me some closure, free me to go on with my life." Despite her best efforts, Carolyn was pretty sure her voice held a hint of tightness.

Though Hannah must have heard the undercurrent of anger, she responded mildly. "I understand all that. But I have a feeling you're not going to like the explanation, whatever it is. You know I was never Gray's biggest fan, but I bet if he thought telling you what happened would help you out he would have done it. There's a reason he's not telling."

Carolyn clamped her teeth shut to keep herself from saying something she might regret later. *Breathe,* she reminded herself. She sucked in a lung-full of air, holding it and then releasing it slowly, trying to let the tension flow from her body. When she spoke again, her voice was much more controlled.

"Gray doesn't get to decide what to tell me and what not to tell me. There's no way I can just let this go."

Hannah nodded gravely. "I wish you would. But, if you're not going to, then count me in."

Carolyn tried to suppress her amused smile, but didn't quite manage it. "Thanks, partner. If I find myself over my head, I promise I'll call you in. But let me try this on my own first."

Hannah wrinkled her nose. "Hey, if you weren't going to accept my help, why'd you ask me here in the first place?"

Despite the grumpy tone, Carolyn figured Hannah understood better than she let on. "I just needed to talk it out. But honestly, Hannah, if things don't go right you'll be the first one I call."

"So, what's your plan?"

She patted her pocket. "I think I'll have a desperate need to visit the Zip Mart next Monday evening."

Hannah's dimples made an appearance. "That would be the Zip Mart about a dozen blocks away from your house, right? Not the one just down the street?"

"Hey, maybe the other one has more selection. It's

right near Penn, so it's got to have all kinds of special college kid . . . stuff. Right?"

"Yeah, sure. Can I make a suggestion, even though you don't want my help?"

Carolyn nodded.

"Don't confront him at the Zip Mart. See if you can tail him to where he lives. That way if he blows you off, you can still get to him."

"Good idea," Carolyn agreed. If Gray did another disappearing act, she could be sure he'd break his Zip Mart pattern and she might never find him again.

She felt a single twinge of guilt over the idea of following Gray like he was one of the philandering husbands her firm had to investigate. But she couldn't help wondering if leaving his coat here—with this evidence of where to find him—weren't a subconscious invitation for her to come looking. And with that admittedly flimsy rationalization, she laid her conscience to rest.

* * *

GRAY YAWNED AS HE headed toward his front door. Usually, he was up the moment the sun set, but ever since last Wednesday when he'd spoken to Carolyn, his daytime sleep had been restless and unsatisfying, and he found himself sleeping into the early evening hours. He glanced at his watch and saw that it was already nearly seven.

Opening the door, he stepped out into the brisk winter night. It was another cold one, with just enough wind to turn the air from frigid to downright arctic. He stuffed his hands into the pockets of his new leather jacket and suppressed a shiver.

Living so near the university, he was used to the sidewalks being crowded with pedestrians—young, boisterous, and too often drunk. The cold tonight discouraged many from venturing out, and the quiet made it feel more like midnight than seven. It also made it painfully easy for Gray to spot his tail for the evening, sitting on a stoop across the street.

A surge of righteous anger warmed him as he glared at the Guardian. Jules must have convinced that sanctimonious Founder of his that Gray was a danger to humanity—ever since Wednesday, whenever he looked out his window he saw at least one Guardian watching his house.

This particular Guardian wasn't quite as unwelcome as many of the others. She smiled at him from across the street, then seemed to decide it wasn't necessary to keep her distance. He waited as she crossed to him, but he still felt an ungentlemanly urge to wring her pretty little neck.

Deirdre MacPherson was hands-down the prettiest of the handful of female Guardians. She wasn't a classic beauty like Carolyn, but her features were so striking she was hard to miss. Large eyes, with ridiculously long lashes, gave her a look of perpetual innocence, although from some of her descriptions of her mortal life, he gathered she'd been a bit of a party girl. Unfortunately, one night she'd chosen the wrong man to party with. The Guardians had rescued her before she'd been forced to kill, and destroyed her maker in the process.

Deirdre looped her hand through Gray's arm, smiling up at him coquettishly. "Lovely night for a walk," she said. "Mind if I join you?"

Gray started walking. "What would you do if I said yes?"

"Silly question."

He grunted an acknowledgment, then shook his head. "You don't really believe I'm a rogue killer in the making, do you?"

"It doesn't matter what I believe. Eli gave the order. I'm just doing my job."

Gray had met the Founder once, when the Guardians had still been actively trying to recruit him. Despite any suspicions they might have about his self-control, the recruitment effort had been intense. Eli couldn't understand how someone could *not* want to be part of the effort to rid the world—or at least Philadelphia—of Killers. Especially when said someone had so much to thank the Guardians for. Of course, maybe it had all been an effort to keep more careful tabs on a potentially dangerous fledgling vampire.

"Is it so terrible to have company every once in a while?" Deirdre asked. She had subtly closed what little distance lay between them, and now her side brushed against his as she clung more tightly to his arm.

A stirring in his southern regions made him grit his teeth. "Stop that."

She gave him a wide-eyed, innocent stare, but he avoided meeting her eyes, knowing that would just make it worse. She laughed lightly, and the stirring subsided.

"You're such a prude," she said as she loosened her grip on his arm.

He snorted. "I'm just not that kind of guy, Dee."

She pouted. "Not the kind of guy who has sex with girls?"

Gray halted and disengaged her arm from his. "Knock it off." He'd never been inclined to give in to her persistent flirting, and he didn't appreciate her attempts to stoke his lust with glamour. "You're a lovely woman, and if I weren't still in love with someone else, I'd probably jump into your bed in a heartbeat." Actually, he doubted that, but there was no reason to hurt her feelings any more than necessary.

Deirdre shook her head. "It's been three years, Gray. Don't you think it's time you let go?"

His heart constricted predictably at her words. "I'm sure you're right," he told her. "But the heart doesn't follow orders. I can't just order it to heal."

"I'm not asking for your heart."

Leave it to Deirdre to tell it like it is! He smiled gently. "I know. But I'm afraid there's an unbreakable bond between my heart and my dick, so you can't have just one."

She rolled her eyes but resumed walking. "You know, most people become *more* horny when they make the transition."

"The subject is closed." He hoped the street lamps bleached the color out of his skin so she couldn't see the flush of his cheeks. It was undeniably true that his libido had been in overdrive ever since that fateful night. Just seeing a pretty pair of legs or a hint of enticing cleavage could make him hard as a brick. It was just that he had no desire to quench his lust with Deirdre.

They reached the Zip Mart, and thankfully she let the subject drop. She wandered the aisles aimlessly while he grabbed his quart of milk and headed to the cashier. Corey, a sophomore at Penn who had an unfortunate predilection toward acne, was on duty tonight. On one very slow night, when Corey was bored and Gray was lonely, they'd struck up a conversation, and now Gray couldn't just get in and get out without at least a little banter.

"You're mighty late tonight, Mr. Gray," said Corey, grinning at him.

When Gray had been forced to disappear, he'd had to change his name. To make it easy to remember, he'd merely switched his first and last names. Now the few mortals who knew him thought his name was James Gray. "Yeah, got caught up on the phone with an old friend."

Corey stopped halfway through ringing up the milk. "Oh? Male or female?"

Gray laughed. "None of your business. Now hurry up. I'm running late, you know." He felt a stab of regret that he had to make up lies even when talking to a convenience store clerk.

Deirdre once again linked her arm with his when they left the store, but at least she gave up her attempts to seduce him. They walked in almost-peaceful silence, and he wondered for a moment if maybe he should accept her offer after all. Maybe a night of mind-blowing sex would ease some of the pressure inside his chest.

Maybe. But every instinct in his body told him that mind-blowing sex with Deirdre was a very, very bad idea.

At his doorstep, Gray had the distinct impression that she expected him to invite her in. He wasn't about to do so.

"You don't know what you're missing," she murmured, standing on tiptoe and planting a dry kiss on his lips.

He felt her glamour wrap around him, pulling him closer. His cock hardened against his will, and his mind filled with images of tasting her delicate mouth, of running his hands over her soft, pliant body. But Deirdre was only a year or so older than Gray, her powers as immature as his, and though he felt her glamour, he had no trouble resisting it.

Afraid to speak lest he say something nasty, he turned from her wordlessly and slipped into his house. When the door closed behind him, he let out a breath of relief. He really, really hated it when other vampires used glamour against him. At least hers wasn't as powerful as Jules's. If it were, he'd be buried inside her by now.

His erection still throbbing uncomfortably, Gray headed to the kitchen and pulled out a water glass. He poured the glass halfway full with milk, then retrieved one of the dark green glass bottles from his fridge and uncorked it with a grimace. Even after three years, he had to force himself to feed. As a mortal, he'd always been just a little overweight, no matter how careful he was with his diet. Genetics, he supposed. But since he'd become vampire, it was all he could do to keep himself from becoming cadaverous.

Gray poured the chilled lamb's blood into his milk,

stirring the sickening concoction into a pink mess. The smell wrinkled his nose, especially the medicinal taint of the anticoagulant. He recorked the bottle, then leaned against the kitchen counter, staring at his meal.

The blood fed his vampire body, and the milk made the experience so distasteful it took a concerted effort not to vomit it up again. Even so, Gray always added the milk. Eli said it was safer, easier to fight the tendency to addiction, if feeding was not a pleasurable task, and Gray wasn't inclined to take any chances.

Pinching his nose shut, Gray tipped the glass to his lips and took a few swallows. The taste made him shudder, but it kept him alive and kept him from feeding on helpless mortals, so he forced it down.

He was only about a quarter of the way through the ordeal when his doorbell rang. He grunted in irritation as he put the glass down, wiping the excess from his lips. He'd thought Deirdre had given up for the night. Apparently, he'd been mistaken. Leaving everything on the counter, he strode toward the front door, his temper sizzling. He was never at his best around the times of his twice-weekly feedings.

He threw the door open, ready to tell Deirdre more forcefully that he wasn't interested.

Words died in his throat when he saw Carolyn standing on his doorstep. A swell of contradictory emotions rose around him as he looked at the woman he couldn't help loving, no matter how much time passed. He couldn't even make sense of what he was feeling, and he just stood there and stared at her like an idiot.

"May I come in?" she asked.

He read determination in her face, along with a healthy dose of the fury she'd already demonstrated. He could just close the door in her face, as he'd done to Deirdre, but he had a feeling Carolyn wouldn't give up as easily. *Stubborn as a mule* was a phrase that everyone who knew her had muttered at least once.

"Are you armed?" he replied with a lift of his eyebrow. No matter how much turmoil she caused, he didn't dare let her see it.

Her eyes narrowed at the detachment in his voice. "Of course, but since we already determined I won't shoot you I don't see why that should matter."

Boy, would Carolyn ever be surprised at what would happen if she *did* shoot him! Reluctantly, he opened the door wider and beckoned her in. She gave his house a thoughtful examination, then turned to him.

"Nice place you have here." But the look on her face told him she thought the place anything but nice.

Being the abode of a vampire, the house was designed for maximum darkness. Small windows, all draped in heavy curtains. Dim lights, though electric light didn't actually bother him. Stranger still to Carolyn's eyes would be the decor and furnishings. Antiques, mostly, with lots of feminine touches. Doilies, rose-patterned wallpaper, lace antimacassars on the ornate arm chairs and sofa.

"I . . . er . . . inherited it," he said as he gestured her into the living room. A parlor, really, though people didn't have "parlors" these days. The place had barely changed since Edwardian times, when Kate Henshaw, his maker, had died and been transformed into a Killer. When the Guardians had destroyed her, they'd arranged for her house to become his. Gray had never been overly curious as to how they'd managed that.

"Really?" Carolyn asked with infinite skepticism as she sat in one of the wing chairs. Gray knew from experience the thing was hard enough to numb your ass, but as he took a seat on the more comfortable sofa he felt it wiser not to invite her to join him. "And how is it that my investigation failed to turn up any sign of this inheritance?"

"What are you doing here, Carolyn? I told you I have nothing to give you."

"And I refuse to accept that. Do you have any idea what these past three years have been like for me?"

As a matter of fact, he did. Despite all advice to sever every link to his past, he'd never been able to let Carolyn go. He wouldn't say he spied on her, exactly, but he had frequently found excuses to wander around her neighborhood.

Of course, for the last few months, he'd found more and more excuses, hence Jules's accusation that he was "stalking" her.

"My last three years haven't been so great either," he assured her. "I'm really, really sorry that I hurt you. But I can't go back and undo it, and even if I could explain what happened it wouldn't change anything."

"I think perhaps you're underestimating me. I *will* find out whatever it is you're trying to hide."

There was that familiar stubborn set to her jaw, the fierce resolve in her sky-blue eyes. She'd let her hair grow out, into lustrous golden-blonde locks framing her face. When she'd been a cop, she'd kept it cropped short in a futile attempt to look butch. She'd looked like a cute blonde pixie instead. A cute blonde pixie who was damn good at her job. But surely this particular secret was safe, even from her. After all, even if she somehow found evidence of the truth, she wouldn't believe it. No, this was one secret she would *not* uncover.

He wished his own logic were doing a better job of convincing him. Somehow, he had to find a way to remove himself from her scrutiny.

"So," she continued, putting a false lightness into her tone, "if you don't want to talk about the past, why don't you tell me about your present? What are you doing with yourself these days?"

Damn, she was going to be hard to get rid of. And anything he said would just give her more fuel. "Carolyn, please." He sounded pathetic even to his own ears, but he didn't know what else to say.

She sighed. "All right. If you don't want to talk

about yourself, how about we just have a quiet drink together and reminisce about old times."

"I'm afraid I don't have anything to drink."

"You have milk."

Ah, that's how she had found him. Just his luck his ex-fiancée was a detective. "I didn't think that was the kind of drink you had in mind."

She smiled. "It wasn't, but as you know I'm not a high-maintenance woman."

But having her here even long enough to drink a glass of milk was a bad idea. "Carolyn—" he started, but she stood up and headed toward the hallway.

"I'll get it myself," she said. "Where's the kitchen? Through there?" She pointed down the hall that did indeed lead to the kitchen.

With a sickening turn of his stomach, Gray remembered leaving his meal arrayed on the kitchen counter. Oh, shit!

He leapt to his feet, sprinting toward her and catching hold of her arm before she'd gotten close enough to the kitchen doorway to spy the contents. He'd moved supernaturally fast, and she gasped in amazement as she raised her gaze to his.

In that split second, he knew there was no logical explanation he could give for his sudden burst of desperate speed, nor for his obvious alarm at the thought of her entering his kitchen. As Carolyn's eyes met his, he knew there was only one thing he could do. Holding her shocked gaze, he used his glamour to push all thoughts of the kitchen and her glass of milk from her mind.

4

CAROLYN COULDN'T BLINK. HER eyes locked
with Gray's, and then refused to budge as she lost herself in those blue-gray depths. Her heart trembled, and
it felt as if the world had taken a sudden step to the
side. Where was she? What had she been about to do?
She wanted desperately to blink away the confusion,
but she couldn't, no matter how hard she tried.

"Wait here," Gray said in a voice barely above a
whisper, and then he slipped away.

Still she could neither move, nor blink. She heard
the sound of a refrigerator door opening and closing,
then the sink running. Then Gray was back, moving
into her field of vision. She couldn't focus her eyes,
but she thought Gray's face looked troubled. He
reached up and stroked her cheek softly with the back
of his hand, just once. The touch made her shiver.

"I'm sorry about this, sweetheart," she heard him
murmur.

Her vision became even cloudier, and suddenly her
knees buckled. She tried to stop her fall with her
hands, but her body's responses were sluggish. The
floor rose up to meet her. . . .

When she opened her eyes, Carolyn's head was

throbbing. A groan escaped her, and she tried to get her bearings.

She was lying down. Gray was sitting beside her, and she felt something cold against the side of her head.

What the hell . . . ?

"What happened?" The words came out mumbled and slurred, as though she'd been drinking.

"You tripped," Gray said. "You hit your head against a table and conked out for a couple of minutes."

Her head seemed to confirm his words with a particularly nasty throb, and she realized the spot of cold on her head was an ice pack. She was lying on the living room sofa, Gray's hip perched on the edge right beside her. "Tripped?" she repeated, trying to get her thoughts lined up. She remembered inviting herself for a drink. And she remembered heading toward the kitchen to help herself when Gray seemed uninclined to play host. Then . . . nothing.

Carolyn furrowed her brow, trying to force the memory to surface. If she'd tripped, surely she'd remember it. She tried to sit up, but Gray laid a hand on her shoulder.

"Take it easy. You've had a nasty knock on the head. How many fingers am I holding up?"

"Two," she answered, rolling her eyes. "I don't have a concussion."

Gray's smile didn't reach his eyes. "Just checking." He moved the ice away from her head, setting the bag down on the floor.

This time, when she tried to sit up, he let her. The pain in her head seemed to be receding, but she still felt . . . strange. Why couldn't she remember falling? Surely she hadn't hit her head *that* hard. She lowered her face into her hands. Her whole body tensed when she felt the warmth of Gray's palm against her back. He rubbed up and down her spine, and his touch dispelled the chill that had settled over her.

God, he had good hands. Some primal instinct in him always seemed to know just where she needed to be touched. She'd forgotten that about him, but now the memories came flooding back unbidden.

His powerful fingers, digging into the knots in her shoulders after a tense day on the job. His short nails scraping gently across her bare back, soothing the itch she hadn't known she'd had. And, most glorious of all—

Carolyn sat up abruptly, shaking her head to clear the images. There were some things she didn't *want* to remember.

Gray moved his hand away and sat quietly beside her. His hands were clasped between his knees, and his shaggy hair hid his face. She swallowed past a lump in her throat. Then her eyes were drawn to a different lump altogether.

Gray's jeans did little to hide the swell of his erection. For one breathless moment, she was tempted to reach out and touch it, feel the power and heat of it in the palms of her hands. A shiver of desire passed through her as she imagined slowly pulling that zipper down.

Luckily, her common sense returned before she did any such thing. Blood heated her cheeks. How could she possibly feel desire for the man who had so thoroughly betrayed her? For all his talk of how miserable his last three years had been, he had apparently not spent them alone, like she had. How long after he'd deserted Carolyn had he waited to hook up with the pretty little brunette she'd seen him kissing?

She moved away from him on the couch, putting as much distance between them as possible. Annoyingly, her heart still tripped over itself, and there was no denying the hint of moisture between her legs.

Gray raised his head and met her eyes, his nostrils slightly flared. Her desire spiked, her throat constricting as her breaths came shorter and faster. She wet her lips, a nervous gesture, not a come-on, but Gray slid closer to her until he invaded her personal space and her head filled with the scent of him. He leaned into her.

What are you doing? a frantic voice shouted in the back of her mind. She wanted to pull away, wanted to put a stop to this right this moment, and yet her body wouldn't obey her. Her mouth opened against her will, and her eyes slid shut. She waited.

His breath caressed her lips, and every inch of her skin was aware of his proximity. She couldn't move, could barely breathe, as she waited for him to take what she offered. Desire like molten lava pooled in her belly, and if she'd been capable of movement she would have lain back on the couch and spread her legs for him. Lust burned out of control, a raging forest fire that threatened to consume her.

When Gray backed away, her sense of loss was indescribable. A groan of protest escaped as she opened her eyes.

There was no doubt he felt the same desire as she. His pupils were so dilated his eyes seemed almost black, and his pants looked about to burst. And there was something else, something she'd never seen in him before, a kind of feral impatience. He looked like a man who would seize what he wanted without asking permission.

The expression should have terrified her. Instead, the heat between her legs intensified.

"Time for you to go," he said, his voice hoarse with lust.

She opened her mouth to protest, but it turned into a cry of surprise when he leapt to his feet, his hand fastening about her arm and dragging her with him. Reality snapped back into place as he headed toward the door, pulling her.

"What the hell do you think you're doing?" she demanded, trying to dig in her heels. Her efforts didn't even slow him down.

"You're leaving." The words came out as a snarl. He paused to open his front door, and she took the opportunity to punch the arm that held her as hard as she could. But it was an awkward, left-handed swing, and the muscles of his shoulder were like corded steel. No doubt she had hurt her own knuckles more than she had hurt him. The door swung open and Gray dragged her up against his body, bringing her face to within inches of his. His erection ground against her belly as he growled at her.

"Stay away from me, Carolyn. I mean it. I'm not the man you once knew." With that, he gave her a shove that almost sent her down his front steps. By the time she regained her balance, the door had slammed in her face.

For a long moment, she stood breathless with shock and outrage, staring at that closed door and wishing she could bore a hole in it with her eyes. Her upper arm ached where his fingers had dug in too deeply, and she noticed once again the throbbing of her head. How could he go from almost kissing her one moment to manhandling her the next? And just what exactly was the matter with her that she'd almost let him do the former?

Slowly, the pounding of her heart calmed, but nothing could calm the turbulence of her thoughts. "All right, Gray," she whispered. "You win this round. But the war isn't over."

She was going to get to the bottom of this. If the direct assault didn't work, well then she'd have to try a little subtlety.

By the time she walked away, she was already beginning to plan her next attack.

* * *

GRAY SAT ON THE floor with his back to the door, his head buried in his hands as he sucked in one breath after another. The beast still raged within him, and it took all his will to tame it, keep himself from flinging the door open and chasing after Carolyn.

How far would it have gone, if he hadn't gotten control of himself? There was no doubt in his mind he would have fucked her, his glamour so fogging her senses she wouldn't have thought to protest. His cock ached with frustrated desire.

What else would he have done? Even now, he felt his fangs pricking the inside of his lips. They had descended the moment he'd scented her arousal in the air, and from the moment they had, his senses had filled with acute awareness of her blood.

He heard the pounding of her heart, saw the pulse beating in her fragile throat. Had it just been his cock he wanted to bury in her?

He banged the back of his head against the door, and that hint of pain helped calm him, gave him something to think about other than his frustrated lust. Breathing slowly and steadily, he willed the fangs to recede. At first, it didn't work, but as the final echoes of Carolyn's footsteps faded, calm gradually returned.

All right. He'd just proved once and for all that he couldn't be trusted around her. Even if he hadn't bitten her, he would never have forgiven himself if he'd slept with her when her mind was too clouded with glamour to make a conscious decision. It would have felt like rape, no matter how eagerly she might have accepted him at the time.

He'd hated being rough with her, but perhaps it was all for the best. If she needed tangible proof that the Gray James she'd once loved and planned to marry had changed, that had been it. It used to infuriate her that whenever they argued, he stayed so calm he didn't even raise his voice while she shouted and raged.

Wishing he could convince himself she would give up after that performance, Gray pushed to his feet. His revolting meal awaited him in the fridge. Maybe after he downed it, the bloodlust that still pulsed just below the surface would ease.

* * *

CAROLYN ARRIVED AT HER office at eight o'clock, though her agency didn't open until nine. She needed to type up all her notes and gather up all the information for her current open cases. Not that this was a massive undertaking. Although the agency did well enough to get by, the same delicate looks that had made her fellow officers overlook her skills hampered her ability to gain the trust of potential clients. She just didn't look the part, and there was nothing she could do about it.

Sighing, she started organizing the files and making sure another human being could understand her cryptic notes. By the time Hannah arrived at quarter to nine, everything was ready.

. They'd never done quite enough business to warrant any secretarial help, so both Carolyn and Hannah had their desks out in the main office. When a potential client came by, he or she was greeted by one of the owners, not some flunky. Of course, there were a couple of conference rooms, where the clients could talk to an investigator in private, but Carolyn and Hannah had tried to make the place more open and friendly looking than most PI offices.

Hannah stepped into the office and reached for the light switch before she realized the lights were already on. She had rolled her frizzy curls into a French twist at the back of her head and wore a gray wool pantsuit that added about five years to her appearance. Her look screamed of capable womanhood, and Carolyn wished she could copy it somehow.

"You're here early," Hannah commented as she moved to the credenza in the waiting area and poured a cup of coffee.

"Yeah," Carolyn agreed, wrapping her hands around her own cup.

"What's up?" Hannah sat in front of Carolyn's desk, regarding her curiously.

Carolyn cleared her throat, then pushed the pile of notes and files across the desk. "I was wondering if you could take over my cases for a little while. They're all pretty simple." She couldn't help the way her nose wrinkled in distaste. "Simple" seemed an understatement.

After all the time and effort she'd put into trying to find Gray, it had seemed natural to become a specialist in locates—finding missing heirs and such, and skip-traces—finding deadbeat dads and others who skipped town without paying their bills. Somehow, it just wasn't as satisfying to hunt down some cheapskate who refused to pay his bills as to bring a murderer to justice. Go figure. But the force had let her down in her time of need, and she was never going back.

Hannah put her cup down and pushed the files to the side, leaning her elbows on the edge of the desk. "This has something to do with Gray."

Carolyn nodded. "I went to see him last night."

"And?"

And I just about jumped his bones. Well, no, she couldn't say that, now could she? She reached up and rubbed her upper arm, where this morning she'd found a set of finger-shaped bruises. She shook her head. "And I don't think I'm going to do anybody any good as an investigator for a while."

"Come on, Carolyn. You've gotta give me more than that."

"There's something very, very strange going on."

"No shit?"

Carolyn narrowed her eyes. "I mean even stranger than I thought."

"That's pretty damn strange."

"Right. Gray still won't tell me anything, but there's no way I can let this go."

"So? What's the plan?"

"I want to do a stakeout. If he won't tell me what's going on, then maybe I can find out for myself." Hannah was silent long enough to convey her disapproval. Carolyn's fingers skimmed over the bruises on her arm again. When Hannah still didn't comment, she had to break the silence. "Okay, come on, tell me what you're thinking."

Hannah reached across the desk and took Carolyn's hand. "Honey, I'm thinking it's time you let this go."

Carolyn jerked her hand away. "No way! I have a right to know why he left me, and, damn it, I'm going to get that explanation if I have to beat it out of him." Not that she had any hope of doing so. What had happened to the gentle, mild-mannered man she'd once known? Last night, she had no doubt he'd intended that vise-like grip on her arm to be brutal. Where had that strength come from? That savagery?

"And then what?"

The question left Carolyn blinking like a fool. "Huh?"

"So you find out what happened three years ago, why Gray disappeared on you. Then what?"

"I don't know."

"Well maybe you should figure that out before you go poking your nose into something you may not want to know."

"Hannah. You've known me what, ten years?" Hannah nodded cautiously. "Do you honestly think it's possible for me to 'just let this go?' "

Hannah's sigh was both exasperated and understanding. "Not unless I hog-tie you and lock you in a basement somewhere."

"So, will you handle my cases for me while I'm busy with Gray?"

Hannah pulled the files over and plunked the pile into her lap. "There, are you happy?"

The tension eased out of Carolyn's shoulders. "Thanks, Hannah. You're the best. Now I'm going to put together my surveillance plan."

She rose from her desk, eager to begin.

"Carolyn."

She turned to see Hannah regarding her with penetrating eyes. "Yes?"

"Why do you keep rubbing your arm?"

Carolyn quickly dropped her hand, but she couldn't have acted more guilty if she tried. "Uh . . ."

Hannah stood up, dumping the pile of folders back onto the desk. "If he hurt you, I'm going to feed him his balls."

Carolyn tried a weak smile. "It's nothing. He just grabbed me and didn't know his own strength."

"Carolyn . . ."

"Look, I shot at him the first time I saw him, okay? We're now even." She stepped in closer, putting both her hands on her friend's shoulders. "I promise, if things start getting out of hand, I'll call for backup. I know my limitations."

"In regular life, I'd agree with you a hundred percent. I'm not so sure I agree when you're personally involved. You could do yourself a world of hurt."

Knowing she would never convince Hannah not to worry, Carolyn decided not to try. "See you later, mom," she said, letting go of Hannah's shoulders and striding to the door.

* * *

JULES LIKED TO THINK of himself as the epitome of dedicated professionalism, but tonight it had taken a supreme effort of will to roll himself out of bed to attend the weekly meeting at Eli's house. His new mortal lover, Courtney, was a masterful bed partner, and when she'd shown up on his doorstep with mischief on her mind, the temptation to skip the meeting had nearly overwhelmed him.

In the end, sense of duty had prevailed, but he'd invited Courtney to wait for him. A smile twitched his lips as he remembered the promise she'd whispered in his ear when she sent him off.

His mind was still half-distracted by thoughts of the lovely Courtney when he stepped into Eli's meeting room. The twenty-odd pairs of eyes that focused on him brought his mind back to the present. Eli looked at his watch pointedly, but refrained from dressing him down.

Even Eli's massive room didn't have enough seats for the entire population of Guardians to sit, so Jules took a seat on the floor. Off in a shadowy corner, he saw Drake leaning against the wall, his arms folded across his chest. The Guardians had put a marked distance between themselves and him, and if Jules didn't know better he would have sworn he saw shades of resentment in the vampire's eyes.

The meeting began with the more mundane aspects of Guardian life—finances, food supply, and a little petty bickering, which Eli quashed before it got out of hand. Then there were reports from various task forces who kept an eye out for news of murders that looked suspiciously like vampire kills. When it came his turn, Jules explained there was nothing to report on the Gray James front.

Finally, the topic made its way around to the Broad Street killer. Deirdre and Fletcher gave a summary of their week's activities, but there had been little progress.

"He's killed again," Deirdre admitted, reluctantly. A quiet murmur passed through the room, then died. "Another young woman on Sunday night, and then there was a break in his pattern." Her pretty brow furrowed with worry. "There was a thirtyish black man found in the subway entrance at Broad and Walnut. Same MO, throat slashed and all, except for the rape."

In the corner, Drake cleared his throat, and all eyes

turned to him. He had said nothing during Deirdre and Fletcher's presentation, letting them speak for him. He'd have to be an idiot not to know he wasn't popular with the Guardians. No doubt it was wiser for him to keep his mouth shut whenever possible.

"There was no break in the pattern," Drake said, pushing away from the wall so he was no longer cloaked in shadows. "That was one of mine."

No one made a sound, but tension crackled in the air. *That's what comes of using a Killer to catch a Killer,* Jules thought in disgust. Only Eli looked unconcerned by the admission. Fletcher's face reddened, and he was the first to break the silence.

"So, not only did you kill some poor fool, you fouled up the evidence so that the police will be thrown off target! Explain to me again how you're 'helping' solve this case."

Drake shrugged. "Do you really want the police getting close to this killer? Mortals are clearly no match for him, and the police would just get themselves killed. Better to throw them off."

"That's not the point!" Fletcher said, his agitation so great he shot to his feet. His fists were clenched tight, his knuckles white, and he looked ready to launch himself across the room. "I won't have you killing people on my watch!"

Drake's eyes narrowed and he took a step closer to Fletcher. "Eli, put your puppy on a leash before it gets kicked."

That sent Fletcher's temper over the edge, and he charged toward Drake with murder in his eyes. Drake bared his fangs and took a single step forward to meet the challenge.

"Stop it!" Eli bellowed.

Jules felt the power of that command down to his bones, even though it wasn't directed at him. The air was still and heavy, stifling almost, and both Fletcher and Drake came to an abrupt halt. They eyed each other across the short distance that separated them, and hostility sparked between them, but neither stepped forward. Jules shivered as he read Drake's face—Drake was *trying* to move, but he couldn't.

"Let go of me, Eli," he snarled, confirming that it was indeed Eli's glamour that held him motionless.

"Will you control yourself?"

Drake's fists loosened, and the aggression eased out of his shoulders. "If Fletcher will do the same."

"He will," Eli responded, and there was no mistaking the command in his voice.

Both Drake and Fletcher relaxed some, and the air suddenly became breathable again. They stared at each other a long moment, but Fletcher's common sense appeared to have returned. If he'd actually managed to close with Drake, Drake could have killed him. Easily. Not that he would have done so in the middle of this gathering of Guardians, but still . . .

"My apologies," Drake said. "I thought throwing the police off the scent was the wisest thing, but I should have consulted you before doing so." He held out his hand. Fletcher eyed it suspiciously, then gave it a brief, insincere shake.

Jules let out a breath he didn't know he was holding and eyed Eli as the tension drained out of the room and the meeting returned to order. The Founder had stopped Drake—a full vampire, with many years of kills under his belt—with nothing more than a word. Just how powerful was he, anyway?

More disturbed by the interlude than he liked to admit, Jules didn't realize until the meeting had adjourned that the last true Broad Street kill had occurred while Gray was under surveillance. Apparently, Gray James wasn't the Broad Street Banger after all.

It perhaps reflected poorly on Jules's character that he was disappointed at the revelation.

5

CAROLYN HUNCHED DOWN IN her car and questioned her sanity. It was ten o'clock at night. The temperature hovered just above freezing. Rain pelted the windshield, making it hard to see anything. And she'd drunk the last of her hot chocolate over an hour ago. She crossed her arms over her chest and shivered, chilled down to her bones.

Gray's house was at the corner of a long row of narrow houses with weathered stucco fronts. From her observations, Carolyn gathered that most of the original row homes had been divided into what had to be cramped apartments, housing anywhere from three to six residents. No doubt these apartments catered to the students at nearby U of P. Gray's house was about twice the size of those around it, and she wondered how it had escaped the neighborhood's transformation from individual residences to student apartments.

At first, she'd focused her surveillance on the daylight hours, when it was warmer and much easier to see. After a full week had passed without Gray showing his face even once, she'd reluctantly moved to a night shift. Aside from being dark and cold and generally miserable, the night watch made her far more conspicuous. During the day, there was enough foot traffic that she could disappear amongst the crowd. At night, she just had to hope no one noticed her. So far, no one had. As far as she knew.

Even during the night, Gray wasn't exactly a social butterfly. He went out occasionally, but he didn't do much more than wander the streets with no apparent purpose. Every once in a while, he'd shop, but never for food. Carolyn wondered how well stocked his kitchen was to keep him fed for three meals a day, this long. It wasn't as if he ever went to a restaurant or ordered a pizza like a normal bachelor.

She'd thought she was getting nowhere. Then she noticed something much odder and more intriguing than Gray's lack of social life: she wasn't the only one watching his house.

There was an all-night coffee shop across the street from Gray's house—the kind of place where the owners probably lived in an apartment directly above. Small and not terribly inviting, it did its best business late at night, when all other restaurants were closed and students needed a place to guzzle coffee while they crammed. Carolyn herself had more than once used it as cover for her stakeout.

Then one day, she'd noticed a man sitting alone in a booth by the window. She noticed him because he was so unlike the coffee shop's usual clientele. *Way* too well dressed to be a student, she could imagine some of the female students pinning posters of him to their dorm room walls. Even sitting down, he looked tall, with broad shoulders displayed to best advantage in his tightly tailored shirt. Auburn hair long enough to run your fingers through, and patrician features that suggested he wouldn't appreciate it if you did.

Carolyn was as fond of eye-candy as the next woman, but after taking one good look, she had dismissed him from her mind. But then she'd noticed he seemed to be staring at Gray's house. A house that was nowhere near remarkable enough to warrant the attention.

He had lingered a long time, nursing a cup of coffee he never let the waitress refill. Then, when Gray emerged, he'd given a little start and hurried out of the restaurant.

Carolyn hadn't set foot in the coffee shop since then. She didn't want whoever else was watching to catch on to her.

After the first time, she'd had no trouble spotting the other surveillance. It wasn't always the same person— there seemed to be a rotation, two men and then the sexy brunette Carolyn had seen Gray kissing. The brunette never made any attempt to hide, though the two men kept their distance. Gray would sometimes pause to glare at his watcher before continuing on his errands.

So, who the hell were these people? The easy assumption was that they were cops of some sort, but Carolyn instinctively knew that wasn't true. For one thing, she sincerely doubted a cop would have kissed Gray while on surveillance.

Which brought Carolyn back to the question she really wished she could stop obsessing over: what was Gray's relationship with this woman? Carolyn hadn't seen any more kisses, but they did sometimes walk together in what seemed like friendly camaraderie, the woman's arm linked with his. If she and her cohorts were antagonists of some sort—which they surely had to be—why was Gray so chummy with this chick? And if they were so chummy, why was she tailing him? All very strange.

Tonight's watcher was the auburn-haired hunk. Carolyn had seen him three times now, and each time he'd been wearing a different expensive coat and a rakish hat. She'd parked her car on Gray's side of the street so that she could keep her eye both on Gray's doorway and on the guy who was watching him. As before, he was sitting in a booth by the window of the coffee shop, paying little or no attention to his coffee. Carolyn wondered why either one of them bothered to watch on a night when any sane person would remain indoors.

By eleven-thirty, Carolyn was so cold her teeth were chattering. Her choices were either to give up for the night or retire to the warmth of the coffee shop. She chewed her badly chapped lips. The snappy dresser hadn't been in the coffee shop the last time she'd used it for cover, so chances were she could go in without attracting his notice. But she would have to keep a careful eye on him to make sure he wasn't getting suspicious. She'd probably never get the information she wanted if the mysterious threesome knew about her.

Carolyn snagged her umbrella and slipped out of the car. Her breath misted, and the damp chill seeped through every opening in her coat. God, that cup of coffee would taste good right now! She hurried across the street, heedless of the puddles, yearning for the warmth of the coffee shop.

The bells on the door jingled when she opened it. Out of the corner of her eye, she saw the hunk glance up. She pretended not to notice the long, hard look he gave her, but it made her wonder if she'd just been made. No matter, it was too late now. She slid gratefully into another booth by the window and could have kissed the waitress's feet for offering coffee. Cupping her hands around its warmth, she took a sip and sighed in contentment.

She put the cup down, and her heart leapt into her throat when Gray's tail for the evening slid into the booth across from her. He piled a beautiful cashmere coat and his black felt hat on the seat beside him, then folded his hands on the table and smiled at her.

It was quite a smile, and he was certainly a treat to the eyes. His hair fell in gleaming waves around his face, tousled in a manner meant to look casual, but was no doubt carefully cultivated. Eyes the color of cinnamon peeked out from under lashes long enough to make a woman jealous. His smile held the self-assurance of a man who knew he was good-looking and made no apologies for it.

Carolyn blinked at him, wondering what on earth she should say in the face of his boldness.

"I thought it might be best to introduce myself," he said, still smiling as he held out his hand across the table. "I'm Jules." He pronounced his name with a sexy French accent—*zhule*—although there was no hint of an accent in his other words.

Carolyn reflexively shook his hand. Who the hell was this guy? Was this some kind of a come-on, or had he noticed her watching Gray just as she'd noticed him?

"Carolyn," she said, extricating her hand from his. "To what do I owe the pleasure of your company?"

He laughed at the stilted formality of her speech. "Mostly I'm just trying to piss Gray off. He'll have quite a temper tantrum if he looks out the window and sees me talking to you."

Well, so much for the come-on idea. Carolyn considered playing dumb for a moment, then decided against it. "Who are you, and what are you doing here?"

His eyes widened in feigned innocence. "Why, I'm just having a cup of coffee. And I already told you who I am."

The waitress stopped by to refill Carolyn's coffee cup, and she took the moment of distraction to try to settle her thoughts. Jules declined the offer of a fresh cup and waited for the waitress to move out of earshot.

"I'm curious why you're out on such a dreadful night, staking out Gray's home," he said.

Carolyn snorted. "I don't know what you're talking about. I'm just having a cup of coffee."

He laughed briefly at her sarcasm, then dispensed with the banter. The smile left his face, replaced by a

look of grave concern. "Let him go, Carolyn. Whatever he may have been to you once, he's changed and
he can't ever go back."

Fury flushed her face, and she had to bite back an
instant, scathing reply. If one more person told her to
"let him go" she was going to scream! Where did this
stranger get off, giving her personal advice? And how
much did he know about her past with Gray? Keeping
a tight rein on her temper, knowing the man sitting before her might be a key to learning the truth, she responded in an almost reasonable tone. "That's none of
your business. Now, tell me why you and your cronies
are watching Gray's house."

"That information is not mine to share."

Oh, but Carolyn was going to convince him to share
it! She just had to figure out how. She was still thinking
about how to frame her next question when Jules suddenly laughed.

"Here it comes," he said, rubbing his hands together. "This ought to be fun."

Carolyn followed his gaze and saw Gray, crossing
the street with murder in his eyes.

✳ ✳ ✳

GRAY TRIED TO CONTROL his rage, knowing he
was overreacting, but had little success calming his
temper.

He'd noticed Carolyn following him two days ago,
and had been debating with himself ever since how to
handle the situation. He should have known that Jules
would push his hand. Gray shoved the coffee shop
door open. The bells jangled harshly. Jules lounged in
Carolyn's booth, an infuriating smirk on his face. Carolyn looked back and forth between the two of them
and said nothing.

Gray came to a stop at the edge of their booth. He

hadn't bothered with an umbrella or raincoat when crossing the street, and a rivulet of cold water trickled down the side of his face. He fixed Jules with a steely stare.

"Leave her alone," he growled as his hands clenched into fists.

"It's a free country, Galahad. I'm allowed to talk to anyone I want."

Gray wanted to smash that goading smile from his face. "Not to her. Go away."

Jules dropped the smile. "Make me."

Carolyn rolled her eyes. "I feel like I'm surrounded by five-year-olds."

Blood pumped loudly in Gray's ears. There'd been a time when he'd had such good control of his temper he almost never raised his voice. Now, it was all he could do to keep from resorting to violence, even when he knew he'd come out the worse in any altercation with the older, stronger vampire.

"I mean it, asshole. Harass *me* all you want, but leave her out of it."

Jules slid slowly out of the booth, rising to his feet. His menace was a palpable force, sucking the oxygen from the air. Gray was momentarily amazed that the waitress and the two other customers in the coffee shop didn't sense the danger.

"You're in no position to make demands," Jules said, leaning forward slightly in his eagerness to begin the fray.

Carolyn cleared her throat. "Gentlemen, can you do your snake and mongoose act some other time? This isn't a good place for a brawl."

Gray wondered how she could speak so casually. Didn't she feel the danger in the air? "You should get out of here, Carolyn."

She snorted. "Yeah, right. Need I remind you that I'm armed?" She pulled her blazer open just enough to give him a glimpse of the shoulder holster concealed within. "Now knock it off!"

Armed she might be, but her gun offered little protection against the likes of Jules. She'd have to put the shot through his heart or his brain, and it would have to be instantly fatal or else the wound would heal itself. However, Jules held up his hands in a conciliatory gesture, his menacing glower replaced with a charming smile. He turned to Carolyn, ignoring Gray like he would an annoying child.

"There's no need for your weapon," he said. "I'll leave you two lovebirds in peace." He picked up his coat and hat, then headed toward the door, giving Gray a hard bump with his shoulder on the way.

The sensible thing to do would be to ignore the provocation and let the bastard go. But Gray's nerves were strung too tight, his temper on a hair trigger. He reached out and grabbed Jules's arm, his other hand clenching into a fist again. Jules whirled, and Gray made the mistake of meeting his eyes. The glamour hit Gray before he could look away.

"Veux-tu savoir comment tu pèses sans tes dents?" Jules asked in a low growl.

Gray couldn't have answered him even if he'd understood the question. He could barely move, trapped in the glamour. Damn it, would he never learn? The macho stare-down was a really bad idea when faced with an older, more powerful vampire.

"Let him go, Gray," Carolyn commanded.

But Gray couldn't have let go if he'd wanted to. Jules pulled his lips away from his teeth, displaying a hint of fang. Then he laughed and let up on the glamour suddenly enough that Gray almost fell. Jules twitched his arm out of Gray's grasp and sauntered out into the rainy night. No doubt he wouldn't go far, but for the moment Gray wrenched his attention back to Carolyn. Anger still simmered in his veins, and his voice came out far sharper than he intended.

"What are you doing here, Carolyn?" He slid into the booth across from her.

"What do you *think* I'm doing here?" was her infuriating response.

He ran a hand through his damp hair, wishing he knew the magic words to make her see sense. "You have a perfectly good life going for you. Don't fuck it up by poking your nose where it doesn't belong." Carolyn looked shocked by his vulgarity, but he didn't dare take the words back. If she thought she could "save" him somehow, there was no telling what kind of danger she'd put herself in. He had to convince her he was beyond her reach.

"I'm a private investigator. It's my job to poke my nose where it doesn't belong. And you have to know I'm not the kind of woman who gives up when things get tough."

"This has nothing to do with your job." His voice rose, and he noticed he'd drawn the attention of the other customers. He doubted his glamour was powerful enough to divert them, and the last thing he needed was more mortal interference in his life. He reached into his pocket and pulled out a five dollar bill, flinging it on the table. Then he slid out of the booth. "Come on, we're going."

Carolyn looked up at him with a slack jaw. "You Tarzan, me Jane?"

"If we're going to argue about this, I'd rather not have an audience."

She crossed her arms over her chest, her chin jutting out stubbornly. "Are you going to manhandle me like you did last time?"

"Honey, I'd drag you by the hair if I thought I could get away with it. Now come on."

"I haven't finished my coffee."

There looked to be maybe two swallows left in her cup, and they were no doubt cold. Gray tried to remember why he had once admired her mulishness.

"Please," he growled in a voice that could not have been more insincere.

She sniffed. "Well, since you asked nicely." She slid out of the booth and headed for the door, leaving Gray to follow behind.

It sure would be nice if I had a plan here, Gray thought as he dashed across the street toward his house. He honestly had no clue how he was going to persuade Carolyn to leave well enough alone. All he knew was he had to try. The Guardians might not be killers, but Gray would feel a lot more comfortable if Carolyn had nothing to do with them. Or with him, for that matter.

Once inside, they squared off in the parlor, neither one of them sitting down. Carolyn eyed him with an infuriating blend of stubbornness and hostility, and he tried to think what he could say to hammer his point home.

"Why are you under surveillance, and who is it who's staking you out?" she asked.

"I'm not answering any of your questions, so you might as well forget it. You don't know what you're dealing with here, and—"

She threw up her hands. "Then tell me, damn it! I'm not some delicate little flower who has to be kept in the dark. Whatever it is you're mixed up in, I'm sure I've seen it before."

He almost laughed, but stifled the impulse and covered it with a feigned cough. Maybe if he made up a story and fed it to her, that would satisfy her curiosity and get her to leave it alone. Trouble was, it was hard to think of a story that would explain things to her satisfaction. Especially on the spur of the moment.

Gray moved over to the sofa, buying himself time as he racked his brain for a creative, convincing lie. Carolyn sat on the very edge of the sofa beside him. The force of her eyes boring into him, willing him to divulge his secrets, was almost as powerful as glamour.

For one moment, he ached to tell her everything, to pour out his anguish and his remorse in an unstemmed tide of bitterness. But he didn't. Carolyn would never believe him. Besides, the last thing he wanted to do was burden her with the knowledge that vampires really did exist. The revelation had set his own world firmly on its ear, and he had no wish to do the same to the woman he still loved.

Carolyn moved closer to him on the sofa, laying her hand on his shoulder. "You can trust me with the truth, Gray," she murmured in a low, coaxing voice. "Even if you're into something illegal, you know I'd never turn you in. Maybe I can even help you."

His throat tightened. After the way he'd deserted her, after his repeated, cruel attempts to chase her away again, she would still offer to help him? Oh, if only he could undo the past! If it hadn't been for one fatal mistake, Carolyn would even now be his wife. Maybe they'd even have a baby on the way. A nice, normal life, with its normal ups and downs. His mind filled with memories of happier times, of Carolyn nestled in his arms, laughing at his jokes, kissing him, rolling with him in a tangle of sheets.

She was sitting too close. He could feel the heat of her body beside him. Her scent filled his senses, a blend of baby powder and apples flavored with her own unique warmth. He turned to her, and she was like a magnet pulling him inexorably toward her.

There was surprise in her eyes, and she licked her lips in apparent nervousness. Her scent changed, spiced by the faint musk of arousal. Gray leaned forward and brushed her lips with his. She gasped, but didn't pull away.

One taste wasn't enough. He stole another kiss, his lips feathering over hers, teasing her, teasing himself. Yearning squeezed his chest, yearning for the life he'd once had, yearning for Carolyn. He cupped his hand around the back of her head, his fingers threading

through the softness of her hair as his mouth pressed
down harder on hers.

Her kiss was every bit as sweet as he remembered,
every bit as sweet as the dreams and memories that
had haunted him since that dreadful night three years
ago when he'd ruined his life. The desire that lit within
raged out of his control. He dipped his tongue into her
mouth, savoring her taste and texture as his erection
swelled and hardened.

When Carolyn's tongue brushed his lips, it was all
he could do not to lay her back on the sofa and start
ripping off her clothes. But that delicate lick reminded
him of the danger he now faced, for in his arousal, his
fangs had descended. He couldn't let Carolyn see them
or feel them with her tongue. But he couldn't tear his
lips away from her, either.

His kiss traveled along the line of her jaw, and she
moaned in pleasure. He traced his tongue along the
shell of her ear, then made his way down her out-
stretched throat. He felt the hammering of her heart
under his lips. The skin of her throat was so fragile.
Unconsciously, his lips had sought out the pulse that
throbbed there and as he traced the vein with the tip of
his tongue, reason and lust battled in his brain.

She's willing, an insidious voice whispered in his
mind. If he were to slip his hand between her legs, he
would find her wet and ready for him. Her skin was
flushed with desire, and her breathing hitched whenever she felt the stroke of his tongue.

Glamour, the voice of reason countered. He wasn't
consciously trying to use glamour, but there was no
way she'd have let him go this far if she were in her
right mind. He'd given up his right to such privileges
when he'd left her stranded at the altar.

The battle raged for what seemed an eternity. Then
Gray realized that his mouth had remained over the
vulnerable vein that pulsed in Carolyn's throat, and
that he was nibbling lightly on the spot. The realization

brought his sense of reason back, and he jerked away, ignoring Carolyn's whimper of protest. He buried his head in his hands and sucked in frantic breaths, willing himself to calm.

The beast within him hungered for something Gray could never let it taste again.

If he'd had any doubts before, they were extinguished now. Carolyn was not safe around him. He *had* to get rid of her, no matter what it took. He forced himself to raise his head and look at her, wondering what on earth she was making of all this. Surely she must be unsettled by the unnatural desire he had inflicted on her with his glamour.

A hint of pink still flushed her cheeks, and a faint furrow appeared between her brows, but she didn't look like she was about to smack him for his nerve. Instead, she chewed her lower lip and cocked her head, regarding him with careful intensity.

"Why did you stop?" she asked.

Not exactly the reaction he'd been expecting under the circumstances. She should be furious with him for taking advantage! But of course, she couldn't know he was solely responsible for what had just happened between them. She would think her own desire—inexplicable as it was—had been equally to blame.

Gray hesitated a long moment as he tried to find a good explanation for his about-face.

"Is it because of . . . that woman?"

For just a moment, Gray had no idea what she was talking about, and he almost uttered a quick denial. Luckily, his common sense took hold before he spoke.

Perhaps Carolyn had just handed him the key to lock the door on his past. "You know about Deirdre," he said, trying to sound guilty. It wasn't hard.

"I've been following you," Carolyn admitted. "I've seen her watching the house. And I also saw her that first night when I followed you home from the store. You kissed her."

No, *she* kissed *me,* he thought, but of course he said no such thing. "Our relationship is a little complicated," he said, improvising. He turned to face her, putting his hands on her shoulders and meeting her eyes boldly. "Carolyn, I can't deny that I still have some . . . feeling for you. But I've moved on with my life, and I wish you would do the same. Deirdre would never forgive me for letting things get so out of hand if she knew. I'm a faithful man by nature, and this was just . . . an aberration."

The flush in her cheeks was no doubt due to anger now, but her voice sounded more reproachful than anything. "If you're so faithful, why is it you were last seen leaving your bachelor party with a stripper?"

Yes, that had been his fatal mistake. "It's not what you think." Boy, was that an understatement! "Her car wouldn't start, so I offered to give her a ride home. There was nothing sexual about it." That was true, as far as it went.

Carolyn pursed her lips. "Anything else you care to tell me?"

Figuring his best strategy was to keep his mouth firmly shut and let her draw whatever conclusions she wanted, he said nothing. He thought he saw a hint of tears in her eyes as she nodded.

"All right, Gray. You've made your point. I hope you and Deirdre have a lovely life together." She stood, averting her gaze quickly. No doubt she was trying to hide the tears. "I'll see myself out."

Gray watched her stride for the door, wishing he could just sweep her into his arms and make everything right again.

"Carolyn!" he called, rising to his feet when she put her hand on the doorknob. She paused, not turning to look at him. "I'm sorry," he said, although the words were useless. "For everything."

She nodded briefly before she slipped out the door and out of his life.

6

DRAKE STOOD OVER THE body of the murdered woman and shook his head. The killer had left her splayed on the floor near the North Broad Street entrance to City Hall.

City Hall took up the entire block, a hollow rectangle of ornate architecture surrounding a central courtyard. Both Broad and Market Streets led right through the building in cavernous walkways for pedestrian traffic only. Even during the daytime, which Drake remembered from his mortal days long ago, the walkways under City Hall were dark and spooky, broken into distinct rooms, each with its own brooding personality. Whoever had designed the place was very fond of columns, which formed pools of shadow within the already dimly lit rooms. Pedestrian traffic was light, especially at this time of night, and the columns and arches and darkened stairways provided ample cover for a lurking hunter of the night.

Drake squatted beside the girl, wondering if the killer meant to leave a message by leaving her here, under the inscription bearing William Penn's prayer for his city: *O that thou mayest be kept from the evil that would overwhelm thee!* Her clothes were torn, and a garish red line slashed across her fragile throat. Her

mouth and eyes were open, and she smelled of fear and
of cum.

"Damn," he muttered softly as he reached out to
close her eyes.

How was the killer eluding him? Drake had spent
the whole night within a six-block radius of City Hall.
If the killer were nearby, Drake should have felt his
psychic footprint. He closed his eyes and reached out
with his mind, and immediately he sensed the presence
of Deirdre and Fletcher. Deirdre's route took her up
and down North Broad, and Fletcher patrolled South
Broad. Drake's psychic radar was strong enough to
sense them when they were three to four blocks away,
but both of them were actually quite close right now.
Not the most efficient use of manpower, to have all
three of them clustered together like this.

At first, Drake had managed to convince Eli to let
him work alone. Then, after the last meeting when
he'd owned up to his kill, Eli had changed his mind.
Drake was pretty sure Eli still trusted him. However,
the Founder needed to appease his restless Guardians,
who were uncomfortable about their alliance with a
Killer.

Footsteps echoed from the next room over, someone
coming through the courtyard toward Broad Street.
Drake looked up to see a policeman passing through. A
faint touch of glamour made the cop overlook the grim
scene against the wall, although in the shadows of the
columns he might have missed it anyway.

When the footsteps had faded, Drake reached out
and swept a lock of hair out of the poor girl's face.
"I'm so sorry," he whispered into the night.

He reached out with his mind yet again and realized
Deirdre was drawing closer, even though he'd sensed
her moving away before. She must have been close
enough to sense him, and was now approaching to see
why he was holding still for so long. Drake scowled

when he felt Fletcher approaching as well. Already, he heard the tap of Deirdre's high heels.

Drake straightened and waited for the Guardians to converge on him. He didn't relish the confrontation, but he supposed there was no avoiding it. If he left the scene now, he would only postpone it.

Deirdre caught sight of him and hurried to his side, looking at the murdered girl with wide eyes. "Oh no!" she cried. "Not again."

Drake clamped his jaw shut, hating that he'd failed. No doubt this was his reward for his arrogant assumption that he'd take the killer down the moment he was on the case.

"What happened?" Deirdre asked.

He sighed. "I don't know. I've been in the area all night and sensed nothing. Then on one of my circuits I decided to cut through City Hall, and I found her. I don't know how long she's been dead."

Deirdre shivered, crossing her arms over her chest. "Eli's going to give us hell for this."

That was the least of Drake's concerns at the moment. "Fletcher's coming."

"I know."

Moments later, a lone figure appeared in the archway leading from the courtyard. Drake braced himself for an unpleasant scene. He'd avoided Fletcher to the best of his ability since the near-fight at Eli's, but there would be no avoiding him this time.

Fletcher joined them and stared at the body without comment for a long time. Drake wondered what the puppy was thinking. Usually he could read Fletcher's face easily—that Irish temper of his was always close to the surface. At this moment, though, that boy-next-door face was closed and shuttered.

"When did you last feed?" Fletcher asked in a low voice without turning his gaze from the body.

Drake suppressed an urge to wrap his hands around

the bastard's neck and give a long, hard squeeze. "Eli's not here to protect you this time, puppy, so I suggest you tread cautiously."

Fletcher's lips pulled away from his teeth and he shot Drake a murderous glance. Drake guessed he was suppressing his own urge to say something stupid about how he didn't need Eli's protection. The man might be a high-strung, irritating son of a bitch, but he wasn't stupid and he knew when he was outmatched.

"Do you suppose the two of you could make nice just once?" Deirdre asked. "This constant squabbling isn't helping our cause any."

Drake had to admit she had a point, but as far as he was concerned, it was Fletcher who instigated all the "squabbling."

Fletcher took a deep breath and some of the aggression eased out of his stance. "Sorry," he mumbled.

Drake blinked. He couldn't remember ever hearing that word from Fletcher's lips before. Perhaps the young Guardian was maturing.

"So," Deirdre continued, "Drake didn't sense anything, I didn't sense anything. What about you, Fletch?"

Fletcher shook his head. "Nothing. Except . . ."

"What is it?" Drake asked.

Fletcher gave him a penetrating look. "Well, I've sensed *you* off and on when I've gotten close enough."

Drake shrugged. "And I've sensed both you and Deirdre, except when you've been at the apex of your patrols. What of it?"

"Well, what if he knows that and uses it against us? What if sometime tonight, one of us thought he was sensing a Guardian but was really sensing the Killer?"

Drake thought about it a moment. "I don't see how he could manage it. He'd have to know our patrol routes, wait for one of us to deviate, then take that one's place and get out before being caught. It's a tall order."

Deirdre chewed her lip. "But what if it were an inside job?"

"Oh for God's sake!" Drake growled, but she hurried on.

"I don't mean you," she assured him.

"Excuse me?" Fletcher asked, sounding as indignant as Drake had.

"Or you either. I just mean a Guardian. After all, being a Guardian does not make one a candidate for sainthood. A Guardian would know our patrol routes. And if he's a Killer, his psychic senses would be stronger, allowing him to track us over greater distances. It might not be as hard as we think."

"It's not impossible," Drake admitted reluctantly. While the Guardians shunned him whenever possible, and while he disliked most if not all of them, he had the utmost respect for their mission and would hate to see their society compromised.

"It's not a Guardian," Fletcher declared, but he sounded like he was trying to convince himself.

"We should mention the possibility to Eli," Drake said.

A long, tense silence followed. Deirdre and Fletcher made eye contact and seemed to share a silent communication. Then, Fletcher nodded.

"All right," he said. "Let's report back." His boyish features were uncommonly grim. "But *I'm* not going to be the one to suggest to Eli that one of his Guardians might have gone bad."

Deirdre raised her hands in a defensive gesture. "Hey, don't look at me. *I'm* not telling him."

Drake wished they'd both grow up. "Fine! I'll tell him. Now let's get out of here." He took one last pitying look at the dead girl. "Let the police find her so she can be returned to her family."

Without another word, they turned their backs on the murder scene and started the long, cold walk to Eli's.

＊ ＊ ＊

GRAY FELT UNCOMMONLY RESTLESS. It seemed he couldn't hold still these days.

Nerves jangling, he stepped to the front window and nudged the curtains aside. Across the street, Jules lounged in a window booth at the coffee shop. The pose looked casual, but the irritating bastard must have seen the subtle shifting of the drapes, for he grinned and raised his coffee cup in mocking salute.

Gray turned his eyes away from the coffee shop, glancing up and down the street. Looking for Carolyn.

He shook his head at himself. He'd wanted to chase her away, and he had. The aching emptiness he felt at the evidence of his success was just pathetic.

Three nights now, his only company had been the trio of Guardians charged with baby-sitting him. But at least Carolyn was safe.

Gray pushed the curtains open a little wider and gave Jules the finger. Jules returned the gesture. Gray was contemplating heading across the street and having another pointless fight with his highly unwelcome shadow when he heard a metallic clank. Frowning, he leaned forward a little, just in time to see a boy, maybe eight or ten years old, scampering down his front steps and running down the street.

Nothing but a neighborhood kid pulling some kind of prank, he told himself. And yet, he couldn't ignore the unease that suddenly seized him. Letting the curtain slide shut, he cautiously walked to the entry hall.

On the floor beneath the mail slot sat a plain white envelope. There was absolutely no reason for Gray to feel such dread at the sight of it. But sometimes he thought his vampire state brought with it just a touch of prescience, and he knew even as he bent to pick it up that it was something bad.

The envelope was unmarked and unsealed. He cautiously opened the flap and pulled out the single piece of paper within. His heart seized when he read the brief note.

> DEAR GRAY,
> CAROLYN IS A LOVELY, LOVELY WOMAN. JUST MY TYPE. NOW THAT YOU'VE TOSSED HER OUT, YOU WON'T MIND IF I SAMPLE HER, WILL YOU?
> YOURS,
> THE BROAD STREET BANGER

Gray crumpled the paper and squeezed it with all his strength. *Don't panic,* he told himself, but it had little effect.

Clearly this was not the childish prank he'd imagined, but it just *couldn't* be serious. He'd read about this so-called Broad Street Banger in the papers. An anonymous serial killer who raped and murdered pretty women. But his pattern was clear, and the police were sure it was only strangers he killed; there was no connection between his victims, and all the crimes seemed based on opportunity rather than planning. And how the hell would he know anything about Gray or Carolyn?

Chest heaving, Gray stalked to the window again and stared out at Jules. Was this Jules's way of torturing him? As far as Gray knew, the three Guardians who'd kept watch on him were the only ones who would know anything about Carolyn. And only Jules hated him enough to torment him like this.

For a long moment, Gray debated once more the option of crossing the street and confronting Jules. He stared at the wadded paper in his hand. If Jules had written this, he would see the prick dead!

But what if he hadn't? A thin sheen of sweat broke out on his face. If Jules had written it, Gray would know its venom was directed solely at him. What if the culprit was actually after Carolyn? Maybe Gray wasn't the only one being followed. After all, in her profession Carolyn had made many an enemy.

Cursing, Gray stuffed the paper into his jeans pocket and snatched his jacket out of the hall closet. He had to warn Carolyn about the danger, whether it was real or not. A phone call wouldn't do it, either. She had to see this note.

Gray let out a deep breath, trying to calm his nerves. Surely Carolyn was just fine—whoever had sent this note would get little satisfaction out of it if she were already dead. Still, his throat cramped tight with worry, and he almost charged out the front door.

He came to an abrupt halt with his hand on the knob.

If he went out the front door, then he would be going to see Carolyn with Jules on his heels. The last thing he wanted was for Jules to see him with Carolyn again. It would just strengthen the prick's conviction that Gray was some kind of dangerous predator. Not to mention that Jules might make a play for her in the ultimate attempt to do him harm.

The damned Guardians thought they were so clever, standing watch outside his house all through the night. But he knew something they didn't.

Giving Jules the finger again—though this time through the closed door, so the other vampire couldn't see it—Gray headed down the steep set of stairs leading to the basement.

The basement was little more than a storage area, filled with discarded furniture and broken household appliances. Kate never had been able to throw anything away, choosing instead to bury her unwanted possessions in the basement. But the basement held a secret.

Moving aside a desk with a broken leg—an "escritoire," Kate had called it when she had him drag it down to the basement for her—he uncovered a faded, moth-eaten rug. When he pulled back the corner of that rug, he unearthed a trap door. He stared at the faint outlines of that door and shuddered.

When Kate had first transformed him, she'd kept him locked in this cursed basement for days on end as the hunger built within him. He'd been too sunk in his misery to search for an escape. He still remembered the cruel light in her eyes when she had showed him the bolt hole he could have escaped through if he'd had the wherewithal to find it. She had, in fact, revealed the hidden trap door right after—

Gray dragged his mind forcefully away from the precipice. He didn't dare let himself sink into despair when Carolyn might be in danger. He yanked open the trap door, sneezing when the sudden motion sent up a cloud of dust. Then, he dropped into the darkness of the tunnel below.

* * *

CAROLYN WRINKLED HER NOSE at the lone slice of cold pizza remaining amidst the crumbs at the bottom of the box.

"You sure you don't want it?" Hannah asked.

Carolyn shook her head, and Hannah snagged the slice. At least it kept her mouth occupied so she couldn't ask any more probing questions during the commercial break. Carolyn stared hard at the TV, willing the commercial to end before Hannah finished wolfing down the pizza.

She got her wish, and she clicked off the Mute button. Jack Nicholson was just waking up after having spent the night as a werewolf, chasing down a deer and killing it. It was her first "Movie Night" with Hannah since she'd given up on Gray, and she should have known the companionable get-together would turn into the interrogation from hell. Hannah had an amazing ability to camouflage her most probing questions so that Carolyn blurted out more than she meant to tell. She had to be constantly on her guard, examining every question tossed her way and measuring her answers carefully.

It was not exactly what Movie Night was supposed to be about. Of course, if their roles had been reversed, Carolyn supposed she might have been just as nosy and persistent.

When the next commercial break hit, Carolyn picked up the empty pizza box, meaning to toss it in the trash. If she could dawdle in the kitchen long enough . . .

"Leave the box, Carolyn," Hannah said, curling her feet under herself on the couch. "I'll stop trying to pry your secrets out of you, okay?"

Carolyn laughed, but sat down anyway. "I'm not stupid enough to fall for that line. You're just trying to put me at ease in hopes that I'll let something slip without noticing."

Hannah tried to look innocent. "Would I do something like that?"

"In a heartbeat."

Hannah shrugged. "Okay, maybe. But I just don't get why you won't tell me what happened. I mean geez, Carolyn, we tell each other everything!"

That was, perhaps, an exaggeration, but not much of one. However, Carolyn didn't dare tell her best friend the truth—that thinking about Gray with another woman had ripped her heart open afresh. Never mind that his relationship with that woman was strange at best. Carolyn hadn't even managed a *date* since he'd left her, and the thought that he might actually be in a *relationship* . . .

"I have my reasons," she said, pinching the bridge of her nose.

"Whatever." Hannah crossed her arms over her chest and slouched back in the couch. It was an attempt to make Carolyn feel guilty, and it worked. But that didn't mean she was going to talk.

The commercial break ended, and Carolyn picked up the remote just as her doorbell rang. She and Hannah looked at each other.

"Who could that be?" Hannah asked.

"I don't know." Carolyn wasn't expecting anyone. It made her edgy enough she almost grabbed her gun out of the coat closet before going to the door. But that, of course, was ridiculous.

The doorbell rang again before she got to it, and the sound was followed by the pounding of a fist on the door. She cautiously approached the door and peeked out the peep hole. And froze.

The fist pounded again, more insistently.

"Carolyn, are you in there?" Gray demanded, with an almost panicked urgency to his voice.

She opened the door just as he was raising his hand to knock again. His shoulders slumped and he let out a harsh breath of relief.

"What's the matter, Gray?" she asked.

He pushed past her without waiting for an invitation to come in. She would have objected, except the look on his face frightened her. She closed the door and locked it, turning to follow him into the living room.

He had stopped in his tracks when he saw Hannah. The two of them were staring each other down, Hannah's lips curled into a grimace of distaste.

"Hello, Hannah," he said, his voice carefully neutral.

"Hello, dickhead," was her graceful response. She turned her gaze to Carolyn. "You want me to serve you his gonads on a plate?"

Carolyn covered her mouth to suppress a giggle. God, she loved Hannah—the most loyal friend she could ever imagine. "No, but thanks for the offer." She fixed Gray with her most penetrating look. "Why are you here?"

He turned to her. Out of the corner of her eye, she saw Hannah move forward. She read the intent on her friend's face, and she tried to bark out a warning. Too late.

Hannah's foot swung in a high arc, her toes heading straight for Gray's groin. She'd studied just about every martial art in existence, and her reflexes were blindingly quick. Distracted as he was, there was no way Gray could avoid that kick. Carolyn winced in sympathy.

The wince turned into a startled gasp.

Gray's arm shot out to block the kick, and his hand wrapped around Hannah's ankle. He gave a sharp jerk, and Hannah's other foot slipped out from under her. With a cry of surprise and distress, she went down, banging the back of her head on the floor.

Gray let go of her foot and shook his head. "Sorry, Hannah."

She sat up and rubbed the back of her head, eyes narrowed in pain. She looked as shocked as Carolyn felt. How the hell had Gray managed that? He'd never been athletic, certainly never been quick. Of course, he *had* lost a lot of weight.

"Are you all right?" he asked Hannah, though he kept a wary distance.

Hannah blew a lock of curls out of her eyes and looked at Gray with a hint of grudging respect. "Yeah. When did you learn self-defense?"

He shrugged. "Thought it might come in handy sometime," he said in a classic non-answer. It was a strategy both Hannah and Carolyn were very familiar with, a way to not answer a question while still giving the appearance of cooperating. Carolyn wondered why he felt it necessary to evade that particular question.

Hannah held out her hand. "Wanna give me a hand up?"

One corner of Gray's mouth lifted in a sardonic

grin. "You don't really think I'm going to fall for that, do you?"

"A girl can hope." She sniffed disdainfully, then popped easily to her feet unassisted. "So, what are you doing horning your way back into Carolyn's life at this late date?"

"Hannah!" Carolyn snapped, knowing it would take a gag or duct tape to keep her friend's mouth shut.

"Carolyn is perfectly capable of fighting her own battles," Gray said.

"I'm not convinced that's true where you're concerned."

"Why don't you let her try, instead of charging in with guns blazing?"

"Because I've spent three years fantasizing about beating the crap out of you for hurting my best friend. And Carolyn's too damn nice to give you the hell you deserve."

"Hannah, *please,*" Carolyn tried again.

Hannah whirled on her. "Well you *are.* I say no matter how good he might have become at self-defense, he's no match against the two of us. Let's tackle him, tie him up, and then ask him nicely to tell you what the hell happened to him for three years."

There was a subtle shift in Gray's posture. One moment he was at rest, his weight settled into one hip as he scowled at Hannah. Now he shifted his weight until it was evenly distributed between both legs, and though he still scowled there was a look of intense focus in his eyes. He was a man prepared to defend himself, and despite Hannah's assertion, Carolyn wondered if the two of them really could take him down.

"I wouldn't suggest trying," he said. The chill in his voice sent a shiver down Carolyn's spine. Even Hannah seemed to feel it, a little of the starch going out of her, though she held her ground.

"Do you actually think you can scare me, Gray?" Hannah asked.

"Yes," was his simple answer.

She *had* to find a way to take control of the situation, Carolyn decided. "Just knock it off, both of you. Hannah, Gray's right: I can fight my own battles. But since Gray has told me in no uncertain terms that he wants me out of his life, I have to admit I'm curious to know why he just showed up on my doorstep. Maybe if you stop provoking him for a moment, he'll actually tell me."

From the look on her face, Carolyn gathered Hannah really wanted to light into Gray some more, but she managed to control herself. "This ought to be good," she said.

"Let's all sit down," Gray suggested.

Carolyn returned to her seat on the couch, turning off the TV. After a slight hesitation, Hannah did the same. Gray reached into his jeans pocket and pulled out a crumpled wad of paper. He uncrumpled it, then held it out to Carolyn.

"Take a look at this," he said.

7

WHEN CAROLYN HAD LET him in the house and
he'd seen Hannah looking daggers at him, Gray's
heart had sunk. Hard enough to deal with one angry
woman, but two? He'd always found Carolyn's temper
somewhat volatile, but Hannah was a veritable fire-
cracker. And she hadn't liked him much even before
he'd jilted her best friend.

However, as the two women bent over the threatening note, he reasoned that having Hannah here might
be to his advantage after all. She could be pushy and
outspoken as hell, and might get away with saying
things that would get Gray eviscerated. Twin furrows
appeared between the women's eyebrows, and he almost smiled to see the similarity of their expressions.

"Where did you get this?" Hannah demanded. She
sounded even angrier than she had earlier, and he
hoped she wasn't armed.

"Someone stuck it in my mail slot this evening."

"Did you see who?" Carolyn asked quickly—trying
to get a word in before Hannah.

"Not really. I saw someone running away, but it
looked like it was just a kid. Whoever sent this didn't
take a chance that I might see him."

Carolyn examined the note again, squinting at it as

though she could pry its secrets out of it. Most people would have been at least mildly disturbed by the threat, but she showed not a hint of fear. Actually, Hannah looked more worried than Carolyn did—hence Gray's thought that Hannah might turn into his unlikely ally.

"I suppose we shouldn't be pawing over it like this," Carolyn said. "We've probably destroyed any fingerprint evidence."

"I still have the envelope it came in back at my house," Gray said. "But I kind of doubt you'd find any useful fingerprints."

Hannah narrowed her eyes and gave him a piercing, suspicious stare. "Why is that?"

Because my prime suspects are vampires, whose fingerprints wouldn't be on file with any law enforcement agency. Too bad he couldn't say that. "Just call it a hunch."

Hannah opened her mouth, no doubt to tear into him, but Carolyn beat her to the punch.

"You think it's Jules?"

Hannah turned to Carolyn, blinking. "Jules? Who the hell is Jules?"

"I wouldn't put it past him."

"So, now will you tell me what's going on?" Carolyn demanded.

"I can't, Carolyn."

"Hello?" Hannah said, waving her hands dramatically. "Excuse me? Would someone like to fill me in on the details here? Who is Jules, and why would he write a note threatening Carolyn?"

Carolyn folded her arms across her chest and looked over to Gray. "Yes, please fill her in, Gray."

He suppressed a snarl. He wished he were a more creative liar. If he had a cover story, this would be a lot easier. However, he had to play the cards he was dealt. "Jules is a guy I know who hates my guts. The feeling is mutual."

"Oh, that explains everything," Hannah said.

"Look," Gray snapped, "I'm not going to explain. I've told Carolyn that, and now I'm telling you. If you want to do your Karate Kid imitation again, feel free, but it's not going to change my mind. I have a good reason for keeping quiet, and you're just going to have to live with it."

Gray couldn't ever remember seeing Hannah speechless before. Of course, he had to admit that during his mortal life, he'd been something of a milquetoast. His new life in the shadows had brought out the darker corners of his soul, and he no longer felt the need to preserve his overly civilized exterior.

"So," Carolyn said, "if you're not going to tell me anything or answer any questions, why are you here?"

"Because I'm not *sure* Jules is behind this, and if he isn't then you may actually be in danger."

"But I'm not in danger if he is?"

Gray hesitated only a moment before answering. "No, probably not. He's a monumental prick but he's not dangerous. At least, not to you." The moment the words were out of his mouth, he wished he could snatch them back. Both Hannah and Carolyn's eyes held a faint gleam he recognized. They thought they were on to something. "Leave it alone. Just . . . Why don't you go stay with Hannah for a little while until I figure out what the deal is."

The women's backs stiffened, and two pairs of eyes flashed with new fire. They both spoke at the same time, their words tumbling over each other so he couldn't understand either of them. However, the gist of the message was crystal clear. They shared a quick glance in which they somehow appointed Carolyn spokeswoman.

"First of all," she said, "I can take care of myself just fine. I'm a former cop, remember?" She didn't wait for an answer. "Second of all, you don't get to give me orders. You wouldn't have earned that privilege even if you'd stuck around for the wedding." Her voice was gaining volume. "And lastly, what the hell makes you think I'm going to cower like a damsel in distress while you charge out into the sunset and play detective?"

"Carolyn—"

She shot to her feet and crossed to him, poking him in the chest with her index finger to punctuate her words.

"You have some nerve! You—"

He grabbed hold of her wrist to stop her poking him. Out of the corner of his eye, he glimpsed Hannah sprinting past them into the foyer. He leaned into Carolyn, glaring down at her from his superior height. "Don't be an idiot. No matter how good you are at your job, you're not invincible. You don't know enough about this situation to defend yourself adequately, and you don't know enough to investigate without getting yourself killed."

"And whose fault is that?"

"Mine! And that's the way it's going to stay, because I refuse to let you put yourself in the kind of danger you would by looking into this. Or by hanging around with me. So go stay with Hannah and let me handle this."

"Bastard!" She tried to wrench her wrist from his grip.

He tightened his hold, not sure what she would do if he let go. Inside, his stomach churned while his heart clenched in pain. He desperately wanted to pull her into his arms, clutch her tight to his chest, tell her everything was going to be all right. And if Jules was behind this, Gray swore he'd make the prick pay. Older and stronger he might be, but Gray would find a way to take him down.

So focused was he on Carolyn's flushed, angry face, that he didn't even notice Hannah returning from the foyer until her hand landed on his arm and the muzzle of a gun appeared in his peripheral vision.

"Let go of her and start talking," Hannah commanded, the gun pointed straight at his head, her finger poised over the trigger. "Carolyn might not have been willing to shoot you, but I would love to."

Gray hesitated, and she moved the gun closer to his head—close enough that he could sense the high iron content of the muzzle and had to fight a reflexive urge to jerk away. If she touched it to his skin and his skin burned, what would she make of it?

"Hannah, put the gun down," Carolyn said in a gently chiding voice, but Hannah didn't move.

"Not until he lets go of you, and not until he quits this cloak-and-dagger crap." She looked at Gray with steely eyes. "If Carolyn's in danger, you sure as hell need to explain why."

Gray let go of Carolyn's wrist, raising his hands and splaying his fingers in a classic gesture of surrender. With his supernatural quickness he probably could have knocked Hannah's hand aside before she squeezed off a shot, but he wasn't about to risk it. Not that he really thought she meant to shoot him. She might talk tougher than Carolyn, but she wasn't a psycho.

Carolyn rubbed her wrist, and he saw the red finger marks that blotched her skin. His heart sank. He hadn't realized his own strength.

"I'm sorry, Carolyn," he said, trying to ignore the gun that still pointed at his head. "I didn't meant to hurt you."

She folded her arms across her chest, her gaze flicking to Hannah, then back to his face. "So, are you going to tell me what this is about?"

"No." He looked into Carolyn's eyes, meaning to capture her with his glamour. He should have known better than to ignore an angry woman with a gun. At the last moment, he sensed the blow coming and raised his arm enough to partially block it.

The butt of Hannah's gun slid off his arm and

slammed hard against the side of his head. Pain stabbed through his skull, and for a moment the world went gray. He managed to keep his feet, just barely. He hated to think what would have happened if she'd caught him squarely! She closed in for another blow, and though he still reeled from the last one, he dodged it.

"Hannah! Stop it!" Carolyn ordered.

"You want to let him get away without telling you diddly-squat?" Hannah countered. "You have handcuffs around here somewhere?"

The beast inside Gray was stirring, fired by pain and the instinct for self-preservation. He wanted to charge into battle, wrench the gun from Hannah's hand and—

And what? Bite her? A tingling sensation in his gums told him his fangs were on the verge of descending. Desperately, he tried to pull back the reins.

"Enough, Hannah," Carolyn said. "Now give me the gun."

Hannah looked vaguely disappointed in her friend's lack of resolve, but handed the gun over with a shrug. Gray closed his eyes and took a few deep breaths, willing the beast to quiet.

"Are you all right?" Carolyn asked. Her voice sounded genuinely concerned.

He opened his eyes and reached up to touch his aching head. The blow might well have knocked out a mortal man, and would certainly have left a lump.

"I'm fine." His voice came out curt and clipped, a consequence of his ongoing struggle for control. He glared at Hannah, who glared right back. "*You* talk sense into Carolyn. Convince her to stay with you, or you stay here with her."

Knowing that neither woman had abandoned her quest to wring information from him, he exerted just a touch of glamour. He wasn't terribly good at it, but he was good enough to achieve his goal. They stood still, looking faintly dazed, as he strode to the door.

By the time the door closed behind him, which would snap them out of it, he would have enough of a head start to get away cleanly.

* * *

So MUCH FOR MOVIE Night, Carolyn thought to herself as she reclaimed her seat on the couch. When they had shaken off their strange paralysis, she and Hannah had both charged out into the night after Gray, but he had disappeared. A brief search of the neighborhood had turned up nothing, and they'd finally had to admit defeat and return home.

Now they both sat in silence, staring at the note Gray had left behind. Hannah was absently playing with one of her springy curls, wrapping it around and around her index finger. Carolyn chewed her lip, trying to understand what had happened.

"So," Hannah said, breaking the silence. "Wanna fill me in on what I'm missing?"

Though she doubted it would clarify things as much as Hannah hoped, Carolyn recounted her last encounter with Gray and the mysterious Jules. Hannah took a moment to digest the information and discover the gaping holes that still existed in their understanding.

"So, this Jules guy . . . You think he's behind this?"

Carolyn shrugged. "I only met him for like five minutes."

"Yeah, but first impressions can tell you a lot."

She thought about it a moment, trying to remember every nuance of her brief encounter. Jules had been conspicuously charming, a smooth-talker who was used to coming on to women. Certainly that kind of charm often hid a dark character. And no one could mistake the antipathy between him and Gray. Still, her instincts told her it was a stretch to go from simple hostility to the kind of vicious threat this note entailed. Gray must have felt the same way or he never would have come here to deliver his high-handed, macho commands.

"My first impression is it wasn't him." She huffed out an exasperated sigh. "I wish we had some idea what the hell Gray is into. Nothing makes any sense!"

"Hey, I was all into gently persuading him to spill the beans, if you remember."

Carolyn shook her head ruefully. "How could I forget? Do you think you might have gone a bit overboard?"

"He was hurting you. I figured if I fetched your gun I could persuade him to stop."

"He wasn't hurting me when you tried to cold-cock him."

"So I got carried away. Sue me."

By all rights, Carolyn should be reading her best friend the riot act. Hannah had never been a cop, didn't own a gun of her own, and had no firearms training. Before becoming a PI, she'd been an investigative reporter. Handling Carolyn's gun at all, much less pointing it at someone and then hitting him over the head with it, was reckless in the extreme. But somehow, Carolyn couldn't find it in her heart to dress her down for it.

"I appreciate the thought, if not the method," she said. "You're a good friend."

"The best," Hannah agreed, smiling. "Will you still think so if I tell you Gray was right and you should come stay with me for a while?"

Carolyn instinctively bristled at the suggestion but gained control of her visceral reaction before she said anything she would regret. Much as she hated to admit it, she knew Hannah and Gray had a point. Yes, she was perfectly capable of defending herself. But not against so vague a threat, with so little information to go on.

Swallowing the stubborn refusal that wanted to tumble out of her mouth, she managed a tight nod.

* * *

JULES WASN'T LOOKING FORWARD to the next meeting at Eli's. True, it wasn't his fault that Gray's house had a bolt hole somewhere that had allowed Gray to sneak out without being followed. But for all the time he'd spent shadowing Gray, Jules should have known about it. If the stupid bastard hadn't come sauntering back through the front door, Jules *still* wouldn't know he had a secret way out of the house!

The first light of dawn was creeping over the city. At his advanced age, Jules could tolerate small doses of weak sunlight, but he was cutting it a little close. He'd been in a foul mood since he'd realized Gray had gotten away from him, and he'd done penance, of sorts, by staying at his post longer than usual.

His mood lifted some when he saw the little red Miata parked in front of his house. He was too tired to take full advantage of her charms this morning, but it would feel nice to fall asleep with Courtney beside him. She was such a sweet little thing. Not noticeably bright—as his fellow Guardians pointed out when they felt like ribbing him—but he'd never minded her lack of intellectual depth. For one thing, it made it a lot easier for him to hide his true nature from her. She was credulous enough to believe just about anything he told her. But she was pretty, she was good in bed, and she was at heart simply a nice person. He found himself smiling in anticipation.

He stepped into the foyer and closed the door behind him. Then he froze as several realizations struck him at once.

The house felt empty—no psychic presence, mortal or vampire, waiting for him in his bed.

His nostrils flared as he scented the distinctive odor of semen, though he hadn't been with Courtney for

two nights now. And under that there was a faint whiff
of blood. Nerves tingling, he crept toward his bedroom, moving in a cautious crouch even though his
senses insisted he was alone in the house.

The door was ajar. Jules took a deep breath to brace
himself, then pushed the door all the way open.

Courtney lay naked on the bed, her legs spread, her
head lolling to one side. A garish red wound slashed
across her throat.

Jules grabbed the doorframe, but his knees still
wouldn't hold him. He slid to the floor, his heart
pounding frantically. He knew without having to examine the body more closely that she'd been drained
of blood. He struggled for breath.

The sun was rising steadily. Lethargy stole over his
limbs, fuzzing his mind.

"Courtney . . ." he croaked as he fought for consciousness. He wanted to go to her, at least cover her
up, give her a kiss goodbye. But he could barely move,
and the need to sleep was an overwhelming force.

He groaned as his eyes slid shut. For now, he could
do nothing. But come sunset, there would be hell to pay.

8

HANNAH WAS STILL HANDLING all the agency's cases, so she headed off to work in the morning and left Carolyn to her own devices. Carolyn promised not to do anything rash or hasty, but she suspected Hannah wouldn't be shocked if she broke that promise.

Figuring her chances of being attacked by the alleged Broad Street Banger in her own place in broad daylight were approximately zilch, she went home. Last night, she'd taken only the bare essentials in an overnight bag. However, if she was going to play along with the paranoia and stay at Hannah's until everything blew over, she would need more clothes. Also, she wanted to take another look at the note, which they had left behind on her coffee table.

It didn't reveal much more this morning than it had last night, Carolyn decided as she sat on the sofa sipping a cup of coffee and staring at it. She remembered that Gray said the note had come in an envelope. She might as well go ahead and check it for fingerprints, despite his claim that she wouldn't find anything. She still had a friend at the fingerprint lab, one who could probably be persuaded to have the print analyzed for her.

Having learned Gray's address the hard way, she had no trouble finding his phone number, which wasn't even unlisted. The number was listed under the name James Gray. He didn't answer, and she left a message on his machine. She frowned at her watch. It was already ten. He was the kind of guy who made "early to bed and early to rise" into a religion. Surely he wasn't still asleep. Though he did seem to keep late hours these days.

When he still hadn't called her back by one, she called his house again. Again she got his answering machine. She left a second message, but now a frisson of doubt assailed her.

In the first week of her surveillance, she'd established that Gray was the ultimate homebody, and she hadn't once seen him venture forth in the daytime. That suggested that he should be home at this hour. Despite his night-owl schedule, he should be awake by now. So why wasn't he answering? Or at least calling her back?

Once the doubt had set in, it nibbled at the edges of her thoughts as she tried to make herself useful. Maybe if Gray couldn't be persuaded to tell her what was going on, she could find someone else who would. Jules, perhaps? She knew only his first name and had no address for him, but at least the name was unusual. She sat in front of her computer and used one of the many locator sites on the Internet to search the city for men named Jules, guessing he was maybe in his early thirties. As it turned out, there were only six thirty-something men named Jules in all of Philadelphia. Of course, there was no guarantee that Jules lived in the city proper, but at least she had a starting point.

She looked at her watch again. Two o'clock. She let out an exasperated sigh and dialed Gray's number again. No answer.

Try though she might, she couldn't dismiss her unease. The man was clearly in some kind of dire trouble. Although the note had threatened her directly,

Gray seemed to think the venom was aimed at him somehow. What if he was right? What if sending her to spend the night with Hannah had been a pointless gesture and it was Gray himself who was in danger?

Carolyn hated the cold terror that settled in the pit of her stomach at the thought. After all the bastard had done to shatter her life, how could she possibly be *worried* about him? *Concerned,* she could have handled. A human being was allowed to be concerned about another's safety, whether or not there was any connection between them. But worry . . . Worry conveyed a much more personal bond. And, damn it, she was worried!

Hannah would skin her alive for this, but Carolyn couldn't just sit around the house and twiddle her thumbs while this worry pounded through her.

Logging off the computer, she bundled up against the cold. Though she'd always been a reasonably law-abiding citizen, and though of course she would never—ahem—dream of using an illegal search to solve a case, Carolyn had taken the precaution of learning how to pick several basic models of locks. She tucked her Glock into one pocket and her lock picks in the other, then took a cab to the Zip Mart two blocks from Gray's house. If possible, she'd really like to avoid being seen by his personal surveillance team. She walked slowly toward his house, scanning the streets for any familiar faces. She didn't see any. Nor did she see any suspicious loiterers.

The coffee shop was doing brisk business, but no one at any of the booths by the window seemed to be paying any particular attention to Gray's doorstep. Still keeping an eye out for surveillance, Carolyn climbed the front steps and rang the bell. She heard the sound echoing through the house, but no footsteps approached the door. She bit her lip.

Maybe he really was out. That would explain why no one was watching the house right now—they'd followed him to wherever he'd gone. Wouldn't she feel ridiculous getting so worked up when he'd just gone out to the movies or something? Logic failed to ease the worry.

A narrow alleyway led around the side of the house. The alley dead-ended at another house, but behind Gray's house was a gated courtyard. Carolyn pushed aside the rampant growth of ivy over the gate and peered into the courtyard.

It was small, shared by five or six row houses and clearly not much used. Here and there, an outdoor grill was locked down against the city's omnipresent thieves. A barren garden looked sad and neglected, tangles of leafless branches spilling over its sides.

There was no sign of anyone watching out of any windows. Knowing she could end up in deep shit if she was wrong about that, Carolyn grasped the top of the gate and hauled herself up. The ivy tangled up her foot for a moment, but she pulled free and slid over the top into the courtyard. She brushed the leaves off her coat, hoping she hadn't left an obvious trail in the ivy.

There was a slight gap between the heavy curtains covering the window in the back door. Cupping her hands over her eyes to fight the glare, she looked inside and saw a stove. No lights on, no sign of life. After one last look around, Carolyn turned her attention to the door itself.

No deadbolt, she noted with a grim smile. That ought to make this easier. She pulled off her gloves and set to work on the lock.

Breaking and entering, Carolyn. Not a good sign. She shook her head at herself, but kept working, her heart racing with adrenaline. She'd be hard-pressed to explain herself if anyone caught her at this, breaking into a house in broad daylight. But she had to assure herself that Gray wasn't lying dead in his house somewhere, had to put her worries to rest.

And if he was?

Her heart clenched and her eyes actually blurred with tears. Damn it! It would be sad if something happened to him, yes. But she would *not* grieve for him! Whatever he'd gotten himself into, he'd made his own bed.

The lock clicked open. Carolyn turned the knob, withdrew her tools, and took a deep breath to steady herself. Then, she pushed the door open and slipped inside.

"Gray?" she called, not expecting an answer.

The house remained silent as the grave. On the kitchen wall, his answering machine blinked the number four. She slid her coat off, drawing the gun from her pocket. Probably the place was empty, but she didn't feel inclined to take a chance. For one thing, it didn't *feel* empty. Keeping her back pressed to the wall, she slid over to the doorway leading out into the hall.

She peeked around the corner, squinting against the darkness. The curtains in this place let in hardly a sliver of light, and she felt as though she'd stepped from daytime directly into night. She waited a minute until her eyes had adjusted as much as they were going to. Then, holding her gun at the ready, she crept down the hall.

There was a staircase to her left, and farther down the hall on her right was the living room. There was a powder room under the stairs, but the door was open and she could clearly see it was empty. She hesitated a long moment, listening intently for any sound, but all she heard were the cars passing by on the street outside. She continued down the hall toward the living room, still keeping watch on the staircase.

The living room was empty. She went in to make a circuit around the room just to be sure. Back in the hall, she had a choice between two closed doors in the foyer, and the staircase. One door turned out to hold a coat closet. No mysterious figures lurked inside. The other door led down into a basement. If she were going to go down there, she'd have to turn on a light. Better to check upstairs first. Unnerved and no doubt overly cautious, she locked the deadbolt on the basement door behind her.

She turned to face the staircase. There was no more light coming from upstairs than from anywhere else. Geez, how could Gray live like this? There was almost no natural light in here. It was downright depressing!

The stairs creaked as she made her way cautiously up, but no one leapt out of the shadows. She tried to take that as a good sign, but her pulse pounded insistently in her throat, and her breaths came quick and shallow. Even knowing that this was all a ludicrous overreaction didn't do anything to calm her nerves. Maybe it was just the aura of this house. It felt oppressive and old, the kind of house a mean old witch would inhabit. There should be cobwebs hanging from the light fixtures!

There were only three doors leading off the upstairs hall. One opened onto . . . a music room? Carolyn blinked and shook her head. An ancient-looking piano with yellowed keys sat propped against the wall, an even yellower sheet of music opened on its stand. In the corner sat a harp, and beside that was another music stand. As far as she knew, Gray didn't play any instrument, and certainly not the harp! No, this house was definitely not him. She remembered him saying he'd "inherited" it, but clearly he had not put his personal stamp on the place.

The second door opened onto a small linen closet, which Carolyn quickly examined and dismissed. The last door had to be a bedroom. Taking a deep breath, she readied the Glock in her right hand and used her left to push the door open.

The bedroom was even darker than the rest of the house, and at first her light-starved eyes saw nothing. Her heart rate shot up, and her palms sweated. Anything could jump out at her from that inky darkness!

When nothing did, she tried to relax, but her nerves remained on red alert.

Her eyes began to adjust, but she knew she'd never be able to make out more than vague shapes. She took one last glance over her shoulder to make sure no one—and nothing—was creeping up the stairs from the basement toward her. She almost laughed at herself. Did she think she was one of those oversexed teenagers in a horror movie who'd get killed by the monster in the first reel?

She groped along the wall until she found a light switch. The light momentarily blinded her, and she had to close her eyes against its searing glare. When she was able to open her lids a crack, she instantly saw the form that lay on the bed, the covers drawn up to his chest.

For one terrible moment, she thought he had to be dead. He couldn't possibly still be asleep! Not after her repeated phone calls or her ringing the doorbell or calling his name from downstairs. Then she saw his chest rising and falling with his slow, steady breaths and relief flooded her.

Carolyn let out a shaky breath, putting her Glock down on the dresser and covering her face with her hands.

The relief made her knees weak, and she was in danger of bursting into tears. She clamped her teeth, willing her turbulent emotions to calm. How could she be letting herself get so wound up over Gray? He was through with her, and she was through with him, and somehow she had to find a measure of emotional distance.

With another deep breath, she told herself that her overreaction was merely an effect of the stress his reappearance had caused. Shaking her head, she approached the bed.

The bedroom was the one room in the house that held a hint of Gray in it. The furnishings all looked as old-lady-like as everything else, but his dirty clothes were scattered over the floor, leaving only the occasional glimpse of the floral rug beneath, and the comforter that covered him was a masculine brown geometric print wildly at odds with the rest of the decor.

Carolyn stood at the bedside staring down at him for a long moment. He was lying on his back, his mouth slightly open, his hair framing his face in a black halo against the white pillow. The comforter revealed his naked shoulders and the very top of his chest. His skin was ghostly pale, almost sickly looking, but his body . . .

She'd always found Gray attractive, despite the extra weight he'd habitually carried. Now she saw the sleek muscles that weight had hidden, and she couldn't help appreciating the view. Broad shoulders, broad chest with conspicuous tone and a smattering of raven-dark hair. When they'd been together, he'd slept in the nude. She wondered if he still did.

She'd reached out and grabbed the edge of the comforter before she realized what she was doing. She started to pull it down, revealing more of his chest, her mouth practically watering.

With a jerk, she pulled her hands away. What was she thinking? She had no right to be looking at him like this! No matter how much she wanted to reveal the rest of his body to her curious stare, she forced herself to pull the cover back up to his shoulders.

Hoping she'd regained every ounce of her self control, she cleared her throat. "Gray?" she said, softly. He didn't respond, and she said it again, louder. Still, he didn't awaken. He'd never been such a sound sleeper before.

Bracing herself for the inevitable pulse of desire, she put her hand on his bare shoulder and gave him a gentle shake. "Wake up, Sleeping Beauty," she said.

Gray groaned and tried to twitch his shoulder out of her grip. Carolyn rolled her eyes and gave him another shake. "Come on already! It's the middle of the afternoon." His eyes fluttered and he groaned again.

"G'way," he mumbled, turning onto his side facing away from her.

She shook him more vigorously and he rolled onto his back again. His eyes were open, but just barely. He mumbled something else, but she couldn't understand him.

"Time to wake up," she said. "Do you need me to make you a cup of coffee?"

He blinked, reaching up to rub his eyes, but despite the movement, he didn't look any more awake. "Tired," he said, and his eyes slid closed again.

"Oh no you don't," she said, and a little hint of worry returned. What was the matter with him? He batted her hand out of the way without opening his eyes. She reached out to touch his forehead, wondering if perhaps he were feverish. Another incoherent protest escaped him. "Gray, what's wrong?" she asked, keeping her voice relatively steady despite the hint of panic that threatened to take over.

"Hangover," he said, and he sounded like he was talking in his sleep. "G'way!"

She finally understood that to mean "go away," but she wasn't at all sure what to make of this. A hangover that had kept him in bed all day? A chill crept up her spine. Drugs, maybe? Was *that* the secret he was trying so hard to hide? She touched a finger to his throat, feeling his strong, steady pulse. She tried to check his pupils to make sure they weren't dilated, but he woke up enough to growl "stop that" and roll away. Gray started snoring softly and she stared at him.

He didn't seem to be in any immediate danger, she supposed, but it wouldn't hurt to poke around a little and try to see what he had taken. She couldn't resist the urge to reach out and brush away a lock of hair that dangled over his forehead. She thought she heard a quiet sigh of contentment at her touch, but maybe that was just her imagination.

The most obvious place to check was the bathroom,

but she saw no signs of drugs in there, not even in the medicine cabinet. Which was very strange. Not only did she not find any illegal drugs, she didn't find *any* drugs. No aspirin, no Tums, no antihistamines. Weird.

She made a thorough check of the two bedside tables, but again found nothing. Next, she tried the downstairs powder room, to no avail. Maybe in the kitchen? She returned to the scene of her earlier break-in.

It was a bachelor's kitchen, to be sure, although unlike most bachelors he didn't have dirty dishes stacked in the sink. There was no sign of any food on the counters, and although there was a teapot on the stove, the layer of dust that coated it suggested it hadn't been used in ages. Carolyn opened the cupboards and found prissy-looking china as dusty as the teapot. It occurred to her that not only had she not found drugs, she hadn't found alcohol either. Just what kind of hangover *was* this? She supposed he could have gotten drunk or high somewhere else, but if he tended to such habits, she would have expected to find some evidence in his home.

Another cupboard held glasses. These were surprisingly clean, compared to the rest of the dishes. Carolyn was getting a distinctly uneasy feeling, but she couldn't put a name to it.

A narrow door in the corner opened onto a pantry. An *empty* pantry. She chewed her lip and frowned. She hadn't once seen Gray buy anything but milk at the store. Nor had she seen him go out to dinner or order take-out, which had led her to assume he kept his pantry well-stocked.

When was he eating? Not during the daytime, when she'd never seen him leave the house. And apparently not at night, as he didn't seem to have food supplies. It just didn't make sense!

She turned to face the refrigerator. Maybe he only ate fresh food, food that had to be kept in the fridge.

Yeah, but then why are all the plates dusty? she asked herself. More unnerved than she had any right to be, she pulled open the refrigerator door.

* * *

JULES PACED THE LIBRARY in quick, angry strides as he waited for Eli to make an appearance. Fury and grief had roused him long before sunset, and his advanced age had allowed him to venture forth into the fading daylight—swathed head to toe like a devout Muslim wife. He'd shown up at Eli's doorstep maybe a half hour before sunset, demanding entrance. Eli had let him in, then instructed him to wait in the damn library. Jules had controlled his temper until the lock clicked shut and he realized Eli had locked him in. He'd cursed the Founder with the foulest Québécois epithets he knew, then repeated them all in English just for the hell of it, but he doubted Eli had hung around to listen.

Jules stopped his pacing for a moment to pound on the door until his fist hurt. "Eli!" he shouted. "Let me out of here, you bastard!" A small, rational corner of his brain told him that he was demonstrating the very explosion of temper that had prompted Eli to lock him in, but that didn't seem to help him regain his self-control. He kicked a small side table, sending it crashing into the wall.

He should have skipped this little trip to Eli's, should have gone straight to Gray's house and ripped the fucker's heart out! God, how he wished he had Gray's mealy face in front of him right now. He wouldn't kill him quickly, that's for sure. That killer of innocents would suffer more than he ever thought possible. It wouldn't really avenge poor, sweet Courtney, but it was the best Jules could do.

It felt like hours that he paced that claustrophobic library, powerless to control the rage that coursed through his blood. But when Eli finally unlocked the door and stepped in, Jules sensed that the sun still had not set, so it couldn't have been long at all.

The fury and the thirst for vengeance were so overpowering that Jules had to suppress an urge to lunge for the Founder's throat. Aside from being an incredibly stupid thing to do, it would never work. That realization helped quell the urge.

Eli stood in the doorway and folded his arms, his face devoid of emotion. "Control the beast," he said, and his voice conveyed both warning and command. "Your anger is awakening it."

"Vas te faire mettre!" Jules snarled. He hated it when Eli went all Yoda-like! Even when the bastard was right. *Especially* when the bastard was right.

"Be careful, Jules. You're standing on the brink of a precipice. I'd hate to see you fall in."

Jules's breath came in short gasps, and he wanted desperately to hit something. He clenched his fists as tightly as he could, making his knuckles ache. "He killed Courtney! I have a right to revenge!"

"You don't know that. You're just making an assumption."

"Damn it, Eli—"

"You're never safe from the hunger, no matter how long you've kept it under control. If you let it control you now, you may never get your humanity back. It's not the human part of you that wants to kill without proof. Is it worth losing yourself to slake the beast's thirst?"

Jules found himself shaking as Eli's words wormed their way into his consciousness. Now that he knew what to look for, he felt the beast within him stirring, uncoiling, ready to strike. That realization chilled him, and with that chill came a modicum of calm. He swallowed hard and unclenched his fists.

Eli stepped closer, watching him with intense concentration. Jules felt as if the Founder were poking about in the dark shadows of his psyche, trying to read his future. Another chill shivered through him. If Eli decided he was losing his humanity, that he would succumb to the bloodlust and become a Killer, he would never leave this house alive.

"He escaped my surveillance last night," Jules said, hoping his voice sounded cool and rational. "And we've . . . had words lately."

Eli snorted, a hint of a grin playing about his lips. "And this is something new?"

The sarcasm eased a bit more of the tension out of Jules's shoulders, and when he spoke he was certain he sounded more like himself. "What are the chances it's a coincidence that he slips away and my girlfriend is murdered on the same night?"

"I agree it looks bad. But I don't believe Gray James is stupid, and only a fool would kill your girl and then advertise to you that he'd gotten out of the house without being seen. If he'd slipped back in the way he'd slipped out, you'd never have known."

Jules shook his head. "Why do you have such a soft spot for him? It's not like he's a Guardian. It's not like he contributes anything to any society, mortal or vampire. He's done nothing but sulk and feel sorry for himself since the moment we saved his pathetic life, and yet you always stand up for him."

Eli sighed. "It's not *him* I'm standing up for in particular. But Jules, I founded the Guardians not just to destroy the Killers, but to save the fledglings who could still be saved. And until I'm one hundred percent certain he can't be saved, I will fight for Gray James and anyone else who's had the misfortune to be transformed."

Now it was Jules's turn to sigh. He felt like a toddler having a temper tantrum in comparison to Eli's supreme calm and noble vision. He ran a hand through his hair, feeling the sweat that beaded his forehead. Everything Eli said was true, and though he hated

Gray with renewed strength, he vowed he would not play vigilante. Maybe some part of him had known this already and that's why he'd come to Eli first instead of confronting Gray immediately.

"I'm sorry, Eli," he forced himself to say.

Eli dismissed that with a wave of his hand. "Not your fault, my boy." He gestured Jules into a chair, taking his own seat across from him. "You have to accept that no matter how well you may control the beast, it is still there. You are no longer fully human, and you never will be again."

Jules winced at the prognosis, but it was nothing he hadn't discovered on his own.

"You can't help the visceral, aggressive reactions. Why do you think you and Gray hate each other, anyway?"

Jules sneered. "I hate him because he's an asshole who'd rather tuck his head in the sand and feel sorry for himself than try to make the world a better place!"

Eli's smile was gently condescending. "If you say so."

"Just what are you implying?"

Eli seemed to think about that a moment before answering. "Vampires are not naturally social creatures, my friend. We're apex predators, territorial and competitive. That I've been able to create the Guardians, convince them to work together, and prevent them from killing each other is a minor miracle. You and Gray are simply reacting to that natural antipathy."

There had to be more to it than that, Jules thought but didn't say. After all, he didn't react so viscerally to any of the other Guardians, with the possible exception of Drake. Still, none of that mattered right now.

"Never mind," he said. "You can psychoanalyze me later. At the moment, I want to know what you're going to do about the murder."

Eli gave him another long, assessing look. "Answer me honestly, Jules—can you keep yourself under control?"

Jules did him the courtesy of thinking about that for a moment, poking at his rage and seeing if it threatened to take over again. But though the rage still simmered, and though he still harbored strong suspicions that Gray had killed Courtney, Eli had instilled enough doubt that Jules believed he could control himself.

"I won't kill him without proof," he promised.

Eli nodded as if satisfied. "Very well, then. I suggest you stop by his house and ask him what he was up to last night. And make sure he shows you his bolt hole and where it comes out. I guess I'll have to assign a second Guardian to the surveillance team each night, but it can't be helped."

"All right." Jules stood, ready to see himself out. His senses told him the sun was almost down, which meant Gray would be up and about at any moment. He turned his back and took a couple of steps toward the door.

"Oh, Jules?" Eli said, and Jules stopped to look over his shoulder. "I don't appreciate being told to go fuck myself. In the future, please watch your language."

To his chagrin, Jules felt the blood rush to his face. It had never occurred to him that the Founder knew Québécois. He cleared his throat. "Sorry, Eli." Then he hurried out.

9

CAROLYN PULLED UP A chair and sat beside Gray's bed, setting the green glass bottle on the bedside table. Her stomach turned over at the thought of what that bottle contained, but she managed to hold off the nausea.

She let out a slow, deep breath as she tried to make sense of the impossible.

Gray apparently never ventured out in the daytime. His house was dark as a tomb. He'd gained strength, and his reflexes were suddenly blinding. She couldn't get him to wake up, and despite his claim of a hangover, she'd found no alcohol in the house. And, his refrigerator was stocked with bottles of . . . blood.

This ridiculous trail of evidence led to an even more ridiculous conclusion. Surely there had to be some more reasonable explanation.

Carolyn stared at the bottle of blood and wondered what rational explanation could possibly explain that away. Then she looked at Gray's pale, pale face as he continued to sleep away the afternoon. What had happened to the man she'd once loved?

She glanced at her watch and was startled to see how the time had gotten away from her. It was six o'clock already! If her absolutely absurd suspicion were correct, then Gray should be waking up any moment now. But of course, her suspicion couldn't be correct, because vampires didn't exist.

Perhaps Gray was merely insane, in desperate need of professional attention.

Carolyn practically jumped out of her chair when Gray moaned and stirred. Her mouth went dry and she grabbed the arms of her chair with white-knuckled hands as he reached up and rubbed the sleep out of his eyes.

The vague, sleepy look on his face disappeared in a heartbeat, and he sat up abruptly, turning to face her as the covers slid down his torso. Despite everything, she couldn't help taking a quick glance at the lean, toned body this revealed. Then she wrenched her eyes away and focused on the bottle. Gray followed her gaze, then cursed under his breath.

He ran a hand through his sleep-tousled hair, huffing out a deep breath. He met her eyes, and she couldn't read his expression at all.

"What are you doing here, Carolyn?"

"I'd been calling you all day and didn't get an answer. I got worried." She bit her lip, wishing she hadn't admitted that, but Gray hardly seemed to notice.

"So you broke into my house and started snooping." Now she *could* read his expression, and it was one of anger.

"I don't think you're in the position to throw any stones right now, Gray." Once again, she stared at the bottle of blood, her stomach threatening to rebel.

"That really needs to stay in the refrigerator or it'll go bad," he said, his voice so bland Carolyn wanted to scream.

"That's all you have to say for yourself? I find bottles of blood in your fridge and all you care about is that I keep them cold for you?"

He swung his legs over the side of the bed, keeping the comforter clutched to his middle. No pajamas, she noted, and hated herself for it.

"What do you want me to say?" he asked softly.

"I want you to explain what the hell is going on."

He nodded. "But you already have a damn good idea."

Her gorge rose, and she swallowed hard. This had to be some kind of dream! "I don't know what to think."

"Yes you do. You just don't like it."

"You're insane." It came out a choked whisper, and it occurred to her to worry that his insanity made him dangerous.

He snorted. "Believe what you like. But those others you've seen watching me . . . they share the same delusion, and they're dangerous, which is why I've tried so hard to convince you to leave me alone."

She wished she would wake up from this damn dream. Immediately! But in her heart of hearts, she knew this wasn't a dream, and though her mind still balked at the conclusions the evidence indicated, that didn't make the conclusions go away.

She jerked her chin at the bottle, unable to suppress a grimace of disgust. "You actually *drink* that?"

He sighed heavily, his face mirroring her own disgust. "Mixed with milk. Yes. And it's lamb blood, not human, in case you're wondering."

She blinked. "And where the hell do you get bottles of lamb blood? I very much doubt the Zip Mart carries it."

His lips twitched at that, but he suppressed the expression before it became a smile. "It's a long story, Carolyn."

She crossed her arms and gave him her most stubborn glare. "I think I deserve to hear it, don't you?"

Gray rubbed his face with both hands. The movement allowed the comforter to slide down a little farther, revealing washboard abs. Again, Carolyn felt an inappropriate tug of desire, but she tried as best she could to ignore it.

"Let's make a deal," he said, raising his head from

his hands. "You put the bottle back in the fridge, then I'll tell you the truth. As much of it as you can stomach."

She didn't relish touching that bottle again, nor did she relish the idea of opening the fridge and seeing the other bottles lined up in the door. But if that was what it took to get Gray talking, then she would do it.

Without a word, she picked up the bottle, holding it gingerly by the neck, and headed downstairs.

* * *

GRAY CURSED REPEATEDLY UNDER his breath as he slipped out of bed and pulled on some clothes. He should have known Carolyn wouldn't sit passively on the sidelines. No matter how badly he disapproved of her profession, he had to admit she was damned good at it. He should never have let her catch sight of him! She could have taken out that street punk on her own if he hadn't come barging in like a frigging hero.

Now she knew. He saw it in her eyes. Oh, she wanted to tell herself he was a nutcase, but she couldn't help but put together the pieces of the puzzle. She'd noticed his increased strength and quickness, she'd recognized the daylight sleep for what it was.

All too soon, he heard her footsteps as she mounted the stairs once more. What were the chances that after she'd heard the story, knew what she was up against, she'd beat a strategic retreat? He almost laughed at the thought.

The door swung open, and Carolyn entered. Her body language screamed of tension and resolve, and if he'd ever entertained a thought that he might put her off, it died.

"Start talking," she said, fire flashing in her eyes.

He sat on the edge of his rumpled bed and gestured for her to sit on the chair. She did so, her back stiff, her movements cautious. Was she afraid of him?

The thought struck him hard, but when he looked into her eyes he saw no sign of fear. Wariness, yes, and she was entitled to it. He swallowed hard. If she hated him for what he was about to tell her, then so be it. No doubt he deserved it.

"On the night of my bachelor party, the guys hired a stripper, as you know."

She nodded, a brisk, jerky movement of her head.

"When her performance was over, she couldn't get her car to start. It was getting pretty late, and the streets weren't exactly flooded with cabs. I offered to give her a ride home."

Even now, he remembered the hint of triumph that had flickered in her eyes when he'd made the offer. At the time, he'd thought it was relief.

"You couldn't have let one of your buddies give her a ride?" Carolyn asked acidly. "They're the ones who hired her, after all."

"We were a bunch of guys at a bachelor party, Carolyn. They were egging me on, and I never would have lived it down if I hadn't agreed to drive her. They already thought I was hopelessly old-fashioned and conservative. If I hadn't—"

"Yes, and it would have killed you if for a moment your macho buddies had had a negative thought about you."

He winced, but as usual she'd seen straight to the heart of things. "You knew this about me when you agreed to marry me. I was a conformist at heart." It seemed so foreign to him now, the way he had let others' opinions direct his life to such an extent. It had been his co-workers' underhanded little comments about how Carolyn would wear the pants in the family—her being a cop while he was nothing but a meek desk-jockey—that had spawned the round of arguments about her job. It had always amazed him that Carolyn put up with him.

A little of the tension eased out of her shoulders at his candid admission. "You're right, I knew that. Sorry. Keep going."

Damn, he hated strolling down this particular memory lane! "So I drove her home, and when I got there, she invited me in for a drink." He remembered the bolt of heat that had shot through his body when she'd made the invitation. Kate was stunningly beautiful, and his mind had filled with visions of her stripping off her clothes, her hips grinding as her breasts jiggled enticingly. He'd hardened painfully, and suddenly he'd known he *had* to have her. Glamour, he knew now.

He hung his head, unable to bear the reproach in Carolyn's gaze. "She was a vampire, Carolyn. She had the power to entice me against my will."

Carolyn grunted in disbelief. "From what I heard when I investigated your disappearance, this little stripper of yours was a knock-out."

He raised his head and forced himself to meet her eyes. "*You're* a knock-out. I couldn't have cared less what she looked like, and if she hadn't screwed with my mind I never would have set foot into her house. But she drew me in and . . ." A shudder choked off his voice for a moment. "She bit me. There was no sex involved. As soon as she had me through the door, she went for my throat." He closed his eyes against the memory.

The glamour had held him still, but he'd felt the sharp pain of her fangs piercing his throat. She'd drunk and drunk while he stood paralyzed, unable to defend himself, until his knees gave out and he collapsed to the floor. She'd collapsed on top of him, her mouth still fastened to his throat as she sucked the life out of him.

In the end, she hadn't needed the glamour anymore, for he had become too weak to fight her. The world had faded to black, and he accepted the reality that he was about to die.

He wished he had.

"She drained me dry," he continued, his voice harsh and hoarse as he tried to beat back the memory. "She brought me to the brink of death. Then . . . This is hard to explain, and unless you'd actually experienced it I doubt you can understand, but . . . I felt like someone was holding out a lifeline to me. It wasn't a physical thing, but a kind of . . . psychic line. On some instinctual level, I think I knew what it was, but I wasn't ready to die. So I reached for it, and I became . . . what I am."

"A vampire." Despite everything she had seen, Carolyn's voice said she didn't quite believe it.

"Yes. Shall I prove it to you?"

Her eyes widened and he heard her hasty intake of breath. "How?"

"It's easier than you think." He flexed his jaw, causing his fangs to descend, then pulled his lips away from his teeth.

Carolyn stared blankly. She was shaking. Quickly, he withdrew the fangs, wishing he could have spared her this.

"I left you because I had to," he said softly. "There was nothing I could tell you to soften the blow. I believed that then, and I still believe it now. You're better off without me, and you would have been better off if you didn't know any of this. Whether you allow yourself to believe me or not."

"I don't know what I believe," she answered. Her face was pale, but she didn't seem to be shaking anymore. "I'll figure that out later. For now, you still have a lot of explaining to do."

He was silent for a long moment, considering how much to tell her. Very likely when she'd had time to process everything, she would hate him, or fear him, or at least be disgusted by him. But there was no reason to make it any worse than it had to be. There were some ugly truths she didn't need to know. At least, that's how he justified it to himself.

"Vampires don't have to kill to live," he told her. "But many of them, like Kate, do it anyway. Once they start killing, it becomes an addiction, worse than any drug a mortal can get hooked on. They lose every touch of their humanity. But there's an organization of vampires in Philly who aren't Killers. They call themselves the Guardians of the Night." He allowed himself a slight, sardonic smile. He always thought the name sounded absurdly pompous. "They hunt the Killers and destroy them. If the Guardians can get to the fledgling vampires before they become addicted, they can be rescued.

"The Guardians tracked Kate down and killed her, and they rescued me. This was her house," he said, waving a hand at the antique furniture that surrounded him. "I've lived here ever since."

Carolyn looked around the room as if seeing it for the first time. "That's why the house looks like some kind of time capsule."

"Yes. It's the house Kate grew up in. Many of the older vampires prefer to live where they did as mortals. There's some kind of comfort to it, I suppose, though I'm not old enough to feel that homing instinct myself."

"And tell me about the blood in your fridge."

"The Guardians provide it. I have to drink it combined with milk to stay alive. It's disgusting, but it keeps me from having to hurt anyone."

"And the people who've been watching your house . . ."

"Are Guardians. They've never quite trusted me. You see, even if you're not addicted to the kill, there's always some level of . . . temptation." His hands were now sweating and he rubbed his palms on his pants legs. "Becoming vampire changes you." He forced himself to look at Carolyn, wondering what she was making of all this. All he could tell was that she was deeply troubled. "I've become . . . more aggressive, as you've no doubt seen. *I* know I'll never give in to the temptation to kill." He said this in a voice of absolute conviction, despite the doubt that hovered always just under the surface. "But *they* don't know that.

"I started watching you a couple months ago. I was just torturing myself, wishing I could turn back time and make everything right. But Jules thought it might be the start of predatory behavior and he sicced the rest of the Guardians on me. Now I can't take a step without being watched."

Carolyn looked like she was about to ask a question, but she was interrupted by the ringing of the doorbell. Gray couldn't help feeling a touch relieved by the interruption, though he doubted the reprieve would last long.

He crossed the room to the window, pushing aside the drapes and looking down at the sidewalk. When he saw Jules standing on his doorstep, he groaned. "Speak of the devil," Gray said. Just what he wanted to deal with right now!

"Who is it?" Carolyn asked.

"Jules." He groaned again as Jules leaned on the doorbell. "I'd better go see what he wants. He's not about to go away." He stood up, and Carolyn rose from her chair to follow him.

"Stay here," he commanded, then internally castigated himself for his tone of voice. Carolyn did not take well to men who barked orders. As her glare told him. "Please," he said, softening his tone. "You don't want to get between me and Jules. As you might have noticed, we don't get along very well. I'd really rather he not know you're here. I don't want him using you to spite me."

Rebellion sparked in her eyes, but to his surprise she nodded. "All right. I'll stay out of sight."

"Thanks." He didn't know what else to say, so he ducked out the door. At this point, he thought he might almost prefer to face Jules than to face Carolyn. At least he knew where he stood with Jules! But that didn't mean this would be any fun.

* * *

CAROLYN FELT LIKE SHE'D gone through the looking glass. Her mind balked at all she'd heard this evening. Surely someone was going to pop out of the shadows shouting "surprise" and admitting she was the victim of a sick prank. Because, of course, there was no such thing as vampires. Hell, if she allowed herself to believe in vampires, then what other myths and fairy tales might she have to reconsider? Werewolves? Witches? Gremlins? The Tooth Fairy?

She heard the front door opening, heard the murmur of Gray's voice, though she couldn't make out the words. She eased through the bedroom door, slinking down the hall under the cover of darkness until she stood at the head of the stairs.

Gray was holding the door just barely open, his posture screaming a message of inhospitality. "Now is not a good time!" he said, his voice sharp, as though this weren't the first time he'd said it.

The door flew open, and Gray stumbled backward, practically falling. Carolyn had to fight an instinct to run to Gray's aid. Ridiculous! The man was a . . . Well, he didn't need her help, anyway.

Jules stepped into the foyer, closing the door behind him. He was wearing the cashmere coat again, the black hat perching on his auburn-haired head at a rakish angle. He was almost as hot as Gray.

Carolyn rolled her eyes at herself. How could she be ogling either of them, under the circumstances?

Jules removed his hat, tossing it onto a side table and brushing at his hair with one hand. Carolyn couldn't help a little smile of amusement. The guy was so vain he had to fix his hair in the midst of a confrontation?

"Well, now that you've invited yourself in," Gray said with poor grace, "what the hell do you want?"

"Where were you last night?"

Gray grunted. "If I'd wanted you to know, I wouldn't have slipped away."

"Don't test me!"

Even from this distance, Carolyn could see the danger that sparked in Jules's eyes. He'd dropped the urbane manner, and his stance screamed of aggression. He looked like a man about ready to snap, and Carolyn hoped Gray could read those signs as well as she. She glanced over her shoulder, wondering if she could make it to the bedroom to retrieve her gun without being noticed.

Gray sighed. "Take it easy, Jules. You didn't miss anything crucial."

"So where were you?"

Gray shook his head. "I'm not telling you that, so forget it. It had nothing to do with you or any of the Guardians so it's none of your business."

"Enculeur de mouche!" Jules snarled, baring his teeth. Carolyn shivered when she saw the fangs he revealed. Okay, if this was a sick joke, then Jules was in on it too. What were the chances?

Carolyn shook her head, not wanting to accept the impossible, but not having much choice.

"I'm going to ask you one more time," Jules said, "and you'd better answer me or I'm going to make you regret it! Where were you last night?"

He looked so dangerous Carolyn decided she'd have to risk the noise of going back to the bedroom for her gun after all. She started to ease her weight backward, then came to an abrupt stop. These were *vampires*! Would a gun do any good? Or did she need a wooden stake?

"There was another murder last night, wasn't there?" Gray asked, his voice devoid of inflection while his shoulders subtly slumped.

Murder? Carolyn thought. What murder? And what did Gray mean *another* murder? Obviously he still hadn't told her everything.

Jules moved so quickly Carolyn felt like she was watching a movie in fast forward. One moment, he was standing at a respectable distance, glaring like a thundercloud about to burst into lightning. The next, he'd crossed the short distance between them, grabbed a double handful of Gray's shirt, lifted him off his feet, and slammed him hard against the wall.

Gray grunted in pain, and Jules slammed him against the wall again. Gray struggled weakly, but it was obvious he was overpowered and struggling for breath.

"Yes, there was another murder!" Jules shouted. "You killed Courtney, you son of a bitch!" He punctuated the accusation with another slam into the wall, and Gray looked like he was near to losing consciousness with the force of those blows.

Carolyn abandoned caution and sprinted down the hall to the bedroom, snatching her Glock off the dresser and hurrying back to the head of the stairs, her heart racing. When she reached the head of the stairs, Jules was still holding Gray off his feet and baring his fangs. Carolyn wondered again if her gun would have any effect and if she was about to incur the same treatment Gray was receiving. She took aim, but couldn't find her voice to announce her presence.

Jules lowered Gray until his feet hit the ground, but retained his grip on his shirt, crowding into his space. "Give me one good reason why I shouldn't kill you right now!"

Gray was gasping for breath, and though Jules was clearly trying to make eye contact, Gray was just as clearly trying to avoid it. "Because I'm not guilty," Gray managed between gulps of air.

"Marde!" Jules said, shaking his head. He let go of Gray's shirt, and Gray slid down the wall until his butt

hit the floor, his head bowed as he sucked in noisy breaths.

Carolyn lowered her gun, although she wasn't at all sure the danger was past. Jules looked like a man on the edge. But she'd promised Gray she'd keep quiet, and she wouldn't break that promise unless she was absolutely sure it was necessary.

"Why should I believe you?" Jules asked.

Gray took a deep breath and rested the back of his head against the wall, his eyes closed. "I didn't even know Courtney, Jules. Why would I want to kill her?"

"To get to me!"

Gray opened his eyes. "Your paranoia is showing."

Jules snarled again. "I promised Eli I wouldn't kill you without proof. But I didn't promise not to beat the shit out of you."

Gray rose to his feet, using the wall as support. "Shit? Gee, Jules, I didn't think you knew any cuss words in English."

Jules looked stunned. "You're making *jokes*? You're one hell of a cold fish, you know."

Gray sighed. "Sorry, Jules." His voice sounded sincere, but his face said he really hated apologizing. "But I swear to you, I didn't kill her. And don't tell me with that massive chip on your shoulder you haven't made any other enemies."

Jules looked like he was about to give Gray hell again, but suddenly Carolyn's cell phone rang. Damn it!

She reached frantically for the Off button, but it was too late. Two sets of eyes turned to stare into the darkness at the top of the stairwell, and she was caught.

10

GRAY CURSED HIMSELF FOR an idiot. He'd known something was fishy when Carolyn agreed to stay out of sight so easily, but he hadn't followed that thought to its logical conclusion. Why did he keep allowing himself to forget she was a detective? For God's sake, the woman had broken into his house!

"Well, well," Jules said with a charming smile completely at odds with his recent rabid-dog impersonation. "What have we here?"

Carolyn, looking sheepish, came halfway down the stairs. "Gray came to see me last night," she told Jules. "I don't know why you would ever think he'd kill your friend, but he has an alibi."

"Why didn't you say so?" Jules asked Gray with a look of pure disgust.

"I was *trying* to keep Carolyn out of this." Gray shot her a reproachful look, which she ignored.

"What time did he get to your house?" Jules asked Carolyn.

"It was about ten, I think. Now, since my cover is blown, would you gentlemen care to tell me why accusations of murder are flying about?"

Gray had a momentary reprieve from the upcoming scene when his phone rang. Probably he should ignore it, but he wouldn't mind a couple of moments to gather his thoughts. His head still felt a little fuzzy from its repeated encounters with the wall. Before Jules could stop him, he darted into the living room and picked up the receiver. When he heard Hannah's frantic voice on the other end of the line, he was glad he'd decided to answer. The last thing he needed was another woman breaking into his house tonight!

"It's all right, Hannah," he said, looking at Carolyn, who, along with Jules, had followed him. She unclipped her phone from her belt and turned it on, grimacing guiltily when she reviewed the calls. "She's here and she's fine," Gray reassured Carolyn's partner.

"Then why the hell didn't she answer her phone?"

"Because she was busy," he snapped, hating the accusatory tone in her voice. Why did everybody think he was some kind of axe-wielding murderer these days? "Carolyn, please come to reassure your mom— er, that is, Hannah—that you're alive and kicking."

"Asshole," he heard Hannah mutter as he handed the phone to Carolyn.

From the look on Carolyn's face, Hannah had some choice words for her too, and he got the feeling Carolyn may have hung up on her at the end. Great to know he was sowing discord with everyone he knew. There was a tight, unhappy look around the corners of her eyes when she put the phone down.

"Why don't we sit down and discuss this like rational adults?" she suggested.

Gray wished he could push Rewind and start over from the moment he'd left Carolyn in his room to answer the door. As a former cop, would she be able to mind her own business after hearing an accusation of murder? Not a chance in hell.

Sighing in resignation, Gray gestured toward the cluster of seats. "Yes, please do come in and join us, Jules," he said, infusing the words with every drop of sarcasm he could muster.

At least Jules chose one of the ass-numbing chairs to sit on. Maybe that meant he wouldn't stay long. Carolyn sat beside Gray on the sofa, and he could just visualize her pulling a little notebook from her pocket and scribbling down notes like some TV detective.

"First, let's establish that I've learned Gray's . . . secret," she said in a crisp, business-like voice.

Jules raised an eyebrow, looking amused. No doubt he underestimated Carolyn's detective skills just like everyone else. "And what is that secret, pray tell?"

Gray suspected that his tone was pissing Carolyn off almost as much as it was pissing *him* off, for her smile was just a little too sweet when she answered. "That he's a vampire," she said.

Gray muffled a laugh at the shock on Jules's face and at the smugness on Carolyn's. He hastened to explain before Jules came to the erroneous conclusion that Gray had blurted out a confession. "She broke into my house this afternoon and found me sleeping. Plus, she looked in my fridge."

Jules shook his head. "And why would you do a thing like that?" he asked Carolyn.

"Because the reason Gray came to my house last night was that he received a threatening letter. The threat was against me, but I was worried it was really directed at him. When I couldn't get him to answer the phone, I thought maybe . . ." Uncharacteristically, she let her voice trail off, and a hint of color touched her cheeks.

A tiny spot of warmth glowed in Gray's chest. She'd been worried about him. No matter how badly he'd treated her, some part of her still cared about him. It was more than he deserved, but he couldn't help being grateful for it.

"What did this note say?" Jules asked.

Carolyn fixed him with a penetrating stare. "Are you sure you don't know?"

He blinked. "You think *I* sent it?"

"Surely that's not any more ridiculous than you thinking I killed Courtney," Gray retorted.

The fire returned to Jules's eyes. "I'm still not convinced you didn't. I'll take Carolyn's word for it that you arrived at her house at ten, but I don't know when you left yours. You'd have had plenty of time to stop by my house and—" He cleared his throat.

Gray felt a moment of sympathy, no matter how much he despised the prick. He'd obviously cared about the girl.

"Just for the sake of argument," Carolyn said, "let's for the moment assume that you didn't send the note and Gray didn't kill your friend, okay?"

Jules nodded tightly.

"So, the note Gray received threatened to kill me, and was supposedly signed by the Broad Street Banger."

Jules started violently, his eyes going wide.

"What?" Carolyn asked.

"The way Courtney was killed . . . The killer used the Broad Street Banger's MO."

"One hell of a coincidence," Gray muttered, though of course none of them could possibly believe it was a coincidence. He wished he had some clue what it meant. He glanced over at Carolyn and could practically see the gears turning in her head as she examined the meager evidence she'd received so far. Her face paled.

"The Banger is a vampire, isn't he?"

Once again, Jules got that surprised look on his face, and Gray smiled. Damn, Carolyn was good. But Jules soon dispensed with his own admiration.

"I think Gray and I have both said more than we should already. You've given him an alibi for last night, but it isn't an airtight one. You've done the best you can under the circumstances, but until I have reason to believe otherwise, Gray remains my prime suspect, and I plan to keep such a close eye on him people will think we're lovers."

Carolyn, true to form, ignored the attempted brush-off. "So, do you two have any mutual enemies?"

"I know you were a policewoman in the past," Jules said, "but this case is over your head. For your own safety, the less you know, the better."

Gray bit the inside of his cheek. Right now, he was actually glad Jules was here. The asshole would say all the things Gray wanted to say, thus sparing Gray from having to have his head bitten off when he voiced them.

"I've already been threatened," Carolyn reminded him, her voice surprisingly mild. If Gray had said something like that, she'd have bristled. "It seems I've been brought into the loop whether you like it or not."

"For all we know, Gray wrote that note himself just to provide an alibi."

"If he were going to do that, he'd probably provide one that would actually hold water."

"I didn't write the stupid note, and I didn't kill anyone. Jules, if you put on the blinders and assume I did it just because you don't like me, then you'll never find the real killer."

Carolyn was looking back and forth between them. She opened her mouth to say something, then froze, staring straight ahead. Into Jules's eyes.

Gray lunged to his feet. "Damn it, Jules! Let her go!"

Jules rose more slowly, and Carolyn watched him, rapt. "She's heard more than enough. The last thing we need is a helpless mortal poking around on the trail of a Killer."

"Helpless" was not a word Gray would use to describe Carolyn, but he supposed under the circumstances it was close to accurate. He hated that Jules was using his glamour against her, but Gray had to admit the older vampire had a point. Too bad they were trying to close the barn door after the horse had escaped.

Gray stopped himself from saying anything to that effect. Who knew to what lengths Jules would go to protect the "helpless" mortal?

"Show me your bolt hole and show me where it comes out. Then I'll get out of your hair for the time being."

Gray glanced at Carolyn, who still sat motionless on the sofa, her eyes glazed, her lips slightly parted.

"She'll be fine," Jules said. "Now come on."

Gray supposed there was no point in fighting it. He led the way down into the basement, showing Jules the trap door and guiding him down the tunnel to its exit in the neighboring courtyard. At least the Guardian who drew this watch duty was going to be miserable—there was no warm, cozy coffee shop to watch from. No, whoever was stuck here would have to sit out in the cold and suffer. Gray hoped for lots of rain and arctic wind-chills.

Carolyn still hadn't moved when Gray and Jules emerged from the basement. Without another word, Jules moved to the front door. Gray grabbed his arm.

"Let her go now!" he demanded.

Jules smiled, picking up his hat from the hall table. "She's all yours," he said, a hint of a sneer in his voice. Then he slipped out the door, and Gray breathed a sigh of relief.

* * *

CAROLYN'S CHIN JERKED SHARPLY upwards, like she'd been nodding off, only she wasn't in the least bit sleepy. She blinked rapidly, disoriented and confused. Shaking her head to try to clear the cobwebs, she looked around the living room.

Jules was gone. And Gray was no longer sitting next to her, he was moving toward her from the foyer. Her heart skipped a beat, and she went cold. What the hell . . . ?

"It's called glamour," Gray said as he returned to the sofa and sat beside her.

"What?"

"The reason you feel all confused right now. It's called glamour. King Jules decided you didn't need to hear any more and put you in a trance."

She swallowed on a suddenly dry throat. *Vampires, Carolyn. These are* vampires *you're dealing with.* The reality still hadn't quite sunk in, and she wondered if it ever would. "So. Glamour. Okay. Vampires are real. They drink blood, they only come out at night, and they use glamour to control us mere mortals. So, know any werewolves? What about pixies? You always used to say I looked like a pixie. Is it true?" She noticed a hint of hysteria in her voice and forced herself to shut up before she started babbling about banshees or any other magical creature she could think of. She took a deep, calming breath.

"Sorry," she said. "I promise not to have a nervous breakdown." Nightmares, definitely, but she'd worry about them later. "So how long was I . . . out?"

She could see him considering his options—press her to talk about her new outlook on life and reality, or pretend she hadn't just started to lose it in front of him. Not surprisingly, he chose the latter. "Just a few minutes. Long enough for me to show him my secret way out and to get him out the door. I'm really sorry about that, but I couldn't do anything to stop him. As well as being the bane of my existence, he's also older and more powerful than I am."

She salted that little bit of information away for later while her mind leapt to the last time she'd felt the kind of confusion she'd just experienced. Her eyes narrowed. "He's not the only one who's used glamour against me, now is he?"

He winced and looked guilty, refusing to meet her eyes. "Well, you were about to go into my kitchen and

I'd left some, uh, incriminating evidence on the counter. I couldn't let you go in there. I'm sorry. But whatever you may think about this, I had your best interests at heart. For all your considerable skills, this task is beyond you."

Rebellion sparked in her veins. Who the hell was he to tell her what was or was not beyond her? "I did uncover your secret you know. I'm a damn good detective."

"Of course you are. Carolyn, I know I've underestimated you in the past, but I learned my lesson. It's just that dealing with vampires is too dangerous for a mortal. Look at how easily Jules overpowered you!"

"Yeah, and if I met some punk with a gun while I was unarmed, he'd overpower me pretty damn easily too. That didn't stop me from chasing down the bad guys while I was a cop."

"But you weren't unarmed."

"Sometimes I was. You know that sometimes it would have blown my cover if I'd had a gun on me." This was starting to feel uncomfortably familiar—like the arguments they'd had as their wedding day neared.

Gray let out an exasperated sigh. "It's not the same. Look—"

"Is there anything I could have done to avoid getting trapped by his glamour?"

"Carolyn—"

"Is there?"

Another exasperated sigh, and he squirmed on the couch. "In theory, yes. But in practice, it's a lot harder than it sounds."

It looked like he was going to try to leave it at that, but Carolyn wasn't about to let him off the hook. "Well?"

"You have to avoid eye contact. But all it takes is the briefest glimpse, and even if you don't look in their eyes you're still somewhat susceptible."

"But as long as you know better, and you avoid the

eye contact, they can't turn you into a vegetable like Jules did to me."

"Depends how strong they are. *I* couldn't. Jules might be able to, though I doubt it. But it's not like glamour is their . . . *our* . . . only power. Remember how I managed to avoid getting kicked in the crotch by Hannah?"

Grudgingly, she nodded. Both she and Hannah had been unquestionably startled by his quickness.

"Well, Carolyn, in the grand hierarchy of vampires, I'm what's known as a fledgling—I've only been vampire for three years and my powers aren't fully developed. Jules can kick my ass without breaking a sweat. And those who kill are even stronger." He put his hands on her cheeks, leaning forward with the intensity of his plea. "You've been hurt enough already because of me. Stay out of this, stay safe."

She relaxed her clenched jaw. There was no reason for her to be angry with him over his protectiveness. Yes, it was infuriating, but he was a *guy* after all. It was in their genes to want to shelter the "little woman."

Gray's thumb stroked absently over her cheekbone and the last of her anger disappeared as her eyes slid closed. His hands felt deliciously warm on her skin, and the echo of Cool Water teased her nose.

When he'd left her at the altar, he'd had what he thought was a good reason. It hadn't been the marriage he was running away from, it hadn't been *her*. The core of bewildered hurt that had ached in her chest for three years eased and she leaned into the warmth of his hand. His thumb continued its idle stroking, and even with her eyes closed she knew he had moved closer to her on the couch.

Her skin shivered under his touch, her hands clenching and unclenching in her lap as her pulse accelerated. She opened her eyes and looked into his gray depths, seeing things there he no doubt didn't intend her to see. Things like longing, and desire, and maybe even the echoes of love.

She closed her eyes again when he leaned even closer and brushed her lips with his. She gasped at the current of desire that coursed through her. Her mouth opened of its own accord, and Gray wrapped his arms around her as he deepened the kiss.

She'd forgotten how good it felt to kiss and be kissed, but Gray had reawakened all those memories the first time he'd pressed his lips to hers again. Now her body came alive, remembering how good certain other things had felt, things she hadn't experienced in three long, hard years. When his tongue teased the seam of her lips, then slid inside, she couldn't control the groan of pleasure that escaped her throat.

His hands slipped under the fabric of her sweater, burning a trail along the length of her back. She crawled onto his lap, desperate to feel more of him, to be closer and drink in his heat, his scent. Under her bottom, his erection pulsed, and she was keenly aware of its heat, even through the layers of clothing that separated them.

Carolyn stroked his delicious tongue with her own as her hands tunneled into his hair. When his tongue withdrew, she followed, tasting the inside of his mouth. His erection twitched restlessly, and she almost smiled at her power to excite him.

Then her probing tongue found something long and sharp and reality came crashing back into place. Fangs. He had fangs! She pulled away. She couldn't help it. Gray covered his mouth with one hand and slid her off his lap.

"It's an involuntary reaction," he said hoarsely from behind his hand. His eyes screamed of misery, and she wanted to offer some words of comfort, but none came to mind.

The heat he had generated in her core cooled, and she wondered if she'd taken leave of her senses.

Again. No matter what she'd learned about the circumstances of his abandonment three years ago, the fact remained that he had left her, severed all ties with her. And he had changed, in ways she'd only just begun to see. She didn't know *this* Gray well enough to be kissing him, certainly not enough to be tumbling into bed with him.

Gray lowered his hand, and through the slight part in his lips she could see his tongue probing at the tips of his canines as if assuring himself that the fangs were gone.

"I'm sorry," he said, running a hand through his hair.

She sighed. "You said it was involuntary."

"The fangs, yes. What I meant was . . ." He met her eyes, a hint of a grimace on his face. "I think I, uh, might have used a touch of glamour there. I didn't mean to, but . . ." His voice trailed off.

Carolyn cocked her head and regarded him closely. "You mean you think it was glamour that caused me to kiss you?" He nodded, one brief jerk of his head.

Maybe he was right. No sane woman would be tempted to kiss a real, live vampire! Especially not one who had jilted her in the past. Even if he *had* turned into one of the sexiest creatures she'd ever seen. Even if she *did* still have feelings for him, jumbled and confused, but there nonetheless.

"Let me take you home, Carolyn. You've had enough . . . excitement for one night."

Carolyn took a step back from the brink. "I think that would be a good idea. If I don't get home soon, Hannah's going to call in the National Guard and storm the building."

That brought a brief smile to his face. "Yeah, she makes you look shy and subtle by comparison." He stood up, holding his hand out to her.

She tried to pretend she didn't feel the pulse of desire that stabbed through her when she touched his hand. She wondered how effective she'd been. Together, they walked to the kitchen, where she'd left her coat. Her eyes were immediately drawn to the fridge, but she dragged them away. There were so many questions she still wanted to ask, so much she still didn't know about vampires, about Guardians, about Gray.

"Now that you know the truth, are you satisfied?" Gray asked softly as he guided her to the front door.

She looked up at him and quirked a brow. "As in, will I stop nosing around?"

"Yeah."

She shook her head, not in denial but in confusion. "I don't know yet, Gray. I understand all the reasons you want to keep me out of it, and they're all perfectly logical. I'm just not sure I have it in me to let this go. Not to mention, I don't know if whoever sent that note is going to *let* me let this go."

He looked like he was going to argue some more, but then stopped himself. Carolyn had to suppress a smile. Was he finally learning?

They had already taken one step out the door when she remembered what had started the whole chain of events that had led to this moment. She put a hand on the door to stop Gray from closing it. "Can I have the envelope that note came in?"

He ran a hand through his hair, and she guessed he was doing some kind of mental countdown to keep himself from snapping at her. "I thought you hadn't decided yet whether you were going to stay out of it or not?"

"I haven't. But come on, how dangerous could it possibly be for me to dust an envelope for fingerprints?"

"You won't find anything."

"What, there's no such thing as a vampire with a criminal record?"

She had him on that, she could tell. With a resigned shake of his head, he went back into the house and retrieved the envelope, holding it gingerly by the corner. She put her gloves on before she took it from him, then gave him an encouraging smile. He didn't return that smile as he offered her his elbow.

Carolyn shrugged and took his elbow. Out of the corner of her eye, she caught a glimmer of movement from across the street. She tried to focus on the area from which she'd seen the movement, but her eyes kept sliding away against her will.

Jules, she decided. Using his glamour as he followed Gray around the city, convinced he was tracking a murderer.

Carolyn's world had tilted on its axis tonight, but one thing she knew for certain: Gray was not a killer.

11

JULES WONDERED IF HE was getting dangerously obsessed. Eli had specifically suggested—in a way that had most likely been meant as an order rather than a suggestion—that he take a night off from his surveillance, let someone else take his place. In fact, Eli had sent in Michael and Thomas, the Freeman twins, for the assignment. Jules had refused to leave, and he outranked the twins, so they'd been forced to back down. Thomas was even now watching the bolt hole, his brother promising to come relieve him in a few hours. Jules had parked himself in his favorite booth at the coffee shop. No doubt he was going to catch hell from Eli about this, but he couldn't bear the thought of going home, where he'd brood endlessly about Courtney.

He didn't suppose that he'd been in love with her, but he had liked her a lot. Certainly he'd never wanted to see her come to harm. More than anything, he hated that she had died because of him. Was the Banger through with him? The threat seemed dire enough that Jules had urged his grandson—the only member of his mortal family who knew what he was—to take a "vacation" in his Lancaster County farmhouse. Jules's elderly son and his great-grandchildren were there too, and he prayed they were far enough away to be beyond the Banger's reach.

The waitress passed by his table, taking a peek at his coffee cup to see if he needed a refill. He gave her his best flirtatious smile, and a pleased blush colored her cheeks. She left without noticing that his cup was still full. Amazing how unobservant mortals were. Night after night, he sat here without ever taking so much as a sip of his coffee, and no one ever noticed. Sometimes he used a touch of glamour to make the waitress think she'd refilled his cup, but he wasn't sure even that was necessary.

His cell phone started beeping an SOS. *"Marde,"* he muttered, his instincts telling him what this had to mean. He flung a couple of dollar bills on the table as he slid out of the booth, shoving his arms into his coat and charging out into the night.

"What?" he barked into the phone as he crossed the distance to Gray's house.

"He slipped by me!" Thomas said, and his distress would have been almost comical under other circumstances.

"Niaiseux!" Jules snapped.

"Huh?"

Jules swallowed another insult. That could wait. "Which way did he go?"

"Down Walnut. He ducked through Gorman, but I lost him."

Jules jogged toward Gorman, which billed itself as a street but was nothing more than a glorified alley. He closed his phone as he caught sight of Thomas at the other end of the street, shifting from foot to foot and looking helpless.

Damn it! Jules should have taken the bolt hole himself. Even Thomas could have handled surveillance on the front door—Gray would have had a hard time losing himself so quickly if he hadn't come out on a side street.

Jules reached Thomas's side and saw how the

younger man was bracing himself for an attack. Jules controlled his temper as best he could. "Do you know which direction he was going when you lost him?"

Thomas pointed halfheartedly down the street, and Jules started to jog in that direction, reaching out with his vampire senses, looking for a familiar psychic footprint. For a fleeting moment, he wished Drake were here, for though Jules was old and powerful for a Guardian, he didn't have a very long range. He thought he felt a hint of a vampire presence in the distance, faint and fleeting. Without a word, he picked up the pace, not caring if Thomas could keep up with him or not.

* * *

SOMETHING STANK, DRAKE DECIDED as he sat huddled against the wall that bounded the subway entrance in the City Hall courtyard.

Tonight, he'd decided that instead of patrolling, he'd park himself here, in the epicenter of the string of murders. He'd been here for hours, reaching out endlessly with his senses, searching for the hint of a vampire in his range. He'd had quite a lively argument with Deirdre and Fletcher last night when he'd insisted they allow him to patrol alone. In the end, when they'd presented their arguments to Eli, the Founder had sided with Drake. If the killer was using their known patrol routes to mask his movements, then Drake would be better off knowing he was the only vampire supposed to be on Broad Street.

He'd have thought that minor victory would have bolstered him. Instead, he was left with this uncomfortable, disturbing sensation that he was missing something.

Certainly he wasn't having any luck in his new strategy. He'd concentrated all his energy on reaching out with his mind, searching for the presence he had yet to touch. His range was considerable, but no immortal presence intruded. Maybe it really *was* the Broad Street Banger who'd killed Jules's little chippie. If so, he'd clearly moved on to a new type of prey, and Drake's usefulness here was questionable.

Stiff and impatient after more than six hours sitting motionless in the cold, he opened his eyes and shook his head. Every instinct in his body told him this was hopeless. It was so late he rarely sensed a mortal presence, much less a vampire one.

The moment he thought this, he felt a pair of mortals approaching from the Broad Street North entrance. He would have dismissed them as completely uninteresting, except they stopped before entering the courtyard. Probably teenagers looking for a good make-out spot, he thought. At two in the morning. In single-degree weather.

Although this had nothing to do with the Banger, Drake rose from his hiding place and crept toward the entrance. His keen senses picked up angry voices echoing through the cavernous spaces under City Hall.

The first chamber of this entrance was easily the most bizarre of the decidedly quirky walkways that tunneled through City Hall. Known as the Crypt of the Tower, because it was directly beneath the tower upon which Billy Penn stood, the room was dominated by four red granite columns. At the top of each column, near life-sized human figures strained to hold the ceiling up. One column was topped by African Americans, one by Native Americans, one by Asians, and one by what looked like classical Greek or Roman figures. The statues' eyes, particularly those of the African Americans, had a tortured expression to them that made Drake uneasy. In stark contrast, faux-columns built into the surrounding walls were topped with jolly cherubs.

The two black teenagers who squared off against each other in the shadows behind the columns no doubt didn't care about their surreal surroundings.

Both were dressed in the kind of baggy jeans and oversized coats that declared they thought themselves dangerous. Their postures screamed of belligerence as they shouted at each other, their slang so thick Drake could barely understand them. Their anger—hatred, even—was a palpable force, a sinkhole of negative energy that tainted the very air. Drake was just old-fashioned enough to label them "evil."

He hadn't fed in over a week, and though he was not desperate yet, the hunger stirred.

In their own little corner, in their own little world, the hoodlums continued to posture and curse each other, a battle that could only end in violence. Sure enough, one of them pulled a knife and lunged. He missed, and his opponent also drew a knife. They faced off against each other, looking more like a pair of mad dogs than like human beings. Drake scented fear in the air, but neither hoodlum showed any inclination to back off.

Drake didn't even need glamour to keep them from noticing him. There was murder in both sets of eyes as they crouched and circled. The knives flashed, and one of the men cried out in pain. The other laughed, his knife now coated with blood. The wounded man fell, clutching his belly. The victor gloated, the virulence of his language so foul that Drake flinched. Then, after kicking the wound, the victor strutted away, proud of his night's work.

The wounded man gasped and moaned, still clutching his belly. The scent of his blood spiced the air. Drake approached and knelt beside him, turning him over onto his back.

Eyes that had moments ago shone with a kind of hate no one of his age had earned the right to feel were now wide with pain and terror. "Help me!" he cried, reaching out to Drake with one bloody hand. Sweat glistened on his face, and his breath came in short, desperate gasps.

"Shh," Drake said, meeting the dying man's eyes and reaching out with his glamour.

The hoodlum's whole body relaxed, his hands sliding away from the still-bleeding wound, the tension easing from his face. The fear in his eyes was erased by a slack-jawed blankness.

A familiar sadness descended over Drake as he slid his arms gently under his victim and raised him to a sitting position. The boy was too young to die, but Drake very much doubted he could survive the wound. And even if he did, he would have learned nothing. When he recovered, he'd be back on the streets, his veins pulsing with hate and violence, a lost soul beyond redemption. His death would likely save lives.

Letting his glamour envelope the boy completely, blanking out every flicker of fear and pain, Drake bent his head and bit.

* * *

CAROLYN STUDIED THE NEWSPAPER with single-minded intensity, willing herself to ignore Hannah's piercing, unwavering stare. It wasn't working.

"Well?" Hannah prompted.

Carolyn folded the newspaper to the article she'd been reading, pushing it across the table to Hannah. "Looks like there's been another Broad-Street-Banger-type killing. A thirty-two-year-old white male, found in his home. His throat was slashed, but there was very little blood. No sign of forced entry." As with the other killings, the police speculated that the man had been killed elsewhere and then transported to where the body was found. A circumstance that baffled investigators—why would the killer bother to transport the bodies? But investigators without Carolyn's new-found knowledge would never guess that the victims were killed by a vampire.

Hannah pushed the paper aside. "I wasn't asking for the six o'clock news."

Carolyn clasped her hands around her cup of coffee, and for the millionth time tried to decide what to tell her best friend. When she'd returned to Hannah's the night before last, Carolyn had told her she needed to sleep on it before deciding how much of what she learned she was willing to share. When Hannah had badgered her yesterday, Carolyn had pleaded for one more day. Now that one more day was up, and she still had no idea what to say.

Hannah was her best friend and a damn good investigator. If Carolyn didn't tell her what she'd learned, there was a good chance Hannah would dig into it on her own. Maybe she, like Carolyn, would get lucky, if you could call it that. Or maybe she'd get spectacularly *un*lucky and get herself killed. Of course, if Carolyn *did* tell her, Hannah would no doubt think she was crazy.

Hannah huffed out an exasperated sigh. "Oh come on, Carolyn. It just *can't* be as bad as that!"

Carolyn grimaced. "It's worse."

"Well then tell me anyway. You look completely miserable. Share the burden. Let me help."

"Hannah, you don't know what you're asking for." *Damn,* Carolyn thought. *Now I sound like Gray.*

Hannah reached across the breakfast table and gave Carolyn's hand a squeeze. "It doesn't matter. I'm your friend, and I'm here for you, and whatever it is you're carrying, I can help. Now come on, spit it out."

With a sinking feeling in the pit of her stomach, she realized she had to tell Hannah. If she herself was the potential target of a renegade vampire, then by staying with Hannah she was putting her in the line of fire. Hannah had a right to know what she was dealing with. No matter how crazy it sounded.

"How open-minded are you?" Carolyn asked with a sick grin.

* * *

FIFTEEN MINUTES LATER, HANNAH looked a bit green around the gills. Carolyn could see that her friend was trying to believe her, but the effort didn't appear to be spectacularly successful.

"Well," Hannah said, "you tried to warn me, I suppose."

"Do you think you can suspend your disbelief for a while? Just *pretend* you don't think I'm ready for the men in the white coats?"

Hannah grinned, but it was a weak grin. "Hey, I'm loyal, remember? I think *Gray's* the one who's ready for the men in the white coats. You're just an innocent victim of his delusions."

Carolyn supposed she would have felt the same way, had their positions been reversed. And if she hadn't seen the fangs come and go, hadn't felt the powerful, inexplicable sway of the vampire glamour, she might even now be trying to rationalize away what she'd seen. "Pretend anyway, Hannah. If you pretend it's serious, and it's all an elaborate hoax, then the worst thing that can happen is you'll feel a little silly when it's all over. If you close your mind to the possibility that it's real, and you're wrong . . ."

Hannah thought about that a moment then nodded. "All right, I can see the sense in that. So, what's our next step, Van Helsing?"

"Ha, ha." The next step? If only Carolyn knew! "Well, I was able to get a smudged partial thumb print from the glue strip on the envelope. I sent it to my friend Ted at the lab. He's agreed to check it out for me. I'm going to have a hell of a lot of questions to answer if it turns out to match the Banger's prints."

"That's for sure! Are you sure the print isn't Gray's?"

Carolyn nodded. "I talked him into giving me his

fingerprints last night. He wasn't thrilled about it." An understatement, to be sure, but when she'd pointed out she could break in during the day and dust his house, he'd reluctantly given in.

"All right, so you've got the fingerprint angle covered. It'll take awhile to get results. What do we do in the meantime?"

"First, we have another interview with Gray tonight." At which time Carolyn would get him to convince Hannah he really was a vampire. Boy, that would be fun! "Then, we gently persuade him to get us another interview with Jules. I've got to think that the killer was purposely trying to frame Gray when he killed Jules's girlfriend, and that suggests they have a common enemy. If we can get both of them to talk, maybe we'll get a lead or two."

"And if Gray goes into his pseudo-macho, protect-the-little-lady mode and refuses to help us find Jules?"

Carolyn grinned. "Well, I did do an Internet search on the name, and there appear to be only six thirty-something men named Jules in the entire city. It shouldn't be too hard to find him."

"Uh, Carolyn?"

"Yes?"

"Aren't you forgetting something? I mean, based on this ridiculous theory I'm keeping my mind open about."

For a moment, Carolyn had no idea what Hannah was talking about. Then it hit her, and she groaned. "I've got to get used to this dealing-with-vampires business. Just because he looks thirtyish doesn't mean he *is*." But still, she suspected the list would not be overwhelming.

"So, Gray should be rolling out of his coffin at what, six o'clock?"

Carolyn rolled her eyes. "He doesn't sleep in a coffin." Unbidden, an image came to her mind of Gray lying asleep on his bed, the covers giving her a tantalizing view of his naked chest. She shivered. "But yes, he should wake up around six."

"I guess we have a date then."

"I guess we do."

Carolyn stifled a yawn and drank another swallow of lukewarm coffee. Vampires wreaked havoc on the sleep schedule. Even though she hadn't gone to see him last night, thoughts of Gray had still kept her awake. When she'd drifted off, he'd invaded her dreams, and though she didn't remember those dreams in the morning, the loneliness that had stabbed through her when she woke was stunning.

* * *

JULES FELT MORE THAN usually reluctant and uncomfortable as he made his way through the hall and into Eli's meeting room. Bad enough that he'd been staking out Gray's house against Eli's orders, but to have actually *lost* the bastard under the circumstances . . . Eli was going to give him hell, and he deserved it.

Jules and Thomas had followed the elusive vampire presence for almost an hour before they'd lost it completely. They'd spent the rest of the night futilely wandering the streets, hoping to stumble upon him accidentally. When they'd returned to Gray's house an hour or so before dawn, a quick check showed that he was safely ensconced within. But where had he gone during the hours he'd been missing?

The moment Jules stepped into the room, he felt a subtle sense of wrongness. The Guardians—and Drake—were all present, most of them sitting in their accustomed positions like schoolchildren. Eli was as usual sitting in his throne-like chair before the fireplace. But something was different.

For one thing, there was not a single smile in the room, nor any hints of lighthearted conversation. Those Guardians who *were* talking looked tense and serious. Jules frowned as a tingle of foreboding buzzed up his spine. Then, he caught sight of Fletcher, sitting on a straight-backed chair instead of in his usual place. His elbows rested on his knees, and his head was bent, a glazed, miserable look in his eyes. Jules's heart sank as Eli beckoned him in.

"What happened?" he asked, directing the question to Eli, for Fletcher looked too miserable to answer him.

Eli's face was impassive, his voice calm, as though he hoped to soothe the situation. "Fletcher's brother was found murdered in his home this morning."

Jules groaned, rubbing his face. "Another Banger victim?"

"So it would appear," Eli confirmed, and the Guardians began to murmur amongst themselves.

"Like hell!" Fletcher cried, his face turning its usual telltale red. He turned to glare at Drake. "Tell me it's a coincidence *he* convinced everyone he needed to be alone last night and that last night my brother was murdered!"

Drake folded his arms over his chest, propping one foot against the wall in a pose that was supposed to look casual but didn't. "Fletcher, dear boy, if I wanted to hurt you, I'd come after *you*, not your brother."

Fletcher looked like he wanted to leap out of his chair, but he didn't. Self-restraint? Or Eli's glamour?

"Look at his coloring!" Fletcher said, sweeping his gaze over all the watching Guardians. "You can see that he fed last night! And who do you think he fed on?"

More murmurs in the crowd.

"Yes, I fed," Drake admitted, "but I didn't hurt Fletcher's brother." He turned to stare at Fletcher. "Unless your brother is a knife-wielding, teenaged black man with a drug problem, who, by the way, was dying of a nasty stab wound when I took him."

"Then why *did* you insist on being alone last night?" a voice called out from the crowd. Frank LaBelle, a relatively new addition to the ranks of the Guardians. His character had been questionable even before he'd been turned, and now his face bore the signs of a trou-blemaker. A couple of other voices murmured agreement with the question.

"Everyone stay calm," Eli said, his voice still that soothing croon, but though Jules felt the touch of glamour Eli exerted, the tension in the room remained high.

"It wasn't Drake," Jules said, glancing over at Thomas Freeman. "Have you told them yet?" When Thomas shook his head, Jules continued. "Gray James eluded us last night. For at least five hours, we have no idea where he was."

Eli shot him a reproachful look but refrained from castigating him in public. A temporary reprieve, surely.

"I don't even *know* Gray James," Fletcher protested. "He'd have no reason to strike out at me. But Drake—"

"Enough!" Eli said, more forcefully. "We don't have enough evidence to convict anyone, so let's stop throwing accusations about like rice at a wedding."

"I think it's about time both of our prime suspects sit down and answer a few questions," Michael Freeman chimed in, his twin nodding eagerly.

"Eli's right," Deirdre said. She practically had to shout to be heard over the muttering and grumbling. "I know both Gray and Drake, and while I won't say I vouch for their characters, I can say that neither one of them is stupid. And that's what you'd have to be to do these killings without leaving yourself an alibi."

"Or maybe they're just arrogant!" Frank said, once again spawning an approving murmur.

"Gentlemen!" Eli said, and Jules thought he heard a hint of worry in that usually calm voice. "And ladies. Please. Don't let emotions get in the way. It's obvious the killer has shifted his focus from anonymous victims to those who are closely affiliated with Guardians. Instead of forming a lynch mob, we need to work together to ensure that no one else dear to us becomes the next victim."

"If we lock Gray and Drake up for a while and another murder occurs, then we'll be sure it's not one of them," someone suggested. Jules didn't see who.

"Yes," Deirdre retorted, "and then another mortal would be dead! Eli's right: our first responsibility is to guard those mortals who are close to us. They're all in danger. And keep this in mind, too: whoever's striking out at us obviously knows who we are."

"You mean, like Drake," Fletcher said with a curl of his lip. "Since Eli includes him in all our meetings."

"Is that a criticism I hear?" Eli asked, and there was something deadly in his voice that hushed all the bickering voices.

Fletcher's face lost its color. Jules felt as if the temperature in the room had just dropped twenty degrees. Eli finally had everyone's full attention. He stood, and though he was not in reality a very large man, his presence was so commanding he seemed huge. "In times of crisis, it's easy to give in to one's emotions and act irrationally. But there is no one here who isn't old enough and experienced enough to know better. If you expend your energy on pointless suspicions, then you will be nothing more than a rabble of witch-hunters who destroy the innocent while the guilty laugh." No one spoke, and more than one head bowed in shame. "Now take tonight to do what you can to secure your loved ones. We'll reassemble here tomorrow night at seven, and we will calmly, *rationally* discuss our options." He scanned the room, his eyes bright with anger. "Any objections?"

Not surprisingly, there were none. Eli dismissed the gathering, but commanded Jules and Drake to remain behind.

12

Drake left his position against the wall and seated himself comfortably in one of the couches before Eli's chair. Jules cast him a wary glance, then sat on the other side of the couch. There was a noticeable flush to Drake's cheeks, as Fletcher had said. Jules almost shuddered, though he managed to control the impulse. Guardians didn't get that telltale flush when they drank their meals of milk and blood.

"So, Eli," Drake said, leaning back into the cushions and crossing one leg over the other, "why did you ask us to stay after class?"

Eli looked back and forth between the two of them, his face inscrutable. "I am . . . concerned . . . about what I saw here tonight."

"Believe me, Eli, not as concerned as I am," Drake said with an ironic smile on his lips. "I make an easy scapegoat, and if your people decide to band together against me . . ."

Jules half-expected Eli to offer some kind of assurance that it wouldn't happen. Then he remembered the Founder's words to him when he himself had teetered on the brink of mindless vengeance: *That I've been able to create the Guardians, convince them to work together, and prevent them from killing each other is a minor miracle*. A miracle Jules and everyone else was taking for granted, perhaps?

"Maybe it would be best if you remained as my guest for a while," Eli said, but Drake just laughed.

"House arrest, Eli? No, thank you. I'll take my chances. Besides, it has occurred to me that the killer may be hoping to remove the two oldest vampires in Philadelphia—save yourself—from the battlefield."

For a moment, Jules didn't follow the argument, for Gray was one of the youngest vampires in the city. Then, he understood. "You think the killer is trying to distract me with thoughts of vengeance."

"Possible, don't you think?"

Jules looked at Eli and realized this was what the Founder suspected as well. He also realized something far more troubling: Eli was worried.

"So, you don't believe either Drake or Gray is the killer," Jules said.

"I sincerely doubt it," Eli answered. "But then it has been a long time since I've been hampered by my emotions. I can understand why others would believe it."

"But Eli, really! The coincidences here—"

"May not be coincidence. You remember what Deirdre said, in the midst of the arguing?"

Jules paused, recalling the discussion, but Drake answered for him.

"She said that whoever's doing this knows who the Guardians are. She thinks the killer has inside help."

"Exactly," Eli said.

"But that can't be," Jules protested, leaping to his feet. "Eli, you can't seriously believe that one of us is a killer!"

Eli raised an eyebrow. "Why not? Guardians are as susceptible to temptation as anyone else. And they have loved ones, just like anyone else. What would you do, Jules, if you discovered your son were a Killer?"

Jules's mouth dropped open in shock and pain, and

he felt like Eli had punched him in the gut. "You think my *son* is involved? He's—"

But Eli was shaking his head and making placating gestures with his hands. "No, no. Don't take it literally. I'm posing a hypothetical question and suggesting a motive that might put even the most dedicated Guardian in a quandary."

Jules must have looked as unconvinced as he felt, for Eli shook his head sadly. "It's happened before, you know."

"What?" Jules had been a Guardian for what felt like an eternity, but he certainly didn't know of any other instances of Guardians turning Killer. Drake looked similarly stunned, though he said nothing.

"Before your time, obviously," Eli continued. "His name was Archer Montgomery. One of my earlier recruits. A talented hunter." He fell silent, lost in thought.

"Well, what happened?" Jules prompted.

Another of Eli's sad smiles. "A woman, of course." He sighed. "Archer had never married, but he'd had a mistress of whom he was very fond. When he'd been with the Guardians for five years, he found her once again. Unfortunately, she'd been bitten, and we didn't rescue her in time.

"She was a ruthless Killer. Archer begged for her life, claiming that we could retrain her somehow, maybe teach her to kill only evil people." He glanced over at Drake. "This was before you came to Philadelphia, and I didn't believe it was possible for a Killer to retain that kind of moral code. So I refused. Archer tried to hustle her to safety, but my Guardians caught up with them before they got away. They killed the woman but they spared Archer. It wasn't his fault he was in love with her, and it was hard to blame him for what he'd done in the name of love. Still, I couldn't take him back after such an open rebellion."

He looked down at his folded hands. "My greatest failure," he said softly.

It was hard for Jules to imagine Eli failing at anything. The Founder seemed damned near invincible at times. But it seemed even the oldest and wisest of them had his moments of weakness. Uncomfortable with this revelation, Jules cleared his throat.

Drake regarded the Founder with a sudden intensity. "Do you think he's still alive?"

Eli smiled sadly. "You mean, do I think he's come back to Philadelphia to get his revenge?"

Drake shrugged.

"No, Drake. I won't say there were no hard feelings, but Archer was a Guardian, and he understood my decision as well as I understood his. We kept in touch for a few years afterward, but eventually he drifted away."

"Okay," Jules said, "I'll admit it's not impossible that a Guardian is involved. But what about Gray? Where does he fit in? Is it just coincidence that he slipped away again last night?"

Eli shrugged off his melancholy and looked more like himself once more. "Maybe. Or maybe the Banger lured him away somehow, setting him up for suspicion. The more suspects he creates, the safer he is."

"All right, you've made your point," Drake said. "Now, what do you want us to do about it?"

"First, I want you to see to your own safety. It seems clear the killer has moved beyond Broad Street, so your surveillance there is no longer necessary. And I highly recommend you change residences as quickly as possible."

Drake dropped all pretense of unconcerned aloofness. "Keep your Guardians away from me, Eli," he said in a deadly voice. "I've proven time and time again that I'm willing to kill to save my own life. If they attack me—"

"If they attack you, it will be in force and there will

be nothing you or I can do to stop them. Unless you're willing to stay here, under 'house arrest' as you put it. I lead only as long as the other Guardians *let* me lead. If the killer has his way, I fear chaos may ensue. So take steps to protect yourself, or the killer really will have eliminated one of his most dangerous hunters."

Drake's eyes still gleamed with anger, but he made no reply save a curt nod. Jules cleared his throat. "And what about me? Why did you want me here for this little discussion?"

"Because I want you to stop playing Lone Ranger. If we're to stop the killing, I need your full cooperation."

"You have it!"

"T'es plein de marde!" Eli retorted with a hint of a grin.

Jules felt an embarrassing warmth in his cheeks, wishing he'd never discovered Eli understood his Québécois. And hoping Drake didn't know Eli had just said he was full of shit.

Drake laughed. "A taste of your own medicine, eh Jules?"

"Trou d'cul," Jules growled. "Not you, Eli!" he hastened to amend.

"You want to call me whatever you just called me in English?" Drake challenged, leaning forward with a glare.

"He called you an asshole," Eli snapped. "Now don't prove him right." Drake made a gesture of surrender and leaned back into the couch, and Eli turned his attention to Jules once more. "You're far more focused on proving Gray's the killer than on finding out who the killer is. That has to change."

Jules bowed his head, knowing that Eli was right. "I'll do my best, Eli, but I'm only human. So to speak."

The Founder chuckled, and Jules took that for a hopeful sign. "My plan should make it easier for you. I want you and Drake to go interview Gray, try to find out where he went last night. And then I want you to put him under a real house arrest."

Drake and Jules shared a look, but didn't comment.

"You told me Kate Henshaw kept Gray locked in the basement when she first took him," Eli continued. "I want him locked in again. That way we don't have to waste any manpower watching him."

"The entrance to his bolt hole is in the basement," Jules said.

"I'm sure you can block it somehow, between you and Drake."

Jules nodded gravely, but his insides practically danced for joy. Oh, this was going to be fun! And, best of all, it was for a good cause.

* * *

CAROLYN AND HANNAH HEADED to Gray's house shortly after the sun set. Hannah had disappeared for most of the day—trying to close out some of the cases they were actually being paid for, Carolyn assumed. Carolyn probably should have gone along, just to have something to do. Until the results of the fingerprint search came back, and until night fell, she was at a dead standstill on the Banger case. The day seemed to creep by with glacial slowness.

Finally, sunset arrived, and Carolyn and Hannah took a cab to Gray's place. Carolyn wondered what Hannah was thinking, whether she believed Gray was a vampire. Chances were, the answer was no, and this might be an awkward interview indeed.

As they mounted the short flight of steps to Gray's front door, Carolyn turned to her best friend and shook her finger at her.

"Behave!" she warned.

Hannah blinked as though she had no idea what Carolyn could possibly mean. "Who, me?"

Carolyn opened her mouth to retort, then thought

better of it. What was the point? Hannah wasn't about to change her stripes now. Hoping Gray would forgive her, Carolyn rang the doorbell.

The door swung open moments later, and both Carolyn and Hannah jumped—there'd been no sound of footsteps. Gray leaned against the doorframe, looking back and forth between the two women, his lips pressed into a thin line of annoyance.

"Yeah, pleased to see you too," Hannah said before anyone else could speak. She shouldered Gray aside so she could enter the house.

Gray's frown turned into a scowl, and he looked daggers at Carolyn.

"Hey, don't blame me for her manners," Carolyn said. "I'm not her mom."

Gray grunted but didn't speak, moving aside to let Carolyn in. Together, they walked into the living room, where Hannah had already made herself at home, picking up some of the antique knick-knacks and examining them.

"Nice place you got here, Gray," she said, peering closely at a porcelain figurine of a ballet dancer. "Very you." She put the figurine down and reached into her suitcase-sized purse. When she turned around again, she clutched a large, gaudy crucifix, holding it before her as she approached. "Back, spawn of Satan!" she cried, and Carolyn wondered if it was possible to die of embarrassment.

"Hannah, please!"

Gray was even less amused, folding his arms over his chest and glaring at Carolyn. The cross didn't seem to be worrying him.

"One down," Hannah said, cheerfully oblivious as she stuck the cross back into her purse. Next, she pulled out a bulb of garlic. "Catch!" she said, tossing it at Gray.

His hand moved lightning quick, snatching the garlic from the air. He held it up for inspection. His face now looked for the most part impassive. Except for his eyes. They smoldered with anger.

"All right, cross garlic off the list," Hannah said. She looked like she was having a grand old time. Next she tried a heavy silver chain. Once again, Gray caught it when she threw it at him, the look in his eyes ever more deadly.

"I don't know," Hannah said, "this whole vampire thing is looking a little shaky. He's not bothered by the cross, or garlic, or silver . . ."

Gray dropped the garlic and the silver chain on a side table. "Actually, it's *iron* we can't tolerate," he said. How he managed to sound so casual and yet so angry, Carolyn didn't know.

"Iron?" Hannah said. "But there's iron in blood! Besides, I thought that was only good against werewolves and fairies. Of course—"

"Don't say it," Carolyn warned between gritted teeth, knowing Hannah was about to make some kind of crack about "fairies." Hannah smiled innocently.

Thankfully, Gray either hadn't read Hannah's mind as well, or chose to ignore what she hadn't said.

"The iron in blood isn't anywhere near concentrated enough to hurt us." He turned to Carolyn. "It would serve you right if I denied all knowledge of this and let Hannah go on thinking this is all some kind of a game."

"I had to tell her, Gray. Thanks to that note, I've been sucked into this, and thanks to me, Hannah has too. She needed to know what we were up against."

Carolyn thought she saw her point hit home, but then Hannah ruined it by opening her mouth.

"All right, kiddies, enough of this shit. Let's all establish that there's no such thing as vampires and Gray has, for whatever sick reasons of his own, decided to play a bizarre practical joke."

Gray's eyes hardened again, and he fixed Hannah with a steely stare. The look in his eyes made Carolyn shiver with superstitious dread, but true to form, Hannah seemed unaffected.

"Oh, don't give me that bad-boy, I'm-gonna-kill-you look!" Hannah said, digging the hole deeper. "Your face just isn't made for it. You—"

Gray crossed the distance between them so fast Carolyn barely saw him move. He grabbed Hannah by the collar of her coat, lifted her off her feet, and pinned her against the wall at eye level. Hannah managed only a squeak of protest. Her feet scrabbled for purchase, and her fingers clawed uselessly at Gray's hands.

"Don't bait me, Hannah," Gray growled in a furious undertone. "You're playing with fire."

Even from across the room, Carolyn could see the glint of his bared fangs. Hannah's face went completely white and her mouth dropped open.

"Put her down, Gray!" Carolyn shouted, finally finding her voice.

He ignored her, leaning in to Hannah, glaring at her, tonguing the fangs he displayed so prominently. A faint whimper escaped Hannah's lips. Carolyn grabbed his arm, trying to loosen his grip, but it was like trying to bend steel. "Stop it!" she said. Gray just shrugged her off.

"Have we reached an understanding, Hannah?" he asked.

"Yeah," Hannah said, her voice barely a whisper.

Gray lowered her feet to the floor, but maintained his grip on her coat. Her knees buckled, and she would have fallen if not for his hold. He helped her slide down the wall into a sitting position. Her face was still bloodless white.

"You bastard!" Carolyn cried, punching him in the arm. She'd never seen Hannah cowed in her entire life.

Anger flickered in his eyes for an instant, then faded. "I didn't hurt her," he said. "Which is more than I can say for her." He held up his hands, displaying the gouges her fingernails had made all along his wrists. He squatted in front of Hannah, meeting her eyes, and his voice gentled. "I'm the least dangerous of my kind. Don't make the mistake of underestimating us. Ever."

Hannah shuddered, but at least a little color returned to her cheeks. "This has to be some kind of bizarre dream, doesn't it?"

Gray sighed heavily. "If only it were." He stood and offered Hannah a hand up. She eyed him warily for a long moment, then accepted his hand.

By the time he'd guided her to the sofa, she looked almost herself again. And, Carolyn noticed, the scratches on his wrists were well on their way to healing.

"Was that really necessary?" Carolyn asked, sitting next to Hannah and putting a hand on her friend's shoulder.

"No," Gray said, "but I seem to have acquired a temper since my transition." He turned to Hannah. "For what it's worth, I'm sorry. But at least everything is out in the open."

Hannah gently shrugged off Carolyn's hand. "Yeah, it's out in the open that you've got Carolyn mixed up in shit with vampires. I thought you'd done a thorough number on her three years ago, but obviously—"

Gray held up a hand for silence. To Carolyn's astonishment, Hannah obeyed, perhaps still cowed by his show of temper. "I can't change what's happened. I don't know why Carolyn was dragged into this, but she has been, and my only concern is to make sure she's safe."

"And the best way to make sure I'm safe," Carolyn said, "is to catch whoever's behind all this. So, I've sent off the fingerprints on the envelope for analysis, and Hannah and I would like to ask you a few questions."

Gray's face darkened. "Leave it alone, Carolyn. There are others looking into this."

"You mean like Jules? The guy who thinks you murdered his girlfriend? Somehow, I don't think he's going to be much help."

"He's not—" Gray's voice was interrupted by the ringing of the doorbell. He looked back and forth between the two women. "Did you call in reinforcements?"

"No," Hannah and Carolyn said together.

Gray heaved a long-suffering sigh. "Great. I just love being Mr. Popularity."

Still grumbling under his breath, Gray stomped to the door. Carolyn stood, putting her hand on the butt of her Glock as foreboding prickled her skin. Maybe Hannah felt it too, for she pasted her back against the wall by the door in preparation for launching an ambush.

Moments later, Gray came flying past the doorway, landing on his butt with a painful-sounding bang. Carolyn drew her Glock and braced herself, taking aim on the doorway while gesturing with her head for Hannah to move away.

Jules appeared in that doorway, his lips twisted in a mean-spirited grin until he saw the weapon aimed his direction. He held his hands up in mock surrender, the grin turning into a pseudo-charming smile. "Why didn't you tell me you had company?" he asked, watching as Gray slowly drew himself to his feet. A bruise was already beginning to darken his jaw.

"Stay back, Jules!" Carolyn ordered. Hannah gasped softly, no doubt recognizing the name and realizing she faced another vampire. Jules turned his head toward the sound. "Don't make eye contact with him, Hannah," Carolyn warned.

"You may lower your weapon," Jules said. "I promise to be on my best behavior."

Gray snorted loudly. "That's not saying much. But you might as well put the gun down anyway. I doubt Jules would be so crass as to kill me in front of ladies."

Jules gave a mocking bow. "Naturally not."

Carolyn wished she had a clue what was going on here. The two men were both bristling with hostility, but she wasn't sure the gun was much help. Wondering if she was making a big mistake, Carolyn relaxed her stance and lowered her gun. She did not, however, holster it.

Carolyn nearly jumped a mile when another man drifted into the room from behind Jules. He'd moved so silently it almost seemed like he appeared out of nowhere. Carolyn thought of the old folklore, vampires turning into clouds of mist, and wondered if the legend had arisen because of that silent tread.

It never crossed Carolyn's mind that the newcomer might not be a vampire. Even if his nature weren't revealed by the company he kept or by the natural stealth of his movements, he had the aura of a predator about him. The same aura that had once seemed so foreign when she'd noticed it on Gray.

He was dressed all in black leather, skintight in some very appealing places, and Carolyn wondered if there was something about being a vampire that made one inherently good-looking. This guy could have made a cover model for *Sexy Bad Boys* magazine.

"Who the hell are you?" Gray asked, directing an unwelcoming look at the leather-clad stranger.

"This is Drake," Jules said with a strangely feral smile. "You've heard of him, I believe?"

Carolyn glanced over at Gray and saw that he had indeed heard of Drake. And that whatever he'd heard scared the shit out of him.

Drake stepped past Jules and offered his hand for Gray to shake. Gray hesitated a moment, then shook with a wary expression on his face.

"I'd say I'm pleased to meet you," Gray said, "but I'm not sure I am."

Drake laughed. "I get that reaction a lot." For all the bad-boy leather look, he had a surprisingly friendly face, with eyes almost as dark as his near-black hair. "I hate to interrupt, but Jules and I need to talk with you for a little while." He turned to look at Hannah. Carolyn followed his gaze and saw the instant that Hannah's eyes glazed over. Drake turned to her. Carolyn hastily lowered her gaze and raised her gun.

"Don't you dare," she said, fingering the trigger. A sudden, almost unbearable urge to look up struck her, and it took all her concentration to keep her eyes focused downward. "No glamour!"

"That's right, Drake," Gray said. "No glamour."

"As if you could stop him," Jules goaded. "You couldn't even stand against *my* glamour."

The urge to look up suddenly left Carolyn. The relief from the pressure almost caused her to look up after all, but she kept her eyes firmly focused on Drake's big silver belt buckle, a Celtic knot that gleamed against the black leather.

"My apologies," Drake said in a voice as smooth as chocolate. "It appears Jules hasn't filled me in on all the details. I was under the impression I was in the presence of mortals who were . . . blissfully ignorant?"

"Well you were wrong," Carolyn said. "Now let Hannah go."

"What the . . . ?" Hannah said, and Carolyn sighed in relief.

Lowering her gun once more, Carolyn glanced at her bewildered friend. "You remember I was telling you about glamour? Well, you just had some first-hand experience."

Hannah shook her head. "Wow. Creepy."

Jules laughed. Carolyn was beginning to understand why Gray disliked him so much.

"Okay," Gray said, "now that the introductions are over, you two want to tell me what you're doing here?"

Jules opened his mouth to reply, but Drake silenced him with a hand on his arm. "Please, let me. You and Gray have enough of an adversarial relationship as it is." Jules visibly swallowed his annoyance, and Drake motioned to the chairs and sofas. "Why don't we all sit down."

Knowing from experience that the chairs were miserably uncomfortable, Carolyn took a seat on the sofa beside Gray. She gestured for Hannah to join her, though the sofa was small and cramped with three people. Her entire leg was in contact with Gray's, and a hint of his cologne teased her nostrils. He shifted to give her a little more room, but it didn't really help. Their shoulders rubbed awkwardly. It would have been more comfortable if Gray put his arm around her, but he refrained.

Jules and Drake sat in the hard-as-a-rock wingback chairs.

Jules slouched casually, but Carolyn thought it had to be an affectation of some sort. The chairs were designed to keep their occupants' backs rigidly straight, and that casual slouch no doubt made him even more uncomfortable. Drake sat on the edge of the chair, making no attempt to lean back.

"Before I get to the point," he said, "tell me how much the ladies know."

"Too much," Gray said, then went on to explain about the threatening note he'd received. A silence descended when he'd finished, and Drake looked thoughtful.

"He could have written that note himself," Jules said. "Personally, I don't think it's much of an alibi."

Beside her, Carolyn felt Gray stiffen, and she figured he was going to rise to Jules's bait. Again. She poked her elbow into his side, drawing an irritated sidelong glance. But he kept his mouth shut.

"I'll agree the alibi is not airtight," Drake said, and Gray stiffened again. "And what about last night?"

Gray looked confused. "What about it?"

"Where did you go? And can someone confirm your whereabouts?"

"I didn't go anywhere!"

Jules snorted loudly. "Don't play this game! It's not like you didn't know you were being watched."

"Yes, I knew I was being watched. And I didn't go anywhere. I was home all night."

Jules shot out of his chair, his eyes glittering. Gray would have met the challenge head-on if Carolyn hadn't grabbed his arm. He tried to jerk his arm out of her grip, but she held tight. He could break that grip if he really wanted to, of course.

"Sit down, Jules," Drake said. "You're not helping the situation."

To Carolyn's surprise, Jules obeyed, though his body language screamed resentment.

"Jules and Thomas are under the impression that you left your house around one in the morning," Drake continued.

"Bullshit!"

Drake patted the air in a calming gesture. "I know you and Jules have your troubles, but even if he were making this up, he has another witness. Do you believe Thomas Freeman has any reason to make up such a story?"

"I don't even *know* Thomas Freeman."

"Exactly my point."

"So you want to drop this 'I was home all night' crap?" Jules growled.

"Perhaps he was," Drake said, before Gray could go for Jules's throat.

Jules gave Drake a look of open-mouthed amazement. "Just what the hell are you implying?"

"That if someone wants to use Gray as the scapegoat for the killings, it would be most inconvenient for that someone if Gray were under constant surveillance."

"You think they used a decoy," Carolyn said.

"I think it's possible."

Jules shook his head. "No. That's just too far-fetched! Why should we look for a complicated answer to a simple question?"

"Did you actually *see* Gray leave the house?" Carolyn asked on a hunch.

"I was in the coffee shop, so no," Jules admitted, but he was conceding nothing. "Thomas saw him, though."

"Did he? Or did he just see *someone*?"

"He saw a vampire!" Jules snapped. "When you see a vampire leaving a house inhabited by a vampire, you can be damned sure it's the occupant who's leaving."

"But the killer's a vampire too," Carolyn protested.

"How do you know that?"

Geez, men could be exasperating. "Women with slashed throats, drained of blood? When you've swallowed the notion that vampires exist, it's pretty obvious, don't you think?"

"It makes sense, Jules," Drake interjected before tempers flared any higher. "The killer knows the Guardians are hunting him. He knows they've eliminated every vampire who's tried to set up shop in Philly. What better way to keep himself safe than to throw suspicion on someone else? And how hard would it have been to pull off last night's little diversion? Especially if he knows about the bad blood between the two of you."

Jules looked like he'd just swallowed sour milk, but he refrained from comment.

"All right," Carolyn said, "if we've now agreed it's possible someone is trying to frame Gray, what do we do about it?"

Jules smiled one of those charming smiles of his, but there was a hard glint to his eyes. "Well, right now the surveillance on Gray is occupying two Guardians every night."

Gray scowled. "It's not my fault you guys are wasting your time chasing red herrings."

"We can't afford the manpower," Jules continued, looking absurdly pleased with the thought.

Carolyn didn't know where this was going, but she was beginning to think it sucked. She folded her arms across her chest, tucking one hand subtly under her jacket toward the Glock. Drake noticed the motion and smiled at her, shaking his head. She made the mistake of meeting his eyes.

✳ ✳ ✳

GRAY WAS AMAZED HIS temper wasn't boiling over anymore. He stood in the cluttered, dusty basement and watched as Drake jiggled the trap door, trying to see if he could open it after Jules had jammed it from the other side.

"It's good," Drake called, and Jules acknowledged his words with a thump on the other side of the door. Drake stood up, dusting off his hands and facing Gray. "I understand this is unpleasant, but your life will be much improved if you're removed from suspicion."

Gray snorted. "In other words, this is for my own good?"

Drake lifted one shoulder in a hint of a shrug. "Maybe so. Keep in mind what's at stake here. Think of how many mortals have already died. Whatever your personal troubles with Jules, he is the oldest and most powerful of the Guardians save Eli. They need his full attention on the case, and as long as he's fixated on you, they won't have it."

"You don't think I'm the killer, do you?" Gray asked.

Drake shook his head. "You're just an easy scapegoat. As am I." He grinned, although the hardness in his eyes denied any hint of humor. "We independent operators must stick together."

Gray bit his tongue to keep himself from making any caustic comments. This wasn't exactly his idea of "sticking together."

"What about Carolyn? If you don't think I'm the

killer, then you don't think I fabricated that letter. She's in danger, and with me locked in my basement I won't be able to help her."

"I don't believe she's in danger. That note was no doubt meant to draw you out of your house so you could be blamed for the death of Jules's . . . companion."

Gray clenched his teeth and stared at the ceiling. Up in his living room, Hannah and Carolyn sat like statues, their minds blank. Drake might be right about the purpose of that note, but that didn't mean Carolyn was safe.

"You don't know Carolyn," he said. "She'll investigate the killings in her own way."

"I wouldn't worry about it if I were you," Drake said, smiling with genuine amusement this time. "If the entire society of Guardians and myself have been stymied, I sincerely doubt your mortal friend will have any greater success."

Gray rubbed his eyes and shook his head. He remembered when he'd first shown himself to Carolyn, remembered thinking he could just disappear from her life once more. Hard to believe he himself had once underestimated her so badly. Now Drake was making the same mistake, and damned if Gray could find a way to convince him of it. He swallowed his frustration as best he could. "Before you and Jules head out, can you give me a few minutes alone with Carolyn?" Drake gave him a penetrating look. Gray refused to look away, despite the threat of glamour. "Let me talk to her and it will reduce the chances that she'll come to the house by day and free me."

Drake laughed. "So now you *want* to remain in your basement?"

"Of course not! But if that's what it takes to get Jules's head out of his ass . . . I don't want people dying because of me. I do have a conscience, you know."

Drake's smile faded. "I know. And so do I. But we've both killed, and if our Broad Street Banger continues his reign of terror, you and I will bear the brunt of the Guardians' wrath. So it isn't just for the good of mortals that we must endeavor to eliminate the Banger as soon as possible."

Gray's stomach turned and he forced his mind away from the memory Drake's words evoked. He nodded an agreement, although as far as he was concerned there was still a vast gulf between himself and Drake. How many had Drake killed over his unnaturally long life? And had all of them really deserved it? It seemed to Gray that a Killer such as Drake wasn't in a position to throw stones.

The basement door opened and Jules peeked his head around the corner. "Let's get out of here."

Drake turned on his heel and left without a word. Gray figured his request to speak with Carolyn had just been denied, but a couple minutes later she ventured down the stairs. Her face was pale, her eyes troubled.

Before he had a chance to think better of it, he'd crossed the distance between them and pulled her into his arms. She was so small and delicate that her head only came up to his shoulder. She wrapped her arms around his waist, accepting his embrace with an ease that shamed him. He closed his eyes and inhaled the scent of her.

"Are you all right?" he asked.

Against his shoulder, he felt her nod. "Yeah. Just a little shaken up is all. You warned me about meeting his eyes, but I did it anyway, like an idiot."

He tightened his arms around her, wishing he could just hold her like this forever. "Don't blame yourself. Drake is probably powerful enough that he doesn't even need any eye contact."

Carolyn pulled away and looked up into his face. "He's more powerful than Jules, then?"

Gray nodded, debating how much to tell her about Drake. Then he almost laughed at himself—what he didn't tell her, she would no doubt discover on her own somehow. "Unlike the Guardians and myself, Drake doesn't feed on lamb's blood."

Carolyn's face turned a shade paler. "What do you mean?"

"He's a Killer, Carolyn. Very dangerous, although he does follow his own moral code. The Guardians tolerate him because they often find his powers useful, and because he only kills people he thinks deserve it. A vigilante, I guess you could call him."

Carolyn shuddered. "And this is one of the good guys?"

"You could say that, I guess. But anyway, Drake isn't the reason I asked to speak with you before you left. He's dangerous, but I doubt he's dangerous to *you*. I just wanted to make sure you didn't get any funny ideas about coming back and 'rescuing' me."

She reached up and touched his face, a gentle smile on her lips. "Don't worry, Gray. I won't break into your house again. If leaving you locked up for a couple of days will clear you of suspicion, then I suppose it's for the best."

He should have known she would be pragmatic about this. He turned his head and kissed her palm. The scent of her skin awakened a deep longing in his chest, and he pulled away before it could overpower him.

Gray knew that his memories would haunt him relentlessly when Carolyn was gone and the door to his prison closed. Memories of the last time he'd been locked in this basement. But worst of all, memories of what had once been his, memories of the joys of life he would never taste again.

Swallowing his bitterness, hoping Carolyn didn't see it on his face, he straightened his shoulders. "You'd better go."

The look in her eyes suggested she, too, was struggling against the memories. "All right."

"You'll stay with Hannah, right? And you'll be very careful, knowing what you're up against." He had to fight the instinct to try to talk her out of investigating, but arguing would only serve to make her angry. And more determined.

"Yes and yes." She took a step closer to him, and he thought she might be planning to give him a hug or a kiss goodbye. She visibly stopped herself. "Take care," she said. Then she fled up the stairs as though being chased.

13

CAROLYN WAS REALLY STARTING to doubt that it was necessary to stay with Hannah indefinitely, but Hannah wouldn't hear of her leaving, so she supposed she was stuck. The first day after leaving Gray locked in his basement, she'd called one of her old friends from the department and casually pumped him for information about the Banger case. What she learned only cemented her conviction that the Banger was a vampire.

One of the pieces of information the police had not revealed to the press was that in not one of the Banger's victims was there any sign of a struggle. No skin under the fingernails, no bruises, no abrasions. Nothing. The best guess was that the victims were subdued with chloroform, which was very hard to detect after the fact. Even so, one would have thought there'd be *some* sign of struggle. But of course, if the killer was a vampire, all it took was a touch of glamour, and the victim would let him do whatever he pleased without a peep of protest. The thought made Carolyn shudder with revulsion.

The other interesting detail she learned was that the police had been unsuccessful in their attempts to obtain the Banger's fingerprints. It appeared he wore gloves to perform his gruesome murders. Carolyn thought that very telling—why would he bother with gloves unless he thought his prints were on file? Mortal killers would do it to avoid prosecution, but she suspected prosecution wasn't the Banger's greatest threat. Her heart leapt with hope, and she put in a call to Ted at the fingerprint lab. Unfortunately, he didn't have any results for her yet.

After that, with Gray locked in his basement, and Jules refusing to talk, there wasn't a damn thing Carolyn could do. It wasn't a situation she took to with much grace, and she was lucky Hannah didn't throw her out, considering how crabby she was becoming.

The Banger was still out there, no doubt ready for his next kill. And the only thing that stood between him and his next victim were a group of amateur sleuths whose only qualification for hunting down a murderer was that they were vampires.

How many more would have to die before the Guardians managed to find the killer?

* * *

GRAY'S FEET HURT FROM pacing, so he forced himself to sit on the faded, dusty divan he'd dug out from under a pile of boxes. The divan had served as his bed for the last three interminable days, and he was royally sick of the thing. However, most of the other furniture in this hell-hole of a basement was broken, so unless he wanted to sleep on the floor, he had few choices.

At the end of his first night, he'd uncovered a box full of books. He'd eagerly torn the box open, hoping for something to distract him from the sheer boredom of his imprisonment. Unfortunately, Kate's taste had run to lurid romance and erotica, and Gray had shoved the box away in disappointment.

He'd avoided even looking at them last night, but by

now the boredom was so overpowering he couldn't stand it anymore. Grimacing in distaste, he picked through the box looking for a book with a cover that didn't make him want to barf. He found one that didn't look too bad, then settled on the divan to read.

Two hours later, he shut the book with a groan and flung it away from him.

The sex scene had snuck up on him from out of nowhere. He'd been reading along, finding the story surprisingly engrossing, until suddenly the lovers found themselves alone and in perfect privacy for the first time in the entire book. For some reason, he'd expected the author to draw the curtains on the ecstatic lovers and let them do their business in private. But the scene had gone on and on, describing in scintillating detail every touch, every kiss, every heated breath. The lovers in the book reached a mind-bending release, but Gray was left breathless and hard and lonely.

He covered his face and tried to take a few deep breaths, tried to dispel the images the book had created in his mind, but it was no use. In his mind's eye, he saw Carolyn, stretched out on her cosy double bed. She was naked and perfect, the sheets twined around her legs while hiding nothing from his hungry gaze. Her cheeks were flushed with desire, her dusky pink nipples hardened into tempting nubs, begging for the rasp of his tongue.

Gray hadn't thought he could grow any harder, but the image, so real he could almost taste her skin, made his groin ache.

Damn that stupid romance book! He readjusted his pants in a futile effort to get comfortable. As if his imprisonment weren't miserable enough already!

He had to stop thinking of Carolyn. No matter how much he ached for her, no matter how desperately he wanted her, she was a figure from his past.

With a pop that made him jump a mile, the overhead light burned out. Gray wanted to scream in frustration.

His vampire eyes could see better in the dark than a mortal's, but even he needed *some* light. This basement was pitch black, and all he could see were the images his horny mind kept conjuring.

Knowing it was the only release he was likely to find, Gray reached down and slid open the zipper on his pants.

* * *

HE STOOD NAKED BEFORE her, his pale, pale skin warmed by candlelight, his deep gray eyes dark with desire. Carolyn wanted to reach for him, but her hands wouldn't move. She craned her neck and saw the gleaming silver cuffs that encircled her wrists, chaining her to the bed.

Gray smiled at her, an expression that bared his fangs. Her breath caught in her throat, and she couldn't tell if the adrenaline that pumped through her was fear or lust or a little of both. The light of countless candles danced and flickered in the room, revealing and concealing in equal measure. She glanced down at herself and saw that she, too, was naked, stretched out on the geometric comforter that covered Gray's bed.

Gray's eyes traveled her body from head to toe, his gaze like a caress burning her skin wherever it landed. He stared at her nipples, and they hardened as though he'd sucked them into his mouth. A moan escaped her, and once more she struggled against the handcuffs. She wanted his touch more than anything in the world, and yet he didn't come any closer, merely stood beside the bed and devoured her with his eyes.

"Please," she gasped, straining toward him, but he just smiled.

His gaze lowered at a leisurely pace, tracing her ribs, then skimming over her belly, lingering at her navel. Then it dipped lower, and another moan rose from her throat. She opened her legs, beckoning to him, wondering what he was waiting for. The tip of his tongue emerged and he slowly licked his lips. Her back arched and she cried out, her body almost feeling that sensuous caress in the place she most wanted it. Her heart hammered beneath her ribs and she could hardly draw breath. If he didn't touch her soon, she was going to scream! He started toward her, eyes gleaming with erotic intent. She spread her legs wider in desperation. Any moment now, he was going to take her and end her suffering.

The heat of his body singed the delicate skin of her inner thighs. "Yes!" she cried. "Now!"

Carolyn woke with a wail of longing on her lips. Her heart was racing, her skin clammy. Her body craved release, but there was none to be had. She pressed her thighs tightly together. Why oh why had she had to wake up at that moment?

She took a deep, slow breath, willing her heart to calm. But that wasn't enough. She slipped out of bed and padded through the darkened room to the bathroom. A splash of cold water on her face helped a little. She met her own eyes in the mirror above the sink and shook her head at herself. Her cheeks were flushed red, and the dream hovered with frightening clarity in the front of her mind. The frustration of wanting him so desperately, and of not being able to have him, brought a wave of despair.

Even her subconscious was telling her she couldn't have him! As Hannah, and Jules, and practically everyone on the planet had told her, she had to let him go.

But oh, how she wished she could stop wanting what she couldn't have.

* * *

GRAY SAT UP ABRUPTLY in the dark. He'd thought he heard the front door open. He closed his eyes and concentrated, sensing the presence of a vampire up-stairs.

Please, let it be Drake! he asked the powers that be. Jules had come by just before dawn last night but had not felt it necessary to replace the burnt-out bulb that left Gray in total darkness. Maybe Drake would be more reasonable. Gray felt like he was holding on to his sanity by a thread, and though he fully understood the circumstances under which he'd been locked up, he had had quite enough of it.

The sound of a deadbolt sliding open echoed down the stairway. Gray stood, but he didn't dare try to find his way to the stairs. Too many boxes and other obstacles in the way. His shins had obtained many a bruise from his previous forays, and though they healed in a matter of minutes, they were still a nuisance.

"Drake?" he asked hopefully. "The light's burned out down here, but there's a flashlight in the top right drawer in the kitchen."

The top step creaked, but no voice answered Gray's greeting. The hair on the back of his neck prickled. There was no reason for either Jules or Drake to refuse to speak to him. He might almost have thought he was hearing things, but he unmistakably felt that psychic footprint.

"Hello?" he called, taking a careful step backward and crouching in preparation for an attack.

He thought he heard a faint laugh. Then he felt his mind sliding helplessly into oblivion.

$$* * *$$

GRAY AWOKE WITH A start, his head aching as though he had a hangover. He groaned and pressed his palms against his eye sockets, fragments of thoughts fluttering through his mind. The world seemed to spin beneath him and for a moment he was afraid he was about to hurl. What the hell . . . ?

He swallowed down the bile and cracked his eyes open.

His first coherent thought was that he wasn't in his basement prison anymore. His second was that he smelled blood in the air. He staggered to his feet, still reeling dizzily.

"Are you back in the land of the semi-living?"

Gray's heart almost leapt out of his chest as he whirled to see Drake standing beside him. The older vampire's expression was dark and hooded, and a hint of memory flitted through Gray's mind. It was Drake's voice that had awakened him.

Awakened him? Had he been asleep? He blinked rapidly, wondering what the hell was the matter with him. He wiped a hand over his face, finding a patch of sticky wetness at the corner of his mouth. His stomach plummeted as he slowly pulled his hand away and saw the blood that streaked his palm. The scent of blood turned into a reek and reluctantly he looked around him.

He was in an unfamiliar bedroom, and he had no idea how he'd gotten here. On the bed lay two bodies, a man and a woman. The woman lay on her back, spread-eagled, her throat slashed. Beside her, the man also lay naked on his back. His mouth was open in what looked like a cry of pain, and his dead eyes stared in horror at the ceiling. His hands were clasped around the length of wood that protruded from his chest.

For the second time, Gray's stomach revolted. If it weren't for the fact that he hadn't fed in days, he probably would have vomited. He drew in a shuddering breath and stared at Drake.

Drake looked impassive, his face giving away nothing as he examined the carnage on the bed.

"That's Thomas Freeman there with the stake through his heart," he said in a bland voice. "He's a Guardian. I don't know his girlfriend's name."

Gray scrubbed at his mouth convulsively, trying to

erase every trace of blood. He didn't know what had happened, how he'd come here, but one thing he *did* know. "I didn't kill them!"

Drake nodded. "I know. It's supposed to look like you did, but despite the blood on your mouth your face isn't flushed like it would be after a kill." He moved to the bed and pulled the sheet up to cover the girl's body. The stake in Freeman's chest made it impossible to cover him completely, but Drake did the best he could.

Gray put a hand on the wall to support himself. His mind was beginning to clear, and he remembered being in the basement, hearing someone start down the stairs. Then nothing.

Glamour. Very powerful glamour. Stronger than anything he'd experienced with Jules. His hands clenched into fists and he looked more closely at Drake. A rosy tint colored the killer's cheeks.

Drake shook his head, looking down at the bodies. "Fifteen minutes ago, Thomas called my cell phone. He said he had to talk to me right away. He sounded scared to death and the call ended abruptly. I came as fast as I could. When I got here, I found the front door open, and you were sitting against the wall with your eyes glazed over."

"Is that so?" Gray asked with obvious skepticism, though a rational part of his brain told him it was unbearably stupid to antagonize a vampire who could squash him like a bug.

Drake cast him an irritated glance. "Don't be an ass. If I were the killer, I'd be gone by now. No, I suspect I was called here to put me under the same blanket of suspicion you're under."

"You said yourself I didn't have the flush of a recent kill. Well, *you* do."

Drake's nostrils flared and anger stirred in his eyes, but he answered mildly. "I've fed tonight, but not on her." He nodded toward the poor dead girl. He shook his head. "Whoever did this, I didn't sense him when I came in. Considering he was powerful enough to hold you under his glamour when he's long gone, I'd say we're in a lot of trouble."

The doorbell rang, repeatedly. Drake moved quickly to the bedside table, picking up the phone and hitting a couple keys. "Damn it!" he said, slamming down the phone and meeting Gray's eyes. "Thomas's last call was to Michael."

"Michael?"

"His twin brother. Also a Guardian."

The doorbell rang more urgently, followed by the sound of a fist pounding on the door. Drake closed his eyes a moment, then shook his head. "There are four of them—Michael must have called in reinforcements."

The pounding sounded more violent, and Gray suspected the door would soon give way. "What are the chances Michael's going to calmly listen to us deny we killed his brother?"

Drake snorted and moved to the window, pushing it open. "I suggest you run for it." He glanced out at the sidewalk below. "You should be able to make the jump without breaking your legs."

Gray really hated to make himself look even guiltier than he already did by running, but he knew from experience just how fierce vampire tempers were. If he hung around, the angry Guardians would kill him first and ask questions later. "What about you?" he asked Drake as he sat on the window sill and swung his legs out.

"I will delay them so you can get away."

Gray paused and looked at the older vampire in surprise. "Why would you do that?"

Drake shrugged. "Because I know you didn't do it." A hint of a feral smile twitched his lips upward. "And because even four of them can't overpower me when I'm ready for them. Now hurry and get out of here before they realize the second vampire presence they sense in here isn't Thomas."

Still Gray hesitated. "Thank you. And be careful."

"You too," Drake said, then started to close the window—with Gray still perched on the ledge.

Gray dropped to the sidewalk below just as a loud bang signaled the front door had given way. Hoping Drake's claims weren't just empty boasting, he ran.

* * *

CAROLYN WOKE FROM A heavy sleep to the sound of a ringing phone. She lifted her head and rubbed the grit from her eyes. The clock beside her bed declared it was three-thirty in the morning. She smothered a yawn.

The phone stopped ringing. Either the caller had given up, or Hannah had answered. Carolyn told herself to go back to sleep, but instead she sat up in the bed and turned on the light. Phone calls at three-thirty in the morning were rarely anything good.

Moments later, the light in the hallway switched on, and Hannah emerged from her bedroom, cordless phone in hand. Her wild curls were loose and tousled from sleep, and Carolyn could see the impression of her pillow on her cheek. Her oversized nightshirt declared her a Naughty Girl. Her eyes were half-closed, and the lack of any obvious alarm on her face eased Carolyn's nerves.

Hannah held out the phone to her without a word, not bothering to smother her yawn.

"Hello?" Carolyn said into the phone, knowing that it had to be Gray. No one else knew she was staying with Hannah.

"Hey," he said, and even in that one word she could hear the strain in his voice. "Everything all right over there? Your governess kept pleading the fifth."

Carolyn snickered and rolled her eyes at Hannah,

who made one of those "who me?" faces. "Everything's fine, except for being awakened at an ungodly hour by a phone call. What's going on?" A chill crawled down her spine as she woke up a little more. "Where are you, and how did you get access to a phone?"

"It's a long story, and I'd rather not go into it right now. I'm at a pay phone. Can I come over?"

"Yeah, sure. Where are you?"

"Look out your window."

She nudged the curtain aside and saw Gray standing at the pay phone on the corner. He waved, and she beckoned him toward the door.

Hannah gave her a penetrating look when she hung up the phone. "Inviting him into my apartment?"

Carolyn smiled sheepishly. "I guess that was pretty rude of me. Sorry."

"Do you suppose it's true that vampires can't enter a residence unless they're invited?"

"My guess would be no," Carolyn answered as she pulled on a battered chenille bathrobe and headed toward the front door, Hannah on her heels. Carolyn quirked a brow at her. "Don't you want to put on a robe or something?"

Hannah grinned. "He already knows I'm a naughty girl. I'm not afraid to flaunt it."

Carolyn smiled and shook her head, though butterflies fluttered in her stomach. What was Gray doing here? The only thing she knew for sure was that it was a bad sign. She buzzed Gray in, then opened the door for him. She couldn't help noticing the nervous glance he cast over his shoulder before she closed the door. His face looked even paler than usual, and trouble brewed in his eyes. Carolyn's mouth went dry.

"I think I'll go make a pot of coffee," Hannah said, leaving the two of them momentarily alone. However, Hannah's apartment was small enough that she could easily overhear any discussion from the kitchen, so it was a false sense of privacy. Carolyn had no doubt her friend's ears were straining to follow the conversation.

Gray declined to sit, instead pacing the length of the cramped living room as Carolyn looked up at him. "What's happened?" she asked again.

He scratched the back of his head, and for a moment she was struck again by how good he looked with long hair. Then she scolded herself for the inappropriate lust attack.

"I am so screwed," he said, letting out a deep breath as he stopped his pacing to meet her eyes. "I don't know exactly what happened, but someone came to my house tonight and hit me with the most powerful glamour I've ever felt. When I snapped out of it, I was at a murder scene."

Carolyn gasped. In the kitchen, Hannah ceased any pretense of making coffee, standing in the doorway and staring.

"One of the victims was killed Banger-style. The other was a Guardian. Someone had driven a stake through his heart. Drake was there, too. He said the Guardian called him in a panic just a few minutes before."

Carolyn beckoned for Gray to come sit beside her on the sofa, and he obeyed, his eyes haunted. Hannah turned back to her coffee-making, and soon emerged from the kitchen carrying two cups of steaming coffee, which she set down on the coffee table.

"I assume you don't drink coffee?" she asked Gray.

"No." He clasped his hands together in his lap. Hannah sat across the table from them on an ottoman, crossing her legs under her. The nightshirt just barely kept her decent in that position.

Carolyn cupped her coffee in her hands, trying to fight off the chill. She had worked countless murder cases as a cop, but she had never before known any of the victims or the suspects personally. This felt massively different, and her mind struggled to retain any semblance of rational thought.

"Not long afterwards, a mob of angry Guardians appeared at the door," Gray continued. "Drake provided a distraction to help me get away."

"Interesting," Hannah said. She no longer looked even vaguely sleepy, her warm brown eyes alight with intelligence. "Do you have any reason to think he's not the killer himself?"

Gray shrugged. "Not really. I suspect he's strong enough to have overcome me with glamour, but . . ."

"But this killer isn't stupid," Carolyn finished for him, "and it would be damn stupid to make himself a prime suspect by hanging around the murder scene until you came to."

"Exactly," Gray said, nodding. "I think he was called to the scene so he would be under suspicion too." He grunted in frustration, leaning back in the sofa and shaking his head. "I can understand why the killer would want Drake out of the picture. The guy is a very dangerous hunter. But why me? I've never been a part of the Guardians. I'm a threat to no one. Before, we thought maybe the Banger was framing me to distract Jules, but now I have to run for it, so it's not like Jules will be stuck guarding my house and following me around. I mean, if he finds me, I'm a dead man. So I don't understand . . ."

"Have you made any enemies since you became vampire?" Carolyn asked.

"Yeah. Jules." His head snapped up. "It would be the perfect cover . . ."

"Huh?"

He met her gaze, a strange gleam in his eyes. "What better way to deflect suspicion from himself than to kill his own girlfriend? He plays the part of revenge-maddened lover, pointing his finger at me as he does so. Then when he's on watch, he tricks Thomas into thinking I've skipped out so he can kill again. It must have been a pain in his ass when I was confined to the basement."

Carolyn saw his hands clenching into fists, saw the

flush of temper in his cheeks. She reached out and put a hand on his shoulder, giving it a squeeze. "Easy there. Don't jump to conclusions. There's been an awful lot of that going on."

For a moment, the expression on Gray's face darkened even further. Then he seemed to snap out of it, the tension draining from his body. He sighed, his fists unclenching. "You're right. There has. But I still think Jules has to take his place on the list of suspects."

"I'll grant you that," she agreed, though her gut told her Jules wasn't the killer. She remembered the look on his face when he'd gone after Gray, just after Courtney's murder. It was possible the guy was a great actor, but she didn't think so. "But keep thinking—do you have any other enemies?"

He shook his head. "Not that I know of."

"There's always me," Hannah said with false cheer, earning herself another of his dark looks.

"I've pretty much lived like a hermit ever since . . . well, just ever since. If you don't interact with people, you don't make enemies."

Carolyn's heart squeezed gently. Gray had always been something of an introvert, but he'd never let that stop him from socializing and making friends. How terribly lonely he must be if he'd cut himself off from all human contact for three years.

"Maybe it's not an enemy," Hannah mused. "Maybe you're just a convenient scapegoat. It might not be anything personal at all."

"True," Carolyn agreed, "but if it's not personal, then we're going to have an even harder time unraveling everything. So for the meantime, I'd like to explore any possible personal connection."

"Unless it's Jules, then I can't imagine it's anything personal," Gray countered. "I'm serious, Carolyn. I haven't been in a position to piss anyone off for three years."

"Then why are you and Jules at each others' throats?"

Gray's face clouded. "We just have a personality conflict is all," he said, but he was a terrible liar.

Carolyn sighed. "How am I supposed to help you if you won't tell me the truth?"

"I didn't ask you to help me!"

"Then what are you doing here at three-thirty in the morning?"

He looked like he was about to snap back at her, but visibly swallowed the words. He crossed his arms over his chest and turned his gaze away from her, every nuance of his body language slamming the virtual door in her face.

"When did you become such a hot-head?" Hannah asked. "You used to be on such an even keel that you might as well have been dead."

"Hannah!" Carolyn barked, wishing Hannah didn't blurt out everything that came to her mind.

As usual, Hannah was undeterred. "Now you seem to fly off the handle at a moment's notice."

Gray squirmed and some of the belligerence faded from his expression. "Sorry," he mumbled. "I'm being an asshole, I know." He raised his chin. "It's like I told Carolyn before. Gray James is dead. I just happen to bear a strong resemblance to him."

Hannah shrugged. "Whatever."

Gray's eyes were shadowed and haunted, his cheeks almost gaunt, but Carolyn could still make out the shadow of the man she once loved in that grim profile. And though it was true that he was much more volatile than he once was, she wondered if the changes were really more than skin deep. Maybe what she was seeing now was the *real* Gray James, set free from the need to conform and "behave."

Of course, she didn't utter a word of this speculation out loud. It was obvious Gray didn't much like the man he had become, and if it was easier for him to pretend that he'd been completely transformed when he'd become vampire, then for now she'd let him cling to that illusion. If illusion it was.

"So," she said, "if you're not here to ask for my help, then what are you doing here?"

He squirmed again and suddenly dropped his gaze to his hands, which were now folded in his lap. "Er—"

Hannah laughed. "He's here to ask for help, of course." She unfolded her legs and leaned forward on the ottoman, quelling her laughter and becoming all business. "You said you thought Jules would kill you if he found you." Gray nodded. "And you said there was a mob of Guardians at the door when you fled the murder scene." He flinched, whether at the memory or at Hannah's bald description Carolyn didn't know.

"Yes," he said.

"So you basically have a lynch mob after you, and they're all vampires."

He lost the hangdog look and sat up straighter. "Yup, that about sums it up."

"Which means you can't go back to your house," Carolyn said, continuing the line of thought. "Which means you have to find somewhere else to spend the day."

"And you decided this would be just the place," Hannah finished.

But Gray shook his head. "No. Jules doesn't specifically know Carolyn is here, but he can make an educated guess. I expect that he will make an appearance here, maybe even before the night is out."

"Oh, great. That should be fun. Thanks a lot, Gray."

"Sorry?" he said tentatively.

"I guess we have to get you out of here, then," Carolyn said.

"No, *we* don't. I was just hoping you'd be able to lend me some money so I can get a hotel room. I had nothing in my pockets when I was abducted, and as you know I don't dare go home."

Carolyn frowned and bit her lip. "Are vampires really as vulnerable to sunlight as the legends say?"

"Pretty close. Direct sunlight would kill me very quickly. Indirect sunlight would hurt like hell and kill me eventually. But if I pull the drapes and bury myself under the covers, I should be all right."

"And when housekeeping comes by?"

"I'll put a do-not-disturb sign on the door and throw the deadbolt. I'll be fine, Carolyn."

"Yeah, Carolyn," Hannah chimed in. "He'll be fine. Now give him some money and let him get out of here before the lynch mob shows up."

But Carolyn couldn't just let him face this alone, not when his life was in danger. "I'm coming with you," she declared.

"Why am I not surprised?" Hannah asked with ill-disguised sarcasm.

"No, you're not," Gray said, his eyes narrowed.

"Then you can't have any money."

He turned to Hannah and raised an eyebrow, but Hannah raised her hands and shook her head. "Don't look at me! I'm not stupid enough to get in the middle of this."

"But you want to keep Carolyn safe, don't you?" Gray challenged.

"Hey, baby, I'm looking out for number one, and if I gave you any money under these circumstances, she'd kill me."

Gray stood up and glared down at Carolyn. "I guess I'll just have to go out on the street and rob someone. Shouldn't be too hard with my glamour." He took two angry strides toward the door.

"Oh for heaven's sake, Gray!" Carolyn said in exasperation, springing to her feet. "You keep telling me how you've changed, but you're still playing this ridiculous, alpha-male, protect-the-helpless-woman game and it's pissing me off." He turned around to face her, and she read his intent immediately, lowering her gaze from his face to his Adam's apple. "And don't you dare use your damned glamour against me. I'm an adult, capable woman and I deserve to be treated like one."

He hissed out an exasperated breath. "Why do you insist on seeing it as a *bad* thing that I want to protect someone I . . . care about? You've got such a massive chip on your shoulder I'm amazed you can walk straight!"

"I think I'll just go to my room, and . . . uh . . ." Hannah crept out of the room without finishing the thought.

"Oh, *I've* got a chip on my shoulder?" Carolyn said, stalking closer to him while still refusing to meet his eyes. "Then what do you call this 'I can handle everything all by myself' crap? You know you need help, but you refuse to take it. That's a chip on the shoulder and a death wish all rolled into one." To her dismay, she felt the distinctive burn of incipient tears in her eyes. Damn, it was like she was reliving every argument they'd had about her job in the weeks leading up to their wedding. "Why can't you have a little faith in me?" she asked, her chest hurting as she fought to keep the tears at bay.

Suddenly, Gray's arms were around her and her cheek was pressed up against his chest. She inhaled deeply. He wasn't wearing any cologne today, so all she smelled was him. His hand touched the back of her head, his fingers running through her mussed hair. Under her ear, she heard the steady thud of his heart, and her mind flashed to memories of lying half on top of him in bed on lazy Saturday mornings. She swallowed hard, the tears still threatening to spill over if she wasn't constantly on her guard.

"Carolyn, I've always had faith in you," he murmured into her hair. "You were a damn good cop, and I'm sure you're a damn good investigator now. I just . . . Can't you understand what it's like to worry about someone? Can't you understand the instinct to keep those who matter to you safe?"

She put her hands against his chest and pushed away, looking up into his earnest eyes, trusting him not to use his glamour right now. "Can't *you*?"

She saw her words hit home, but he looked even more miserable. "If I let you come with me, and something happens to you, I'll never forgive myself."

She managed a weak smile. "Well if I let you leave without me, and something happens to you, *I'll* never forgive you."

His face softened and he laughed. "You're a priceless gem," he said, then leaned forward to kiss her lightly on the forehead.

Even when he moved away, she felt the touch of those lips searing her skin. Desires long suppressed stirred in her center, and though Gray tried to act casual she noticed the dilation of his eyes. And the bulge in his pants.

Yes, there was more than one reason she wanted to convince Gray to let her come along to his hotel room tonight. His nostrils flared slightly, and she was reminded of some predatory animal scenting its prey on the wind. "Go put some clothes on," he said in a voice that would have sounded more natural if he were saying "take those clothes *off*." "I promise I'll wait for you."

Carolyn wasn't sure she could trust him to wait. But she also knew that if he really wanted to leave the house without her, there was nothing she could do to stop him. Nodding briskly, she hurried to her room to change at top speed.

14

THE STREETS WERE DEADLY quiet as Gray and Carolyn made their way to the convention center area, where she was reasonably certain they'd be able to get a room. She'd wanted to call ahead, but she figured it was more important to get out of Hannah's house before any Guardians came knocking. For security purposes, they'd be staying under a false name and paying in cash.

They stopped at an ATM on the way, where Carolyn made a maximum withdrawal. Gray was silent and brooding, his eyes distant as he fought whatever internal demons he wanted to hide from her. His hands were shoved into his coat pockets as he walked, his head bowed.

Carolyn slipped her hand through his elbow and he seemed to start out of some reverie. "We'll get through this," she assured him, giving his arm a squeeze.

The expression on his face lightened into something almost like a smile. "Nothing ever intimidates you, does it?"

She raised her free shoulder in a half-shrug. "It does, but I'm damn good at hiding it."

He laughed, the cold turning his breath into a misty white cloud. He withdrew his hand from his pocket and slung his arm around her shoulders. It was only natural for her own arm to slip around his waist. His body felt wonderfully warm in the frigid night. Carolyn matched his long stride as deep down inside her a revelation unfurled.

I've never stopped loving him.

She closed her eyes for just a moment, wishing she could stuff that thought back down into her subconscious where it belonged.

The silence between them shifted from companionable to tense, and Carolyn couldn't for the life of her tell if it was just her imagination. His arm tightened around her shoulders, and something stirred in her center.

Three years. Three years she'd been alone, her heart irreparably broken by Gray's desertion. Three years she hadn't had sex, or even a kiss, for God's sake! Hannah had repeatedly told her she wasn't over Gray, and Carolyn had repeatedly denied it. Well, denial wasn't getting her anywhere anymore. She cleared her throat.

"So, about that woman . . ." Her voice came out husky, so she cleared her throat again. "You said you were in a relationship with her, and yet it's *me* you came to."

He sighed. "I lied about that. I was trying to protect you, keep you out of all this craziness, but you're so damned stubborn. I thought telling you I was in a relationship with Deirdre might be the one thing I could do to get you to back off."

And he'd been right, as far as it went. "But then you got that letter from the Banger."

"Right. I got that letter, and I knew it was too late to keep you out of it completely."

"So what about that time I saw you kissing her?"

He made a sound somewhere between a snort and a laugh. "*She* kissed *me*. She's been flirting with me on and off since the beginning."

Carolyn came to a stop, looking up into his face. "And why haven't you taken her up on it? She's awfully pretty."

He said nothing, just stared down at her, his jaw clamped so tightly shut that a muscle twitched in his cheek. A lump formed in her throat as she came to her own conclusions, but Gray abruptly dropped his arm from around her shoulders and shook his head.

"Let's keep moving," he said, walking on without waiting to see if she was coming.

Carolyn hurried to catch up with him, her teeth worrying at her lower lip. His head was bowed, his shoulders hunched, his hands back in his pockets. She wanted to break down the wall that separated them, but he had reinforced its weak spots and she doubted she would get through.

They spoke not a word to each other as Carolyn checked them into the Marriott, paying a cash deposit. When the guy at the reception desk balked at the idea of cash, Carolyn convinced him she was a battered woman trying to hide from her abusive ex-husband. She was probably being paranoid, for it seemed unlikely the Guardians had the resources to track her by her credit card, but she wasn't inclined to take chances. She chose a non-smoking room with two double beds.

Carolyn's heart sped as she and Gray rode the elevator. He wasn't looking at her, and his expression was still closed and shuttered, and yet there was a tension in the air that wasn't born of awkwardness. She chewed her chapped lip some more, wondering if she was imagining it, sure she was not.

Once they were inside their room, the deadbolt secured, the tension rose another notch. Carolyn slipped out of her coat, tossing it over a chair. Gray stood in the middle of the room, looking indecisive, his hands still stuffed in his coat pockets.

"Aren't you hot?" she asked, moving to the thermostat and sliding the temperature down. Of course, she didn't think it was the heater that was generating her body heat.

Gray hesitated a moment, then shook his head and shrugged out of his coat. When he turned to drape it over the chair with hers, Carolyn saw why he'd been reluctant to take it off. He followed her gaze down to the bulge in his jeans, then raised his eyes to hers again.

"Carolyn . . ." he said, his voice conveying a vague warning.

She moved closer to him, her pulse throbbing insistently in her throat as warmth flooded her body and pooled between her legs. But Gray held up both hands to ward her off. She might have felt hurt, except there was no denying the desire that shone in his eyes.

"It's glamour, Carolyn," he said in a husky, strained voice. "I'm not trying to use it, but it seems to be a reflexive reaction. Don't come any closer."

She raised an eyebrow as a few puzzle pieces fell into place. She'd never thought of glamour as something to cause sexual desire, but now she remembered how badly she had wanted him when they'd gotten carried away on his living room couch. At the time, her desire for him had been totally inappropriate, and she'd attributed it to her long abstinence. Apparently, there'd been more to it than that.

Carefully, she poked at her feelings, wondering if they were genuine or whether they were artificially created by Gray's vampire glamour. She didn't have to think about it very long.

Shaking her head, she continued to move closer as Gray continued to back up. "It's not glamour."

"Yes it is!" he insisted, and he sounded almost panicked. His butt hit the dresser and he couldn't back up any farther. His eyes had gone almost black with desire, and his erection looked like it was about to burst out of his pants. Still he held up his hands, keeping her away.

She began unbuttoning her blouse, smiling at him. "No. I remember what that felt like, and this isn't it." She thought the sight of her unbuttoning might push him past his resistance, but instead he reached out and grabbed her wrists, stilling her hands.

"Please, Carolyn," he said, anguish in his voice and eyes.

"I'm not expecting this to turn back into what it once was," she assured him. "But we're two adults who've gone without for too long. We can still enjoy each others' bodies, no matter what's come between us before."

Gray shook his head, not letting go of her hands. "That's not why I'm fighting this." He took a long, deep breath, letting it hiss out slowly between his teeth. His Adam's apple bobbed as he swallowed hard.

"Then why?" she asked, mystified.

"Because I can't trust my self-control. I'm afraid I might . . . hurt you." His eyes closed in pain and he bowed his head.

Gently, she extricated her wrists from his grip. Perhaps a more sensible woman would be frightened by that admission, but she only felt more keenly her body's desires. She stepped into him, pressing her belly against the glowing heat of his erection. His eyes popped open in surprise.

"I'm not afraid of you, Gray," she whispered, reaching up to cup her hand against his heek. "You won't hurt me."

The fire in his eyes flared higher, and he pulled his lips away from his teeth, baring the two sharp fangs that had appeared where his canines once were. A tremor passed through her body at the unspoken warning, but she slid her hand along his jaw, then speared her fingers through his silky dark hair and pulled his head down to hers.

For one agonizing instant, he resisted. Then with a guttural moan, he wrapped his arms around her and pulled her hard against him. His lips pressed against hers, his tongue demanding entrance, which she eagerly granted. It was a bruising, hard kiss. She welcomed it with all her being.

One of his hands grabbed her ass and pressed her even harder against him, fingers digging into her flesh in a grip that should have been painful but wasn't. His other hand tunneled into her hair and held her head still while his tongue ravaged her mouth. Fire coursed through her veins, and she could barely breathe. Even through the thickness of his jeans, she could feel his erection throbbing and pulsing. She moaned deep in her throat, and Gray let out a feral growl.

He raised his head from her lips, his breath coming in short gasps. His fangs were bared, his eyes dark as a moonless night. Carolyn's breath caught in her throat as she looked into the face of lust and danger. Her heart hammered, and for a handful of beats a flicker of fear sparked in her belly.

Gray lifted her easily off her feet, his hands under her butt. Instinctively she wrapped her legs around him to keep from falling. His mouth descended on hers once more, hot and fierce and needy. She held tight to his neck, sucking on his tongue whenever it slipped into her mouth, the spark of fear overwhelmed by the inferno of her desire. He surged forward, setting her down on the foot of one of the beds.

Carolyn let out a moan of protest when he tore his lips from hers. He towered over her, his chest heaving with his hastened breaths. She wanted to reach for him, but he kept her trapped with his eyes as his fingers tore at the buttons of his shirt. She bit her lip to stifle another moan when the shirt fell from his shoulders. His chest was all lean, toned muscle that rippled when he moved. God, he was beautiful! She reached for his belt, desperate to get him completely naked, but he batted her hands away. She gasped in surprise.

Baring his fangs again, Gray pushed on her shoulders until she lay back on the bed, her legs still dangling over the edge. He practically tore off the button on her jeans, then his fingers curled into the waistband, snagging her panties at the same time. Before she knew what was happening, both jeans and panties were bunched up around her knees. Gray was still tugging on them, and she wriggled to help free herself.

Her skin glowed with the heat of her body, and she held her breath in anticipation. This was so unlike anything she had ever experienced with Gray before. She had no idea what to expect, what he would do next. She was on a roller coaster, being inexorably dragged up the endless incline, knowing the drop—terrifying and exhilarating at once—was waiting for her.

Gray jerked open his belt with hands that visibly shook. Carolyn watched, fascinated, as he popped the button open and yanked the zipper down. He didn't bother to remove his jeans or shorts, just pulled them down far enough to free himself. Carolyn's throat closed as her eyes fastened on his enormous erection. She had almost forgotten the mind-boggling size of him, and after three long years of abstinence, he looked even bigger than she remembered.

There was no hint of gentleness to his touch when he urged her legs apart. He seemed a creature of raw, unbridled passion, all trappings of civilization gone as he bent over her.

He buried himself to the hilt in one hard thrust. A choked cry escaped her lips, mingled pain and pleasure. Always when they'd made love before, he'd entered her slowly and carefully, letting her body stretch to accommodate his impressive girth. Now, his hips pistoned, driving his rock-hard shaft deeper with every thrust. She gasped for breath, her back arching under his assault, her hands fisting in the covers, holding on for dear life. She lifted her legs and clamped them around his hips. Mindless whimpers escaped her lips.

The headboard banged rhythmically against the wall. Tension built in her center, a meteoric rise she tried to control. Not yet! She wasn't ready for this to end yet!

Gray's hands slid to the back of her knees, powerful fingers urging her to release her hold. She would have done anything he wanted at that moment. He pulled her legs forward until her ankles rested on his shoulders. The change of position awakened new sensations, and no matter how hard she tried to hold it off, orgasm seized her by the throat. Her whole body arched into the pleasure, wringing a rapturous cry from deep within. Gray roared in triumph, exploding inside her as he continued to pump.

Releasing her legs, he collapsed on top of her, his body slick with sweat, his heart thudding so loud she could hear it. Or was that was her own heart she heard? She wrapped her arms around him, burying one hand in his sweat-dampened hair as she sucked in gasps of air. There were tears on her cheeks, though she didn't remember crying.

Gray raised his head and saw those tears drying on her cheeks. His eyes widened. "I hurt you!" he cried, his face filling with anguish.

"No!" Carolyn hastened to assure him. "It was just . . . powerful."

Carefully, he pulled out of her. She bit her lip at the fiery burn between her legs, but it wasn't an entirely unpleasant sensation. It was like he'd imprinted himself on her body, branded her as his in some primal way that should have offended her feminist sensibilities but didn't.

For a moment, he looked torn between the alternatives of pulling his jeans back up or taking them off entirely. He glanced at her face, then made the correct decision, letting them slide to the floor and then stepping out of them, along with his shoes. Sitting up gingerly, Carolyn finished unbuttoning her shirt, then tossed it and her bra aside as Gray pulled back the covers. She started to get up so she could get into the bed, but Gray swept her into his arms and laid her down.

When he slipped into the bed beside her, she curled herself into his arms, laying her head on his chest and twining her legs with his. The drumbeat of his heart under her head soothed her raw nerves and she played absently with the sparse hair on his chest.

"Are you sure I didn't hurt you?" he asked, his voice hoarse and tentative.

She pressed a kiss against his chest, savoring the salt of his skin. "Not in any way I feel inclined to complain about." She folded her hands on his chest, then rested her chin on them, smiling up into his face. He'd always been a good lover, reveling in her pleasure as much as in his own. But he'd always been so terribly gentle, knowing that he was particularly well-endowed, and she was a small woman. She'd appreciated the care he took with her, but every once in a while she'd wished he would just let go of the reins. "You were magnificent," she told him, and to her surprise he actually blushed. She laughed and laid her cheek against his chest once more.

"I was a rutting beast with not a hint of finesse, and you call that magnificent?" Laughter mellowed his voice, and she felt wrapped in a cocoon of warmth.

"There were times in the past when you were making love to me that I wished you would just fuck my brains out instead," she admitted.

He was silent for a moment before he spoke. "Why didn't you ever tell me?"

"You would have taken it as criticism, and that wasn't how I meant it."

"Jesus, Carolyn, was my ego really that fragile?"

She chose not to answer that one. Gray sighed and ran his fingers lightly through her hair. She practically purred with contentment. She traced his chest with her fingertips, finding a hardened nipple. She tweaked it experimentally, smiling at Gray's sharp intake of breath. She smiled even wider when she saw how the sheets were tented below his waist.

"Would you like me to fuck your brains out again?" he growled, his fingers tightening in her hair.

Something quivered in her center like the flap of butterfly wings. She found his other nipple and flicked her tongue over it. "Yes, please," she said as he groaned in pleasure.

Gray was happy to oblige.

* * *

MICHAEL FREEMAN HISSED IN pain, but Drake didn't slacken his grip. He didn't dare. The other three Guardians glared at him, newly roused fanaticism in their eyes. Michael shifted, trying no doubt to ease the pressure on his shoulder, which must be screaming in protest. Drake nudged his wrist a little higher up his back, and Michael held still.

"You'll pay for this," Tim Carter snarled, his hands clenching and unclenching at his sides.

"Yeah, yeah," Drake said, and the blandness of his voice made the Guardians even angrier. Drake bared his own fangs, dangerously close to Michael's throat, and the Three Musketeers refrained from charging him. "Now get your car over here." A pedestrian passed by their little gathering, but Drake turned the mortal's attention away from the violence before his eyes.

Carter hurried down the street to get the car and Drake eased a little of the pressure on Michael's arm. The poor kid was shaking, from fear, from grief, from impotent fury. "I'm sorry about Thomas," Drake said in a murmur so low only Michael could hear it. "I didn't kill him, and don't want to hurt you either." Not surprisingly, Michael didn't respond. When Carter pulled the car up to the curb, Drake motioned for the others to get in before him. After another round of resentful glares and snarls, they obeyed.

Drake couldn't really keep his grip on Michael's arm while getting into the car. He shifted so that his forearm pressed tightly against the Guardian's throat. Michael instinctively reached up and grabbed at the arm that pressed against his windpipe.

"Let go," Drake said quietly. "I can break your neck with one quick move if I want to." Michael's hands dropped back to his sides, and Drake maneuvered him into the car. "We're going to Eli's," Drake informed Carter.

Carter met his glance in the rearview mirror. "Eli's not going to take your side against us!"

Drake shrugged as best he could while retaining his choke hold. "Let's go ask him, shall we?"

The car started, and Drake allowed himself to relax just a little. None of the Guardians seemed to realize that Drake was not the only vampire on the scene when they arrived, which meant Gray had a good chance of escaping. For now. But Eli's control over his Guardians was slipping, and Drake had the sinking feeling that things were going to get worse. Much worse.

Something wet dripped onto his forearm, and Drake realized Michael was silently crying for his dead brother. He cursed under his breath, wishing he didn't have to make an intolerable situation worse. However, it had been quite clear from the moment the four Guardians had burst into the house that they were not prepared to listen to reason. Grabbing one as a hostage was the easiest way to make sure no one got hurt, and Michael had come at him first.

Carter called Eli during the drive over, so by the time they arrived at the house, the gate was standing open. Eli was waiting for them by the front door when they pulled up. Trusting that Eli could keep the Guardians contained, if not exactly controlled, Drake released Michael's neck. "Sorry about that," he said, pushing the door open and pretending not to notice the kid swiping at his eyes.

Michael was far enough gone that when he stumbled out of the car, he reached out to steady himself by putting his bare hand on the open door. He yelped in pain, snatching his hand away and sticking it under his arm. It was a testament to how enraged the Guardians had been that they'd risked the dangers of an automobile to hurry to the scene—it was so easy to carelessly brush against the exposed, iron-laden steel and gain a nasty burn.

"Thomas is dead!" Carter proclaimed loudly, though he had already conveyed this fact on the phone. Michael flinched, and Drake wished the asshole had had more tact. "What are you going to do about it, Eli?" Carter continued.

Eli's eyes looked old and tired suddenly, but he spoke in his habitual calm tone. "Let's all go inside. It's cold out here."

But Carter shook his head. "I'm not going anywhere with *him!*" He jerked a thumb at Drake. His flunkies murmured agreement, though Michael stood still and quiet, perhaps in shock.

"As you wish," Eli said, then turned to Drake. "Come inside." Drake started forward, and the Guardians grumbled loudly. Eli swept them with a commanding glance, but it didn't still their grumbling. "You should at least come in and get that hand tended to, Michael," Eli continued.

"We can take care of his hand, you heartless bastard!" Carter spat. "You're protecting a Killer! That's not what the Guardians are about, Eli."

Eli snorted. "I founded the Guardians, Tim. I know perfectly well what they're about, and it's *not* about killing anyone they merely suspect of wrongdoing."

"He was at the scene!"

"Thomas called me!" Drake retorted. "He sounded

panicked, and the line went dead before he finished. I was *trying* to help him."

He might as well have been speaking to stones for all they listened—except for Michael, who frowned like he might actually be considering Drake's words. He, who had the most understandable cause to be reacting with pure emotion, seemed still to have a spark of intelligence in him.

"I want to hear the rest of it," he said, but his three companions were unmoved.

"If you want to sit down with your brother's killer, then you can do it alone!" Carter said, stomping over to his car and jerking the door open. The other two followed his lead. Carter slammed his door and started the car, giving Michael a long stare before realizing he wasn't coming.

The tires shrieked, filling the air with the reek of burning rubber. The car roared down the driveway and out the gates. Michael stared after it for a moment, then mounted the short flight of steps up to the porch where Drake and Eli stood. He regarded Drake with flat, dead eyes.

"If I find out you killed my brother, I'll find a way to kill you. I don't care how much older or how much stronger you are. I'll find a way, and it won't be quick."

Drake nodded an acknowledgment, but he was only being . . . polite. If he *had* killed Thomas Freeman, and if he'd thought Michael capable of making good on his threat, then the young fool would have just signed his execution order.

Realizing it could be quite some time before he stepped out again, Drake entered Eli's house.

15

CAROLYN EMERGED FROM AN extra-hot, extra-steamy shower feeling relaxed and languid, despite the lingering soreness between her legs. A smile played about the corners of her mouth as she cleared the steam from the mirror and toweled her hair. That had been some of the best sex she'd ever had, though admittedly her experience was scant with anyone but Gray. She hoped the rooms adjoining theirs were empty—or that the occupants were very sound sleepers.

She pushed open the bathroom door and padded quietly into the room. Not that it mattered if she was quiet. She knew from experience how soundly Gray slept during the daytime. The bedside clock declared it was ten, and hints of sunlight glimmered around the edges of the heavy drapes. Gray was buried under the covers, only a few stray locks of black hair peeking out from underneath. Naked, she sat on the bed beside him, running her hand over the solid muscles of his hip and thigh, wishing she could touch him skin to skin instead of through the layers of covers.

Gray was out cold, giving no hint that he felt her caress. She sighed. It was going to be a long, long day if she was just going to sit here keeping watch.

Reminding herself that she didn't have to be quiet,

she picked up the phone and dialed Hannah's apartment. Hannah answered on the third ring.

"Hey, girl," Hannah said. "You still with Dracula?"

Carolyn rolled her eyes. "Yeah, I'm still with Gray. He's asleep now."

"Dead to the world, even."

"Ha ha ha. So, anyone come looking for him last night?"

"Matter of fact, I did have another nocturnal visitor."

"Jules?" Carolyn guessed.

"Yup. He seemed a little peeved."

"I'll bet. What did you tell him?"

"I tried to stonewall him at first, but that wasn't working. So I told him the truth—you and Gray left together and I didn't know where you went." She cleared her throat. "I, uh, blanked out for a while in the middle of everything. I assume he tried to pry the truth out of me with glamour, which means I probably mentioned you were at a hotel. Sorry."

"Don't worry about it. Do you have any idea how many hotels there are in the city?"

"No, but I suggest you move to a different one tonight. You should have called on your cell. Thanks to the wonders of caller ID, I now know where you are. It's probably better that I don't know."

"Thanks for the warning."

"So, what's the plan?"

"First, I want to stop by Gray's place and dust for fingerprints. Whoever let him out last night must have touched at least the front door and the basement door."

"Yeah, but he could have been wearing gloves."

"True," Carolyn agreed, "but he might not. Why should he be so cautious at Gray's place? It's not like he'd be expecting the CSU to be dusting for fingerprints there."

"Good point. So you going to leave Dracula alone in the room while you're gone?"

Carolyn grimaced at how easily Hannah read her

mind. "I was kinda wondering if you'd keep watch on him for a couple of hours."

Hannah's sigh was dramatic and long-suffering. "The things I'm willing to do out of friendship!"

Carolyn laughed. "My heart bleeds for you. Now move your butt."

"I'll be right over."

After hanging up, Carolyn got dressed, picking up Gray's clothes and folding them neatly. She wondered if the room smelled like sex. She sniffed, but if the scent lingered she was too acclimated to notice. No doubt she'd be subject to a lecture or two from Hannah if her best friend guessed what she'd been up to in the night.

* * *

HANNAH'S IDEA OF "RIGHT OVER" and Carolyn's differed by at least a half hour, so it was almost noon by the time Carolyn got going. This annoyed Carolyn, because she had to do her investigative work during the daytime and there were only so many hours of daylight available this deep in the winter. Hannah had given her an uncomfortably knowing look when she'd stepped into the room, but blessedly refrained from comment. Maybe that was just because Carolyn hurried out so fast.

She stopped by her house to pick up her digital camera, then took a cab to Gray's. She strode up to his door as if she belonged there, and no one gave her a second glance. Carefully, she twisted the doorknob with her gloved hand. As she'd expected, the door was unlocked—if the killer had removed Gray from the premises under glamour, she'd figured he wouldn't stop to lock the door on the way out. Much more convenient than having to break in again.

She pushed the door closed. She would dust the front doorknob only if she didn't find any other usable prints. She figured even in the live-and-let-live city someone might notice her dusting the front door and wonder what the hell she was doing.

The inside of the front door yielded a number of good, clear prints. She had Gray's fingerprint cards in her pocketbook and did her best to identify his prints by eyeballing them under a magnifying glass. She wasn't exactly what you'd call an expert, but she managed to eliminate some of them with a reasonable level of certainty. She photographed all of them anyway, then moved on to the basement door.

The fingerprint dust revealed another generous collection of prints. Again, she photographed them, then carefully lifted them, sticking them on the backs of index cards and documenting where exactly she'd found them.

The whole process took about two hours, and she had to fight against impatience. She'd never before been quite this aware of the ticking clock during an investigation, and the added pressure was distinctly unwelcome.

She hurried home to download the pictures onto her PC. Then she began the painstaking business of trying to separate the prints into groups. At a generous magnification on her screen, it was reasonably easy to identify which prints came from different fingers. Once again, she compared the prints to the ones she'd taken of Gray, dropping from consideration the ones that looked to be his.

From the remaining prints, she was able to discern at least two individuals based on nice, clear thumb prints. She brought up the file containing the pictures of the smudged partial she'd lifted from the envelope. Her pulse kicked up a notch when it seemed to match one of the thumb prints. Of course, it was only a partial, and she was doing her matching by the incredibly scientific method of eyeballing, but she still felt she had reason to suspect she was looking at the killer's print.

She glanced at the time on her computer's Start bar and cursed. It was already after five o'clock. The sun would be down soon. Hannah was probably going to read her the riot act for being gone so long. Carolyn quickly dialed the Marriott to assure her friend she wasn't dead.

"Where are you?" Hannah demanded the moment she answered the phone.

"At home, but I'm just about to leave."

"Yeah, well you'd better move it. Dracula isn't sleeping so soundly anymore."

"Will you stop calling him that?"

"Yeah, yeah, whatever. Just move your ass. I don't particularly want to be the one to explain to him where you are, okay?"

"I'm coming," Carolyn assured her. "I'll catch a cab and be there in fifteen minutes, tops." Which should be just in time to be there when Gray awoke, as long as she didn't have any trouble finding a cab. She hung up, then printed out a couple large-scale images of the suspicious prints. Hoping she wasn't forgetting anything in the sudden rush, she hurried to the door.

She pulled the door open, then swallowed a scream when she almost slammed into a dark figure blocking the doorway. A rakish hat shadowed his eyes, and a cashmere scarf wound around his nose and mouth, but she had no trouble recognizing Jules. Her heart leapt into her throat and she glanced up at the sky. The sun was still up, but barely.

"May I come in?" Jules asked, his voice muffled by the scarf.

She stammered and he stepped into her, forcing her to take a step backward. He took the door from her nerveless fingers, pushing it shut behind him, then pulled the scarf away from his nose and mouth. His handsome face held a sardonic smile and no hint of threat.

"How can you be awake right now?" she asked.

"The light bothers us less as we get older. I am one of the oldest vampires in the city, so I can venture forth a little before sunset." His smile turned from sardonic to smug. "I figured you wouldn't know that and I might be able to run into you."

Mentally, she recited a list of the foulest curses she'd ever heard in her years on the force. If Jules was the Banger, as Gray seemed to suspect—or hope—then she was dead. Careful not to make eye contact, she crossed her arms over her chest. It was supposed to look like a defensive posture, but she managed to snake her fingers into the gap of her coat. If she moved slowly enough and kept him distracted, maybe she could get to her gun.

"Gray didn't do it," she said.

Jules chuckled. "Your loyalty is touching. But the evidence is rather damning, my dear."

"Of course it is," she agreed, her fingers working their way steadily deeper into her coat. "If you're trying to frame someone, you do try to make the evidence look damning."

"How does he explain his presence at the scene of the crime?"

Her chin started to lift almost of its own accord. She closed her eyes and fought the pull of his glamour. "He said someone came to his house and hit him with a very powerful glamour. He thinks *you* might be that someone."

Another chuckle, tinged perhaps with a touch of bitterness. "Yes, he would try to point the finger in my direction. *Trou d'cul.*"

"I was at his house today. I dusted the basement door for fingerprints, and I found a couple I couldn't identify. They weren't Gray's."

"And?"

"And one of them seems to match a print I lifted off

the envelope that threatening note came in. It wasn't
Gray's," she repeated. If Gray's suspicion was correct
and Jules was the Banger, no doubt she was well on the
way to getting herself killed. But though the man was
unquestionably a jerk, her gut told her he wasn't the
killer. "Would you be willing to give me your thumb
print?"

Jules hesitated for a long moment, and her pulse
rose another notch. She risked a quick glace at his face
and saw the furrow of puzzled concentration between
his brows. Then he seemed to come to a decision.

"I will give you a thumb print if you will take me to
Gray."

"No deal," she answered immediately. "You've already tried and convicted him in your mind, and I already know you can overpower him."

"Your mysterious fingerprint has created a shadow
of a doubt. I'm willing to withhold judgment for the
time being."

"How generous of you. No deal."

He sighed. "You don't understand. I can *make* you
take me to him. Instead, I'm asking politely, and offering you something in return."

She shut her eyes tightly. "You can't make me do
anything as long as my eyes are closed." Her fingers
brushed the butt of her gun, but her triumph was short
lived when Jules's hand closed around her wrist.

"How long do you think you can resist the pull?" he
asked, and the compulsion to open her eyes became almost overpowering. "I have time."

A thin sheen of perspiration broke out on her face
and she bit her lip hard.

"This isn't necessary," Jules continued. "I give you
my word that I won't harm him unless there is absolute
proof he is the Banger."

"And I should trust your word?"

"When you know you have no alternative, yes."

She let out a long, slow breath, knowing he was right. Hoping she wasn't condemning Gray, she opened her eyes.

*   *   *

GRAY STRETCHED, SLOWLY AND thoroughly. His muscles were pleasantly stiff from his . . . exertions last night, and he had the vampire equivalent to the morning hard-on. Would Carolyn be up for another go? He smiled and pushed the covers away from his face.

The smile vanished when he saw Hannah sitting cross-legged on the other bed. She held a hand up over her eyes.

"Please don't get up," she said, snickering.

He shifted his position under the covers, hoping she hadn't noticed his boner. "What are you doing here?"

She dropped her hand away from her eyes. "Gee, Gray, I'm glad you appreciate me spending several hours of my life standing guard over you so you wouldn't get burned to a crisp by the sunlight. Your gratitude just gets me right here." She thumped her breastbone.

"Enough with the dramatics! You know what I mean."

Hannah wrinkled her pert little nose. "Carolyn Mathers, girl detective, is doing a little crime-scene investigation. I talked to her not too long ago, and she's on her way." Her eyes darted to the clock then slid quickly away. It didn't take a genius to catch the worry on her face.

Gray cursed himself for a fool. Why had he thought Carolyn would stay out of trouble while he slept? Surely he should know better by now. "Turn your back or close your eyes or something." He grabbed the edge of the covers and threw them back without waiting to see if Hannah obeyed. His clothes lay neatly folded on a chair. He snatched his briefs from the top of the pile and pulled them on.

"Nice ass," Hannah commented as he grabbed his jeans.

He glanced over his shoulder to see her watching him. Once upon a time, this would have embarrassed him. Now he was just annoyed. "Weren't you the one who wanted me to stay under the covers so you wouldn't be traumatized for life by seeing me naked?" He stepped into his jeans.

"You moved so fast I didn't have time to look away. Besides, you should know better than to expect me to follow any orders you bark my way."

He shook his head in exasperation, but arguing with Hannah was a losing battle. He stuck his arms into his shirt.

"Uh, don't you want to shower before you go out in public?" Hannah asked. Her nose wrinkled, though he wasn't sure she knew she was doing it.

He supposed he smelled like sex, but right now he didn't care in the least. "I'll shower when I know Carolyn's all right. Your face is an open book, Hannah, and I know you're worried about her. So tell me where she was when she called and we'll go meet her." He started to button his shirt.

Hannah shook her head. "She was going to get a taxi. If we go charging out into the night, she'll probably show up here the moment we leave. Just hang tight. She probably just had trouble finding a cab."

Hannah's words made sense, though Gray hated to admit it. He ran his hands through his hair, combing out some of the worst of the tangles. His feet were still bare, his shirt only half buttoned, when he heard the sound of a card-key sliding into the lock. Hannah heard it too and quickly ran to the door to take off the deadbolt.

Gray's heart lurched with relief when Carolyn stepped into the room. Then it almost came to a stop when Jules stepped in behind her. Carolyn was chewing her lip furiously, a pinched, strained look on her face. Jules wore his habitual smirk as he stepped around her and took off his hat and coat. He left the cashmere scarf draped around his neck, and Gray had visions of grabbing both ends and pulling tight.

Jules plopped down in one of the chairs and folded his hands over his belly, making himself quite at home. At least he hadn't gone straight for Gray's jugular.

"Sorry, Gray," Carolyn said sheepishly. "Apparently, he's up and around before sunset. I didn't know."

Gray blinked and took another good look at his nemesis. "I didn't know that either."

The smug smile on Jules's face made Gray want to punch him, but of course he knew better.

"He's not the Banger, Gray," Carolyn said, drawing his attention away from Jules.

"How did you determine that?"

"I checked his fingerprints, and they don't match the print on the envelope."

"But we don't know for sure the print on the envelope is the Banger's."

"Well I found one that looks suspiciously close to a match on the door to your basement. I don't think that's a coincidence."

Gray sat on the edge of his rumpled bed, wondering how close Carolyn was to solving the case. Could it really be so simple as checking fingerprints?

"Of course," Jules said, "we know that Drake touched that door also, so we have to make certain the mysterious print isn't his."

"Did he make it out all right last night?" Gray asked, figuring Jules would know all the details.

"Yeah. He's at Eli's, and will be for the foreseeable future. Things are kind of going to hell. But I'm sure I can get you his fingerprints so we can officially eliminate him as a suspect." He turned his gaze to Hannah. "Hannah, my dear, I suggest you rent yourself a room in this lovely establishment. I'm not the only one who can connect you to Carolyn and from her to Gray. I don't think it's safe for you to go home."

"Oh, peachy!"

"My apologies," he said, and to Gray's shock he sounded almost sincere. "I've shared too much information with the masses, but I never expected . . ."

"Never expected what?" Gray prompted.

Jules sighed. "Never expected things to get so out of hand." He met Gray's eyes, and his lips pursed like he was eating a lemon. A very bitter one. "Now that I see others acting like I did, leaping to conclusions without proof or consideration . . ." He shrugged and let the words trail off.

"This reconciliation thing is very touching," Hannah said, "but I think I'm going to go reserve a room so I can barf in the privacy of my own bathroom." She hopped off the bed and headed for the door. "Don't anyone do anything important until I get back," she called over her shoulder.

For a moment, all three of them stared at the closed door. As far as Gray was concerned, Hannah was a loose cannon. How much did she hate him? Enough to go to her house and wait for the Guardians to find her?

Carolyn seemed to read his thoughts. "She didn't have to stand guard over you all day," she said. "She talks big, but she's really a pussycat."

Gray snorted and Jules laughed. "More like a battle-scarred alley cat," Gray said, earning him a dirty look from Carolyn.

The mood in the room shifted subtly. Gray's shoulders tensed in anticipation as he asked the question that burned in his chest. "So," he said, turning to Jules. "Are you here to take me in or kill me or what?"

"Pick the right answer, Jules," Carolyn said, drawing her gun and aiming it squarely at his chest. As soon as she took aim, she cast her eyes downward.

Jules laughed, a sound that once again grated against Gray's nerves. "You would need perfect aim to kill me with a shot to the chest," he said. "You'd have a greater chance of success if you aimed at my head."

Gray could almost hear Carolyn grinding her teeth at the condescending mockery in the prick's voice. "Your head's a mighty small target," she snapped. "Maybe a shot to the chest wouldn't kill you immediately, but I'm betting it would still hurt. And I'm betting the pain would be distracting enough that I could get off a kill shot." Jules no longer looked so amused. "If I feel any hint that you're using glamour against me, or if I see any hint that you're using it against Gray, I *will* shoot you."

Jules sucked in a quick, startled breath, then looked at Gray with fear in his eyes. For the space of one heartbeat, Gray thought about doing just what Jules feared he would—pretend to be affected by glamour. But much as he despised the prick, he wasn't going to stoop to what amounted to murder, and he certainly wasn't going to put Carolyn in the position of pulling the trigger.

Feeling for the first time like he was in control of a situation involving Jules, Gray smiled. "Checkmate."

"*Enculé,*" Jules snarled, but the pallor of his face weakened his venom.

"Gray, this is no time to gloat," Carolyn chided.

"Sorry," he said, not meaning it.

Jules leaned back in his chair and crossed his ankles. Tension still tightened his jaw, but from the calculating look on his face Gray guessed he'd regained some of his composure.

"Your loyalty is admirable, Carolyn, but do you have any idea what you're protecting with such ferocity?" Jules asked, raising an inquisitive eyebrow.

Gray's stomach dipped as he realized what a dreadful mistake it had been to gloat. "Shut up, Jules!"

"What's the matter, Gray? Afraid of what I might say? Afraid I might tell her the whole, ugly truth about you?"

Gray's throat tightened with panic, and though he wanted to tell Jules to shut up again, he couldn't get a sound out. He must have looked as panicked as he was, for Jules laughed his mocking laugh again. Then he turned to Carolyn.

"You may put down your weapon. I'm not here to kill anyone. You've raised sufficient doubt in my mind that he's the Banger and I won't act unless I'm sure. As I've told you before."

Her laughter held no hint of amusement. "Yes, but before you were trying to talk me into bringing you here, so your claims were highly suspect. I'm not going to lie to you, Jules: I still don't trust you." The gun still pointed unwaveringly at his chest.

"And I still don't trust Gray, so I suppose we're at an impasse. However, I would really like to know whose print was on that envelope, so with your permission I would like to track down Drake and confirm it isn't his."

"You don't believe it is," Gray said.

Jules shook his head. "No. I don't trust him any more than I trust you, but even *I* have to admit last night's tableau was too contrived. Someone worked very hard to make the two of you look bad. Even if you're both as bad as I think you are, there's another party at work here."

"All right," Carolyn said. "Go get me Drake's fingerprints. Then we'll figure out where we go from there. But move slowly."

Jules raised his hands and splayed his fingers as he rose carefully from his chair. "I would suggest none of you leave this hotel tonight. You should be safe here, but I very much doubt that would be true if you ventured out into the streets." He picked up his coat and hat, moving slowly as ordered. Carolyn was watching him through her peripheral vision, the gun following his movement. He paused with his hand on the door, turning to look over his shoulder with an evil grin.

"Make sure you convince Gray to tell you what he's been hiding from you. Maybe then you'll understand why I hold him in such contempt." He slipped out the door before Gray or Carolyn could respond.

Slowly, Carolyn lowered the gun, then reholstered it. She let out a deep breath and shook her head. "Sorry about that, Gray," she said. "I had no idea he could be out and about before sunset. He ambushed me at my place, and I had no choice but to bring him here."

Gray rubbed his face, though the last remnants of sleep had left him long ago. "It's not your fault," he assured her, dreading what was going to come next.

A tense, waiting silence filled the room. Gray rubbed his palms up and down his pants legs, betraying his nerves. Carolyn slipped her shoes off and crossed her legs under her on the bed.

"Don't leave it hanging over your head, Gray," she said, her voice soft and full of sympathy he didn't deserve. "Just tell me whatever it is Jules says I should know. No doubt he'll tell me himself if you don't, and he'll put the worst possible spin on it."

Gray nodded, knowing that was true. That didn't make it any easier for him to tell her. He sprang to his feet, too agitated to hold still. Pacing the length of the small room, he forced the words out of his mouth.

"The woman who transformed me, Kate Henshaw. She was a very old vampire. Very powerful. She'd managed to live in Philly for a century or more without the Guardians ever guessing she was here. I guess she got arrogant, thinking she could outwit them forever, so she decided to make a fledgling. Me." He licked his lips nervously and continued to pace.

"I think her idea was to create an army of fledglings, all loyal to her, who could take down the Guardians and make Philly a safe place for Killers to live and hunt. I was her first project.

"Of course, for me to be of any use to her, I had to become a Killer myself. She knew perfectly well when she took me that it wasn't something that would come naturally to me." He heard the bitterness that had crept into his voice but saw no reason to try to hide it. "She could have taken some gang-banger or hardcore criminal who would have been perfectly happy to kill over and over again so he could be immortal. Instead, she chose me.

"She locked me in the basement and left me there as the hunger built and built in me. I fought it as best I could, but . . ." He shuddered, remembering those terrible days, when he could feel the beast growing stronger within him, threatening to overwhelm him. Worst of all, he remembered his moments of weakness, when the siren call of the beast had tempted him to give in voluntarily.

His life before then had been a monument to control, to civilization, to conformity. The beast whispered that he could throw it all away, drop all the restraints society forced upon him, live in a state of total selfishness, denying himself nothing that he wanted, repressing none of his feelings or desires.

"I lost track of time down there, but I must have been there at least a week, starving, when Kate brought a mortal to the house. He was a street person, stinking drunk and probably clinically insane on top of that. She locked him in the basement with me."

The torment had been like nothing he'd ever experienced in his life. The hunger was unbearable, and the guy was such a pathetic specimen of humanity. His clothes stank of alcohol and urine and body odor. He mumbled incessantly, words that made no sense, and when Gray tried to talk to him, he got no response. The stink and the constant mumbling grated on Gray's nerves, adding to the pressure of the hunger.

He watched his feet as he paced, unable to face Carolyn as he told her the rest. "She left him there with me for days as the hunger continued to build. Until one day—" His voice choked off, and for a moment he wasn't sure he could finish. He cleared his throat. "I killed him. I couldn't help myself."

And try as he might, he would never forget how heavenly the blood had tasted to him, nor could he forget the ecstasy he'd experienced as the wino's life force had slowly weakened, then died.

"The kill is addictive," he continued, still not looking at Carolyn. "Stronger than the strongest drug known to mankind. Some vampires are lost to it after the very first kill. Some can hold out longer. But the addiction is incurable. I think I'm very vulnerable. If I had killed one more time. . . ." He swallowed thickly.

"After the kill, Kate still kept me locked in the basement. She knew I wasn't addicted yet, so she kept me there and starved me some more. When she thought I was ready to break again, she brought me another mortal, a prostitute this time. A crack addict, with the most grating, offensive personality you could imagine. Kate knew I'd have a harder time restraining myself if she trapped me with the most distasteful mortals she could find.

"But she made a terrible mistake when she grabbed this prostitute. The Guardians were finally on to her, and they saw her grab the woman. They followed her back to the house. They killed her and freed me."

"And the prostitute?" Carolyn asked softly, her voice betraying nothing of how she was reacting to his confession.

"I bit her. I would have killed her, if Jules hadn't intervened." A grim smile stretched his lips. "I bit *him* too, so crazed I couldn't recognize a rescue attempt when it slapped me in the face. He wanted to kill me then and there, but the rest of the Guardians thought it was best to take me to Eli, their founder and leader. And Eli, as you can see, decided to let me live."

The story over, he sat back down in his chair, his breath whooshing out. He felt exhausted, body and soul. And he didn't dare raise his head from his hands to see how Carolyn was reacting to his tale.

16

THE SITUATION WAS EVEN worse than he'd originally thought, Jules realized when he stepped into Eli's meeting hall, a few minutes late as usual. Eli had called a meeting of all Guardians tonight, meaning to do his best to restore order. Many had come as requested, but there were some notable absences. Fletcher, for one. And the three Guardians who'd accompanied Michael Freeman on his witch hunt last night. Plus two more of the younger Guardians. Almost a third of their number missing. Drake wasn't there either, but Jules could sense another vampire presence lurking in the next room over. No doubt Eli had thought it best not to stir the pot.

Shaking his head, he took his seat and shared a look with Eli.

"Lest anyone worry that our missing brethren have come to harm," Eli said, "I've been informed that they cannot possibly take time out from their duties to attend a meeting when this Broad Street Banger is still out and about." That started a murmur amongst the gathered Guardians.

"Maybe they're right," Michael Freeman said, and many a head nodded in agreement.

Eli's eyes narrowed. "If you truly believe that scattered packs of blood-crazed vigilantes are more useful against this threat than an organized, controlled investigation, then feel free to leave at any time."

The temperature in the room seemed to dip, the murmuring voices quieting. An angry Eli was an intimidating sight, no doubt about it.

"Sorry," Michael said, hanging his head and looking terribly young. He'd only been twenty-two when he'd been transformed, and although he'd lived many years since then, his face remained a picture of boyish innocence.

Eli's shoulders relaxed, and the pall that had settled over the room lifted. For the moment. "We're all angry. We're all upset. And we all want to stop whoever's behind this. But the more fragmented we become, the more easily the killer will elude us."

"And the easier it will be for the killer to pick us off, if that's what he intends," Deirdre added, causing another stir.

Jules wished she'd kept that thought to herself, and from the look on Eli's face, the Founder did too.

Kelly Hammond, the oldest of the female Guardians, raised her hand like she thought she was in school. Then she proceeded to speak without awaiting an invitation. "But if we think the killer might be one of us, when we get together like this and share information, we're telling him everything he needs to know about how to avoid us!"

Jules wondered if the fingerprint Carolyn had found might not be the perfect way to exonerate the Guardians who were present and thereby heal the rift that was still widening. He opened his mouth to speak, then swallowed his words. Given the atmosphere of suspicion, he feared that by seeking to get the Guardians' fingerprints, he might draw suspicion upon himself. He could just hear one of the young hotheads accusing him of falsifying the fingerprints. No, before he made any move, he needed to discuss what he'd learned with Eli.

"I understand your objection," Eli said soothingly, "but I don't think our other options are terribly appealing. There's no evidence that the killer is one of us—just that the killer knows who we are. That could have happened any number of ways."

"So what do you suggest?" Kelly asked.

"I suggest we work on the assumption that the killer is not one of us and we start looking into others who have reason to know of our existence. Take a close look at any mortals you've befriended. They could have learned things you never intended them to learn, and they could have shared with the killer unknowingly. Remember, mortals have no way of knowing that they're talking to a vampire. Perhaps the killer hired a private investigator to help him figure out our identities."

Jules bit back a curse and hoped his thoughts weren't showing on his face. A private investigator. Like Carolyn Mathers? She'd been following Gray, supposedly, after that little incident with the mugger. Had she really been gathering intelligence, finding out the identities of the Guardians who were watching Gray? After all, Gray didn't know all of their identities, only the ones who'd interacted with him. If he was really the Banger, then he would have needed to identify as many Guardians as possible. Love made people do crazy things—like cover up for a cold-blooded killer.

Heart suddenly pounding, Jules held his tongue. He'd gone off half-cocked enough times lately. He wasn't going to do it again. So he'd wait until the gathering of Guardians broke up, and he'd get Drake's fingerprints. But once again, Gray James had jumped to the top of his suspect list, with Carolyn Mathers as his willing accomplice.

* * *

IT TOOK ALL CAROLYN'S self-control to sound normal when Hannah called to announce she was in a room two floors up. Her fingers dug into her palms. Gray's eyes bored into her, no doubt trying to guess her reaction. She couldn't read the expression on his face. There'd been anguish and horror and shame there when he'd told her of his first days as a vampire. Now he'd schooled his features into a mask of blandness. A defensive measure, she supposed.

"So, what's the next step?" Hannah asked brightly, oblivious to the turmoil that filled Carolyn's mind.

"Uh, I'm not sure," she said, trying to keep her mind focused on the conversation. If she let slip that something was wrong, Hannah would rush down to "help," and Carolyn didn't think she could take that right this minute. "Jules is going to try to get prints from Drake. Let's wait and see what he comes up with before we go plunging back into danger."

There was a telling silence on the other end of the line. "It's not like you to suggest we sit and wait."

"Sometimes that's the wisest option. I don't particularly want to go poking around when there are riled-up vampires roaming the streets, do you?"

Hannah sighed. "Okay, I guess you have a point. You want me to come down and keep you company?"

"No thanks, Hannah."

"Hmm." Carolyn could almost hear the gears in Hannah's mind turning. Luckily, her best friend decided to let things slide. "Call me if you need anything," she said.

"Will do."

With a deep breath, Carolyn hung up the phone and turned to face Gray. His lips twisted into a brittle smile that looked more like a grimace.

"So, are you measuring me for a nice big stake?" he asked.

She rolled her eyes. "Of course not." She shifted uncomfortably on the bed, wishing her feelings would just line up in an orderly fashion and make sense. "I won't tell you that story isn't . . . disturbing."

"That's one word for it." Gray rose from the chair he'd collapsed into when he'd finished talking. "Look, the reality is that there's no guarantee I can keep the beast under control at all times. That's why Jules is so suspicious of me. And that's why you should walk away and have nothing more to do with me."

Unbelievably, he started toward the door. Carolyn leapt to her feet, confusion replaced by fury. "Don't you dare!" she shouted, loud enough that his shoulders hunched as if he expected a blow.

"Carolyn—"

"No! Don't give me your pitiful excuses about how you have to keep yourself away to protect me. That's the decision you made three years ago. It sucked then, and it sucks now. Let me decide if I need protecting instead of making these goddamn unilateral decisions of yours." Her chest heaved with anger and pain and fear, for if she allowed him to walk out that door she doubted she'd ever see him again. She might not be entirely clear in her mind how she felt about him these days, but she knew she didn't want him to storm out of her life with all these issues unresolved.

He took a couple of steps closer, his eyes shining with a ferocious light. She had to fight an irrational urge to retreat.

"You know what I'm capable of," he growled, leaning into her space. "You've seen how much I've changed, you've seen my temper. Now you know what happens to me if I'm pushed to the extreme. You're better off without me."

God, she wanted to slap him and see if that would jiggle his common sense back into place. "You don't get to make that decision for me, asshole!" Fury heated her cheeks and she poked him in the chest to punctuate her point.

Gray's hand darted out and seized her wrist with what felt like bone-crushing force. She yelped, and his grip loosened immediately, though he didn't let go. The part of her mind that was still capable of rational thought noted that this "ferocious," "dangerous" man who thought he might be a danger to her had shied away from hurting her even when he was in high temper.

"What are you trying to do, Carolyn?" he asked, his voice softer now but no less fierce. Behind the anger in his eyes, she thought she glimpsed the shadow of a lost little boy, looking for someone to show him the way home. "Do you think you can save me? Surely you've learned from your work on the force that there are some people who are beyond help."

"You're not one of them!" she blurted, an instinctive outcry rather than a reasoned response.

He blinked a couple of times, and his Adam's apple bobbed. "You don't know that," he said, but he sounded less sure of himself.

"I know *you.*"

He flinched, finally letting go of her wrist. "You know the man I used to be. I keep telling you, he's dead."

"It's easier for you to think that, isn't it? Easier than to think—"

Gray raised his hand as if he were about to hit her. His eyes had gone wide and wild, but she knew a feint when she saw one. Even when he started to swing, she didn't flinch.

"Goddamnit!" he shouted as his hand fell back to his side, his shoulders heaving as he panted for breath. Sweat beaded his face and stained his T-shirt.

Carolyn reached out and put her palm against his chest, feeling the frantic hammering of his heart. "I don't scare easy, Gray. Remember?" She said it very softly, slowly sliding her hand up his sternum and over to his rigidly tight shoulder.

A strained laugh escaped him and he shook his head. "As far as I can tell, you don't scare at all."

She wouldn't have gone that far herself, but if that's what Gray wanted to believe, at the moment she was happy to let him. Somehow, in the midst of all the shouting, she'd figured out that his revelation didn't change anything. Whatever Kate Henshaw had made him do all those years ago, he was no longer under her power. And no matter how uncomfortable he was with his new, more volatile self, he had much more self-control than he gave himself credit for.

She almost smiled when it occurred to her that in a way, he seemed more human now, when he was capable of having a world-class temper tantrum, than he had in the old days when he refused to raise his voice.

Gray sucked in a quick, pleasured breath when she squeezed the tight knot she found between his shoulder and his neck. Wordlessly, she guided him to the bed and urged him to sit down. Then she climbed onto the bed behind him and started to work his shoulders in earnest. He sighed in pleasure, the muscles relaxing under her hands.

Her fingers kneaded the nape of his neck, brushing away damp tendrils of his silky hair. He made a sound almost like a purr, and she smiled. Sliding her hands down his back, she leaned forward and pressed her lips against his nape. His purr turned into a moan as she tasted the salty skin with the tip of her tongue. She pulled his T-shirt from his pants and slipped her hands inside, her fingers exploring his well-muscled back while she continued to lick and nibble around his neck. Her lips brushed over his pulse point, and she could feel the renewed throbbing of his heart.

Gray started to turn, no doubt to grab her and pull her into his arms.

"No you don't," she said, her hands bracing against his back to keep him still. Her words might have been a tad indistinct, seeing as his earlobe was between her teeth at the time, but he seemed to get the message.

At her urging, he raised his arms, letting her draw the T-shirt off over his head. She kissed her way down his spine, loving the taste of him, loving his little gasps of pleasure, loving the way his fingers dug into the edge of the bed to keep him from turning around.

"You're killing me," he complained breathlessly.

She chuckled. "Just you wait," she warned, and he groaned. She figured she'd given his back enough attention for now. "Why don't you lie down and make yourself comfortable?" she said, moving out of the way so he could comply.

He looked at her, a wolfish grin on his face. "The only way I can make myself comfortable is to bury myself inside you. Now."

His words shot a bolt of desire through her entire body, but she wasn't ready to give up control yet. She smiled at him. "Lie down."

He stuck out his lower lip in an exaggerated pout. She leaned forward and took his lip between her teeth, giving it a little suck before letting go. His eyes glittered as he lay back on the bed, folding his arms and resting his head on his hands. She could only describe his smile as smug.

She flattened both her hands on the middle of his chest, rubbing up and down his sternum, enjoying the texture of his skin, the firmness of his muscles beneath. His eyes slid closed and he sighed in quiet contentment.

But quiet contentment wasn't what Carolyn was aiming for. She leaned over and planted a soft kiss in the center of his chest. Her fingers brushed over his nipples, which pebbled at her touch. When her kisses started heading in that direction, he sucked in a sharp breath of desire and pulled his hands out from behind his head. She flicked his already hardened nipple with her tongue and his back arched under her. She played with his nipple, using teeth and tongue and lips, until he squirmed desperately beneath her and buried his hands in her hair.

"Carolyn, please," he begged, his voice so breathless she could barely make out the words.

She chuckled and raised her head, checking out the impressive bulge in his pants. "That looks uncomfortable," she said, meeting his heavy-lidded eyes.

"Only you can make it better."

His words made her heart constrict in a strange way, but she refused to let her tumultuous emotions overwhelm her. Instead she smiled and trailed a finger up the length of him, so hot and hard and tempting under the heavy denim of his jeans. He reached down to open the button, but she quickly grabbed his wrists.

"Uh-uh," she said. "Let *me* do that."

He growled low in his throat. "Then hurry up." His chest rose and fell with shortened breaths, and when he opened his eyes wide enough she saw that they were almost black with desire.

"Patience is a virtue," she chided, but she popped the button loose anyway. He let his hands fall away to lie clenched into fists beside him. Slowly, she dragged his zipper down. His hips lifted in an attempt to increase the pressure of her hand against his erection, but she moved with him, keeping the touch as light as possible.

When she slid her fingers into his jeans and rubbed lightly against him, only the thin cotton of his briefs separating skin from heated skin, he practically jumped off the bed. Under her hand, his erection pulsed. His fists clenched even more tightly beside him, until the knuckles turned white. His eyes were screwed shut, his face glowing with sweat. Carolyn smiled faintly. For a man who supposedly had no control over his primal urges, he was doing an impressive job of holding still for her sensual torture.

She pulled on the waistband of his jeans and he eagerly lifted his hips to let her pull them off. For a moment, she considered leaving his briefs on and teasing him further through the layer of cotton, but she wasn't sure she could stand that herself. She wanted to feel him naked under her fingers, wanted to see his cock bob and twitch with every new sensation.

Gray opened his eyes again when she'd maneuvered his briefs off. His lips pulled away from his teeth in an expression between a wolfish smile and a grimace. His tongue played dangerously with the point of one fang. It was a threat, of sorts, but Carolyn was not intimidated. She licked her lips.

"Behave," she told him, and he groaned in pleasured anguish.

She turned her attention to his erection, newly released from its confinement. Heavily flushed, it jutted stiffly upward, then seemed to swell even more under her fascinated gaze. With a touch as light as butterfly wings, she traced the length of it from base to tip, drawing a deep-throated moan from Gray's throat. A drop of moisture glistened on his crown and she touched her finger to it. His hips jolted upward and she decided he had earned a firmer, more gratifying touch.

"Oh God, Carolyn," he gasped when she closed her hand around the thick shaft and squeezed.

She dragged her hand slowly up his length, squeezing and pulling the skin taut as he writhed and tried to thrust. Her delicate hand was too small to fully encircle his girth, so she added her other hand to the effort, moving with deliberate slowness despite his growing desperation.

"Please," he moaned. But though he writhed and begged for release, he made no move to take charge. The powerful predator lay yielding on the bed, ceding the control he so cherished.

Carolyn bent over him, pushing his legs apart so she could prop her elbow between them. The scent of his arousal, the sight of his flushed and swollen cock, almost shattered her own self-control and she pressed her legs tightly together. This slow seduction was too much fun—she wasn't ready to end it yet.

She flicked her tongue over his crown, and she thought for one moment she'd pushed him beyond his endurance. His hands dug into her shoulders and his breath wheezed in and out of his chest. But though his hands and body quivered in conflict, he made no further move to make her stop.

There was no way she could take that impressive specimen of manhood fully into her mouth, so she settled for tasting him with her tongue, exploring each throbbing vein. Her fingers sought his balls and found them clenched tightly. The touch provoked a choked curse, and she realized he couldn't hold out much longer.

Although she hated the necessity, Carolyn had to let go of him so she could wriggle out of her jeans and panties. He started to sit up, but once again she stopped him, pressing firmly on his chest. She was running the show this time, and she was going to finish the way she'd started.

She straddled him, letting his erection nestle among her damp curls. His back arched again as he tried to create more friction. She shuddered at the feel of him gliding over her most sensitive flesh. He reached up and started unbuttoning her blouse. She decided to let him as she moved slowly up and down the length of him. Matching groans of pleasure escaped both their mouths, and they smiled at each other in the midst of the sensual haze. Gray found the clasp of her bra and snapped it open. When his hands cupped around her breasts, she realized *she* couldn't wait any longer.

"Carolyn," he breathed as she grabbed the base of his shaft to hold him steady. The pads of his thumbs traced delicious circles around her nipples, each stroke making something clench in her core.

Slowly, she lowered herself onto him. His erection was so hard it might as well have been marble, and despite his size he slipped easily inside her. His hips thrust upward, the sweet friction so good it brought tears to her eyes. She wanted this to last forever, wanted to forget all the issues and troubles that lay between them, wanted to forget their tenuous future. If she could just live in the now, and make the now stretch out forever.

Clenching her inner muscles, she lifted up as slowly as she'd lowered herself until only his crown remained inside. His moan now sounded more like a wail, and his hips lifted desperately in an effort to keep himself buried. And yet still he allowed her to lead, resisted what must have been a nearly overpowering desire to flip her onto her back and pound into her.

Her downfall came when he slid his hand from her breast down her belly, then plunged his fingers between her legs. With unnerving accuracy, he found the swollen bud of her arousal. When his fingers toyed with it, her careful restraint shattered and suddenly she couldn't get him deep enough within her. He thrust upward, and she met him stroke for stroke as his wicked fingers teased and coaxed. She planted her hands on his chest, giving herself better leverage, feeling the pounding rhythm of his heart. She looked into his night-black eyes, watched the pleasure gathering behind them as her own climax inexorably approached.

With a guttural cry, she broke. The spasms seized her whole body, waves upon waves of bliss shaking her to her core. She heard Gray's matching cry, felt his body surge upward, every muscle straining. His pleasure only served to heighten her own, and for a moment she saw stars before her eyes.

When the spasms finally ceased, her muscles were too loose and sated to hold her up any longer. She collapsed on top of him, resting her ear against his chest and listening to the drumbeat of his heart. Sweat drenched her body and she gasped for air.

The tears hit her from out of nowhere, her defenses

too shattered to hold them off. A sob tore from her throat and the floodgates opened. Her rational mind tried to reel her emotions back in, but it was too late.

She loved him, damn it! And he was a *vampire*. He'd killed someone.

And he'd left her.

Gray's arms wrapped around her, and if he found her childish sobs odd or out of place, he didn't show it. He pressed her head firmly against his chest, his lips feathering over her hair as he gently rocked her and murmured soothing endearments.

17

GRAY LEANED BACK IN his chair, folding his hands over his belly as he watched Carolyn sleep. She looked mind-numbingly beautiful, lying there naked amongst the tangle of sheets, her hair tousled, her inviting lips slightly parted. Despite how thoroughly she had pleasured him not so very long ago, he hardened painfully. He'd never felt tempted to complain about their sex life when they were engaged, but man! He hadn't known how much better it could be.

He had pulled his jeans back on when he'd slipped out of bed, and now he had to readjust himself within them. He wanted her again. Badly. But she needed to get some sleep, so he did his best to restrain himself. The pangs of desire were no doubt made worse by his hunger. If he'd kept to his regular feeding schedule, he would have fed last night. He had to make sure he fed tomorrow night. No doubt Jules could be persuaded to bring him one of those dreaded green bottles, despite his antipathy.

Carolyn shifted on the bed, the sheets sliding away enough to reveal the swell of her breast. Gray's heart constricted with longing. God, what he would give to turn back the clock three years, to have a second chance to make her his wife! What a shallow, callous fool he'd been back then, not to recognize how lucky he was to have her. Even before he'd been bitten, he'd been in danger of driving her away with his insistence that she quit her job.

He sighed heavily, pain and regret making his chest ache.

How long did they have before he would have to disappear from her life once more? For the time being, their fates were inexorably twined together, but when the Banger was caught and the threat was gone . . . Carolyn needed to move on with her life. Even if she really *were* safe with him, how could such a relationship survive? He couldn't be with her in the daytime, and he couldn't ask her to change her life around to be with him in the night. They would have only the few stolen hours between sunset and her bedtime, and though at first she would probably stay up too late and make herself miserable from lack of sleep, eventually she would realize that they were not meant to be.

It would tear his heart out afresh to lose her now. If he allowed himself to hope for something he could never have, it would kill him.

Unable to sit still, he rose from his chair and crossed to the bed. Using just a hint of glamour so he wouldn't awaken her, he straightened out the sheets and tucked them under her chin. Then he brushed a gentle kiss across those tempting lips and told himself not to think about what tomorrow might bring.

* * *

CAROLYN WAS GOING POSITIVELY stir-crazy. When she'd awakened this morning, she'd called to check the messages on her home answering machine. She had a message from Ted, her contact at the fingerprint lab. To her disappointment, but not surprise, there'd been no match for the partial thumb print on the envelope.

Ever since that, Carolyn had been pacing the suddenly cramped-feeling hotel room, trying to figure out her next step. Gray was no more than a man-shaped lump under the covers, and Hannah had gone to her house to pack a bag, so there wasn't even anyone here she could bounce ideas off of. The only good news was that Jules had left Drake's fingerprints for her at the reception desk, and she was able to eliminate Drake from the suspect list.

Why was the Banger so careful to avoid leaving fingerprints at the scenes of his kills if his fingerprints weren't on file? With his glamour, surely he didn't fear being *arrested*. Carolyn couldn't help thinking his fear was of being *identified*. Of course, just because his fingerprints weren't in the AFIS database didn't mean they weren't on file somewhere. Chewing her lip, she continued to pace. Where else might his fingerprints be on file?

Carolyn wished Hannah would hurry up and get back to the hotel. Her best friend and business partner had also promised to bring Carolyn's laptop, printer, and scanner. The hotel had broadband access, and Carolyn's fingers were just itching for the Internet.

Finally, at ten-thirty, Hannah made her grand entrance, her arms full of computer equipment. Together, they set everything up. Carolyn wondered if the silence that hovered over them when they worked could be considered companionable, or whether it was just tense. Hannah obviously knew Carolyn and Gray were sleeping together. She hadn't voiced any disapproval, but it wasn't hard to read on her face. Carolyn wasn't about to explain herself, not even to Hannah.

"So," Hannah said, when everything was hooked up and Carolyn booted up the computer, "if it's okay with you, I'd like to get a little work done today. I brought my computer too, and I have some research to do. If I leave, will you promise not to go haring off without me if you find something?"

Carolyn smiled. "I promise not to go haring off without *telling* you if I find something. After all, if I leave I'll need someone to keep watch."

Hannah's pretty face scrunched in displeasure. "When did I volunteer to be a baby-sitter?"

"Hannah . . ."

Hannah sighed dramatically. "I know, I know. If you need me to, I'll stand guard. But if you leave this hotel room alone, then you're going to have to check in with me every hour. And you'll have to promise to be back long before sunset."

"Yes, mom. Now go on upstairs. Get some work done. And don't worry about me."

Hannah gave her a penetrating look. Carolyn stiffened, bracing herself for whatever her best friend was going to say. But Hannah shook her head and restrained herself. Her eyes said quite clearly that she had no intention of not worrying, but thankfully she beat a strategic retreat.

Carolyn hit the Web and started searching for possible fingerprint repositories. The more she searched, the more her heart sank. The list was intimidating, and she didn't know how she could possibly narrow it down. There were a surprisingly large number of businesses that fingerprinted their employees. There were fingerprints of children, to help find them if they were lost. Fingerprints of military personnel, of FBI-wannabes, even some of medical professionals.

None of these repositories was public record, of course, which meant if she wanted to examine them she would have to come up with a convincing pretext. And she'd probably have to have a different pretext for each source. If she didn't whittle the damned list down, it would take her forever and a day to conduct her investigation. Too bad she knew diddly-squat about the Banger, other than that he was a male, a vampire, and a Killer. No personal details, and she didn't even have a profile for him. You needed a body of knowledge for comparison to create a profile, and she didn't have a body of knowledge about killer vampires!

But then again, maybe she *did* know something. Gray had said that vampires got stronger as they got older. And all the evidence pointed to the Banger being very, very strong, which no doubt meant he was quite old. Carolyn wasn't sure just how old was "old" for a vampire, but the more she thought of it, the more she suspected it meant too old to be in any of the current fingerprint databases. Perhaps what she really needed was to find historical data, perhaps some kind of fingerprint archive.

She surfed the Web some more, and the results at first were disappointing. Fingerprints had been taken as far back as the early 1900s, when the army had started fingerprinting its soldiers. But the chances that any of these fingerprints still existed a hundred years or so later seemed slim, and the chances she could gain access to them if they did, even slimmer.

She was about to take a break in an effort to calm the frustration when something caught her eye. Each time she'd come up with a list of search results, she'd done a screen print, knowing from experience that after hours of surfing it could be really hard to remember where she'd seen a particular link that she hadn't yet examined. At the bottom of one of those pages of screen shots was something that looked like it might actually be a public-access fingerprint repository.

Carolyn typed in the Web address for a company called Origins. The Flash intro displayed a series of images of artwork, each followed by a fingerprint image with a name written beneath it. When the home page opened, she was amazed at what she saw.

The founders of Origins were a pair of art historians who had frequently been consulted to verify the authenticity of newly discovered works by well-known painters. They'd done their best to authenticate the works based on traditional methods, but had then hit on an exciting concept—what if somewhere on the paintings, you could find a fingerprint you could match to the artist's?

At first blush, it sounded far-fetched to Carolyn, but the owners of Origins claimed to have had success with the technique. Paintings had often been handled extensively since they were originally created, but occasionally the artist's prints survived. Whenever they had a chance, Origins tested paintings for prints. When they found the same prints repeatedly on paintings by the same artist, they considered it a strong possibility that the prints belonged to the artist. Origins had built an impressive collection of artists' fingerprints—mostly of more modern artists, to be sure, but "modern" in the art world was a relative term. They'd also gathered a large number of collectors' prints, a necessary step toward eliminating those prints that *didn't* belong to the artist.

What had started as an experiment and a hobby had turned into a business and expanded. Origins worked with museums around the world, as well as with private collectors, authenticating paintings and even identifying those who once owned them.

Surely she wouldn't be so lucky as to find a match there. And yet . . . To Carolyn's mind, it seemed like the Banger feared being identified by his fingerprints, and he seemed to be very old. Here was a database of historical fingerprints. So, might the Banger be an old, wealthy vampire who had once collected art?

Only one way to find out.

* * *

FOUR HOURS AND FOUR hundred dollars later, Carolyn was obsessively checking her e-mail for the results. She'd told the nice lady she'd called at Origins—Ellen Hadley—that she was trying to authenticate a painting she'd inherited from her grandmother. Her grandmother had claimed it was by a famous artist, but Carolyn couldn't remember the name of the artist, and could find no signature on the painting.

Ellen was a little taken aback that Carolyn had already lifted a print—supposedly from the inside of the glass that protected the painting—but she didn't seem to find it suspicious. Carolyn had promptly e-mailed a digital image of the partial print, and had paid a premium to expedite the search. If Ellen's time estimate was anywhere near accurate, the results should be arriving any time now.

Hannah had come downstairs to keep Carolyn company during the tense wait. When Carolyn checked her e-mail for the umpteenth time, Hannah clucked her tongue.

"Relax already. You know this is a long shot."

Carolyn shrugged and tried to relax as her friend suggested. "Maybe it's wishful thinking, but somehow I feel convinced I'm on the right track. I feel it here," she said, thumping the middle of her chest.

"Uh-huh," Hannah replied, sounding entirely unconvinced.

All right, so maybe it *was* crazy. But knowing that didn't change the way Carolyn felt, and she wished Origins would just hurry up and give her the answer one way or another.

It was almost four o'clock when her computer announced a piece of incoming mail. Carolyn's heart leapt into her throat, and she shared a nervous look with Hannah. When she saw that the e-mail was from Origins, her pulse accelerated even more.

Holding her breath, she double-clicked the message.

Hannah was leaning over her shoulder to see, and Carolyn heard her friend's startled gasp.

The fingerprint appeared to belong to a man named Archibald Montgomery. Born 1865. Died 1902. Ellen was sad to report that Montgomery wasn't the artist, but instead a filthy-rich collector of Impressionist paintings. He'd had neither wife nor children when he'd died, and his estate had passed to a distant cousin who'd sold everything at a spectacular auction.

But apparently, he hadn't really died.

Hannah cleared her throat. "Of course, this ID is based on only a partial print, and a smudgy one at that. We can't be certain—"

"What are the chances that our partial would match someone who supposedly died more than a hundred years ago when we're hunting a vampire, and it would be nothing but a coincidence?" Hannah had no answer for that.

Carolyn sent a quick thank-you to Ellen, then immediately began searching for information about Archibald Montgomery.

He wasn't famous enough to warrant tons of Web pages, but after an hour or so of searching, Carolyn found another interesting fact about him that practically cemented his place on top of the suspect list. While he had officially been declared dead in 1902, he'd actually disappeared mysteriously in 1899. Was that the year he'd become vampire? Another interesting tidbit—when the cousin had sold the estate, he'd claimed that much of Archibald's money had gone missing.

By now, even Hannah was grudgingly convinced that they'd found their man. The question remained, how could they put their knowledge to good use? Carolyn chewed her lip as she stared at her computer screen and thought furiously. Hannah hoisted herself onto the desk beside the computer, her legs swinging freely, and appeared to do the same.

Another idea entered Carolyn's mind, and she quickly typed in the Web address for the Philadelphia Department of Records.

"Onto something, Sherlock?" Hannah asked.

"I don't know. Maybe this is a little nuts, but . . . Gray said Kate Henshaw was still living in the same house she'd lived in as a mortal. He said he thought she found that comforting. What if Archibald Montgomery is still living in the same house?"

Hannah's nose wrinkled. "That seems unlikely. Rich people in his day could afford mansions they'd never be able to support in this modern age. If the house still exists, it's probably been made into a museum or fancy condos or something."

"Hmm, maybe. But filthy rich people also tended to own *lots* of property." She navigated the Records site until she found the page she wanted, one she'd stumbled on accidentally on one of her long-ago skip traces.

Hannah hopped off the desk and came to peer over her shoulder once more. "Historical data?"

Carolyn nodded. "Believe it or not, they have scanned records of transfers of deeds, dating back to the 1600s."

Hannah's eyes widened. "No shit?"

The scanned images were laid out in various folders, with a folder for Grantor, a folder for Grantee, and a folder for Miscellaneous. The Grantor and Grantee folders had subfolders to let you narrow your search by century and by decade. However, the Miscellaneous folder had the information she *really* wanted. Unfortunately, that information was not so clearly sorted. Worse, it wasn't searchable. She double-clicked on the first folder, then brought up the first image—of an old handwritten document, listing the grantor and grantee names, as well as the address of the property in question. Smiling smugly, Carolyn magnified the view so Hannah could see.

Hannah groaned. "Crap. I know where you're going to go with this, don't I? You're going to suggest that we go through these lists page by page, line by line, hoping to see Archibald Montgomery's name, aren't you?"

Carolyn nodded, grinning at Hannah's sour expression. "Good, old-fashioned detective work. And we don't even have to leave the privacy of our own hotel rooms to do it." Hannah's expression soured even more. "Come on, Hannah. At least we don't have to do this in the bowels of some musty old courthouse!"

"I'm jumping for joy." She sighed. "But I suppose I have to help you. I'll go up to my own room and log in. You start at the top of the list, I'll start at the bottom, and we'll meet in the middle."

"Sounds like a plan," Carolyn agreed cheerfully.

Not quite so cheerful, Hannah trudged to the door. "Behave yourself while I'm gone," she said. She didn't wait for Carolyn's answer.

* * *

GRAY YAWNED AND PUSHED the covers away, rubbing at the grit in his eyes. Carolyn was sitting with her back to him at the desk, peering at her computer's screen, hunched slightly forward.

"Good morning," she said without turning.

He smiled and sat up straight. "Good evening." He wanted to grab her immediately and tumble her beneath him onto the bed. But she seemed very much absorbed in whatever she was doing, so he restrained himself. "Whatcha doing?" he asked, slipping out of bed.

She finally turned to look at him. Her eyes fastened immediately on his burgeoning erection, but though her cheeks flushed with desire, she made no move to act upon it.

"The Banger is one Archibald Montgomery, who supposedly died in 1902."

He sank down onto the bed once more, all thoughts of sex momentarily taking a backseat. Carolyn explained her day's activity.

He shouldn't have been so amazed. The woman was incredible, an amazing detective with an indomitable will, and that so-frequently annoying stubbornness of hers served her well in her chosen career.

"So now," she continued, "I'm making myself go blind by poring over scanned images of transfers of deeds. Real exciting, let me tell you. And I'll have you know Hannah is upstairs doing the same thing, so you be nice the next time she comes down."

He snorted. "I've been nice to her! She's the one who's constantly trying to do me bodily harm."

Carolyn laughed at that and turned back to her work. "Why don't you take a shower, then you can help me look. My eyes are starting to glaze over." She pointed to the armoire. "I brought you a change of clothes."

His first impulse was to scold her for setting foot anywhere near his house, but he swallowed it. There was no reason to think it was dangerous to go there during the day, and she'd obviously come to no harm. "Thanks," he said, and though he suspected there might have been a slight edge to his voice he seemed to have avoided offending her.

The appeal of a hot shower was undeniable, but Gray couldn't help noticing the heightening of his senses—the first warning signs of his growing hunger. The scents of the room were dizzying, and very faintly under the sound of the mouse-clicks, he heard the beat of Carolyn's heart. He took a deep, calming breath and picked up the phone.

He hated to be dependent on Jules for anything, and he hated to have Carolyn in the room when he made his request, but perhaps it was for the best. She needed to remember what he was, and that he was dangerous.

Jules answered on the second ring, his tone of voice changing the moment Gray identified himself.

"Well," Jules said, "you're about the last person I expected to hear from."

"And you're about the last person I wanted to call, but . . ." The words stuck in his craw, and he waited for Jules to start mocking him for his reticence.

"You're hungry," Jules said, and there was no mockery in his voice.

"Yes," Gray forced himself to say. "I should have fed night before last, but as you know things kind of got out of hand."

"Control yourself or you can bet I'll make you sorry you were ever born."

Gray suppressed a surge of temper. *Don't cuss out the man you're asking a favor of,* he reminded himself. "Don't worry, I'm not desperate. Besides, Carolyn has some very interesting information to share, so I've decided to let her live." She looked over her shoulder and raised an eyebrow at him. He mouthed the name "Jules" and she nodded sagely.

"I'll be right over," Jules said, then hung up without awaiting an acknowledgment.

* * *

Twenty minutes later, Jules arrived, bringing with him a thermos. "Pre-mixed," he said as he stepped into the room, slapping the thermos against Gray's chest. The liquid inside sloshed, and Gray couldn't help his grimace of distaste. "You're welcome," Jules said over his shoulder as he strode into the room and made himself at home.

Gray put the thermos down and glared at the older vampire. "Do *you* actually like this stuff?"

Jules raised one shoulder but didn't respond. "You said you'd found something?"

Gray smiled a secret, proud smile watching Jules's face as Carolyn explained how she'd discovered the name of their adversary. Jules's mouth dropped open, and a furrow appeared between his brows.

"Archibald Montgomery?" he whispered. "Where

have I heard that name before?" He cocked his head, his face a study in concentration. His eyes widened when he figured it out.

"Who is he?" Gray asked.

Jules let out a deep breath. "*Archer* Montgomery. Eli told me about him. He was a Guardian once, long ago. He and Eli had a . . . falling out. Eli kicked him out of the Guardians. Supposedly, it was a relatively amicable parting of ways, considering the circumstances. But Montgomery's had a lot of time to stew about it. I can imagine how he'd come to hate the Guardians."

"This means that the Banger isn't a Guardian after all," Carolyn said. "Surely Eli would recognize him."

Jules frowned. "You're right, of course. But he *must* have help from the inside. There's no way he could know who the Guardians are a century after he left them."

"At this point, I think we'll have more luck trying to track down Montgomery than figuring out who the insider is. Gray told me that vampires like to live in familiar surroundings. I'm going over old records, trying to find out where Montgomery lived when he became vampire."

Jules nodded. "Good idea. I'll check with Eli to see where he lived when he was a Guardian, but that probably wasn't his mortal residence. Usually you can't return to your mortal residence until everyone you'd known in mortal life has moved away or died."

"I'll let you know if I find any addresses associated with him during his mortal life," Carolyn said.

Jules nodded. "Yes, do. But of course, you won't do anything foolish like try to confront him yourself, right? He's old and a Killer, a hugely dangerous combination."

Carolyn's lips thinned in annoyance. "No, I'm not an idiot."

"Glad to hear it. Now, I've got something I have to take care of. Let me know as soon as you find anything."

Gray ground his teeth as Jules made his exit. Where did the prick get off ordering Carolyn around like that? "What if *Jules* is Archibald Montgomery?" he asked. "His little story could be a complete fabrication, and we could be feeding information to the enemy."

Carolyn turned to give him a pointed look. "If he were the Banger, and we'd discovered his name, you can bet we'd be dead by now."

Gray couldn't argue her logic, though he wanted to. Perhaps his nerves would feel a little less raw if he fed. Wrinkling his nose, he picked up the thermos, twisting off the top. The scent of blood stirred his appetite while his stomach simultaneously flipped over in distaste. Would he never get used to this?

Someone knocked on the door.

"I'll get it," Gray said, hastily putting the top back on the thermos. He should just drink the shit and get it over with, but he couldn't help being grateful for the reprieve.

He'd assumed that it would be either Jules or Hannah, so when he opened the door and saw Deirdre standing there, he came to an abrupt halt.

"Dee?" he said, frowning. "What are you doing here?" And how had she found him?

Deirdre smiled up at him. And the glamour struck him like a speeding truck.

18

"PLEASE JUST TRUST ME on this," Jules told David, his forty-two-year-old grandson. "It's not safe to bring your father back to the city yet."

David sighed and leaned back in his chair, his handsome face tight with strain. "Dad wakes up in the middle of the night screaming because he doesn't recognize his surroundings. My daughters are wondering when they're going to go back to school. Maria nags me night and day for an explanation for why we can't come home. What do you expect me to tell her? Am I supposed to tell my wife we're living in exile because my grandfather the vampire thinks we might be targets for the Broad Street Banger?"

Jules ground his teeth in frustration. He hated this. But until the Banger was caught and killed, it was just too dangerous for his son or his grandson to remain in the city. Courtney had already been killed because of her association with him; he wasn't going to start losing family members too! He felt like grabbing David by the scruff of the neck and giving him a violent shake for forcing this meeting between them. Jules's senses were on high alert, searching for any sign of a vampire stalking him, but just because he didn't sense anything didn't mean someone wasn't out there. And by meeting him, David was making a target of himself.

How many other Guardians had Jules counseled to sever all ties with their mortal lives? And why couldn't he do so himself? Even if the Guardians killed the Banger, Jules knew his son didn't have long to live. The man was eighty years old and suffered from Alzheimer's. How badly was it going to hurt to lose his only son to that dreaded disease?

"I'm sorry, David," Jules said. "I should never have intruded on your life. Then you wouldn't be in danger. But I can't turn back time, and I can't make the threat go away. Please go back out to the country and stay there until this is over." His cell phone beeped an urgent message, and Jules looked down to see that it was from Eli. "*Marde,*" he muttered under his breath. "I have to take this. Please—"

David held up a hand to silence him. "I'm going. My car is just over there." He pointed at the shiny blue Volvo. "As long as no one jumps me before I get in, I'll be safe, right? So go ahead and play bodyguard, Gramps."

Internally, Jules cringed at the anger in his grandson's voice, but he didn't let it show on his face as he answered the phone. "What's up, Eli?" he asked, keeping a careful eye on David as he got into his car and drove away.

"There's been another murder." Eli sounded exhausted, like he hadn't slept in three days.

"Who?"

"Frank LaBelle."

Jules let fly a stream of expletives in Québécois, not caring that Eli could understand him. LaBelle had been a troublemaker in the making, but still. . . .

"A stake through the heart, just like Thomas Freeman," Eli continued. He hesitated a moment. "There's more." Jules tensed at the warning tone in Eli's voice. "There was a note at the scene."

"Well, what did it say?" Jules prompted when Eli hesitated once again.

"I want you to promise to stay calm and rational."

"I'm not going to stay calm and rational if you don't finish what you started here, Eli. What does the note say?"

Jules could almost hear the Founder debating himself. Finally, Eli spoke. "The note says '*Vas chier*, Jules. You should have killed me when you had the chance.' It's supposedly signed by Gray James."

Adrenaline surged through his veins as Jules glanced at his watch. It had been two hours since he'd left Gray at the hotel room. Plenty of time for the bastard to run out and kill again! Maybe the whole Archibald Montgomery story was a load of crap, though Jules wondered how Gray could have known that name. But Carolyn had already proven herself a masterful detective. Maybe somehow she'd learned the story of Montgomery and Eli's falling out, and had fed the information to Gray. Just another red herring, amongst the many others.

"Are you staying calm and rational like I asked?"

"Hell no! Eli—"

"No, don't give me your list of reasons why you think he's guilty. I've heard them before. Just go check and see if he's in the hotel where you left him."

Jules shook his head. "He won't be."

"But maybe he will. You and I are the only ones who know where he's hiding. The Banger may have just screwed up, thinking we don't know where Gray is and can't check his alibi."

Reluctantly, Jules had to concede the point. "All right. I'll go back to the hotel and check it out. But if he's not there . . ."

"If he's not there, we'll deal with it, one way or another. But be careful. If he really is the Banger, then he can probably overpower you. Don't hunt him alone."

Jules resisted the urge to snap at the Founder, irritated that the old man found it necessary to deliver such an elementary warning. "Don't worry, Eli," he said in a relatively calm voice. "I'm not quite the hot-head you seem to think I am. I won't take him on alone. I'll call you from the hotel." He hung up the phone, already moving at a steady jog.

∗ ∗ ∗

GRAY BLINKED AND SHOOK his head to clear the fog from his brain. His eyes focused sluggishly and he swayed on his feet. A quiet, malicious laugh sent a chill down his spine and the world snapped back into focus.

He was standing in a barren room, surrounded by windowless walls of dull gray stone. A bare bulb shone dimly from the ceiling. A flight of wooden stairs led upward. Perched on the edge of those steps, Deirdre sat with her arms wrapped around her knees and a nasty smile on her beautiful face.

"Dee?" he said, his voice sounding as shaky and confused as he felt.

"Welcome back to the land of the living, Gray," she said, smiling more broadly.

A soft groan beside him told him that they were not alone, and he saw Carolyn sitting on the floor, her back against the wall, her head hanging halfway to her chest.

"Carolyn!" he cried, crossing the distance between them in a quick bound. He knelt beside her and seized her arms, his heart thudding against his breastbone in panic. She groaned again, but her eyes opened and she squinted up at him.

"Don't worry, Gray dear," Deirdre said. "She's un-harmed. The glamour just hit her a little hard is all."

Carolyn's eyes cleared and she took a deep breath. "I'm all right," she told him quietly, accepting his hand up.

Putting an arm around Carolyn's shoulders, Gray positioned himself between her and Deirdre, trying to make sense of things. "How did you find us?" he asked.

"You think that was hard? I followed Jules, of course. You're lucky half the Guardian population didn't find you or you'd have a stake through your heart by now."

"You mean to tell me I won't have a stake through my heart in the near future anyway?"

She sniffed daintily. "If I were going to kill you, I'd have done it already while you were . . . shall we say, indisposed? No, I have other plans for you."

Something ugly gleamed in her eyes, but Gray still felt confused. He shook his head. "You *can't* be the Banger. You don't have the proper . . . equipment."

She giggled. "Amazing how single-minded you and all the Guardians can be. Unfortunately, I don't feel like explaining everything to you just this moment. You'll just have to piece things together yourself, I'm afraid."

"You can explain why you've just kidnapped us at least."

"That I can do." Her smile became even uglier—malice, perhaps even madness, shining in her eyes. "You are now thoroughly screwed over, my friend. I've set up another lovely crime scene for you, and while you were under the influence, you wrote a particularly incriminating little note. If you set foot on the streets again, the Guardians will hunt you down and kill you. In the past, they would have tried to get to the bottom of things before taking such drastic action, but I've reduced them to a pack of mad dogs, ready to tear the throat out of anything that looks at them funny."

"Why?"

She laughed with what sounded like genuine amusement. "Damn, Gray. Are you that naive?" She controlled her mirth. "You might have noticed that Philadelphia is a hostile environment for a Killer. My choices were to move away—and hope the Guardians

never came after me—or to make the city more wel-
coming. As you no doubt realize, I can easily overpower a Guardian or two, but as long as Eli held the
society together and kept their efforts organized, I was
doomed. I wasn't stupid enough to think I could remain here and fly under their radar indefinitely, like
your poor Kate Henshaw. Now they're at each others'
throats, broken into warring factions and bands of useless vigilantes."

She was very proud of herself, her lips twisted into a
smirk, her eyes glowing with superiority. Gray hoped
he was doing a fair job of keeping his reactions to
himself—he didn't want to give her any satisfaction, if
he could help it.

"You still haven't answered my question—why
have you framed me?"

"Oh, just a little extra motivation."

"Motivation for what?" he demanded, his voice rising as he lost his cool despite his intentions. Carolyn
slipped her arm around his waist and gave him a warning squeeze. He tried to reel in his temper.

Deirdre stood, descending the stairs until she was
eye level with him. "To join me."

He blinked a few times as his brain tried to make
sense of that. What the hell . . . ?

"The Guardians are weak now," Dee continued, "but
it's still possible Eli can manage to pull them together
eventually. So far, I've been more than a match for
him, but I'm not so foolishly arrogant as to think I'm
unstoppable. No, I need my own army to help me take
him down, my anti-Guardians, so to speak. And you're
to be the first member."

Gray was beginning to follow her train of thought,
but he really didn't want to reach its conclusion. He
swallowed hard, his body tensing as his stomach
dipped.

"You've already taken the first step toward addiction," Deirdre said. "And once the addiction takes hold, there's no escaping it. You'll lose your humanity and become a Killer, as you were meant to be. All you have to do is take another step down the road."

Her eyes shifted to Carolyn, and Gray's heart seemed to stop. "No," he gasped.

"You're hungry, aren't you?" Deirdre asked in what was meant to be a seductive murmur. "I saw the thermos Jules brought you. You hadn't drunk it yet. How long has it been since you fed?"

Gray couldn't have spoken if he'd wanted to. Cold sweat bathed his face and body, and if it weren't for Carolyn's arm around his waist he might have collapsed to the floor, his knees felt so weak.

"Please," he choked. "Let Carolyn go, at least."

"I'm afraid I can't do that. She's been making quite a nuisance of herself. Last night, I overheard Jules when he asked Drake for his fingerprints. I figured that wasn't Jules's idea." She smirked. "Not that she was going to learn anything with her little game."

Neither Gray nor Carolyn saw fit to contradict Deirdre's assumption.

Deirdre's face softened, as did her voice, but there was no hint of mercy in her eyes. "I know it hurts right now. But once you give in, that pain will go away." She stepped closer. "You have no idea what the Guardians have deprived you of." Her voice dropped to a low, coaxing murmur. "You have no idea what it feels like to stop fighting the beast within, to let it take you, to let it fill you with power and strength!"

Gray lunged at her desperately, though his rational mind knew it was a hopeless and foolish effort. Deirdre dodged him easily and countered with a brutal jab to his kidney that stole all his breath. He collapsed to the floor, his teeth gritted against the pain. Carolyn knelt beside him, her face drawn with strain as she took his hand in silent moral support.

"The sooner you give in to the urge," Dee said, starting up the stairs, "the sooner your pain will end." And then she was gone, and he heard the distinctive sound of a key turning in a lock.

* * *

CAROLYN WAS VAGUELY AWARE of a current of fear that ran through her veins, but she had no intention of letting Gray see it. He stood still and tense, staring up at the doorway through which Deirdre had disappeared, his face stricken, a world of pain in his eyes. She let out the breath she'd been holding and approached him, putting a hand gently on his shoulder. He jerked away from her.

"Don't touch me!" he barked, a wild light flaring in his eyes.

"Easy, Gray," she said in her most soothing voice. "You're letting her screw with your head. You weren't anywhere near desperate before she brought us down here. She's just got you thinking about it, worrying about it. You're fine."

His hands clenched into fists at his sides, and his rapid breaths seemed to echo through the small room.

"Don't panic," Carolyn continued in the same tone. "Instead of worrying about what might happen, let's concentrate on trying to find a way out of here, okay?"

His Adam's apple bobbed as he swallowed hard. "You don't understand—"

"Yes, I do. But if you give in to panic now, then we'll never get out of here. It's a self-fulfilling prophecy. So take a deep breath, relax, and tell me if she's still in the house. You can sense her, right?"

For a moment, she thought he was going to argue with her, but then he took the deep breath she'd suggested and some of the wildness faded from his expression. There was still fear in his eyes, but at least he seemed to have controlled it. "How can you be so calm?" he asked. "*You're* the one who's in danger, and *I'm* the one who's panicking!"

She moved to him, and though he took one quick step backward, he halted his flight and let her put her arms around him for a quick, hard hug. "I trust you, Gray. You'll fight it with every drop of your will."

When she tried to end the hug, he held on, pressing her head against his chest, his fingers burrowing into her hair. "I'm so sorry, Carolyn. So sorry I got you involved in all this."

She pushed away and looked up into his eyes. "Don't be sorry. This isn't over yet, and it's possible my investigation could be the key to stopping the Banger."

Gray frowned and shook his head. "I have to admit I'm very confused. Deirdre *can't* be the Banger."

"But she's obviously his partner or accomplice."

"Yes, but she was acting as if this were all her plan."

Carolyn nodded. "She's still trying to cover for him. She's being cautious, in case by some chance we escape."

"Of course, she doesn't know we already know who the Banger is," Gray mused.

"Right. And let's keep it that way, shall we? If she doesn't realize how far we've come, she won't realize her danger."

Gray laughed, genuine mirth sparkling in his eyes. "Only you could claim *she's* in such great danger when you're locked in a room with a hungry vampire with questionable self-control."

She grinned at him. "Hey, I'm an optimist. But really, we aren't completely sunk yet. If Deirdre knew about Hannah, you can bet Hannah would be down here with us."

"Or dead," Gray agreed grimly.

"Right. And if she were dead, I suspect Deirdre would have gloated about it. So Hannah may still be able to locate us."

Gray shook his head. "Yeah, then she'd have to

convince Jules and company that the note Dee made me write was a fake, otherwise they'd just ignore her findings."

Carolyn smiled again. "Hannah can be quite persuasive. Now tell me, is Deirdre still in the house?"

He closed his eyes and a furrow appeared between his brows. He sighed, then opened his eyes. "Someone is. Don't know if it's Dee or her buddy the Banger."

"Well let's sit tight for a while then. We don't want them to hear our escape attempts."

Gray took a seat on the floor, his back against the wall, then beckoned for her to sit beside him. She did, resting her head against his shoulder and twining her fingers with his.

* * *

JULES USED THE KEY he'd conned out of the front desk clerk to let himself into Gray and Carolyn's room. Not surprisingly, it was empty. Fury burned through his veins, but he doused it. He'd promised Eli he wouldn't jump to conclusions. He frowned when he noticed Carolyn's pocketbook sitting on the floor, and his frown deepened when he saw her laptop still on. In his experience, women never went anywhere without their pocketbooks. He picked up the purse and searched through it. Her wallet was in there, containing her driver's license and her PI license, as well as a couple hundred dollars in twenties.

If she was Gray's accomplice and had helped him slip away, why wouldn't she have taken her purse—and her money—with her?

Jules checked out the laptop and saw the page of handwritten entries she'd left up on the screen. Why would she have taken her pretense of having found the identity of the culprit to the extreme of poring over these records if she already knew Gray was the killer?

Of course, there was always the chance that Carolyn

was an unwitting accomplice and that she'd been his dinner tonight. Jules grimaced at the thought, noticing the thermos he'd brought to Gray earlier in the evening. He picked it up and shook it, confirming that it was still full.

Conflicting instincts warred within him, his old enmity urging him to believe the hard evidence, while his more rational mind suggested the evidence had been badly overdone—just like it would have been if someone was attempting to frame Gray.

The phone rang, nearly startling Jules out of his skin. He picked up on the second ring, not speaking.

"Hello?" Hannah's voice asked from the other end of the line, sounding puzzled.

Jules sighed. "Hello, Hannah."

"Jules? Where's Carolyn?"

He wished he knew. "I think you'd better come down here," he said.

Hannah gave a gasp of dismay, and the phone went dead immediately.

* * *

GRAY SAT WITH HIS back against the wall, his eyes closed in concentration, as Carolyn examined the only possible exit from their prison—the door. He heard her up there jiggling the handle, but though she would usually be capable of picking a lock given enough time, she didn't have any equipment on her. She'd fashioned a primitive pick from the O-ring on her key chain, but said she needed something called a tension wrench to get the lock open. That didn't stop her from trying, of course.

The hunger stirred restlessly in his center, a feeling so unlike mortal hunger it was amazing they shared the same name. Even at this distance, he could hear the beat of Carolyn's heart, could smell the scent of her skin. With his eyes closed, he sensed her as a pocket of heat when he himself was freezing. He clasped his arms around his knees to stop himself from going to her.

It didn't matter what Deirdre thought—he would *never* join her. He might lose his humanity, or even his soul, but he refused to surrender to the fate she'd drawn out for him. If she made him hurt Carolyn, then he would dedicate his life, whatever remained of it, to making her pay.

He opened his eyes when he heard Carolyn descending the steps. Her face was grim, but still she showed no fear, despite the danger. An extraordinary woman, all around. Love and regret warred in his chest.

"No luck?" he asked as she came to sit beside him once more.

She shook her head. "It's a sturdy deadbolt. I'd suggest trying to break the door down, but there's no way to get any leverage or momentum on those stairs."

"Besides, I'm sure Dee would have guarded against it. The door's probably reinforced."

"I'm not giving up yet."

He chuckled, earning himself a dirty look. "Don't get mad at me," he said. "It's just that I never thought for a moment you were giving up."

Her frown eased into a wry smile and she leaned her head against his shoulder. He put his arm around her and rubbed his chin over the top of her head, wishing he could stop his ears against the throb of her pulse. She sighed and laid the palm of her hand against his chest.

"Do you have any idea how much I missed you for the three years you were gone?" she murmured.

He closed his eyes in pain, his arm tightening around her. He'd known when he'd walked out on her how badly he was going to hurt her. The decision had been mind-numbingly painful, and he'd hated to do it. But he'd honestly thought he'd had no choice. In fact, he *still* felt he'd done the right thing under the circumstances.

"Believe me, I missed you too," he said, restraining himself from qualifying the statement.

She snuggled closer. "No matter what happens, I'm very glad you came back into my life."

He gritted his teeth, once more restraining himself. Everything that had happened only served to validate his conviction that he had to stay out of Carolyn's life. No matter how much it hurt them both. But that wasn't a conversation to have now.

Her finger started tracing idle circles against his chest, and he sucked in a quick, startled breath. Desire surged through his veins, a wave of feeling more powerful than anything he'd felt before. He grabbed her hand to still it, but already his pulse was racing and he'd hardened painfully. His fangs pricked his lower lip.

Carolyn smelled of citrus shampoo, of floral perfume, and of aroused woman. The drumbeat of her heart filled his ears, and images of her lying naked beneath him filled his mind. His mouth went entirely dry and his body quivered with strain as he fought for control. The desire to rip her clothing from her body and bury himself within her was near overpowering, but he knew that if he gave in to his sexual urges he stood a terrible risk of giving in to his other urges as well. He could almost taste the strangely spicy tang of her blood in his mouth, the tantalizing, intoxicating flavor that would fill him with strength and power. Where the blood-and-milk concoction he drank to stay alive made his stomach revolt, the taste of pure human blood, hot from the vein . . .

He groaned and stuck his fist in his mouth, his hand visibly shaking. Carolyn moved away from him and said nothing, watching him with a neutral expression as he battled himself.

It seemed to take forever, but eventually he gained a

semblance of control. The fangs slowly receded, and
he was able to breathe normally again, though his body
was drenched in sweat as if from great physical exer-
tion. He might have thought Carolyn would be frightened now that she'd seen how thin a thread his control
hung on, but she smiled at him.

"I guess this isn't a good time for a roll in the hay,
huh?" she said.

For a moment, he had to fight back a resurgence of
desire, but then he was able to laugh and shake his
head. "You'd think by now I wouldn't be surprised by
you anymore, wouldn't you?"

Her face sobered. "I'm not afraid of you, Gray.
Whatever happens."

He shook his head. "You *should* be. Honey, if Dee
leaves us down here long enough, then it doesn't matter how hard I fight it. I won't be able to help myself."
His voice choked off in horror.

"I understand that," she said gently. "But you see, I
still love you, Gray. Even after all these years. Even after what's happened to you."

A lump formed in his throat, and he ached to return
her declaration with one of his own. But he'd didn't
dare. Their situation was grave indeed, but there was
still a chance that they could escape, that Hannah
would find this house and the Guardians would listen
to her and send a rescue party. If they did get out of
this, he *had* to keep Carolyn out of his life. Their current situation just served to underscore how dangerous
he was to her.

And so he let her declaration hang between them,
unanswered save by his aching heart.

19

DAWN WAS FAST APPROACHING, and Jules's eyes were gritty and heavy as he tried to focus on the glowing computer screen. Hannah sprawled over one of the beds, her heavy breaths proving that she was sound asleep. She'd come downstairs at around three in the morning with the addresses of two properties she'd found under Archibald Montgomery's name. Jules hadn't recognized the addresses but had called Eli to have him send someone to check them out. Eli had also checked out Montgomery's last known address, from his Guardian days, but the house had long since been demolished.

Hannah had dark circles under her eyes, and he'd suggested she get a few hours of sleep. She'd made a counter-suggestion, of the physically impossible kind, at which point he'd used his glamour to enforce his will. After all, he didn't want her missing an important listing just because she was too tired to see straight.

His own search had uncovered yet another property once owned by Montgomery, but until he heard back from Eli as to whether any of these addresses panned out, he wasn't going to stop looking. Now, however, it was time for him to head home for the day. He wasn't about to sleep unguarded in this hotel room!

Closing the folder he'd been searching through, he stretched and yawned. No doubt Hannah still hadn't had enough sleep, but he decided it would be ungentlemanly to leave the room without waking her. He rose and shook her shoulder gently. She awoke with a start, sitting straight up and looking momentarily disoriented. Then she narrowed her eyes at him.

"You glamoured me!" she accused.

He grinned. "I've never heard 'glamour' used as a verb."

"Asshole," she muttered, rubbing her eyes and shaking her head. "How long was I out?"

"About three hours. I'd advise you to sleep some more if I thought there were any chance you'd listen to me."

She cast a sour glance in his direction. "Thanks for refraining from giving me unwanted advice."

"I have to retire for the day," he said. "While you were sleeping, I found another address to pass by Eli, but I haven't heard any news yet. You'll keep looking, I presume?"

She slid off the bed, yawning again. "Yeah. And I promise, if I'm too tired to function, I'll quit for a while. This is my best friend we're talking about—I'm not going to take any stupid chances with her life."

Jules felt a twinge of unexpected pity. "Hannah, you have to accept the possibility that she may already be dead."

Hannah's face flushed bright red and her eyes flashed. "The hell I do!" she snapped. "I've never been Gray's biggest fan, but I've seen enough to know he's not a goddamned serial killer! And he would never hurt Carolyn."

Jules swallowed a protest and refrained from pointing out the flaws in Hannah's logic. Even if Gray *weren't* the Banger, the odds were that he and Carolyn had fallen victim to him. But if hope would allow Hannah to continue functioning, then he would not deny it to her. Whether Carolyn was alive or dead, the Banger was still out there, killing wantonly, and the faster they tracked him down, the better. Having someone on the Guardians' side who was capable of working the case during the daylight was an opportunity they needed to take full advantage of.

"Write down any addresses you find for Montgomery," Jules continued as if he hadn't heard Hannah's outburst. "I'll be back by sunset, and we'll check them all out, one by one."

Hannah held her hands up and bowed from the waist. "Yes, master."

Half irritated, half amused, he shook his head and left her to her own devices.

* * *

Gray lay down on the hard, cold floor, his hands crossed over his belly, his head resting in Carolyn's lap. Her fingers toyed with his hair, her touch oddly restful and soothing even though the hunger loomed. The only light in their cell came from the dim bulb hanging from the ceiling, but even so he could feel the languor of the approaching dawn in his limbs. Soon, he would sleep, and when he woke again, the hunger would have grown stronger.

"When I wake up in the evening," he said, his voice sounding smoky even to his own ears, "keep your distance."

"Gray—"

"No!" He forced his heavy eyes open. "It's going to be worse tonight. Keep your distance. Don't touch me, don't talk to me. Let me concentrate all my energy on fighting the hunger."

"All right," she said, her voice low and soothing. "Sleep now, Gray." Her fingers caressed his brow, and his eyes slid closed.

His mind slid away into the darkness, but not before he felt the phantom brush of her lips against his. And the warm, wet trickle of her tears.

* * *

JULES PRIED HIMSELF FROM his bed the moment he could string two thoughts together without falling asleep in between. His eyes still heavy with the need for sleep, he hastily pulled on some clothes and quaffed a meal of blood and milk. Swathed in his coat and hat and scarf, he made his way through the dying daylight to the Marriott. By the time he knocked on the door to Hannah's room, the sun was just beginning to set, and even the younger Guardians would now be waking.

Hannah looked positively haggard when she opened the door. Her room smelled strongly of coffee, and Jules guessed the tar-scented swill on the warmer was not the first pot she'd consumed during this long day.

"Any progress?" he asked.

She brushed her uncombed hair away from her face and nodded. "Yeah. I found three more addresses for him. I've been through all the folders. If he's still living where he was when he died . . ." She giggled, and Jules thought she might be on the verge of exhaustion-induced hysteria. She swallowed hard and bit her lip and somehow got herself under control. "If he's still in the same house, we have its address. We just have to figure out which one."

Together, they moved to the desk, where Hannah had scrawled the addresses she had found. Jules picked up the piece of paper. And froze when he read the list.

"What?" Hannah cried. "What is it?"

Jules put the paper down, his heart thudding painfully against his ribs. Damn it, they'd *known* there had to be someone on the inside. Someone who knew who all the Guardians were, and knew their plans and movements. Why had he and Eli insisted on believing the insider was male?

Jules pointed at the address. "We'll find Archibald Montgomery right here," he said, hating the sense of hurt betrayal that stabbed through him.

"What?" Hannah cried. "How do you know?"

"Because that's Deirdre MacPherson's house." Now that he thought about it, he realized how very easy it would have been for Deirdre to manipulate the situation from her position of "innocent" invulnerability. And he remembered how she'd subtly planted the seeds of dissension among the Guardians, with her innuendos and suggestions.

It was Deirdre who'd first voiced the opinion that the Banger had an in with the Guardians. She'd been telling nothing but the truth, but that suspicion had stirred the rising sense of distrust among a formerly unified society.

Hating that he had to do this, Jules picked up the phone to call Eli and tell him about Deirdre's betrayal.

* * *

IF THIS DIDN'T WORK, she was going to feel like the world's biggest idiot, Carolyn thought as she pulled her shirt back on. But hey, her choices were to sit around brooding helplessly all day while Gray slept, or to try any hare-brained escape plan that came to mind. She'd pick the hare-brained scheme any day. And so she set her teeth to the underside of her bra cup and ripped. She spit out a mouthful of thread and was pleased to see the faint metal gleam of the underwire already exposed. She widened the rip until she was able to pull the length of wire out.

When she'd examined the lock last night, Carolyn had determined that it was a standard pin-and-tumbler design, but though her stretched-out key ring wire would have made a perfectly decent pick, she still needed something to serve as a tension wrench, the element of a lock-picking kit that would actually turn the lock.

In a pin-and-tumbler design, pairs of pins passed through the lock and wedged into the housing. The right key would lift each of the top pins until they were lodged entirely inside the housing, allowing the tumbler to turn freely. The way to pick this kind of lock was to turn the tumbler as far as it could go—just a few millimeters—and then use the pick to coax the top pins up until they rested on the tiny ledge formed by the slight turn. If you could tell by sound and feel when you'd gotten the pins lifted into place, you could pick the lock.

The underwire from her bra was supposed to be flexible so it wouldn't bite into the skin—yeah, right!—but when she tested it out, she thought it might be just stiff enough to do the trick. The ends of the wire were covered in a rubbery coating, but by bending and twisting she was eventually able to snap one end off. Then she climbed the stairs and got down on her knees, peering at the daunting keyhole.

"Nothing ventured, nothing gained," she muttered as she poked the wire into the lock and tried to turn it. She smiled when she realized the wire was just stiff enough to make a passable tension wrench. She then inserted the wire from her key ring. Taking a deep breath, she closed her eyes to better concentrate all her attention on the feel of the pins inside the lock. She felt and heard the first pin lift into place, but the surge of adrenaline that small success triggered made her hand shake and she lost the pin.

"Damnation," she grumbled, then took another deep breath and tried again.

As time crawled by, she found that she had a relatively easy time with the first couple of pins, but keeping the pressure steady on the makeshift tension wrench was a bear. Its flexibility meant that if she moved the hand that was holding it even a little bit, the tumbler would move enough to dislodge any pins she'd managed to lift. By the time she gave herself permission to take a break for a while, her hands were shaking with frustration.

Three more times during that long morning and afternoon she knelt down before that lock and tried to coax it open. Some times she had more success than others, but each time she failed, she came closer to giving up. She told herself she'd give the lock one more go. Trying to relax as much as possible, she inserted the wires again. One by one, the pins lifted into place. She was so attuned to this lock by now that she no longer had any doubts as to when a pin had "clicked" into place.

Four pins gave in to her persistence. Perspiration coated her face as she tried to keep herself from getting too excited by her success. Just one more pin to go and she'd be able to open the door. She sucked in a couple of deep breaths, her arms aching from the strain of holding so terribly still. Gently, she wiggled the wire that was holding up the last pin.

When she felt and heard the click of the pin lifting into place, she held her breath. Maybe it had been just an illusion. Or wishful thinking. But when she increased the pressure on the "tension wrench," it turned in her hand and the deadbolt slid open with a gratifying thunk. She practically wept with relief.

If only it hadn't taken her so long! It was nearing six o'clock already, and Deirdre could be waking up any moment now, and for all she knew Montgomery was now in residence as well. Carolyn glanced at her watch, chewing her lower lip. Below her, Gray lay fast asleep on the floor of their cell. He would expect her to run for her life immediately, but she couldn't just leave him here. If there had been more hours of daylight left, she could have armed herself and tried to kill their captors, but if they were already stirring, she'd be doomed.

Carolyn hurried down the stairs and knelt before Gray, putting her hand on his shoulder and shaking him urgently.

"Gray? Wake up. We have to get out of here." He made a vague, incoherent sound of protest. She shook him harder. "Gray! I got the door open. Now come on, you're not completely unconscious. Move it!"

His eyes opened to slits, but he showed no inclination to move. He mumbled something and his eyes closed again.

Carolyn's heart thumped behind her breastbone, every nerve on high alert. Montgomery was an old vampire, and she'd already learned from Jules that older vampires could rouse themselves before the sun had set. How much longer did she have before the Banger awoke and cut off their retreat?

Gray remained a dead weight as she grabbed his arm and slung it over her shoulder. She shouted down her doubts as best she could as she dragged him toward the stairs. He grumbled some more and took some of his weight onto his legs, though his head still lolled. Holding his arm around her shoulder, she put her other arm around his waist and dragged herself up the first step.

Already her lungs were straining for air and her muscles were quivering with strain. Thin though he was, he outweighed her by at least fifty pounds. She was in decent shape, but she wasn't a bodybuilder or anything. Gritting her teeth against her muscles' protest, she forced herself up another step.

Despite being mostly still asleep, Gray tried to help, supporting a little of his own weight and lifting his feet from one step to the next. Halfway up, Carolyn had to stop for a rest, though she was terrified she wouldn't be able to start up again once she lost whatever slight momentum she'd gained. Gray almost fell down the stairs when she eased him into a sitting position. His eyes slid closed, and in frustration she slapped him across the face.

"Damn it, Gray! Wake up! Our lives depend on it."

He didn't open his eyes, but he nodded. "Soon," he said, or at least that's what she thought she heard.

"Now!" she insisted. She still needed more rest, but she was too conscious of the time ticking away to hold still for long. Slinging his arm around her shoulders again, she dragged him to his feet and climbed one more step.

The next few minutes went by in a blur of pain and exhaustion as she labored up one step after another. Gray helped more and more with each step as he slowly roused from his unnatural slumber. By the time they reached the top of the stairs, he was yawning and his eyes were open, though he still leaned against her for support.

"Hurry," she urged him as she reached to push the door open.

"Too late," Gray said, finally standing on his own power.

The door swung open, and Carolyn's heart sank. Standing in the doorway, smiling in malicious condescension, was a man she'd never seen before.

Too tired to think before she spoke, she said, "Archibald Montgomery, I presume?"

✳ ✳ ✳

JULES AND HIS MAKESHIFT raiding party watched Deirdre's house from the cover of one of the city's ubiquitous dark alleys. Jules tried to suppress his scowl, but the expression only deepened when Drake returned from his recon mission.

"I sensed three vampires in the house," he said, shaking his head as he, too, seemed to calculate the odds and find them lacking. "There's a window at the back of the house on the second floor that looks like it might be breachable, but we'd have to scale the wall to get there, and we'd only be able to get one man through the window at a time. If we attracted any attention to ourselves on the way in, the window would be a choke point and they'd be able to pick us off one at a time. Even with all of us attacking together, we'll be at a disadvantage. Perhaps we should have allowed the mortal to accompany us after all—she could have provided some distraction, at least."

Jules snorted. "Yeah, but it's *us* she would have distracted. The last thing we need is another helpless mortal to protect. This is going to be hard enough already." He'd been an idiot even to mention to Hannah that a rescue party was being organized. Even based on their admittedly slight acquaintance, he should have known she would insist on coming along to try to save her friend. It was a minor miracle that he'd gotten her to see sense without having to use glamour.

"Hard?" Michael Freeman complained. "This is beginning to seem like a suicide mission!"

Jules resisted the urge to snap at the youngster. Personally, he would have preferred that Eli kept the puppy at home, but considering what they were up against, he supposed the extra manpower was necessary.

Usually, when the Guardians needed to attack a Killer, they attacked in greater numbers, for the Killers were much stronger. However, right now many of the Guardians couldn't be trusted to heed Eli's call. And so Jules was stuck with an untried fledgling and a Killer he disliked as his partners.

"Anyone know why Eli wouldn't come himself?" Michael asked. "I mean, he's the most powerful vampire I've ever seen!"

"Eli doesn't leave the house," Jules answered. "Ever."

Michael's mouth dropped open. "Ever?" he repeated. "But why?"

Jules shook his head. "Never mind that. Keep your mind focused on the task at hand." Drake chuckled faintly, and Jules glared at him. Of course Drake knew the answer that Jules had avoided giving—"I don't know." No one knew why Eli remained in his self-imposed imprisonment, but Jules supposed it was something more than a whim, or the current situation would have drawn him out.

"So, what's your plan, fearless leader?" Drake asked, raising an eyebrow at Jules.

"We need a diversion," Jules answered, thinking furiously. "I can go to the door, and Dee will probably open for me. I've stopped by before, so she shouldn't get suspicious. But if the two of you were with me . . ."

"She'd slam the door in our faces, then she and Montgomery would batten down the hatches."

"And possibly use Carolyn as a hostage, assuming she's still alive."

"I understand the reasoning," Drake said, "but what's your *plan*?"

"I go to the door like I'm just here to discuss the Banger case. I keep Dee talking as long as possible, and you two try to get in from the back. Break a window if you have to, just make sure you can both get in. We need all three of us there and at the ready when she realizes the jig is up."

"Of course, she might not open the door," Drake said. "After all, she's not alone in there and if she lets you in, you might learn things she doesn't want you to learn."

But Jules shook his head. "She'll let me in. She's dead-set on framing Gray, isn't she? What better way than to make me the next Banger victim?"

"I don't like it. If she wants to make you the next victim, you could easily be dead before Michael and I find a way in."

"We'll just have to chance it," Jules said, smiling grimly. "Besides, I expect Deirdre thinks she's terribly clever for having fooled us for so long. Chances are if she has me in a position where she thinks she has the upper hand, she'll want to gloat a bit."

Drake and Michael didn't appear entirely convinced. However, neither of them professed to have a better plan, and so, hoping his plan wasn't going to get them all killed, Jules gave Drake and Michael five minutes to get into position at the back of the house, then crossed the street and rang the bell.

20

SO MUCH FOR KEEPING the bad guys from learning how much she knew, Carolyn thought, wishing she could swallow back the words as soon as they'd left her mouth. Montgomery smiled and bowed from the waist in a mockery of a polite greeting, but she hadn't missed the way his eyes widened in surprise at hearing his name on her lips.

At first glance, Carolyn would have said he looked quite ordinary. Of medium height and medium build and medium weight, he wouldn't warrant a second look if she passed him in the street. His hair had been prematurely thinning and going to gray when he'd "died," making his high forehead look even higher than it was, and his gently rounded cheeks lent his face an aura of innocence. His eyes, however, were far from innocent, a shockingly deep and cold shade of blue that glittered with malice.

"I can't tell you how pleased I am to make your acquaintance, my dear," the Banger said when he stood up straight. He reached out to her with the clear intention of touching her face.

Gray snarled and yanked her out of reach, which seemed to amuse the Banger to no end. His pudgy cheeks dimpled when he laughed, and if it weren't for those eyes he would have looked positively harmless.

"Such gallantry, Mr. James," he said, still laughing. "I can understand your desire to protect such a beautiful woman, but since you'll be killing her in the near future, the effort seems wasted." The dimples vanished, and he looked Carolyn up and down with blatant appreciation. She shuddered when he licked his lips. "Of course, she might prove an enjoyable diversion. Perhaps I should send you down to the basement by yourself, let your hunger build while I indulge my own appetites."

Gray stepped in front of her. "You'll have to kill me first!"

But Montgomery just laughed at Gray's bravado. "You think so?"

Carolyn saw that Gray was carefully avoiding Montgomery's gaze. And she saw that moment when Montgomery's glamour got to him anyway. Montgomery put a hand on Gray's shoulder and pushed him aside.

Carolyn's heart slammed in her throat and a trickle of cold sweat chilled the small of her back. She was unarmed, and she had none of Hannah's martial arts skills. Even if she did, she would be helpless before this creature, with his glamour and his strength. She shuddered as he licked his lips again, slowly and with exaggerated relish. He took a step toward her and it was all she could do not to retreat. He couldn't miss her terror—she wasn't a good enough actress to hide it entirely—but she would give him as little satisfaction as possible.

"What's the matter, Montgomery?" she asked, her voice shaking a bit despite her best efforts to sound sarcastic. "Can't find a woman to sleep with you willingly?"

He chuckled and bared his fangs. "Happens I prefer a little more excitement than I get with a willing woman."

She snorted. "Yeah, I bet it's real exciting to rape a

woman who's like a zombie because of the glamour. Must make you feel like a really big, powerful man."

His eyes narrowed, and Carolyn hoped she'd managed to irritate him a little. At least he hadn't trapped her with glamour yet. As long as her mind and body were still her own, she would hope she could find a way out of this.

"When one is willing to allow one's victims to be found," the Banger said, "one is well-advised to leave a minimum of evidence at the scene. Which leads me back to the question of how you knew my name."

Carolyn mentally cursed herself for letting that slip. He was dangerous and elusive enough when he thought he was completely safe from his pursuers. Now unless she could find some story to allay his suspicions, he'd be even more cautious, maybe even flee to a safer location, where he could go on killing with impunity.

"You're not as clever as you think," she told him, stalling for time.

He dropped all pretense at charm, freezing her to the marrow with the menace of his glare. "Careful what you say, my dear. I have refrained from satisfying some of my more outrageous appetites since I've come back to reclaim my city, but the Guardians are descending into chaos as we speak and I am free to indulge my every whim." His nostrils flared. "And believe me, you would not enjoy it if I indulged them with you."

Her nerves were stretched so taut the feminine giggle nearly startled Carolyn to death.

"Now, now, Archer darling," Deirdre said, coming up behind him and putting her hands on his shoulders, "it's not polite to play with your food."

His eyes crinkled, but he didn't quite smile as he covered one of her hands with his. "Gray's food, dearest, not mine. But your point is well taken."

Deirdre pressed her body up against his and then turned her attention to Carolyn, a faint smile on her lips. "Gray never stopped loving you, you know," she said.

Carolyn blinked, more than a little confused by the change of subject.

"I've been trying to win him over for years, and he used your memory like a suit of armor to hold me away. I knew once he had you in the flesh I'd never be able to get him on board without . . . extraordinary measures." She slipped out from under Montgomery's arm and came to stand mere inches away from Gray, who might have been a statue for all the life that shone in his eyes. Deirdre reached up and stroked his cheek, and it was all Carolyn could do not to snarl and pull him away as he had done when Montgomery had tried to touch her.

"He's spent three years in hell," Deirdre continued, and if Carolyn didn't know better she would have sworn there was a hint of compassion in her voice. "The Guardians have always treated him like dirt because—" She paused and furrowed her brow. "You do know that Gray has killed already, don't you?"

Carolyn didn't answer, but Deirdre shook her head as if it hardly mattered.

"Cut off from the life he once knew, unable to embrace his current life, constantly under surveillance . . . I don't know how he managed to tolerate it as long as he did. It's time for him to shake off the brainwashing and rise to his potential."

"Are you telling me you think he'd be happier if he were out there indiscriminately killing people?" Carolyn asked, unable to believe what she was hearing.

Deirdre smiled. "Don't knock it till you've tried it, lady. The rush is indescribable." She pouted. "If you really love him, you'll encourage him to stop fighting it, to let himself become what he's meant to be."

The weird thing was, Carolyn got the sense Deirdre actually believed what she was saying. "So you'd like him to be like your boyfriend the Banger here, raping and killing women without—"

Deirdre cut her off with a hiss. "Don't be ignorant!

Vampires are predators, just like lions and wolves and hawks. We kill to live, and we have as much right to live as mortals."

"Wolves don't rape their prey before killing them!"

Deirdre and Montgomery snorted in unison, but it was Montgomery who answered. "The Guardians try to teach that it is a sin to be what we are. They teach their fledglings to put everyone else's well-being above their own. Deirdre and I are merely existing as we were meant to exist. That we take pleasure out of our lives and our natures is not a source of shame!"

"But you don't have to live that way," Carolyn said. "The Guardians manage to be vampires without being wanton killers."

Montgomery bared his teeth. "Don't canonize them, Ms. Mathers. They are every inch the predators we are. They've merely chosen to hunt other vampires instead of mortals." His eyes narrowed. "They hide behind a cloak of respectability and righteousness, but you should never forget that they are beasts and killers all."

"Ever heard of the pot calling the kettle black?" Carolyn expected her snide question to irritate him, but he merely shrugged.

"One might question who is the pot and who is the kettle. Tell me, what else have you learned about me, other than my name?"

Carolyn hesitated only a moment before speaking. He was more likely to be appeased with partial truths than stubborn silence. "You disappeared in 1899 and were declared dead in 1902. You were a very wealthy man, and you liked to collect Impressionist paintings."

He shook his head, a rueful smile on his lips. "You found me through Origins, didn't you?"

Carolyn blinked in surprise. "How did you know?"

"Over the years, I've attempted to regain possession of some of my favorite works." His eyes drifted to a lovely watercolor of a field of lilies that hung above the mantel. "Imagine my surprise when I bought one from a collector and he proudly announced it was from the collection of Archibald Montgomery! I asked him where he'd learned that interesting tidbit, and he told me. Now, tell me what else you've learned."

His penetrating stare told her he believed she knew more than she was telling. Did older vampires have any psychic abilities? She suppressed a shudder. The only fact she truly had to hide was that Hannah was right now actively looking for this house—assuming, of course, it really was one of his original properties, but his quest to buy his favorite paintings back added credence to the possibility. Taking a deep breath, she said, "I've learned that Deirdre's story about how you just want to make Philly safe for vampires is bullshit."

"Oh?" he said, a hard glitter in his eyes. "How did you learn that?"

"Because I told Jules your name. He said you were a Guardian once and had a falling out with Eli."

Montgomery looked sharply at Deirdre. "I thought you said no one knew about that!"

She patted his arm reassuringly. "I didn't know anyone did. But once I started planting suggestions that a Guardian had gone bad, I suppose it's not surprising the subject came up. It doesn't matter, really. So Eli knows you're back. So what? It's too late to mend the rifts now. Half the Guardians won't even answer the phone when he calls anymore."

Carolyn shook her head at Montgomery. "How could you go from being a Guardian to being a psychotic murderer?"

"I got out from under Eli's influence is how. He did me a favor when he kicked me out. If I'd stayed with the Guardians, I'd probably still buy into all his holier-than-thou, suppress-the-beast-within nonsense." He sneered. "He's not the saint he pretends to be, anyway."

Disgusted, Carolyn turned to Deirdre. "So, what's *your* excuse?"

Deirdre smiled sweetly. "Oh, I was never a Guardian, not really. We figured the best way to take Eli down was to get someone on the inside. So I took up residence with another of Archer's fledglings and we lured the Guardians to our door." She sighed and put a mock-sorrowful expression on her face. "The poor fledgling thought we were setting a trap for the Guardians, and Archer was going to kill them. But the Guardians killed him instead."

"And took a Trojan horse into their midst," Carolyn finished for her.

"Precisely," Deirdre said with a brisk nod.

"And now," Montgomery said, "while I have greatly enjoyed our little chat, I think it's time for Deirdre and me to reap the rewards of our labors." His smile was pure evil as his eyes swept over Carolyn once more. "You won't mind if I amuse myself with the mortal woman before Gray kills her, do you my dear?" he asked Deirdre.

Her smile was just as vicious and just as chilling. "Not at all, Archer darling. As long as you don't mind if I amuse myself with Gray. I've always let him resist my glamour in the past. I look forward to showing him what I'm capable of."

Carolyn was on the verge of panic when the door-bell rang. She started to turn toward the door, a scream rising in her throat as she hoped against hope that help might be on the way. But the sound died before it escaped, and her mind descended into what was becoming a familiar darkness.

* * *

JULES SMILED HIS MOST charming smile when Deirdre opened the door. Was it his imagination, or was there a hint of worry in her eyes? She returned his smile easily enough, brushing her hair away from her face in a coquettish gesture.

"Jules!" she cried. "What a pleasant surprise. Please come in."

He stepped past her into her house, his mind searching for the other two vampires. His eyes flicked to a closed door against one wall, a door with a deadbolt lock on it. Behind that door, he sensed two vampires lurking. He hoped like hell one of them was Gray, not a third accomplice he didn't know about. As casually as possible, he strolled into the living room and made himself comfortable on the couch, crossing one leg over the other. Deirdre joined him, her face a mask of polite inquiry.

"What's up?" she asked.

He let out a slow sigh while his senses reached out a little further, searching for a sign that Drake and Michael were inside. He could sense them, above him and to his left, but the tingle was faint and he knew they weren't inside yet. A faint scraping sound sent a bolt of adrenaline through him, but Deirdre didn't seem to have heard it.

"I'm . . . wondering what you think of the note Gray left at the latest murder scene." It seemed like the most likely topic of conversation, for it wasn't the first time he'd discussed his distrust of Gray with Deirdre. "I keep feeling like . . ."

Dee raised an eyebrow. "Yes? Like what?"

He frowned. "I don't know. Like it wasn't him, maybe?"

If he hadn't been looking for it, he was sure he would have missed the flicker of fear that passed briefly over Dee's face. *Careful, Jules. Don't go too close to the truth.*

"What makes you say that?" she asked, leaning forward on the couch ever so slightly.

"It just seems so blatant. He's been denying it so long, I don't understand why he'd suddenly announce to the world that he's a Killer." He heard a couple of faint tapping sounds upstairs. Still, Dee didn't seem to hear anything, though her eyes looked more troubled than ever.

"Well, Jules, he does rather dislike you, you know. Perhaps he decided to come out of the closet—so to speak—so he could rub your nose in it. After all, you knew where he was and you didn't bring him in."

"True," he conceded. "But—"

From upstairs came the sound of shattering glass, followed by a heavy thud.

There was no time to think, only to act. As Deirdre rose to her feet with a cry of alarm, Jules charged her.

* * *

GRAY CAME TO WITH a start. The first thing he noticed was a shadowed shape charging out the door at the top of the stairs. The second thing he noticed was that he was standing with his weight split between two steps somewhere around the middle of the staircase. Unfortunately, the third thing he noticed was that his head was spinning. He put out a hand to steady himself against the wall, but he missed and his weight tipped backward.

Flailing for balance, he teetered for a second, then fell, his back smacking the wooden steps before he rolled head over heels. He plowed into something warm and soft, and heard Carolyn's cry of distress. Then she, too, went down, and they landed together at the base of the steps in a tangle of limbs.

"Gray!" Carolyn cried. "Are you all right?"

He disentangled himself as best he could. His back screamed where he'd hit the stairs, but he could bear the pain, and even bone-deep bruises would heal in minutes. "I'm fine," he said. He spared her a quick glance, assuring himself that she, too, was all right. "Stay here!" He bolted up the stairs, heading toward the sound of combat.

When he burst through the basement door, Gray had to stop a moment to make sense of the melee.

Drake and Jules were both struggling with Montgomery, who was roaring like some kind of medieval warrior. Standing slightly apart from them, Deirdre was staring into the eyes of another man Gray didn't know. The man's jaw had gone slack, his eyes glazed over. Deirdre grabbed his arms and drew him roughly to her, sinking her fangs into his throat.

Lowering his shoulder, Gray barreled into her, hoping he wasn't too late. She gave a squeak of surprise, losing her grip on her victim's throat. The three of them collapsed to the floor together. Gray wrapped his arms around Dee and tore her away from the wounded man, whose eyes were still glazed despite his wound. Blood poured from his throat and pooled on the floor, soaking into the carpet. The scent filled the air, and Gray's fangs descended in instant reaction to it as the hunger stirred.

Deirdre turned in his arms and pressed her bloody mouth to his. He shoved her away violently, using his sleeve to wipe the blood off his lips before even the smallest drop touched his tongue. She laughed at him, her eyes glowing with manic delight.

Behind him, he heard Jules cursing, but he dared not ignore Deirdre, who was even now rising to her feet. He averted his eyes, though he already knew her glamour was strong enough to overpower him even if he wasn't meeting her eyes. The man she had wounded groaned feebly. The river of blood that had flowed from his throat slowed to a trickle. So, he wasn't a man, exactly, but another Guardian, healing at supernatural speed. Still, Gray didn't think he'd be strong enough to rejoin the fray anytime soon.

Amidst all the shouting and cursing, Gray heard another sound, the frantic pounding of a fist on the door. But he didn't have time to ponder that puzzle, for Deirdre was upon him again, her hands wrapping around his throat and squeezing.

The Guardian's blood still coated her lips and chin as she bent over him, pinning him easily despite her diminutive size. He struggled, but she was far too strong, his own strength no match for that of a Killer. She grinned down at him, her hands at his throat squeezing just tight enough to cut off most of his oxygen supply while not crushing his windpipe. She couldn't kill him this way, but she could sap his strength and make him damned uncomfortable. He clawed at her hands and labored to suck in tiny gasps of air. She let him breathe just enough so the scent of blood filled his nostrils, and within him the beast stirred.

"Give in to it, Gray," Deirdre coaxed, breathing the smell of blood over his face. "Help us. You know you want to. It would be so much easier." She was leaning down again, bringing the tantalizing scent of blood closer.

She was right—it would be so easy to give in. All he had to do was put his humanity aside and let himself do what he wished to do with every fiber of his being. Spots began to dance before his eyes as the lack of oxygen played tricks with his brain. His hands fell away from hers, for he was too weak to keep fighting. The room seemed to be spinning around him, the floor bucking around under him. She wasn't letting any air into his lungs anymore, and her hands squeezed ever harder, until he feared his neck might soon break under the pressure.

The sound of Jules's curses suddenly grew louder. Then Deirdre's hands ripped away from Gray's throat, her nails leaving painful, burning trails in his skin. He gasped desperately for breath and lay still, the world still spinning around him.

Beside him, Jules and Deirdre rolled on the floor, locked together in mortal combat. Jules's eyes were squeezed closed against her glamour, but he didn't appear to be having much success against her. She was snarling and snapping, and when Jules tried to pin her, she merely flung him off.

A few feet away, Montgomery had gained the upper hand against Drake, now that Jules was otherwise occupied. Montgomery pinned Drake against the wall and now bared his teeth in an obvious preparation to bite. Gray tried to rise, some vague idea of charging to the rescue flitting through his mind, but his oxygen-starved limbs weren't up to obeying him yet.

Suddenly, the cursing and grunting and banging were drowned out by a deafening roar, and everyone went momentarily still.

Gray blinked away the black spots in his vision and saw Montgomery crumple to the ground. Drake nearly fell with him, but managed to keep his feet. Blood spattered Drake's face, and he turned his head slowly to the left, his eyes wide.

Gray followed Drake's gaze and saw Hannah standing in the foyer, her gun still trained on the Banger's inert body. Behind her, Carolyn pushed the front door closed.

An ear-piercing shriek rent the air, as Deirdre leapt away from Jules and flew toward Hannah, fangs bared in fury. Hannah started to turn the gun toward her attacker, but would never have made it in time. Fortunately, Drake managed to throw himself in front of Hannah just in time to intercept Deirdre.

The struggle that ensued was surprisingly brief. Either Drake was just too powerful for Dee, or Dee was too maddened with rage and grief from losing her mentor. Either way, they closed for maybe ten seconds before she stiffened and the life disappeared from her eyes.

Drake withdrew a long, bloody knife from the center of her chest, then lowered her gently to the floor. Silence reigned as everyone took in the carnage. Carolyn moved toward Hannah and plucked the gun from her hands.

"This is mine, I presume?" she asked. Hannah's

eyes were wide and frightened-looking as she nodded. She shivered and looked at Montgomery's body. Blood seeped from a gaping wound on his temple.

"Beginner's luck, I guess," she said, but her shaking voice belied her bravado.

Drake and Jules shared a significant look, then Jules folded his arms over his chest and glared at Hannah.

"I thought we had an understanding that you would remain at the hotel!" he growled.

Hannah grinned, but it was a feeble expression. "I saw no reason to disabuse you of that notion."

Drake chuckled quietly, earning him a pair of matching glares from Jules and Hannah.

Across the distance that separated them, Gray met Carolyn's eyes. And didn't like what he saw there. Didn't like the hint of softness, and of longing.

The Banger was dead. Carolyn was safe, and there was no longer any reason for him to remain a part of her life. The problem was, he feared she wasn't ready to let him go. And she *had* to. He loved her too much to condemn her to a life spent in the shadows, and he loved her too much to risk that someday, somehow he might fulfill Deirdre's prophecy and hurt her.

The scent of blood that filled the air was overpowering to his sensitive, famished senses. The beast inside him was still stirring, and even now, with the melee over, his fangs were out. He drew in a shaky breath, knowing there was one way he could demonstrate to Carolyn beyond a shadow of a doubt that she was better off without him. Of course, there was a reasonable chance that Jules and Drake would kill him if he tried it. But it was worth the risk.

Slowly, reluctantly, Gray forced himself to relax, to stop fighting, to let go of his control. It didn't come easily. He was so used to fighting it was almost like his brain was hardwired for it. But then he closed his eyes and inhaled deeply the scent of blood that filled the room. The beast uncoiled in his belly and his eyes shot open on a surge of adrenaline.

Carolyn was looking at him quizzically, her head tilted to one side, when he let go of the reins entirely and the beast took over.

Some part of the real him was still there, watching like a concerned observer, when he rose to his feet in one quick movement and hurtled across the empty space that separated him from Carolyn. Her eyes widened in shock, and her mouth opened to voice some kind of protest, but he was on her before any words escaped. His body slammed against hers, knocking her hard to the floor as he pulled his lips away from his teeth and snarled. The sound of her hammering pulse, so close, fueled his hunger, and he grabbed her hair to stretch the skin taut over the thin blue vein of her throat.

The part of him that was still Gray James mentally urged Jules and Drake to hurry up. The part of him that was the beast crowed in triumph as he lowered his head to bite.

Hands like vises fastened onto his arms and tore him away from her. The beast growled and snapped, trying to tear free of the restraint, finish what it had started. Jules slammed him hard against the wall, knocking the wind out of him then holding him pinned. Hannah helped a dazed-looking Carolyn to her feet. Gray struggled and kicked, eyes boring into Carolyn, willing her not to run away, willing her to come to him and offer her throat.

She took a step toward him, and Hannah grabbed her arm to stop her. A brutally hard punch to his gut broke Gray's concentration on the glamour.

"Get her out of here!" Jules yelled to Hannah.

Hannah obediently dragged on Carolyn's arm, but Carolyn didn't budge. "Promise me you won't hurt him!" Carolyn said, her eyes shining with tears. "He can't help himself." One of those tears slid down her cheek.

"I won't hurt him," Jules said, and if Gray hadn't

still been struggling for air after the vicious punch, he might have laughed.

"Come on," Hannah urged, pulling harder on Carolyn's arm. "We need to go. Now!"

Finally, Carolyn allowed Hannah to guide her out the door.

As soon as the door closed, Jules released his grip on Gray, shocking him so much Gray almost fell down. He glanced sharply upward to meet Jules's eyes.

"Why'd you let me go?" he asked as he realized he'd regained full control.

Jules smiled at him, one of his crooked, mocking smiles. "You never told me you were an actor."

Gray scowled. "I wasn't acting!"

"You forget—I was there the last time you truly lost control of the hunger. I know the signs."

Gray was pissed enough to lower his fangs again, though with Jules it could never be anything but an empty threat. "If you knew I was faking, then you didn't have to punch me!"

Jules grinned. "Hey, I was helping you make it look real."

"Prick!"

"Asshole!"

"Gentlemen," Drake said, before it could get any uglier. They both turned to see him kneeling beside the injured Guardian. The wound had closed over, but the poor guy looked dazed and sick. "We should get Michael out of here. He needs to feed as soon as possible. Take him to Eli."

Jules came to squat beside him. "And what are *you* planning to do, other than give orders?"

"Clean up this mess," Drake said, with a sweeping motion of his hand. "And make sure that if the gunshot draws any police attention, it gets deflected." Even now, Gray heard a siren howling its way toward them. "Now hurry up," Drake urged, helping Michael to his feet.

Jules slung the injured Guardian's arm around his shoulders. "Let's go, Gray," he said, heading toward the door.

Resisting the urge to argue just for the sake of arguing, Gray followed.

* * *

BACK IN THE SAFETY of her own home, Carolyn bawled helplessly, a pile of tissues clutched in her fist. Hannah hugged her tightly, rocking her and murmuring soothing, meaningless words. Carolyn's throat was choked and tight with tears, her chest aching with sobs she couldn't seem to contain.

"Let it all out, honey," Hannah said, stroking Carolyn's hair. "You've been bottling all this up for three years and it's time to let go."

Carolyn gulped a breath of air, but though she wanted to dispute her friend's diagnosis the relentless tears wouldn't let her. Whenever they seemed about to ebb, she'd remember the look on Gray's face, eyes filled with madness as he bared his fangs and prepared to bite her. To kill her.

A shudder rocked her whole body. It wasn't his fault. Deirdre had been starving him. And the room had reeked of blood, which must have maddened him. It *wasn't* his fault.

"I never stopped loving him," she sobbed, and Hannah's arms tightened around her.

"I know. But it's just like he told you—the man you loved died three years ago. It's time you finally let yourself mourn him, and then let him go."

Carolyn squirmed out of Hannah's embrace, scrubbing at her eyes with the already soaked tissues. Her nose was so stuffy she could barely breathe, but at least the flow of tears seemed to be slowing. "I kept thinking . . ." She hiccuped and almost lost it. She tried again, her voice little more than a whisper. "I guess I thought it was all in his mind somehow, that he really was in control of himself. I never really allowed myself to think he might hurt me."

The sympathy in Hannah's eyes only made the pain worse. "He tried to warn you, I think."

She nodded. "Yes, he did. And I didn't listen. I only heard what I wanted to hear."

A gentle smile touched her friend's lips. "Human nature, I suppose." The smile faded. "I can't pretend to understand how you're feeling right now. I've never loved anyone like you loved Gray, and I can't put myself in your shoes. But I have to think that when the worst of the aftermath is over, you'll finally be able to start healing. As long as you didn't know what had happened to him, there was always some part of your heart that believed hope was still alive. I don't know if you were ever going to get past it. Now maybe some day . . ."

Carolyn was glad Hannah didn't finish the thought. It was too soon to think about healing. Right now, all she could think about was trying to weather the storm, trying to contain the pain and keep herself from going stark, raving mad. She wanted to scream, wanted to hit something. Surely there was some way she could make herself feel better!

But there was nothing she could do. Only time would ease the pain, and right now Carolyn had her doubts about even that.

* * *

GRAY SAT ON A plush chair in front of the fire, sipping from a glass of blood and milk, not even noticing the foul taste that usually turned his stomach. He was very much aware of Eli and Jules staring at him, but he couldn't tear his own eyes away from the flickering flames. His whole body ached, and though rationally he knew that this was no physical pain but an emotional one, he couldn't shake the illusion.

"You did the right thing," Jules said softly, and Gray reluctantly dragged his gaze away from the fire. For the first time he could ever remember, he saw no hint of animosity on the older vampire's face. "I know from firsthand experience what it's like to cling to one's mortal life, to refuse to sever the ties." Jules shook his head and looked at the floor, his voice dropping even lower. "My son is eighty years old. My grandson is forty-two. My great-granddaughters are ten and eight." His Adam's apple bobbed as he swallowed. "Soon, my only child will die of old age. It would have been better if I'd heeded Eli's advice eons ago and just let them all go."

Gray sighed heavily and finished up his meal. "You know, it's much easier to hate you when you're being a prick."

Jules laughed, and though the sadness still sat heavily on Gray's shoulders he allowed the corners of his mouth to lift in a slight smile. "I'll keep that in mind," Jules said.

"Perhaps it's too early to ask," Eli said, his voice conspicuously gentle, "but have you given any thought to what you're going to do now?"

For half a minute, Gray was tempted to play dumb, his heart too sore and his thoughts too jumbled to deal with a serious conversation. But in the midst of the turmoil, he sensed a paradoxical calm at the center of the storm. The one and only thing that was clear to him right now was that he couldn't go on the way he had before Carolyn waltzed back into his life. He couldn't go on just . . . existing.

Gray cleared his throat. "Three years ago, you tried to get me to join the Guardians and I turned you down. Is the offer still open?"

"Of course," Eli said.

Jules let fly another stream of his French cuss words, but Eli silenced him with a raised eyebrow. Jules folded his arms over his chest and leaned back in his chair. "Well, *I'm* not working with him!" he declared, his expression dangerously close to a pout.

"Glad to see you're the same old Jules," Gray muttered, earning himself a withering look. "And before you start acting your usual self and pissing me off with every word that leaves your mouth, let me thank you for saving my life."

Jules looked like he'd just swallowed a live toad, his face so comical that even Eli laughed. Gray's mood lightened just a bit. Life was full of surprises—he'd finally found a taunt to get under Jules's skin, and it was because of Jules's good deed!

"I'm regretting it already," Jules grumbled.

21

"I THINK I'M GETTING carpal tunnel syndrome," Carolyn complained as she shoved her chair back from her desk.

At the other desk, Hannah switched off her computer and raised an inquiring eyebrow. "What? You don't enjoy spending eight to ten hours a day pushing your mouse around and staring at a little glowing screen? But Carolyn, just think how rewarding it is when you find the missing heir." She frowned theatrically. "Or is it a deadbeat dad this time?"

Carolyn scowled at her best friend and business partner. "Make fun of my misery, why don't you."

Hannah sighed and shook her head, pulling her chair over to Carolyn's desk and sitting down. "It's self-imposed misery, honey." Carolyn opened her mouth to protest, but Hannah cut her off before she had a chance to get a word out. "Face facts, Carolyn: you became a cop because you wanted to do some good in the world, and then you gave it all up because of the man who shall remain nameless. You've never liked being a private investigator."

Carolyn's scowl deepened. "That's not true!" she protested. "I love being my own boss. I love not having to fill out twenty different forms to explain every move

I make. And I especially love picking and choosing the cases I want to work on."

"Are you fooling yourself with this shit, because you're not fooling me."

"Hannah—"

"Look, you're a perfectly decent PI. You get the job done, and your clients have no reason to complain. But you were a *great* detective. You had passion. You were excited by what you were doing."

Carolyn narrowed her eyes. "We've been working together for three years. You've never complained about my lack of enthusiasm before."

"I'm not *complaining*. I'm just pointing out what I see." Hannah bit her lip and looked uncertain.

Carolyn braced herself—if Hannah was unsure of herself, then she must be thinking of saying something pretty scary. Finally, Hannah blew out a loud breath.

"From the moment you started looking into the Banger case, you had this . . . sparkle in your eyes. A sparkle I hadn't seen for three years. Me, I was scared shitless the whole time and I wanted it all to go away. But Carolyn, you wanted to take the Banger down. And face it, if it weren't for your investigation, he'd probably still be out there killing people right and left. *You're* the one who figured out who he was. *You're* the one who figured out *where* he was."

Carolyn squirmed and refused to meet her friend's eyes. The police were baffled by the sudden cessation of the Banger attacks. It had seemed to them that the killer's pace was accelerating, and they'd expected it to keep getting worse and worse. Now eight weeks had passed without another killing, and they were beginning to think perhaps they'd gotten lucky and arrested the perp for some other crime. Or that he'd died violently, the way violent criminals often did.

"What does that have to do with anything?"

"It has to do with you wasting your talents doing locates and skip traces. It's kind of like Ernest Hemingway deciding he'd rather be a typist than a writer."

Carolyn gritted her teeth. "So what? It's my life, and I get to choose what to do with it."

Hannah glared at her with genuine annoyance. "Well if that's your choice, then don't complain about freakin' carpal tunnel syndrome!"

Carolyn looked away from the anger in her friend's eyes, turning off her computer even though she hadn't finished the tasks she'd set herself for the afternoon. "Just what is it you're suggesting I do, anyway?"

"The only reason you left the force was because you were too pigheaded to quit chasing after Gray," Hannah started.

"Don't go there," Carolyn warned, her cheeks heating with angry color. Hannah would probably never understand it, but Gray hadn't been the only reason she'd left the force. Yes, her insistence on investigating his disappearance was the catalyst that had caused her to leave, but there had been more to it than that. She'd always felt like a cog in the wheel in the midst of that huge, urban PD, and a part of her had longed for a kind of independence she never would have found there. Unfortunately, while she now had the independence, Hannah was right that she'd lost a lot of excitement and sense of urgency that had come from working cases that were truly important.

Not that tracking down deadbeat dads wasn't important, she reminded herself. The kids who suffered because of those men's neglect were very much in need of any help they could get.

"All right," Hannah said, "maybe you don't want to go back to the force. Maybe you burned your bridges when you left. Maybe you should apply to the FBI. That would give you a brand new start, and you'd be back in the hunt where you belong."

Join the Feebies? Carolyn could honestly say the thought had never occurred to her. "I'll think about it," she said. Of course, if she'd felt like a cog in the wheel in the Philly PD, how would she feel in the FBI? Assuming she managed to get in, of course.

"Is that 'I'll think about it' as in I'll think about it, or is that 'I'll think about it' as in 'no way in hell, but if I pretend I'll think about it, maybe she'll leave me alone'?"

Carolyn couldn't help laughing at her irrepressible friend. "I'll let you know when I've figured it out myself, okay?"

"Deal!" Hannah declared.

* * *

IT WAS A LOVELY evening, so Gray decided to walk home from the weekly meeting at Eli's, though it would take more than an hour. Eli wasn't ready to send him out on assignments yet, so he still had many hours to fill during the long, lonely nights.

The Banger had taken a deadly toll on the Guardians, and it wasn't just because of those he'd killed. Eli had persuaded all of the Guardians except for Tim Carter to return to the fold, but though Gray had only been a Guardian for eight weeks, he knew things had changed drastically since the pre-Banger days. The tension Deirdre had planted had grown roots, living under the surface but always unavoidably there. A rumor circulated that Carter was dead, that Eli had learned his lesson from the Banger and would never again let a Guardian leave the organization alive. Gray wondered if it was true, but no one was about to question Eli.

Gray still found himself the recipient of many a hostile glare, for though he had been completely exonerated of the killings, the suspicions clung to him in a lingering taint. He found himself scowling as he walked.

"Don't take it too personally," Drake said from close beside him, and Gray jumped a mile into the air.

He whirled on the older vampire and glared at him, putting his hand to his chest where his heart thumped vigorously. "You scared the shit out of me!"

Drake grinned. "If you're going to be a Guardian, my friend, you should learn to be a little more conscious of your surroundings. You should especially be conscious if a Killer is coming up behind you."

Gray let out a deep breath as his pulse rate slowed to normal. He started walking again, and Drake fell into step beside him. "Are you following me around to lecture me, or did you have something else in mind?" Gray's voice came out surly, but in truth he and Drake had formed a friendship of sorts, both existing on the fringes of the Guardian society.

Drake shrugged. Across the street, a pair of college-age girls stared at him and whispered to each other. Drake noticed their attention and grinned at them. Twin blushes colored the girls' cheeks.

Gray couldn't help laughing. "Anyone would think you're a rock star, the way women eye you," he muttered. Personally, he couldn't quite understand what women found so appealing. He supposed Drake was a good-looking guy, but to Gray's admittedly untrained eye there didn't seem to be anything extraordinary about him. Not enough to warrant the kind of attention he got, at least.

"Women are attracted to men who are comfortable in their own skin," Drake explained, as if reading Gray's mind.

Gray thought about that a moment, then nodded. There was something about Drake that set him apart, and Gray could easily see confidence as that magical something. For a long moment, they walked in silence, but now Gray's curiosity was roused and he had to ask. "So it doesn't bother you, being a vampire?"

Drake shook his head. "Not in the least. I didn't *choose* to become what I am, but I have always been determined to embrace it. I'm immortal, forever young, forever healthy." He smiled. "I have little cause for complaint."

Gray shivered, even though the night wasn't particularly cold. "But you kill people."

Drake shrugged as though it hardly mattered. "Had I encountered Eli before the addiction took hold, my life would indeed be much different now. Better, even. But I'm not one to moan and whine over what might have been. I can't help the killing. All I can do is choose victims who will not trouble my conscience."

Gray stuck his hands into his pockets, the chill deepening. "Now you sound like Deirdre. She and Montgomery kept trying to tell us how they had every right to keep killing people right and left."

Drake stopped in his tracks, and Gray stopped too. He hadn't meant to be a judgmental jerk, but now that the words were out of his mouth, he couldn't very well call them back.

Drake, however, didn't look particularly angry or offended. He regarded Gray with a penetrating gaze, so knowing that Gray had to look away.

"It's like this, Gray—you can only control what you can control. I can't control my need to kill. I can control *who* I kill, and to a certain extent how often. Montgomery couldn't control his need to kill either. But he could have controlled his choice of victim, and he could have controlled the way in which he went about it. He didn't have to rape them. He didn't have to drive stakes through Guardian hearts. He didn't have to try to destroy the Guardians from within. And he certainly didn't have to try to create more Killers.

"If I could live on lamb blood and milk, then I would. But I can't, and I refuse to wallow in guilt over something I can't control. Perhaps that's a lesson you should look toward learning."

Gray turned away and resumed walking. "I'm not wallowing in guilt."

"No? Then why did you chase Carolyn away?"

Anger surged through Gray's veins and it was only

with a concerted effort that he managed to contain his temper. "That's none of your business!"

"Any fool can see you love her," Drake continued, undaunted.

"Quit it!"

"So one could come to the conclusion that you chased her away to punish yourself. Only, you may well be punishing her just as much."

Gray ground his teeth and clenched his fists, reminding himself that Drake was even more powerful than Jules. If Gray couldn't control his urge to throw a punch, he'd find himself flattened to the sidewalk in a heartbeat.

"Of course, that's your choice to make," Drake said. "It's just that you should do yourself and Carolyn the courtesy of thinking it all the way through before—"

"Enough!" Gray snapped, and this time Drake must have seen how thin a thread his control hung on, for the older vampire shrugged casually and shut up.

They stood there for maybe a minute or so, each trying to stare the other down. Then Drake shook his head. "Coward," he said softly, then turned his back and walked away.

* * *

CAROLYN DROPPED HER PEN and closed her eyes, shoving the pile of papers away from her as she propped her elbows on her dining room table cum work desk. She didn't need a PhD in psychology to know that her inability to fill out the application without making stupid mistake after stupid mistake was a big, blaring warning message. She opened her eyes again and shook her head at the botched mess she'd made of the first page. It looked like it'd been filled out by a first-grader! The FBI would take one look at that page and toss her into the rejects pile without bothering to read any further.

Carolyn crumpled the application into a tight wad and tossed it at the trash can. She missed. She unfolded her legs from under her and walked over to dispose of the botched application, her teeth worrying at her lower lip.

Okay, so her subconscious was trying to tell her—none-too-subtly—that she didn't want to join the Feebies. And Hannah was trying to tell her—even less subtly—that she didn't want to be a PI anymore. What did that leave her? She paced the length of her dining room, then threw up her hands in frustration.

Nothing! It left her with freaking nothing!

"What do you want to be when you grow up, Carolyn?" she muttered under her breath.

Her thoughts were interrupted by the ringing of the doorbell. She frowned. She wasn't expecting anyone. But even talking to a wandering Jehovah's Witness might be better than being alone with her muddled thoughts, so she went to the door and peeked out.

Her heart did a strange flip-flop when she saw Gray standing on her doorstep. He reached out to ring the bell again, and she wiped suddenly sweaty palms on her pants legs. Then she opened the door.

He reminded her somewhat of a turtle, ready to retreat into its shell at the slightest hint of danger. His hands were stuffed into the pockets of his leather jacket, his shoulders were hunched, and uncertainty bordering on fear shone in his eyes. Her heart did another of its roller-coaster dips, and she opened the door wider.

"Come in out of the cold," she said, although the temperature outside was comfortable enough.

He stepped through the doorway and headed for the living room. He sat down on the edge of the couch, but didn't take off his jacket. His posture was still defensive, and he looked poised for flight. Carolyn sat in a chair across from him and leaned back. The devil in her made it impossible to resist teasing him.

"You can relax, Gray. I promise I don't bite."

That brought a reluctant smile to his lips and he eased back into the couch a little more comfortably.

"Well, you *have* shot at me in the past."

She grinned. "If I'd been shooting *at* you, I would have hit you."

He managed a small laugh, but it was a strained sound. He cleared his throat. "So. How've you been?" He had the grace to blush at his inane question.

A tense, uncomfortable silence descended. Carolyn broke it by asking, "Why are you here?"

Gray winced, although she'd kept her voice carefully neutral so it wouldn't sound like some kind of accusation.

He sighed. "I'm sorry it's taken me so long to get around to it. But I need to at least . . . apologize to you. For what I did."

Carolyn rose from her chair and went to sit beside him on the couch. He looked so miserable that her heart went out to him. "You couldn't help it," she said softly, putting her hand on his back and rubbing the supple leather, suddenly wishing he'd taken the jacket off so she could feel the warmth of his body. "I hope you don't think I've spent these weeks cursing you or anything."

The memory of his attack haunted her at times, but after the initial shock had worn off, her emotions had run more to sadness than to fear. Sadness that this man she loved had to live with that specter hanging over his head, sadness that she hadn't found a way to push that specter away.

"So, you and Hannah don't spend your evenings sticking pins in a Gray doll?" he asked.

She laughed. "I can't speak for Hannah, but *I* don't." She sighed and couldn't resist resting her head against his shoulder. She inhaled deeply the scent of leather, touched with a hint of Cool Water and a dash of Gray. "I've missed you," she whispered, and damn if her eyes didn't start to tear up.

Gray slid his arm around her shoulder, and she gratefully snuggled closer. Despite the affectionate gesture, his voice when he spoke was tight with strain. "You could have come to see me. Or called."

She grasped the zipper on his jacket and slid it down, then rested her hand against his chest. "I was afraid you'd slam the door in my face."

He put a finger under her chin and lifted her face so he could look into her eyes. "Why on earth would you think that?"

She narrowed her eyes. "I don't know, Gray. Maybe it's because you've done it a few times in the past. You practically threw me down your front steps once, if you remember." She sat up, though her body screamed in protest, wanting to lean into his warmth once more. "The only reason I'd been able to break down your defenses was because of the Banger's threats. If it hadn't been for that, you would have washed your hands of me. After . . . what happened, I knew the truce was over. I couldn't have borne to have you shut me out again. So I didn't give you the chance."

His eyes were wide with shock as he stared at her. "So you weren't avoiding me because of . . . what I did?"

Almost, she allowed herself to answer glibly. But Gray deserved total honesty, so she gave it to him. "I won't say I wasn't disturbed by it. And I won't say it didn't scare me. But no, that's not the reason I stayed away. Please believe me—I'm not angry with you."

He was silent for so long she almost thought he wasn't planning to speak to her anymore. Then he smiled grimly. "I think I can remedy that."

"Huh?"

"Do you have your gun on you?"

"I repeat, huh?"

He grinned, but it was a decidedly forced expression. "I'm just wondering how much bodily harm I'm risking by pissing you off right now."

She shook her head. "Whatever it is, just spit it out."

Still he struggled with it for a while. Three times he opened his mouth as though about to speak, and three times he swallowed his words. When he did it the third time, she punched his upper arm.

"Now you really *are* risking bodily harm!" she said. "What is it?"

He raised his chin defiantly, though who he thought he was defying, she couldn't guess. "I was faking it," he blurted.

She blinked, not instantly understanding what he meant "Faking it?" He nodded, and her brain snapped all the pieces into place. "Faking it?" she cried, remembering the feral glow in his eyes when he'd gone for her throat, the brutal strength of his hands, the glint of his fangs. She delivered another punch to his arm. "You bastard!"

He winced, whether at her words or at the blow she didn't know. She wanted to grab his shoulders and shake him until his teeth rattled.

"Why the f—" She cut herself off, for she'd never been as fond of vulgarity as Hannah. "Why the hell did you do a stupid thing like that?"

He rubbed his hands up and down his pants legs and grinned sheepishly. "Because in some things I haven't changed. I'm still an opinionated, old-fashioned, caveman-like Neanderthal who thinks he has the right to call all the shots and make all the decisions in a relationship. I decided for like the third or fourth time that you were better off without me, and I was going to prove it to you."

"And you call Jules a prick!"

He winced again. "You really know how to hit a man when he's down. Comparing me to Jules is a low blow." He was trying for humor, but the uncertainty in his voice destroyed the attempt.

She was still furious, and her instincts urged her to shout at him until she was hoarse. But he looked so miserable she couldn't help throwing her arms around him and hugging him tightly. "You're an idiot," she told him, her voice muffled against his shoulder.

"No doubt about it," he agreed, wrapping his arms around her. "A moron."

"A bastard."

"A jerk."

"A *trou d'cul.*"

He pulled away and raised an eyebrow at her. "Excuse me?"

She grinned. "I heard Jules call you that once. I looked it up on the Internet."

"Let me guess, he was calling me an all-around great guy."

"Asshole, actually, but then who cares what he thinks."

Gray's eyes softened and he brushed his fingers down the side of her face. "I care what *you* think."

She turned her head to kiss his fingers. "I love you," she said simply. "I never stopped."

He closed his eyes as if the words hurt him. "Carolyn, we live in different worlds. I'm a creature of the night, and you're a creature of the day. We'll—"

"We'll work around it. Maybe I can cut back my hours at work, or—" An idea struck her, and suddenly she was filled with an almost overwhelming sense of hope.

"Or what?" Gray asked, his head tilted to one side.

"Would you agree that I was instrumental in hunting down the Banger?"

"Of course! If it hadn't been for you, he might have won. The Guardians are still reeling from the poisonous influence he had on them through Deirdre."

"And do you think I might be instrumental on other cases?"

He looked doubtful, his protective instincts no doubt triggered once again. "I don't know . . ."

"Yes you do. I can do things the Guardians can't. There are loads of records in courthouses that Guardians would never be able to get to because they can't go out during the day."

"Carolyn—"

"And I have contacts they don't have, like my friend at the fingerprint lab."

"But—"

"Of course, if I was working for the Guardians *and* trying to get stuff done in the daylight, I'd have to shift my sleep schedule around a bit. But there are lots of people who work night shifts and get along just fine."

Gray grabbed her shoulders and stopped her babbling with a firm kiss. She would have melted under his lips, but he pulled away too soon, his eyes boring into hers. "Think about what you're saying, Carolyn. You weren't willing to give up your career three years ago. Why would you be willing to do it now?"

She smiled and raised her hand to his hair, running her fingers through it until her hand was cupped behind his head. "Don't you see?" she murmured. "I wouldn't be giving it up. I'd be helping the Guardians root out Killers like Archer Montgomery." She tried to pull his head toward her for another kiss, eager to drop the more mundane topic of her employment, but he resisted.

"Eli might not go for it," Gray warned. "He's very protective of mortals."

"If he's protective of mortals, then he should be willing to accept any help he can get. Especially if the Guardians are in the kind of disarray you've suggested."

Gray shrugged out of his leather jacket, letting it fall casually to the floor. "It won't be easy," he said, but his voice was growing noticeably husky. "All our issues won't heal overnight."

"I know," she murmured as she slid onto his lap and wrapped both arms around his neck. His erection was a prominent lump under her bottom, and her body flushed with desire.

"Hannah will castrate me when she finds out!" he said, tugging the tail of her shirt out of her jeans.

Carolyn straddled him, squeezing her thighs around his hardness. "Just let her try!"